Shadows of Fog

J. D. NICHOLS

J.D. NICHOLS
www.authorjdnichols.com

Printed Worldwide
First Printing 2023
First Edition 2023

Library of Congress Cataloging-in-Publication Data
Names: Nichols, J.D., author
Title: Shadows of Fog / J.D. Nichols
Description: First Edition. | Missouri, Crepe Myrtle Press, 2023.

10 9 8 7 6 5 4 3 2 1

Book cover design by Sadia Shahid

Shadows of Fog is a work of fiction. Names, characters, places, and incidents either are the product of the author's imagination or are used fictionally. Any resemblance to actual persons, living or dead, events, or locales is entirely coincidental.

Shadows of Fog

For my grandmothers.

Someone once told me digging up the past has two sides: The pro is that you remember things you had forgotten about. Unfortunately, the con is the exact same thing.
—Pete Wentz, *Gray*

I

E mma Campbell was drowning.
   Drowning in guilt.
   Drowning in regret.

Drowning in memories.

She sat on the edge of her bed, vacantly staring down at the decrepit sock monkey in her hands. A remnant of a time long past, his threadbare skin had split open in several places, revealing puffy white stuffing inside. His tail—long since a victim of childish roughhousing—was gone, a clumsily stitched stump the only reminder it had ever existed. He was missing one eye and the other—a decades-old mother-of-pearl button—was fractured into three pieces.

"Just you and me now, Rover."

Plastered over the walls around her were hundreds of Polaroids, a living record of the past year. Every smile. Every laugh. Every triumph. Every defeat. They had chronicled it all. Gran had insisted. It had even been her idea to use Polaroids.

"I want you to have something you can hold in your hand," she had said just after her diagnosis. "Something you can see and touch. Not some digital re-creation on a cell phone screen. Something tangible you can't just swipe left or right on to make it go away."

The collage spread around the room and gave Emma's bedroom a slight teenage vibe even though she was nearly thirty years old. The Polaroids' tangibility was now both comfort and curse to Emma, a reminder of what she'd had and lost.

She wanted to rip them down, wanted to bury herself under the covers and wallow in her grief.

Limp tears—too feeble to be more than a nuisance—formed in the corners of her eyes. Emma had cried herself dry these past few days since her grandmother's death. All that remained was emptiness.

Nausea made her unsteady as she gripped the sides of the bed with her hands. She closed her eyes, willing away the smiles and laughs that washed over her walls and tumbled over her like she was some unsuspecting beachgoer.

"Breathe. Just breathe."

Someone rapped on the bedroom door.

"Yes?" Emma said, her voice scratchy and constricted. She released her grip on the bed.

"Emma?" It was Nessa. "Can I come in?"

"Sure."

African American and in her late twenties, Nessa had been Emma's best friend since they both started working at the same CrossFit gym in Columbia.

"You okay, girl?"

Emma shrugged and glanced back down at Rover. "I'm here, I guess. Okay? TBD." She looked up at Nessa and gave a half smile. "You look nice."

Nessa smiled, her broad grin a shining beacon, and struck an exaggerated modeling pose. She wore a pair of freshly pressed black slacks. Formfitting through Nessa's toned midsection, they flared outward bell-bottom style and stopped just high enough to show off a stylish pair of black open-toed heels. A matching V-cut long-sleeve blazer with a white satin blouse underneath completed Nessa's outfit. Her impossibly curly hair had been pulled up into a top knot, showing off gold chandelier-style earrings that danced in the morning light streaming through the window.

"Thank you, dahling," Nessa cooed. "I do look fabulous, don't I?"

Emma laughed. It was the first time she'd laughed in . . . How long had it been? Days? Weeks? Emma couldn't remember.

"Wow," Nessa said, stepping toward the photo collage. "This is amazing, Emma. I had no idea you had so many."

"Every day. Sometimes two or three a day."

"It's beautiful." She pointed at one photo of Emma and her grandmother in a sea of yellow sunflowers, their warm smiles as bright as the flowers around them. "Oh! I remember that day. She was so excited for that trip."

"She loved Van Gogh."

"Yes, she did." Nessa moved along the wall, glancing from one photo to the next. "I'm glad she made you do this."

"Yeah," Emma replied, noncommittal.

"My grandfather was in bad shape the last few years of his life. You remember that?"

Emma nodded.

"My dad and his sisters took it pretty hard. But all they remember are the bad days, never the good ones. They forgot about those. Miss Nellie— she gave you a gift, Em. All these photos. All these memories. Good memories, girl. Every single one—"

There was another knock on the door. A prim middle-aged woman stuck her head in. "It's just about time to go, Emma."

The door closed behind her before Emma managed to respond. "Yes, Mother."

She didn't move to get up though. Couldn't move. Heavy limbs anchored her to the end of the bed. "I don't know if I can do this, Nessa."

Nessa sat down on the bed and took Emma's hand. Her skin was warm. Alive.

"The world spins every time I move. And I can't catch my balance. I can't concentrate."

"Em—"

"I haven't slept in days. Every night I wander through this house, and I remember. I picture Gran sitting in her favorite chair every time I walk through the living room. I still hear her humming in the shower. I get anxious every time I walk into a room and she's not there. And I freak out because for that brief moment, I'm scared she's fallen somewhere. Or wandered off. And then . . . then I . . ."

Fresh tears ran down Emma's cheeks, and she brushed them away with a trembling hand.

Nessa finished Emma's sentence. "Then you remember."

Emma collapsed into Nessa's chest and sobbed. "I feel like I'm falling through that rabbit hole in *Alice in Wonderland*. And I don't know how to make it stop."

Nessa slid a tender hand across Emma's back, but before she could speak, Emma pulled away suddenly and sat up straight. She shook her head, shaking off the moment of weakness, and held her head high and proud.

"But we can't do that now, can we?" Emma asked in a stilted voice. Cold. Professional. "We have to present the perfect family image to the community, mustn't we?"

She swiped at her tears as she stood. Unsteady in heels, Emma's legs wobbled under her, and she grabbed hold of the bureau to steady herself. As she got her bearings, she moved around the bed toward the door.

"I'm stuck with this robot of a mother"—her words, full of frustration and resentment, grew louder with each step—"who cares more about what people think of her."

She stood there, legs splayed, fists balled tight, shoulders squared back. She was ready for battle.

Nessa went to her friend. As she wrapped her arm around Emma's waist, Emma wilted. Her strength emptied.

"I can't do this, Nessa."

"Yes, you can, Emma Campbell. You know why?"

Emma turned to face her, and Nessa took Emma's hands into her own.

"Because you're not alone. You hear me?" She shook Emma's fists. "You're not alone. I'm right here. And I'm not going anywhere."

Emma's lips pressed into a tight line as she fought off fresh tears. "Thank you."

"Now come on. Let's get out of here before your mother tries to cite us for contempt of court."

"Nessa?"

"Hmm?"

"Before your grandfather passed, did he . . ."

"Did he . . . what?"

Emma walked across the room to the mirror and checked her outfit. She sighed. "I feel stupid for even asking this."

"Go on."

Emma turned back to Nessa. "Did he ever talk about . . . *seeing* . . . people?"

"You serious?"

"Never mind." Emma shook her head, embarrassed. "Forget I said anything." Emma moved toward the door, but Nessa's next words pulled her up.

"He saw his older brother. Carried on full conversations with him there at the end."

"Was he—"

"Died in a car accident when my grandfather was nineteen. But no one in the family talks about that kind of stuff."

"I see."

"Who did Miss Nellie see?"

"I don't know."

"She never said? Never called her name?"

Emma shook her head. "She said she didn't know who it was. Only that she appeared like a shadow. Like a fog."

"That's creepy, Emma."

Emma's mother's raised voice from the other side of the house ended the conversation. "Time to go, girls!"

"Talk about this later?" Emma asked.

"Sure thing." Nessa held up her index finger and pointed to Emma. "Just not after nightfall. Just promise me that."

They laughed and set off for the car, where the rest of Emma's family was waiting.

"She comes like a shadow in fog."

Her grandmother's last words tossed and turned in Emma's mind like a restless night's sleep. She had initially dismissed it as drug-induced confusion, a side effect of the physical and mental maladies that had plagued Nellie's last months. Still, even now, days after her death, the words would not settle no matter how hard Emma tried to shelve them away.

As Emma sat listening to the minister's polite, but completely dull, eulogy, Nellie's words bounced off the domed ceiling of the memorial chapel, splintering into shards of glass as they showered down upon the unsuspecting audience. And despite the preacher's best efforts, his dulcet, calming Midwest tones gave no comfort to Emma.

"Stop fidgeting, Emma Louise," her mother, Angela, said.

The family had been positioned so they could be seen. Her mother's idea, Emma assumed. Always the center of attention, even at her own mother's funeral.

"Sorry. The cleaners used too much starch on this shirt."

"I don't care if they marinated it in starch," she whispered through gritted teeth. "You're drawing attention."

Emma hated her mother's "lawyer voice." Her words in this mood had the same bite as the Missouri summer sun outside.

Emma's skin crawled as if with ants as the overstarched black cotton blouse rubbed against her bare flesh. The skirt she wore was only slightly better. Emma loathed dressing up. Athletic gear was more her style.

A cold bead of sweat ran down her spine, temporarily cooling her. She would need a bath after this just to get the creepy-crawlies off her. She hated funerals. So had her grandmother.

So much regret at funerals, Nellie had once told her.

Emma glanced around the small collection of relatives and close friends who had been invited to her grandmother's memorial service. Emma knew them all. Rocheport, Missouri, was a small town, and most everyone knew one another. One figure stood out, however.

Tucked in between one of her cousins and a local police officer stood a teenage girl. Her vacant eyes were fixed on the funerary urn in the center of the round chapel. It wasn't the girl's presence that struck Emma as odd. Small-town funerals brought out everyone and their extended relations, so it was possible the girl was there with some of the townsfolk. No, what Emma found strange was the girl's dress: a green jumper with white polka dots and a long-sleeve white blouse underneath. It was at least fifty years out of fashion. She looked like something from the pages of a Laura Ingalls Wilder novel. Her shoulder-length hair was parted down the center and braided into pigtails. She just looked . . . odd. Against the suits and dresses of those around her, the girl stuck out. It was true that no one in attendance qualified as "runway ready"—apart from her mother, that was.

She nudged her mother's arm.

"Mom?" she said under her breath, trying not to move her lips. "Who is that?"

"Who?"

"The teenage girl directly across from us in the green dress. Standing next to the police officer."

Angela slowly turned her head to look in the direction her daughter had indicated. "Where?"

"She's right next to the cop. Tall, slender man with short blond hair."

"I see *him* just fine." The tension in her mother's voice betrayed her mounting agitation. "But I don't see this girl you're talking about."

Emma laid her hand on her mother's right leg and slowly began tucking in her fingers, leaving only her index finger extended. It was a trick they had played when Emma was a little girl when one of them wanted to point something out but didn't want other people to see them doing it. When only her index finger remained, Emma slowly turned her hand and pointed across the chapel.

"There."

Emma watched her mother's eyes flicker across the room toward the minister. He was going on about the virtues of a well-lived life and the beatitudes, but Emma was barely listening. Angela stared in the direction Emma was pointing for a few seconds before she sighed. She ran her slender manicured fingers through her hair casually, tucking any strays behind her ears.

"Point her out to me after the service."

"But—"

"Shush." She gave Emma a stern look. She was interrupting her mother's moment of "expected display of public emotion." Sensing the fire in her mother's eyes, Emma could see how grown men would confess their transgressions in open court with just one cold, stern look from this prosecuting attorney. "Remember where you are, Emma Louise."

Emma withdrew her hand as Angela smoothed out the nonexistent wrinkle in her skirt where her daughter's hand had been. Emma clasped her hands together in her lap and leaned back in her chair. She looked across the room. The girl was still there. Only now her attention had shifted.

Now—with vacant dark eyes—she stared directly at Emma. All the warmth seemed to leave Emma's body.

A small tug on her shirtsleeve pulled at her attention, and Emma smiled down at her niece.

"I see her too," the five-year-old said.

Emma's pulse quickened as her palms began to sweat. "You do?"

The girl nodded. "She was at the hospital when Gramma died."

Emma's stomach churned, and the mint in her mouth turned bitter. "She was?"

Another nod.

"You saw her?"

"We played with the LEGOs."

Emma remembered that moment in the hospital. They had been in the waiting room, and Emma had set Julia in a chair, given her a picture book to occupy herself with, and walked across the room to where the other adults were talking with Nellie's doctors. When Emma turned to check on her moments later, Julia had abandoned her picture book and was occupied in the corner of the room, playing with LEGOs.

And talking to herself.

Emma had thought nothing of it at the time; a child's imaginary friend was hardly something worth noting for most adults.

Emma glanced back at the girl. She was still there.

"Did she say what her name was?" Emma whispered.

Julia shook her head. "She seems sad."

Sad wasn't exactly how Emma would have described the girl, but she said nothing. She gave the child's knee a comforting pat before turning her attention back to the priest, willing herself not to look back at the stranger.

II

Emma was grateful to have Nessa with her that night after the house had finally emptied of people. Most of the family had gone back to their lives, except for Emma's mother, who was staying with her brother and his family.

After returning from the funeral, Emma and Nessa had spent the rest of the day cleaning out closets. Six extra-large garbage bags of clothes now sat atop Nellie's bed, ready for donation to the local Goodwill. Backs aching, tired and hungry, the women trudged into the kitchen.

Evening light flooded in through the large front windows as they poured themselves glasses of water and sat down at the bar.

"You hungry?" Nessa asked.

"I could eat, I guess. You?"

Nessa nodded. "Did they leave us anything?"

In true small-town hospitality, the community had been dropping off food for the family over the past few days. For Emma, this seemed perfectly natural. She had lost count of how many casseroles, pies, and such she had helped her grandmother make when someone in their hometown had passed away. It was just something you did in a small town. Neighbors helping neighbors. For Nessa, who was Yankee through and through, it was weird.

As Emma's extensive family had made their way through the house once last time before leaving, each had taken several dishes with them. The sink was piled high with plates, bowls, and platters—all scraped clean. Nellie's Tupperware drawer, on the other hand, was empty.

"I think there's a baked spaghetti in the fridge. Unless someone in the family took it."

Nessa slid off her stool and walked across the linoleum floor—careful not to step on the cracks in her bare feet—and opened the refrigerator door.

"Yeah, it's here." Nessa leaned in to check something else. "And a full loaf of garlic bread."

"That'll do."

Nessa turned the oven to *Warm* and slid the dish inside. She picked at a bit of parmesan-crusted chicken before closing the oven door.

"Mmm. That's good."

"Hey!" Emma teased. "Save some for me too, okay?"

"Maybe. Why don't you grab a shower while this is warming up?"

"Good idea."

Emma slid off her stool and made her way through the kitchen. She paused in front of the sink as she set her glass down.

"I can start on those while you're washing up."

"Oh, no!" Emma protested. "You've done quite enough already, Ness."

"I don't mind, Em."

Emma hugged her. "You're the best. You know that?"

"Yeah," Nessa joked. "I know."

They laughed as Emma pulled away.

"We can do them together after dinner."

"Fair enough."

The warm water felt calming as it cascaded over Emma's face, and for the first time in days, the tension in her body finally began to ease. Blindly, she reached for the shampoo. The scent of lavender struck her with the force of a linebacker. She opened her eyes, but they filled with water, and Emma closed them again as she stepped out of the shower stream. She blinked rapidly several times to clear her vision, and once it had been restored, she looked down at her hand.

There was next to nothing left in the bottle. Maybe enough for one use, Emma surmised. But it was her grandmother's shampoo. *Nellie's* favorite shampoo. Emma could not use this. She would get in trouble. She'd gotten in trouble several times over the years for using it.

But Nellie was gone now. Still, Emma stood there, the tepid water slowly turning colder, and she couldn't do it. Her hand trembled as grief overtook her, and she returned the bottle to the metal basket hanging from the showerhead.

The dam she had spent the past six months erecting to hold back her grief finally broke inside her as she slumped to the floor, pulling her knees to her chest and wrapping her arms around her legs. Her face buried between her knees, she sobbed. The jagged, unrelenting pieces of her grief tore at her insides as they rose to the surface. She wept, tightening her grip around her trembling limbs in a desperate attempt to rebuild the shattered wall around her heart. But it was no use. As she reset one brick, two more broke away until all that remained was the exposed pulsating flesh of a vulnerable organ no larger than a human fist. Such a little thing.

She cried for her grandmother. For her mother. For their broken, disjointed family scattered to the four winds. She cried over lost opportunities that would never come now and for memories that would never be.

"Gran," she whispered.

There was no answer, of course. There would never again be an answer.

Lost to her grief, Emma slowly became aware of something else. She was not alone.

"Hello?" she finally said. The words faltered in her mouth and came out in a childish stutter. "Nessa? Is that you?"

No one answered.

She stood and turned off the tap.

"Hello?"

The only response to be heard was that of the water dripping off her naked frame. The droplets landed with a dull thud on the porcelain tub floor. She stepped out of the tub tentatively, wrapping a towel around herself.

"Nessa? This isn't funny."

Silence.

Emma tucked her hands into her armpits, clutching the towel close. Beneath her towel, her heart pounded. Shoulders tense, Emma inched toward the locked bathroom door. The beige linoleum underfoot was clammy with steam, causing a soft *splat* each time she took a step. She flinched with each one, certain someone else was there. Emma's labored breathing created ripples in the steam. It swirled and moved around her, a lazy river of condensation shrouding the room's features.

Halfway to the door, Emma caught a movement out the corner of her eye. She jerked sideways, and there, in front of the bathroom mirror, stood the shadowy figure of someone watching her.

Emma screamed as she stepped backward. He feet slipped on the wet floor, and she fell against the wall, her head bouncing off the bathroom closet door as she collapsed into a heap. Eyes wide, her head pounding from contact with the door, Emma scrambled back against the wall.

"Emma!" Nessa pounded on the door. The doorknob jiggled as she tried to open the door. She pounded again. "Emma? What's going on in there? Emma! Let me in!"

But Emma couldn't move. Her limbs wouldn't move, wouldn't function. The room had the warm, humid temperature of a rain forest, yet Emma lay curled in a ball in the corner, her body trembling with cold.

Emma wasn't sure how many times it took, but the door finally splintered open, and Nessa burst into the bathroom. Cool air rushed into the steamy room as she fell on her knees by Emma's side.

"Emma, what is it? What happened?"

Her words came out in a terrified jumble, and Emma was reduced to pointing at the oversize bathroom mirror. Nessa looked but saw nothing. The open door had altered the temperature of the room. The steam, along with Emma's guest, had melted away.

She watched as Nessa walked to the mirror, her expression a mixture of confusion and trepidation. Nessa turned back to Emma, who still lay curled up on the floor.

"Did you see something?"

Emma's eyes gave Nessa all the answer she needed. Grabbing a nearby hand towel, Nessa made quick work of wiping down the mirror. When she was done, she hung the towel back on its rack and went to help her friend off the floor. She set Emma on the toilet seat.

"There. That's better."

Emma clutched Nessa's hands, squeezing them tightly.

"Dang, your hands are cold!"

"So-sorry."

"It's okay, Em." Nessa sat down on the floor in front of Emma. Her hands were still shaking. "It's all right."

"I-I s-saw someone in th-the mirror."

"There's no one here but us, Emma," Nessa said, trying to reassure her. "I pro—"

The smoke alarm in the kitchen cut Nessa short.

"The garlic bread!" Nessa exclaimed as she scrambled to her feet. "I completely forgot about the bread."

She dashed out of the bathroom, leaving Emma to collect herself. Emma could hear her in the kitchen muttering to herself over her forgetfulness.

"I'll be right back, Em," she called out from the kitchen. "Just give me a minute to deal with this first."

Seconds later, the alarm ended. Emma stood and cautiously stepped in front of the mirror. It was vacant save for her own reflection. She was still staring at it when Nessa returned.

"You good?" Nessa asked.

"Yeah." Emma swallowed. Her throat was dry from screaming. "I'm good."

Nessa wrapped her arm around Emma's shoulders.

"It was nothing, Em. Just a trick of the light. And all the steam."

"Yeah."

"Come on." Nessa nudged her playfully. "Get dressed. Dinner's ready."

"Okay."

III

Emma's nerves were still frayed when she walked into the dining room ten minutes later. A collection of hostas, ivy, and cut flowers—small arrangements Emma had taken after the memorial service—sat in a cluster on the floor in front of the bay window to catch the last rays of the setting sun. Eight high-backed wood chairs, some of them missing a spindle or two, were scattered around the room. The past few days had seen a rush of friends and neighbors filling the house, and the dining room had been used to hold the spillover once the living room had reached its capacity.

"About time, girl." Nessa was already seated at the head of the vintage midcentury table, and she had set a plate for Emma to her right. A chilled can of Diet Coke sat unopened next to Emma's plate.

"Thanks." Emma pulled a chair to the table and sat down. Her stomach rumbled as she inhaled the heavily seasoned aroma of the parmesan-crusted chicken and spaghetti. It was heavenly.

Her hand was too shaky to hold her fork properly, so Emma reached for the piece of buttered garlic bread. But her hand-eye coordination was still off-kilter, and Emma practically crushed the bread into a gooey ball of dough. She caught sight of Nessa watching her in dismay, a forkful of food suspended halfway between her plate and mouth. Her ears burned with embarrassment as she dropped the bread onto her plate and cupped her hands in her lap beneath the table.

"Sorry."

Nessa took a deep breath. "Do you wanna talk about it?"

"I'm not crazy, Nessa," Emma protested. "And this isn't misdirected grief over Gran's death."

"Uh-huh."

Emma threw her a defiant glare. "I saw something—someone—in the mirror."

Nessa set her fork down. "Who was it?"

Emma's shoulders slumped in defeat. "I couldn't make out a face. It was just . . . a figure. Like the silhouette of someone, ya know?"

"You asked me before the funeral this morning about Miss Nellie seeing people before she passed. Could this . . . figure . . . you saw be who she saw before she died?"

Emma was clutching her hands together so tightly she could feel her nails digging into her skin. "I don't know. Gran never said who it was she saw."

"But you said they were familiar to her, yeah?"

Emma shrugged. "She never said. But with the drugs she was taking by then. . . I mean, Gran was pretty well medicated there at the end."

"I still can't believe she never got treatment."

"It wasn't that she *couldn't* get treatment. She turned it down. Didn't want it. Said she'd had a full life and if it was her time, then her house was in order and she was ready to go."

"Tough ole broad, Miss Nellie."

"I begged her to take the chemo. Begged her to keep fighting."

"She wouldn't do it?"

Emma shook her head.

"I always admired you for stepping up the way you did."

Emma turned, surprised at Nessa's confession. "You what?"

"The way you moved in to help take care of her. Driving back and forth between Rocheport and Columbia for work. Taking her to all the doctors' visits."

"Nessa—"

"You were a godsend for Miss Nellie."

"Stop."

"I'm serious, Em. It takes a special kind of person to just—"

"Just stop, okay!" Emma shouted. "I'm not a saint!"

Nessa fell silent. Emma searched her friend's eyes for a shred of understanding. Finding none, she broke down into sobs.

"I didn't move in here to help Gran," Emma confessed.

Nessa set her napkin on the table and leaned back in her chair. The midcentury spindles creaked as she settled in.

"There's something I never told you about why I moved."

Nessa arched an eyebrow but said nothing. Emma stared across the table, inhaled slowly, and blurted, "Tom asked me to marry him."

"He what?" Nessa sat up in her chair. "When did this happen?"

"Right before Gran's diagnosis."

"And you said no, didn't you?"

Emma nodded.

"Emma! Why?"

A noncommittal shrug was the only response Emma could offer.

"I don't get you, Emma Campbell." Nessa forked a piece of chicken into her mouth and chewed as she continued speaking. "The man is gorgeous, but not conceited. Educated. Owns his own place. Isn't hung up on mama and daddy issues. And can carry on a conversation with anyone. Heck! He's the American version of Mr. Darcy, for crying out loud. Why would you turn that down?"

Emma slammed her fork down, rattling their plates with the force of the impact. "Because it wasn't what I wanted, Nessa!"

"You don't know what you want!"

"I don't want kids!"

The surprise confession caught them both off guard, and a stunned moment of silence passed between them.

"His family was already starting to pressure us to have kids right off. And I didn't want to get sucked into that. Not right now anyway."

"What did Tom say about it?"

"I know you think Tom's not a mama's boy, but—and I hate to break it to ya—he is. He laughed it off as the impatient in-laws just wanting grandkids before they get too old to enjoy them, but not once did he ever speak up when his family started teasing. If I'd said yes, I would've been pregnant by the time we got back from the honeymoon.

"I moved in with Gran because I was running away from Tom. I was running . . . running away from adulthood, I guess. It was an excuse, Nessa, that's all. Call it selfish. Call it cowardice. Call it whatever. But I didn't move in with Gran because I'm any kind of saint. I moved in because I didn't want to deal with Tom, and I knew if I was here taking care of Gran, he and his baby-obsessed family would leave me alone."

"Wow," Nessa said between bites of spaghetti. "That really was selfish."

Emma crossed her arms in front of her, a sullen expression on her face. "Gee, thanks . . . friend!"

"Look here, *friend*." Nessa shook her index finger at Emma.

"No more lectures, Nessa. Please."

"Let me finish."

"Fine."

"Whatever the reason," Nessa said, "it doesn't matter."

Emma turned in surprise. This wasn't the chastising she'd been expecting.

"What matters," continued Nessa, "is that you *stayed*. What matters is even after Tom walked away—and we'll come back to that subject another day, believe you me—you still stayed. You were here when Miss Nellie needed you the most. *You* were the one who took her to the doctors. *You* were the one who took off work when she couldn't be left alone. *You* were the one she turned to when she needed help. That was all you, Em."

Guilty tears ran down Emma's cheeks, staining her gray Mizzou T-shirt the color of charcoal. She buried her face in her hands.

"What matters is you stayed."

"I almost hated her at times." Emma sobbed. "Hated her for not taking the chemo. Hated her for getting sick. Hated her for interrupting my life."

"You think you're the only one who ever felt like that? My father turned into an alcoholic while taking care of Grandpa. It brought out demons in that man none of us knew were there. So don't you go all 'woe is me' with me, girl. Death does things to families. Changes them. Turns them into people they don't recognize."

"I just . . . I just miss her so much."

Nessa reached out and took one of Emma's hands in hers. "Look at me." She waited for Emma to stop crying and look her in the eye. "Now do you understand why Miss Nellie made you do that photo collage? She knew there was gonna come a time when you felt like this. She made you take all those photos to remind you of all the *good* times, Em. So you wouldn't forget them. Ya hear me?"

Emma nodded. "Yes, ma'am."

Nessa laughed. "Let's talk about something else, shall we?"

Another nod.

"You coming back to work tomorrow?"

"Evan gave me the week."

"Oh, did he now?" It was Nessa's turn to be surprised. "Guess you're not the only one feeling guilty."

"Nessa—"

"Don't." She shook her fork at Emma. "Don't sit there and defend that guy. He made your life a living hell every time you needed off to help Miss Nellie. He's a crappy boss suffering from a Napoleon complex, and that's that. You know what?" Nessa swiped her hand through the air as if she were swatting away an errant fly. "No more negativity tonight. Deal?"

"Deal."

"How old is your niece now? The one who sat next to you at the service. I barely recognized her this morning she's gotten so big."

"Julia? She's five now. Going on thirteen, of course."

"God." Nessa sighed. "Seems like only yesterday she was a little baby. I remember you bringing her into the gym that day. Such a sweet baby."

"Julia!" Emma stood up so quickly that her chair fell backward onto the floor. "That's it!"

"That's what?"

Emma rushed out of the room. "Hang on a minute!" she shouted as she ran to her bedroom.

Nessa finished the last few bites on her plate and rose from her chair. "Are you finished eating?" she called out to Emma.

"Yeah, I'm done," came the response from the back of the house.

Nessa collected the plates, and took them to the kitchen sink. She was just about to turn on the tap when Emma returned with her laptop.

"I don't know why I didn't think of this before."

"Think of what?"

"Julia saw her too."

"Saw who?"

Emma set the silver Samsung computer on the counter and connected to the internet.

"There was a girl at the service I didn't recognize."

"A girl?"

"Yeah. Dressed in a weird-looking dress."

"I don't follow you."

Emma turned around to face her. "Mom couldn't see her, but I did. And Julia said she was at the hospital the night Gran died. But no one else saw her that night. Only Julia."

Nessa's confused expression slowly changed to consternation. "I'm not sure I like where this is going, Em. Who was she?"

"Don't know. But now I'm beginning to wonder if *she's* the one Gran was seeing before she passed away." Emma turned back to her laptop before Nessa could say anything further.

"So, why do you need your laptop?"

"The funeral home does live streams of their services."

"They film their funerals?" Nessa was incredulous. "Is that a white-people thing?"

Emma smiled, half laughing at the question. "No. It's a 'half the family is out of town and can't make it to the funeral service' thing."

"You're serious?"

"Yeah."

"They filmed your grandmother's funeral?"

"Yeah." Emma turned back to Nessa, who was still half confused, half repulsed over the revelation.

"You know that's weird, right?"

"Well," said Emma as she logged into the funeral home's webpage, "it wasn't my decision if that helps."

Nessa shook her head. "Not really."

"Here we go."

Nessa stepped closer to the monitor and watched as Emma scrolled down the page to the link to Nellie York's funerary service that morning. She clicked *Play*. A new screen opened, and the two women watched the service play out. Multiple cameras placed in various locations around the chapel captured the service in fifteen-second intervals before fading into the next camera shot. The whole system had been laid out to give online viewers a view of the minister, casket, family, and those friends and family in attendance.

"What exactly are you looking for?"

"She was right behind the minister," Emma said.

Emma scoured the screen, looking for the strange girl she had seen. Each time the camera angle changed, she leaned closer, searching for the unknown visitor. But each time, Emma came up empty-handed. The girl was not there. After several camera changes, Emma hit the *Pause* button.

"There." She pointed to a spot behind the minister.

Nessa took another cautious step forward and peered at the screen.

"I thought you said it was a girl. That's two men."

"She was right there, Nessa. Standing in between those two men."

"Well, she's not there now."

"I'm telling you! She was *right there!*"

"Look, Em, it's been a long day, and my back is killing me. Can we pick this up tomorrow?"

Emma stared at the computer. Where was she? She distinctly remembered seeing the girl right there behind the minister, standing between her cousin and a uniformed police officer. Julia had seen her too. So, why couldn't she find her?

"I'm not crazy, Nessa."

"I know, Em." Nessa gave her a hug. "You're just dealing as best you can."

"The girl *was* there. We both saw her. I'm not making this up."

"I believe you. But if this is a ghost or spirit or whatever, maybe she's focused on you for some reason."

"Me? But why me? I've never seen this girl. Even Gran didn't know who she was! She just said she—"

"Look, I don't know, Em. Maybe figuring out who this girl *is* is why she keeps popping up. Maybe she needs you to figure it out so she can have closure."

"Oh, for God's sake. You make it sound like a daytime soap opera."

"Call it whatever you want, Em." Nessa turned and walked away. "You're the one being haunted. I'm going to take a shower. Don't solve the case without me, Nancy."

"Nancy?"

"Nancy Drew."

"I hate you!" Emma yelled.

"Yeah, whatever."

Nessa's laughter faded as she made her way down the hall to the guest bath. Minutes later, Emma could hear Nessa singing in the shower. She turned back to the computer screen and pressed *Play*.

"I'm not crazy," she told herself.

Three camera changes later, Emma found herself watching footage of the family. She watched the exchange she'd had that morning with her mother, the way Angela had brushed her daughter's hand from her leg after Emma had tried to point out the strange guest. She watched the brief conversation she'd had with Julia. Sweet little Julia.

Emma watched as she turned away from Julia back to the minister, who was nearing the end of his sermon. As she did, little Julia turned to the person sitting on the other side of her. Emma leaned in closer to see who it was. One of her uncles, no doubt. Or Julia's mother, maybe. Emma couldn't be certain who'd been sitting there that morning, and the video from this angle ended right at Julia's shoulder. But whoever it was reached out and held the girl's hand.

The camera angle changed once more, and Emma felt her blood pressure drop. She gripped the counter to keep from crumbling to the floor.

There, sitting just to Julia's right, was the teenage girl. She smiled comfortingly at Julia, who gazed up at the older girl. No fear. No trepidation. Julia was completely comfortable with whoever this girl was.

Had Julia seen her before the hospital? Emma's mind raced with possible explanations.

"She seems sad," Julia had said.

Emma watched as the girls shared a tender moment and turned their attention back to the minister. Emma was about to yell for Nessa when the girl's gaze changed again. She looked straight into the camera. Straight into Emma's eyes.

Emma stood momentarily frozen. That chair had been empty during the service. She remembered that now. No one was sitting there. No one. She was certain of it. Just before the camera angle changed again, the girl smiled.

"Who are you?" Emma whispered.

The video changed to the minister talking. Emma dragged the time bar back twenty seconds to watch the scene again.

She and Julia talked, and then they turned to listen to the minister. Change of camera. Julia's hand moved, and she looked right and smiled. Only this time . . . the chair was empty. The girl was gone.

IV

Over the week that followed, Emma began to question her sanity. She felt stalked. Hunted. She took to leaving the hallway light on at night despite the fact she locked her bedroom door before going to sleep. She walked into rooms and paused, trying to gauge whether she was alone. Every corner she turned became a test of nerves. Every closed door she opened became a potential threat. Every creak of the old house became a gunshot through Emma's frazzled nerves.

Twice she had seen the specter's shadow outside her bedroom window. She'd closed the drapes—first in her bedroom, then the living room. The entire house soon followed suit, plunging the warm, loving home Emma had once shared with her Gran into something more akin to a tomb. Each time Emma began to feel herself clawing her way out of the abyss and into humanity, the little ghost dragged her back into the shadows.

Three days after the funeral, Emma had driven the fifteen miles to Columbia, where the family met with the attorneys to discuss her grandmother's estate. It was the first time she had been out of the house since the funeral. Nellie's house had been left to Emma, which infuriated Angela. The ensuing argument had nearly escalated to a shouting match; however, a security guard had interrupted them. Emma glanced at the middle-aged man in his crisp white shirt and navy trousers standing in the open doorway, a look of consternation on his tanned face, his free hand hovering close to a taser gun. Shame reddened Emma's face, and she was about to apologize for causing a scene when she saw the young girl dressed in her green-and-white dress standing in the hallway just behind the man. Emma had panicked and fled through a secondary exit. Returning home, she was pulled over by a state trooper, who took one look at the grief-stricken young woman in the driver's seat and ordered her to slow down and let her off with a warning even though Emma had been going eighty-five in a seventy-mile-per-hour zone.

By Friday afternoon, Nessa—who was still staying with Emma—had had enough.

"You're getting out of this house," Nessa demanded. She forced Emma into the shower, her first since the meeting with the lawyers. The shattered bathroom door was an incessant haunting reminder of the week's events.

The warm afternoon air felt good against Emma's skin as the two women walked the few blocks into town. A handful of neighbors were out tending their lawns, and the scent of freshly mown grass wafted in the air. For the first time, Emma felt life returning to her body. Her muscles relaxed as she walked alongside her best friend through the neighborhood toward downtown Rocheport.

"Feels good to be out of that house, eh?" Nessa said. She plucked a primrose from a hedgerow of rose bushes that defined the old Dickerson property, sliding the stem behind her ear. Its sun-washed petals gleamed even brighter against her dark hazelnut skin. "All the flowers in bloom. I love being outdoors in the summertime."

"Me too," Emma said softly, still afraid of expressing the slightest joy out loud for fear it would be snatched away. "I'm sorry I've been such bad company."

"That's putting it mildly, don't ya think? You've been wandering around that house scared of your own shadow."

"I just—"

"You're grieving, Em." Nessa slipped her arm into her friend's and smiled.

"It's not just that."

They reached the end of the block and turned right onto Central Street, which ran through the center of town. A woman jogged by, waving as she passed.

"Hey, Sara!" Emma and Nessa yelled in unison, waving back at the young woman.

"So, what is it?" Nessa prodded after a few steps as they walked past the antiques shop.

Emma stopped in front of a vintage chest of drawers. Its polished mahogany finish shone like warm caramel under the May sun. She looked pensively at Nessa, sizing her up.

"Promise you won't laugh?"

Nessa put a hand on Emma's shoulder. "Best friends always laugh."

Emma's mouth fell open in hurt and anger until she caught the mischievous glint in Nessa's eye. She let out a heavy breath and stuck her hands into her pockets.

"Well, at least you're honest about it, I guess."

Nessa tugged on her sleeve as she resumed walking. "Come on. Food first, then confessional."

They stopped by the Rocheport Diner, where Nessa bought a takeout order of their famous "extreme" nachos and three bottles of Diet Coke. Two blocks down, they spread their wares out on one of the wooden picnic tables. The small park stretched lazily along the Missouri River. Joggers and cyclists taking advantage of the warm weather passed them as they made their way up and down the famous Katy Trail—one of Missouri's countless hiking trails—which ran along the river's edge for miles in both directions.

Emma watched as a young athletic jogger sprinted by. Wearing a black tank top with matching running shorts, he was the picture of health. Emma's gaze followed the man's frame as he receded into the distance.

That was once my life, she thought. She loved jogging along the river early in the morning before the world started waking up. The crunch of gravel beneath her feet, the silence of nature around her. That perfect time when it was just her . . . and Tom . . . and the trail.

But that was before. Before Gran became too ill to be left alone. Before she broke up with Tom. Before the funeral. Before this ghost who, for whatever reason, would not leave her alone.

"He's cute, huh?" Nessa asked, clocking Emma's gaze. She was still staring at the jogger.

"What?"

"The jogger. He's cute, don't ya think?"

"I guess."

Nessa opened the Styrofoam to-go box and handed Emma a plastic fork. Between them lay a heaping mound of freshly fried corn tortilla chips submerged under layers of steaming nacho cheese sauce, shredded iceberg lettuce, diced white onions, black olives, chopped tomatoes, and jalapeños. Strips of grilled chicken—still hot—were piled atop this and finished with a dollop of rich sour cream right in the center.

"Mmm," they both said in unison.

"Now," Nessa said, reaching for a crispy chip along the edge, "tell me what's going on with you."

Emma watched as Nessa piled a little bit of everything onto the massive chip—the perfect bite—and popped it into her mouth.

"God, these are good," Nessa mumbled as she chewed.

"How much do you wanna know?"

Nessa paused at this, setting her fork down. Emma saw the caution in her eyes. The fear. And then . . . something of understanding, maybe? Nessa closed the carton, then wrapped her fork in a napkin and tossed it into the bag with the nachos. She set it aside and reached across the table for Emma's hands. It was only then Emma realized she was trembling.

"I'm your best friend, Em. I want to *know* everything. Whatever it is. I know you've been struggling since Miss Nellie passed, but—"

"It's not just that."

"Okay, so tell me what it *is*. Tell me how I can help."

Emma took a deep breath and exhaled slowly, counting backward from ten. She could do this. She had to do this. She had to tell *someone*.

"You remember the girl at Gran's funeral I told you about? The one Julia saw at the hospital?"

Nessa nodded. "The ghost."

Emma waited for the smirk. She expected Nessa to smirk, expected her to laugh it off. But she didn't. Instead, Nessa leaned forward and tightened her grip on Emma's hand.

"I'm . . ." Emma's voice faltered, and she closed her mouth tight. Saying it out loud would make it real. Saying it out loud would change everything.

"Go on," Nessa said. "Tell me."

"I'm . . . I'm still seeing her."

There. She'd said it. Emma glanced around the park, expecting to find the girl watching them, observing as Emma and Nessa talked about her. No one was there. The park was vacant save for the two of them. The only sounds Emma heard were the gentle rush of the river, the rustling of the willow trees around them, and the crunch of gravel under a cyclist's tires as she rode by.

Nessa said nothing at first, just nodded. She watched the cyclist speed by. Emma couldn't gauge her expression. What was going on inside Nessa's head right now? Did Nessa think she was crazy? Did she think she making it up?

Emma's chest tightened as beads of sweat appeared on the edges of her forehead.

God, I could just die, she thought. *Why the hell did I say anything?*

"Is she here now?"

Emma sat up straight, shocked by the question. Tears welled in her eyes. Leave it to Nessa to go at the problem head-on.

"Hey." Nessa shook her hand, pulling Emma out of her thoughts. "Don't do that."

"Don't do what?"

"Shut me out."

"Oh, Nessa!" Emma cried, finally breaking down. She covered her face with her hands and lay her head against the table.

Nessa came around and sat next to Emma, taking her into her arms.

"She won't leave me alone," Emma cried into Nessa's chest. "She shows up everywhere I go. And I don't know why. Gran is gone. And I can't ask her what to do. I can't ask why she's here."

Nessa stroked Emma's hair in silence, letting her get everything out in the open. Emma told her about the episode at the lawyer's office. How she had seen the girl in the bathroom mirror that night. How she had seen the girl standing outside her bedroom window.

"I wondered why you'd taken to shutting all the curtains."

"This isn't funny!" Emma recoiled, yanking a napkin from the table to wipe her eyes.

"Oh, I ain't laughing, trust me! You tell me you've been seeing a ghost the past week and a half! All the while I've been sleeping there? Uh-uh, trust me, Emma Louise Campbell, *laughing* I ain't."

Emma almost felt abandoned as Nessa slid out of the park bench and went around to where she had been sitting previously.

"I'm sorry."

"We don't do ghosts!"

Emma laughed. The whole thing seemed ridiculous, and Nessa's retort was the cherry on top.

"You think I'm playing?"

"Well," Emma managed to say between fits of laughter, "whether you do them or not, it's still here."

Nessa humphed, folding her arms across her chest in indignation. When Emma continued laughing, she reached for the nachos and resumed eating.

"Laugh it up, girl. You'll be sleeping by yourself tonight too."

"Afternoon, ladies."

Emma's head turned to the unexpected visitor, and her laughter fell suddenly silent.

"Tom!"

"Hey there. Heard you girls laughing half a block away and thought I'd come see what was so funny."

"You didn't hear me laughing," Nessa protested, pointing a finger at Emma as she shoved another loaded chip into her mouth. "That's all this one."

"What are you doing here?" Emma asked. He looked good.

Tom shrugged. "Had the munchies for nachos. And the diner's got the best around."

Nessa motioned him to sit down before Emma could turn him down. "Hmm! Come join us! We've got plenty."

"You sure? I don't wanna intrude." Tom raised his hands in half protest.

"Absolutely," Nessa ordered. "There's enough here for a party. Come and sit down."

"Ah, thanks, Nessa." Tom slipped in beside Nessa and took a nacho covered in cheese sauce and jalapeños. "Mmm. That's good."

"Help yourself," Nessa prodded despite the protest kick Emma had given her under the table. She slid the container closer to him. "Here, have a soda."

Emma's mouth fell open. "You little sneak."

Tom and Nessa both turned from their conversation in mock dismay.

"You set this up, didn't you?"

Nessa shrugged. "Maybe."

"I don't believe you! What else did you tell him?"

"Hey!" Tom interjected. "Don't be mad at Nessa. She's been worried about you since your grandmother passed away and asked if I'd stop by."

"So, this is *what* exactly? An intervention? A 'Come to Jesus' meeting to keep me from jumping off a bridge or something?"

"Calm down," Tom said sternly. He looked around them. Passersby were starting to notice the raised voices coming from the park, and he knew small-town gossip traveled fast.

Emma could feel the blood rushing to her face, the angry heat radiating off her ears, the humiliating tears forming in the corners of her eyes. She crossed her arms across her heaving chest and looked out at the river. She wanted to scream. She wanted to cry. She wanted to bang her fists against something. Anything. Anything that would make this whole thing go away.

"I'm not crazy."

"We're not saying you are, Em," Nessa said between bites of chicken. "But you've got me running scared here."

Emma hadn't expected that. Her shoulders relaxed as she turned back to Nessa. She was crying.

"I'm scared, Em. This past week, I . . . I feel like I'm losing you one piece at a time."

Emma started to say something, but Nessa cut her off.

"Every time I leave that house, I never know who I'm coming back to. What I'm coming back to. It's like you're getting smaller and smaller every day, Em. And I can't sit by and watch my best friend turn into someone I don't know."

Emma reached across the table and took her hand. "I'm sorry, Nessa. I didn't—" Emma's throat tightened with the guilt swelling inside her. "I didn't know."

Tom reached out his left hand and placed it tenderly on top of the two women's.

"We know you're not crazy, Em," Tom said. "And we may not understand everything you're going through, but that doesn't mean you have to go through it alone."

His hand was warm. Strong. Gentle. Emma looked from Nessa to Tom and back again. She couldn't look at him right now. Not without remembering the strength of Tom's arms around her. The warmth of his breath against her neck when he buried his face in her hair. The way his five-o'clock shadow tickled her skin.

"Emma's been seeing a ghost." Nessa's words cut through the air like a razor across a man's throat.

"Don't!" Emma cautioned.

"No more hiding, Em," Nessa argued. "If you don't figure out *what* this girl wants and *why* she's coming to you, you may never get a moment's peace ever again. And you *will* end up going crazy."

"Uh, okay." Tom withdrew his hand. "Will one of you fill me in? How long has this been going on?"

Nessa and Emma exchanged glances, each one waiting for the other to speak.

"You tell him," Emma said, a tinge of defeat in her voice. "You'll be more objective than I'd be."

Nessa nodded. Still clutching Emma's hand, she turned to Tom.

"She's been seeing this girl since Miss Nellie's funeral. And it turns out Miss Nellie was seeing her too in the months leading up to her death."

Tom said nothing, only listened as Nessa recounted the events of the previous week: The impact it was having on Emma's mental health. The drawn curtains. Her lack of appetite. Her fear of leaving the house. Her fear of staying in the house.

Several times Emma saw him glance in her direction. The sting of humiliation was dulled only by the realization that Emma *knew* she needed help. She needed to figure this out, and she couldn't do it on her own.

When Nessa finally stopped talking, the park fell strangely quiet around them.

"Did your grandmother ever mention her?" Tom asked. "Say who she was?"

Emma shook her head. "She didn't know."

"Like a distant cousin or something, maybe?"

"It's possible."

"Anything's possible at this point," Nessa joked.

"Where did she grow up?"

"St. Louis, I guess." Emma shrugged. "Only child. Older parents. She never really talked about her childhood that much."

"Would your mom or one of your aunts or uncles remember?"

"My mom is a nonstarter; I can tell you that much. The two of them never got along. Not sure what happened—no one's ever talked about it—but whatever it was, it cut deep. For both of them. She just wants to sell the house and be done with the whole thing."

"But you don't?"

Emma paused. It was the first time anyone had bothered asking her what *she* wanted.

"I don't know," she finally said. "I was thinking of renovating the old place and sticking around for a while."

Nessa looked at her with hurt astonishment.

"I thought . . . I thought we were going to move up north," Nessa said. "Take on the big city. Be celebrity trainers."

"You've both been saying that for years now," Tom added.

"I know. I just . . . I don't know. I'm not ready to leave it now."

"Oh."

Emma could feel the hurt in Nessa's voice, and it stung knowing she was the cause. She glanced at Tom, who—recognizing Emma's silent plea for help—changed the subject.

"What about your uncles and aunts? Would they know anything about Miss Nellie's upbringing?"

"My uncle in Columbia is older than Mom." Emma smiled, grateful for the save. "He might know something."

"Did she leave any family documents? Old photos or anything?"

"No," Emma said. "She—"

"That's not true," Nessa said. "Your mom brought by a stack of old papers that day you went to the lawyer's office."

"When was this?" It was the first time Emma was hearing about her mother's visit—not that she minded missing her sudden appearance at the house. "You never told me she came to the house."

"I'm sorry. I completely forgot. You were so upset when you got back that I lied when she came by a couple hours later. Said you were out on a run."

"Thanks for that."

"I could tell when you got back it hadn't gone well. And your mother was ready for a fight when she arrived. I think she was madder you were out than she was over what happened at the lawyer's."

"What *did* happen?" Tom asked. "If you don't mind me asking, that is."

"*She* turned up," Emma said flatly. "Scared me so bad I took off."

"Oh."

"Yeah. *Oh.*"

Tom turned to Nessa, changing the subject again. "So, did you look at the papers?"

"Of course not! They weren't mine to go through."

"Where'd you put them?" Emma asked.

"They're still on the dining table, I guess. Unless you moved them."

"No, I haven't been in there in a couple days."

"Why don't we go take a look at them?" Tom suggested. "It might point us in the right direction."

"Right." Nessa snatched up the to-go box of half-eaten nachos and slipped it back into the plastic bag. She was up and walking away before Emma or Tom were even standing. "I'll put these in the fridge before they ruin. No sense in throwing away good nachos, right?"

Emma's limbs felt heavy as she watched Nessa walk away. She knew she had hurt her, knew Nessa had been counting down the months. Moving to New York City was all they'd talked about since finishing their certifications. And now, when Emma was finally free, when it seemed like the universe was finally opening a door, Emma didn't want to leave.

Tom's muscular arm wrapped around her shoulder, and Emma leaned into his chest.

"Give her time," he said. "She'll come around."

"I feel like I stabbed her in the back."

"You didn't."

"Am I wrong for wanting to stay?"

Tom sighed and sat back down. "I'm not sure I'm the person you should be asking, Em."

"What's that supposed to mean?" Emma asked, whirling around on him.

Tom raised his hands in surrender. "I don't wanna fight."

"You're right." She took a step back, shoving her hands into her pants pockets.

Tom smiled. "I miss that about you."

"What?"

"The way you always put your hands in your pockets when you're trying to *not* get in an argument but secretly *want* to get in an argument."

Emma gasped. "I do not!"

"Do too." Tom laughed. A hearty laugh. It reminded Emma of all those long nights spent on Tom's sofa watching black-and-white movies.

He stood and motioned her on to the house. She fell in step beside him, still eyeing him warily.

"You didn't answer my question."

"Em, why did you break up with me?"

"You wanna talk about that *now*? Seriously? With all the crap I'm going through right now?"

Tom stopped, grabbing hold of Emma's elbow. "You left because you didn't want to be tied down to Columbia."

"No, I didn't—"

"Yes, you did."

"No, I—"

"You said it yourself. Don't you remember? You told me you weren't ready to settle down. Said you still had dreams to pursue."

"Tom, I—"

"Love was never our problem, Emma. I knew you loved me. And God knows I loved you. Hell, I still love you. But you never loved me enough to stay *here*. To let go of everything else"—Tom motioned his arms at the world around them—"out there."

Emma didn't know what to say. Tom extended his hand as she reached for it. Bringing it to her lips, she kissed his knuckles.

"If you want to stay in Rocheport, that's fine with me. Maybe give us another try." He withdrew his hand and cupped Emma's chin between his thumb and index finger. "But if you're staying because you feel guilty over something that happened with Miss Nellie or obligated to some romantic idea of 'the ole family homestead' . . . Emma, what the hell are you doing? Get out of here. Go. Live your life. Move to the city the way you always wanted to. Be the best, most exclusive personal trainer New York's ever seen."

Emma laughed, fighting back tears.

"Just go," Tom continued. "Okay?"

"Tom." The word seemed more a prayer than a response, but for what, Emma wasn't sure. Forgiveness? Understanding? Or maybe, perhaps, an acceptance that this man knew her better than she knew herself.

He wrapped his arms around her and pulled her close. They stood there for several moments, warmed by the late afternoon sun peeking through the treetops, oblivious to the comings and goings of the neighbors around them. A passing car honked at them, cutting short their reverie.

"Right," Tom said. "Guess we better get back to your place and sort this mystery girl out."

V

By the time Emma and Tom reached the house, Nessa had switched on all the lights, drawn back the curtains in all the rooms, and opened the packet of documents Emma's mother had dropped off. A pot of fresh coffee was percolating in the kitchen. Three lemon-yellow Fiesta mugs sat on the counter in front of the filling pot, patiently waiting to be filled.

"Nessa?" Emma called out as they passed through the kitchen.

"In here," came Nessa's cheerful reply.

They walked into the dining room, where Nessa had spread out several piles of documents.

"Thought we could divide and conquer," Nessa said. "We've got photographs, documents, and letters and postcards." She pointed to each stack as she spoke. "Be right back. Just going to grab my laptop in case we need to search anything online."

She disappeared down the hall, and Emma, still standing in the doorway between the dining room and kitchen, looked up at Tom. With the crook of his head, he motioned Emma to follow after Nessa.

"Go. Talk to her. I'll grab the coffee. You still take two creams, one sugar?"

"Yeah." Emma glanced apprehensively across the dining room to the hall beyond. "What do I say?"

"Tell her the truth, Em. She deserves that much at least."

"Right." Emma sighed. She left the room to find Nessa as Tom turned back to the kitchen to pour coffee.

Minutes later, the women returned to the dining room, wiping tears as they found Tom already seated at the table and leafing through a manila folder of documents. Steam wafted over three mugs of coffee situated in front of him. The warm aroma of fresh coffee lured Emma and Nessa to the table, where Emma sat opposite Tom and Nessa sat at the head of the table. Emma gave him a quick wink and a smile, letting him know things had been patched up with Nessa, and she could see the relief on his face as he relaxed into the high-backed modern midcentury chair.

"Check this out." He handed Emma three aged brown pieces of paper. "Didn't know you were Canadian."

"What?" Emma yanked the documents from Tom, almost ripping one in her excitement.

"Careful, Em!" Tom scolded. "These are pretty old."

"What are they?" Nessa asked.

"Immigration papers."

"From where?"

"Nova Scotia, Canada," Emma said, scanning the documents. Her pulsed quickened as she read.

"Well?" Nessa prodded. "What do they say?"

"They're immigration papers for Gran and her parents. Nelda Rosemary Roberts. Rosemary. I didn't know that."

Emma's throat felt as dry as the desert. She reached for her coffee, which had been carefully prepared by Tom, and took a quenching sip. It burned as it trickled down her throat. She looked up from the paper. Tom and Nessa were both leaned forward against the table, eagerly anticipating what Emma would say next.

"Go on," Tom said encouragingly.

"Nelda Rosemary Roberts moved from Canada in 1948 with her parents, Tobias Eugene Roberts and Marian Cecilia MacDonald Roberts."

"That's a pretty name," Nessa said. "Cecilia."

"Tobias," Emma continued, "was a former member of the Royal Canadian Mounted Police."

"A Mountie?" Tom said. "Your great-grandpa was a Mountie?"

"That's hot," Nessa joked.

Emma laughed, taking another sip of her coffee. "Cecilia was a seamstress. Gran is listed as three months old."

"Anyone else mentioned?" Nessa asked.

Emma scanned the three documents and shook her head.

"No. No mention of anyone else. Nessa, you were here when Mom brought these by. Did she say anything about them when she was here?"

"All she said was they were in your grandmother's safe-deposit box at the bank."

"Do they know how long they'd been there?"

"A long time from the way your mom talked."

"Like . . . years?"

"More like decades, Em. Most of this stuff your mom and aunts and uncles had never seen before."

"What made her bring it here?"

"She said no one else wanted it."

"Okay," Tom said, changing the subject. "That means that whoever this girl is, she must be from Nova Scotia, right?"

"Not necessarily," Nessa said, thumbing through several black-and-white photographs. "She could be someone Miss Nellie met here when she was little."

"Right," Nessa added, "like someone she was supposed to know but couldn't remember."

"Yeah."

"So, back to square one is what you're saying," Tom said.

Emma sighed. "How do you find a needle in a haystack?"

"The answer's here somewhere," Tom said. "We just have to keep looking."

As the light faded to darkness outside the dining room window, the three friends scoured the items Emma's mother had left. Every photo was scrutinized for any sign of Emma's ethereal visitor. Family documents were read and reread with each tidbit of information discussed. At one point, Emma had left to grab a notebook from her room, and now she had over a dozen pages of notes and questions that were still unresolved.

"All these photographs," Emma said, holding an 8 × 10-inch family portrait. Seven smiling faces beamed back at her. Emma didn't recognize a single one. Some pictures had names written on the back, some had dates, and some were blank.

Emma's hopes were dimming. "This is hopeless. Even if we were staring right at this girl, we *still* wouldn't know it. She could be any *one* of these people. At *any* given point. *Any* given year. There's just not enough to go on."

Tom was looking at a group photo dated 1931. "Maybe we're looking at this the wrong way."

"How so?" Nessa asked.

"We've been trying to figure out who this girl is."

"Right," Emma said.

"Maybe we should work backward instead: figure out who she isn't and then go from there."

"Who she isn't? Tom, that doesn't make any sense."

"Hang on, Em. Hear me out. You have all these family photographs. Plot everything out."

"You mean like a family tree?" Nessa asked.

Tom snapped his fingers and pointed to her. "Exactly."

Emma wasn't convinced. She propped her head in her hand. "I don't know."

"A family tree," Nessa countered, "however crude, might help if you do end up going to Nova Scotia. It'd at least give you a place to start looking and who to start asking."

"True." Emma gazed out the dining room window. Burnt-orange shadows covered the yard as the Missouri summer sun slowly ducked beneath the horizon. "But I don't even know if this girl *is* family."

"At least it's a start, Em," Nessa said.

"And I," Tom added, "know just where to start." He flipped over the weathered photograph in his hand and handed it to Emma. "Your great-grandfather's four brothers."

"What? How do you know?"

"I have three brothers. I know this photo. These guys are brothers, count on it."

Emma examined the photo carefully. "They do look a lot alike." Her tone was still wary.

"Believe me, I know a sibling lineup when I see it."

Emma turned the photo over and read the names aloud. "Matty, Bart, Sam, Toby, Jules—1931."

Nessa leaned over. "Which one is your great-grandfather?"

"I'm guessing it's Toby, but I'm not sure. Gran's parents died before I was born, and she never talked about them that often."

"What was his full name again?" Tom asked.

"Hang on. I have it here somewhere." Emma dug through a stack of discarded documents until she found the right one. "Here it is. Tobias Eugene Roberts."

"Toby would certainly seem to fit," Nessa said.

"So, these others," Emma said, contemplating the photograph, "would be my great-uncles."

"Take a look at this," Nessa said. She handed Emma two brittle brown pages—birth certificates for Tobias and Marian. Both documents identified Digby, Nova Scotia, as their place of birth.

"Where's Digby?" Emma asked.

Nessa opened a web browser on her laptop and did a quick search. "Digby, Nova Scotia. Seaside town in southwestern Nova Scotia. Population 2,060 according to the last census. Famous for scallops and lobster."

"Sounds picturesque," Tom added.

"Well, if these pictures are anything to judge by, yeah, I'd say so."

"So, if Tobias and Marian and Gran were all born in Digby, there must be a larger family presence there."

"You might have extended family still living there," Tom said.

"You should go check it out, Em," Nessa said.

Part of Emma wanted to. Part of her knew she would eventually have to. The other side of her . . . No. It wasn't possible.

Emma shook her head. "I can't go to Nova Scotia. I've got to be at work on Monday. I've got this house to deal with. I can't go running off on a wild-goose chase."

"I think you should," Nessa said.

Tom nodded. "I'm with Nessa. I mean, look. We've been at this for hours now, and we haven't uncovered anything that helps you figure out who this girl is. Maybe the answer's up there."

"What if it's not? Nessa said it herself. Apart from the photographs, none of these documents mention anyone other than Gran, Tobias, and Marian. It's possible—even likely—this girl is someone she met *after* she moved to the US."

"Maybe," Tom countered.

"I think Gran recognized her. I can't be certain of it, but the way she talked about this girl, it always seemed to me that she was someone from Gran's past. But according to this, she was only a few months old when they immigrated to America. She wouldn't remember anything from that time. She was too young."

Nessa sighed and looked down at the picturesque images on her laptop screen.

"Ya know, Em," Nessa said, looking down the table at the painting on the opposite wall. "Miss Nellie's painting does kinda look like Digby."

The trio stared across the room at the oversize oil on canvas. A great tree anchored the shoreline along the left-hand side. In the background was a mass of boats at harbor, their masts all bobbing peacefully in the gentle waters. Two girls swung from a rope swing hanging off the largest branch.

"Maybe," Emma said. "Gran never said if this was a real place or something made-up."

"Miss Nellie painted that?" Nessa asked, eyebrows arched and mouth agape.

"No, her mother, Marian, painted it."

"It's beautiful," Tom added.

"Gran said it was a wedding present from her mother. Apparently, she made Gran promise to never get rid of it." Emma now stared at the painting with new interest. "But I can see your point, Nessa. It does look like it could be Digby. Anyway . . ." Emma turned away from the painting and flipped to a fresh page in her notebook. "Let's scrape together this family tree, shall we?"

The amber shadows outside had turned pale white as night fell. Once again, they scrutinized each photograph, postulating what the occasion could have been and the relationship between the people in each one. In some they could identify couples, which helped flesh out the makeshift family tree filling up Emma's notebook. Several branches had been x'd out—usually after they found a photo that corrected an earlier assumption about the family line. After the fourth correction, Emma lost patience with it and got up from the table.

"Where you going?" Tom asked.

"To get a bigger piece of paper."

Tom and Nessa exchanged a confused shrug. When Emma returned a minute later, she was carrying a roll of Christmas wrapping paper. Before either of them could say anything, Emma pulled out a piece as long as her arm and ripped it from the roll. Laying it out on the table back side up, she began anew at the top of the page, writing in Sharpie this time instead of pen. Tom and Nessa watched, amused grins plastered across their weary faces, as Emma copied each name from her notebook onto the sheet of wrapping paper. Finally, after several minutes of work, Emma stood and stretched.

"There," she proclaimed. "Done."

Tom and Nessa rose and walked around the dining table. They admired their work. Most of the major players had been identified. Tobias and Marian. Tobias's brothers and parents. An assortment of spouses. Marian's mother and father.

There were holes, to be sure, but at least Emma had somewhere to start. She reached for her notebook to check her names and lines one more time and caught sight of a photograph where Nessa had been sitting. Picking it up, Emma felt her legs wobble, and she collapsed into her chair.

"Emma!" Tom cried out in alarm. "Are you okay?" He stepped to her side and knelt beside her, his hand on her arm. "Jesus, your pulse is racing. What's wrong?"

Emma didn't answer, couldn't answer in that moment. Her hands trembled as she forced the muscles in her arm to turn the photograph over. The hand went numb as Emma read the name.

"Oh, God."

"What?" Nessa asked. She had pulled a chair close and now sat on Emma's other side. "What is it?"

"It's . . . her."

"Her who?" Tom asked.

"The girl. The ghost."

"Really?" Nessa snatched the photo from Emma and flipped it over. "Marian."

"Your gran's mother?" Tom said.

"The ghost . . . is your great-grandmother?" Nessa said. "I thought you said she was younger. A teenager."

"She is," Emma said, taking the photo back. "But this is her. I'm sure of it. The same nose. Same facial expression. Same shoulder-length hair. This is her. She's older in this photograph, but I know this face. I'm telling you . . . this is her."

"You're sure?"

"Nessa, this . . . is her."

"Well, that's one mystery solved," Tom said, looking across at Nessa.

Emma was still too stunned to move. She kept staring vacantly at the photograph, into those haunting eyes that had stared back at her at the funeral, eyes that had twinkled with mischief as she looked directly at Emma when she watched the video playback.

"Dang, is that the time?" Tom said, glancing at Nessa's laptop screen.

"Yeah. Just after eight."

"I have to go," Tom said, rising from the table. "Gotta be at work early tomorrow."

"Thanks for stopping by, Tom," Nessa said, still seated at the table.

"Yeah, no problem." He patted his pockets and scowled. "Now where'd I put my keys?" He glanced across the table, finding them next to his cell phone. "Just wish we had found more to help. But at least now we know *who* we're dealing with, right?"

Emma felt unexpectedly light-headed as he began walking toward the front door. She wanted to say something, knew she needed to say something.

"It's all right," she blurted out. She looked to Nessa for help, but Nessa's focus was on her laptop screen. "It's late. I think we should call it a night anyway."

Tom shoved his phone into his pocket. They stood on opposite sides of the table, each one waiting for the other, each one too afraid to take the first step. After a brief awkward silence, Nessa finally looked up.

"I . . . think my battery's about dead," Nessa said, getting up quickly. "Better go plug it back in. Night, Tom."

"Night, Nessa. Good to see ya."

"You too." She disappeared down the hall but reappeared a moment later. "Hey, if you wanna take the rest of those nachos home with you, be my guest."

"You sure?"

"Yeah, knock yourself out."

"Thanks."

"Bye." Nessa waved as she retreated down the hall.

"I'll walk you out."

The night was warm, like a hot bath that'd been left out for a while. Lightning bugs danced in the grass, creating a mini fireworks show across the front lawn. A sliver of a moon played hide-and-seek amongst the trees as Emma and Tom walked away from the house.

"Where are you parked?" Emma finally managed to ask.

"Downtown. In front of the antiques store."

"Oh."

"You don't have to walk me to my car, ya know," Tom teased. "I'm a big boy. I can ask for directions and everything."

He laughed when Emma's face reddened.

"I don't mind."

"I know. I was just teasing. But I do think you need to head back."

"Why do you say that?"

"Because you left Nessa all alone in that house with a big scary ghost." She punched his arm in mock anger.

"And Nessa doesn't do very well with ghosts and stuff."

"Fine." Emma cocked her head up in indignation. The effort only made Tom laugh harder. "I'll leave you to your own devices, then, Tom Evans."

She spun on her heels and was about to step away when he caught her by the arm. In the process, he nearly dropped the plastic bag containing the to-go box of nachos.

"Aw, Em. Don't be like that."

His teeth glimmered in the moonlight. Emma wanted to get lost in that smile. She smiled back. Was he about to kiss her? Did she want him to kiss her? Yes, she wanted to. No. No, she didn't. They weren't together anymore. But tonight had been so wonderful. He was still smiling.

"Th-thank you," Emma finally stammered. "For tonight, I mean. And . . . for listening."

The moment was over. She had killed it. And worse, Tom knew it was over too.

"No problem, Em." He fist-bumped her shoulder and continued down the street to his truck.

She watched him walk away.

Go after him! she yelled at herself.

I can't.

Yes, you can! He's right there! Go after him!

"One thing doesn't make sense to me," Tom yelled out from two houses down.

Emma laughed. "Just one?"

He laughed. It rode the summer winds to her ear like a blissful melody she wanted to keep listening to.

"If Marian really is the ghost . . . why you?"

The question abruptly silenced the conversation in her head. She took a few steps forward. Tom, in turn, took a few steps back toward her.

"What do you mean?"

"I mean, Marian never knew you. She died before you were born. She wouldn't know you is all I'm saying. Miss Nellie makes sense. That was her mom. But she has no connection to you. Apart from family, that is. It doesn't make sense for her to come to you after Miss Nellie's gone."

"You think it's someone else?"

They were only a few feet apart now.

Tom shrugged. "I don't know. You were pretty certain from the photograph, and—having never seen this ghost—I can't say one way or the other. It just seems . . . strange that she would come to you and not your mom or one of your aunts or uncles who were alive when Marian and Tobias were still alive. Why not go to one of them? Why you?"

"Maybe she wants me to do something."

"Maybe. But I still think you need to go visit Nova Scotia. I think the answers you're looking for are gonna be up there. Not in that house."

"You may be right."

"Well . . ." He sighed. "Whatever you decide, I support you."

"Thanks."

"Any time." Tom motioned behind him with his keys. "But now I really do have to get going."

"Early shift?"

"Six a.m."

"Ouch."

"Yeah." He started walking away. "Keep digging."

"Will do."

He walked to the end of the block, where he turned and yelled back, "Try talking to her."

His laughter echoed off the tree-lined street as he moved out of sight. The night seemed colder in his absence, and a shiver ran down her spine as she turned back to the house.

From the shadows, a teenage girl with pigtails stood watching. Waiting.

VI

The weekend passed without incident, and by Sunday Emma was already beginning to question her decision to visit Nova Scotia. She knew who the girl was now, right? There was no reason to go traipsing off to Canada on a wild-goose chase. They'd solved the mystery. End of story. Right?

But Tom's parting words Friday night kept pestering her: Why Emma? She had no recollection of her great-grandmother, and Marian had no recollection of her. She'd been gone years before Emma was even born. Her appearance to Emma's grandmother made sense; Nellie was Marian's daughter. The mother had come back to help her daughter cross over or something like that. But it didn't explain why Marian's spirit wouldn't rest.

Sunday morning, Nessa left for work, but only after forcing Emma to promise she wouldn't sit inside all day, dwelling on the situation.

"I'll go for a run on the Katy Trail," Emma finally said, acquiescing to her friend's demands. She had worn the same T-shirt and sweatpants all weekend. Her appetite was gone, her stomach in perpetual knots.

"I'm gonna hold you to it," Nessa said, racing out the door.

But Emma couldn't let it go. She'd start a task, then have a random thought about Marian and go back to the dining room. Time and again, she went back to the family tree still lying across the dining table. She scanned the names, hoping for something—someone—to jump off the page. She flipped through photos, searching faces for a clue. Every time she reached the photo of her great-grandparents in their youth, it unnerved her. Her mouth went dry, and she was suddenly queasy.

"What am I missing?"

She shuffled into her grandmother's room. The family had cleared most of the personal mementos when they left. Emma's cousins and aunts had raided Nellie's jewelry box. The polished mahogany case sat open on top of the bureau. The necklace hooks on the doors were empty. The drawers had all been pulled out and pilfered. Only a handful of pieces were left. The open closet door exposed the vacancy of the space. Emma had cleaned out part of Nellie's clothes during the final months of her illness. The rest she and Nessa had bagged up and donated to the local Goodwill after the funeral.

Emma sat down on the edge of the bed. One of her uncles had laid claim to the top quilt, leaving only the bedsheets and pillows. The metal frame creaked as Emma settled. The room still smelled of lavender, and for a moment, she could close her eyes and imagine Nellie was still there. A La-Z-Boy recliner sat unwanted in the corner, abandoned by the rest of the family. It was too big. Too dated. Too threadbare.

"Best to just throw it away or give it to someone in town if anyone wants it," the family had declared.

But Emma knew every stitch on that chair. She knew where the stuffing was worn out, knew where it had bunched up and created a knot. She knew just the right position she could stretch out in to get a decent night's sleep. Not that she'd had many of those over the past months.

As Nellie's illness progressed, Emma had dragged the chair into the room. Each night after she got her grandmother settled into bed, she would pull the recliner close, and Emma would sleep there. Emma remembered every single night. She remembered Gran's fear of being alone. She'd been terrified of dying alone. She remembered the exhaustion, the slow progression of disease as it stole Gran away one piece at a time. Worst of all, Emma remembered her own internal conflicts, a three-way war of emotions going on in her head: love for her grandmother, anger and frustration over being saddled with the responsibility, and the subsequent guilt she'd felt because of her anger. Gran had never asked her to move in. It had been Emma's decision from the beginning.

Punctuating the bad nights was an endless number of good ones. Emma remembered the countless conversations they'd had. Gran's little life lessons, Emma called them. The funny anecdotes from her youth, stories from her courtship with Nellie's grandfather. Each night, Nellie would fall asleep with Emma's hand resting gently on her leg. The touch was a comfort to an old woman afraid to be alone and a reassurance to a young one that life was still there. Emma's silent tears on those nights glazed over her vision until she'd swipe them away.

I want more time had been Emma's consistent prayer those nights.

It had been during one of their bedside chats that Nellie had first mentioned the girl in the shadows. Always in fog. Always silent. Familiar, yet unfamiliar. Emma had dismissed it as a side effect of the medication. Now she wished she had listened.

Emma fell backward into the bed, pulling her feet up and curling into a fetal position. Heavy sobs fought their way out, and Emma buried her face in one of the pillows. But that only worsened her grief, for each time Emma inhaled, the residual fragrance of Nellie's shampoo filled her body. Emma pulled the pillow close and cried.

"Help me, Gran." Emma sobbed. "Tell me what I should do."

Through the haze of grief, a fragment of conversation pushed through, grazing Emma's subconscious.

"You must promise me not to get rid of it."

Emma's eyes flew open, and she stopped crying.

"What?"

The room remained silent. Nellie, it seemed, had given the only clue she felt Emma needed.

Emma sat up, running through a subconscious inventory of the house. She remembered the words, remembered Gran saying them. But what had they been discussing at the time? She stood and looked around the room. Nothing seemed familiar. Shoving her feet back into her slippers, Emma scuffled out of the bedroom and began wandering the house, pausing in each room to take stock. What was Gran talking about?

She found her inquiry in the dining room: the painting.

Emma stared at the large seascape. Nessa was right: it did look like Digby. Had that been the artist's intent? Was Marian drawing her back to Digby *specifically*? Or was it more nostalgia for the old homestead?

Emma couldn't remember a time when there had been anything other than the large oil canvas hanging there. A grassy shoreline ran along the lower edge of the painting's foreground and curved up the left side of the piece as it faded into the distance. A handful of boats lay anchored in the harbor—some sailboats, others fishing boats. Far in the distance lay the opposite shoreline and the faint lights of a small village nestled amongst rolling hills.

A lone tree, its branches spreading out across the water, anchored the foreground in the lower left-hand corner. A rope swing had been tied to the largest branch, and a young girl swung happily while gazing out across the sea. From this angle, Emma wasn't sure how old the girl was. In her lap sat a toddler. The younger girl's legs were kicked out in front of her in delightful abandon as the duo swung. The older girl's right hand held firm to the rope while her left was wrapped securely around her sibling.

A familiar prick pained Emma's heart as she remembered the sisterly scene had always hurt growing up since she'd had no sisters to play with, only two older brothers who'd seemed to want to make her life miserable growing up. They were all friends now, of course, now that her brothers were both in their thirties. But Emma remembered hating them as a child. She had cousins, but their family was so spread out, holidays were the only times they saw one another. And besides, a cousin wasn't the same as a sister.

More than once after she'd moved in with her grandmother, Emma had said Nellie should get rid of it. *"Replace it with something more suited to the space,"* Emma had said. Its intricately carved Victorian-style wood frame was out of step with the midcentury modern furnishings in the room. Compounding the problem was its size. It was much too large for the room, yet it was the only wall in Nellie's house that could accommodate such an oversize painting.

Emma walked across the room and sat down at the table, her eyes never leaving the canvas. She thumbed the edge of a photograph, remembering their last conversation on the matter.

"No, Emma."

"But, Gran, why not? The room could use a freshening up, ya know? New coat of paint. Some new furniture. Lose the plastic wrap on the table. Maybe some smaller art pieces. This thing's gotta be as old as I am, maybe older."

"Midcentury modern is due for a comeback," Nellie had said with a knowing wink. "You just wait and see."

Emma laughed. "Oh, Gran. No one's buying this old stuff anymore."

"Classics are never old, my dear. And one day"—Nellie shook a playful finger in her granddaughter's face—"you will understand that."

"What about the painting? It's not midcentury . . . whatever. Can we get rid of it?"

Emma remembered the wistful look on Nellie's face at that moment. Back then, she hadn't understood where in her memory Nellie had retreated to. But now, years later, sitting in the same chair her grandmother had been seated in all those years ago, Emma understood. These "old things" of her grandmother's were as much a part of the fabric of her life as Nellie herself had been. They were part of her.

"My mother gave me this painting," Nellie had explained, gazing lovingly up at the canvas. "She painted it herself just after my father died."

"Oh." Emma blushed with awkward embarrassment. "I'm sorry, Gran. I don't think I ever knew that."

"It was a wedding present," Nellie continued. "She made me promise to always keep it. She never said why though."

Emma reached out a hand and slipped it into hers. "I'm sorry, Gran. I didn't know, or I would've never suggested getting rid of it."

"Tsk, tsk."

Nellie's eyes were half-filled with tears, and the guilt and remorse over putting them there silenced Emma and any further discussions of home makeovers.

"You must promise me not to get rid of it."

Emma nodded. "I promise, Gran."

"Change the frame if you want. Change where you put it, that's fine. But it should always stay with the family."

Recounting that day, Emma sat staring up at it and wondered why her great-grandmother had placed such significance on keeping it and why Gran was pointing her back to it now.

"What were you trying to say, Marian?"

Emma rose and walked around the table. Up close, the painting was filthy.

"Alexa!"

From the kitchen next door, a mechanical female voice answered.

"How do you clean an oil painting?"

A moment passed between them.

"Here's something that I found: Methods of cleaning an oil painting on canvas include brushing the surface with a soft brush or rubbing the surface with a soft damp cloth dabbed with dish detergent. However, art conservators caution these methods are damaging to a painting and recommend a professional cleaning if the painting is valuable."

"A damp cloth with dish detergent," Emma repeated. "Okay then."

She walked back to the kitchen and returned with a dishrag in hand. She started with the girls.

With delicate movements, she dabbed over the girls. With each touch, they sprang to life, a teenage girl holding a smaller child, possibly a toddler. The other girl's hair came just below her shoulders and was braided into pigtails. Her freshly cleaned dress now shone in the light, billowing in the wind. But on closer inspection, Emma realized it was not a dress; it was a jumper. A vibrant hunter-green jumper with small misshapen white dots on it. Underneath her jumper, the girl wore a long-sleeve white shirt.

Just like the girl at the funeral.

Just like the girl outside her bedroom window.

Every hair on Emma's body stood at attention. Every muscle froze in place.

"No," Emma whispered.

Intuition said otherwise.

"Marian?" she said to the empty room. Emma prayed there would be no response. In the stillness, she heard a shuffle just to her right. Slowly, very slowly, Emma turned her head and bit her lip to stifle the scream that wanted to come out. Emma stepped back so quickly she lost her footing and ended up on the floor.

Barefoot and older than Emma had thought at the service, the girl was a teenager, fifteen or sixteen, perhaps. Possibly seventeen, but no older than that, Emma was certain. There was a slight ruffle to the collar of her white undershirt. With the apparition now standing over her, Emma saw the dots on the girl's jumper in the painting were gardenias, beautiful full blooms evenly spaced across the hunter-green fabric.

Her eyes were a fiery blue that stung when Emma tried to look directly at her. She averted her gaze but felt the piercing intensity of the girl's stare. It felt like she was seeing straight through Emma. Her dark brown hair was parted down the middle and braided. Little white ribbons had been tied up at the end of each braid. She was real.

"Try talking to her," Tom had said.

All right. No harm in trying, right?

"Marian?" Emma asked again. She managed to stand back up but refused to step closer to the apparition. Raising a trembling hand, she pointed to the painting. "Is this you?"

The girl said nothing.

Emma turned back to the canvas and pointed at the toddler.

"Is this your daughter? Is this my grandmother? Nellie?"

"I'm sorry." Alexa's mechanical voice echoed in the silence. Emma turned to the kitchen, surprised by the unprompted response. "That's not something I can do."

Emma turned back. A tiny finger pointed at the painting between them. She was speaking. Emma heard nothing. But in the room next door, Alexa heard.

"I'm sorry. That's not something I can do."

"Marian."

The girl stopped speaking and lowered her hand. She stood there, a figure of stone in color, looking back at Emma. Emma took a tentative step forward.

"Wait," Emma said. Her eyes widened as a new thought formed in her mind. Was it possible? It couldn't be possible. Gran would've said something. Emma's feet felt nailed to the floor. It was an impossibility. But Emma had to know for certain.

She reached for the photograph on the table. Her muscles clenched so tightly she almost screamed, but she managed to half raise her arm. The photo danced in her grip as gooseflesh ran up and down her arm. She pointed out Marian in the photograph.

"Is this you?" Emma managed to squeak out.

No response. Emma tried again.

"Are you Marian?"

No response. Emma drew in a breath and prepared herself for her next question.

"You're not Marian, are you?"

The girl's eyes flicked between the photo and Emma. Emma dropped the portrait onto the table and tapped the Roberts family tree.

"Are you part of this family?" Emma asked. Her words were shaky, her legs Jell-O, her knuckles white from the grip she had on the table edge. If she didn't sit down—and soon—she was going to end up on the floor again.

The girl glanced down and back up to Emma. No response. No change of expression. Nothing.

"Not Marian," Emma chanted. "Not Marian."

The women stared at each other. Emma searched the painting for an answer. When it came, Emma's legs gave out, and she collapsed into a chair.

"Oh my God," Emma cried. She stared at the canvas and realized seeing this painting had hurt because Emma didn't have a *sister*. A sister!

Emma's cell phone—still on the table from Friday night—rang, and she shrieked as the painting slid off the wall. The paper backing ripped as Emma lunged for it, catching it just before it hit the linoleum floor. Another ring. She looked up. The girl was gone. Another ring. Emma stood and laid the painting facedown on the dining table. Still on the floor, she reached for her phone and hit *Answer*.

"Hello?"

"Hey, kiddo!"

"Hi, Uncle Adi." Emma leaned against the table leg, pulled her knees into her chest, and tried to sound as cheery as possible.

"Just wanted to call and check on you. Hadn't heard from you in a few days. Everything okay?"

"Yes, sir. I'm okay." Emma scanned the room for something to say. "Just . . . doing some cleaning today before I go back to work."

"You going back tomorrow?"

"Yes, sir."

"Okay."

Emma could sense he wanted to say more. Had Tom or Nessa said something?

"Well, why don't you come for dinner tomorrow?"

"Tomorrow?"

There was a pause on the other end.

"Or some night this week," her uncle said. "Doesn't have to be tomorrow if you're busy."

"Okay, I'll do that," Emma lied. "Let me check my schedule at work this week and get back with you."

"Sounds good, kiddo. Well, let me get off here. I'm at work at the moment and can't really talk. Just wanted to call and check on you."

"Thanks, Uncle Adi. I appreciate that. I'm good. I promise."

"Glad to hear it—"

"Hey, Uncle Adi?"

"Yeah?"

"Can I ask you a strange question?"

"I guess. What's up?"

"Did Gran ever mention having any brothers or sisters?"

"Jesus, Emma. That *is* an odd question. Why do you ask?"

"I was just . . . wondering. There's a. . .possibility. . .that I'm exploring."

"Possibility, huh? You sure you're okay, Em?"

"I promise. I'm fine. I've just been . . . going through some of Gran's papers and old photographs, and something just felt off."

"Off? How do you mean?"

"I . . . I don't really know yet. Just something I was thinking about. Did Gran have any siblings you know of?"

"No, she didn't." His words had a cautious tinge to them. His happy-go-lucky conversational style was gone. "Mom was an only child."

"Did she know she was Canadian?"

"Yeah, that much she did know. But Poppy and Mimi never talked much about their lives before they moved to St. Louis, so I doubt Mom knew anything, truth be told."

"Did something happen?"

"I don't know, kiddo. We were still kinda young when they passed away, and you never think to ask those kinds of things when you're young, ya know?"

"Yes, sir. And by the time you do think to ask . . ."

"Exactly."

"And you're sure Gran didn't have any siblings?"

"I'm sure. Mom never talked about any siblings, and Poppy and Mimi never mentioned anyone else either."

"Do you remember any odd photos around their house when you went to visit? People you didn't recognize, maybe?"

"Em, these are a lot of really strange questions for just a—what did you call it?—a possibility. Did you find something in Mom's papers about a sibling?"

"No, I'm sorry. I didn't mean to go snooping in the family's business. I was just curious."

"That's all right, kiddo. But let me put your *possibility* to rest. Mom was an only child. And Poppy and Mimi weren't the kind of people who would've kept that kind of knowledge away from Mom if there were other children."

"Thanks, Uncle Adi. And thanks for indulging me."

"No problem, kiddo. Let me know about dinner, all right?"

"Yes, sir. I will."

"Okay, talk with you later, then."

"Thanks for calling."

"Love ya, kiddo. Bye now."

Emma stood back up, bracing her wobbly legs against a chair for a moment while she righted herself. When she was confident she wasn't going to fall again, Emma reached for the painting. The aged brown paper was brittle to the touch and came away in flakes as Emma maneuvered around it to see if the frame or canvas had been damaged. Underneath she could see the faint lines of a pencil marking. She ripped away the remaining paper, exposing the canvas beneath.

A circular brown stain the size of a man's fist stood out against the cream canvas—water damage. The edges were dark and defined, and Emma wondered for a moment what had caused it. It wasn't perfectly circular, but close. Inside the stain, the writing was smeared and illegible. The writing to the left and right of the stain, however, was still faintly visible. To the left, someone had written the word *Home,* and to the right was written *and Nellie.*

"Okay, Gran. I'm listening. What are you trying to tell me?"

Using both hands, Emma delicately separated the canvas from its frame and flipped it over. A chill danced down her spine as she caught sight of the two girls once more. Her gaze landed on the lower right-hand corner. There was writing she hadn't noticed before, writing that had been covered for decades under the frame.

Digby, Nova Scotia, 1950

"Nessa, looks like you were right after all."

"Welcome home."

Alexa again. Emma's eyes flew up. As expected, the girl had rejoined her. Still pointing. Still speaking.

"Welcome home, Emma."

"Home," Emma repeated. "Digby is home."

"Welcome home, Emma."

Emma summoned what remained of her courage to ask one final question. Taking a breath's pause, she finally said, "Are you Gran's sister?"

Outside, someone honked their horn in greeting as they drove by, and Emma turned to look out the window. When she turned back, the girl was gone.

"Digby it is, then."

VII

After the incident in the dining room, Emma decided visiting Digby was the only way she was going to find the answers she needed. Finding a flight and accommodation was simple. Dealing with everyone else . . . not so much. Her boss was sympathetic but needed her back taking care of her clients. They had argued over Emma's return date: Emma wanted an extra week to take care of "family matters," but her boss wanted her back on Monday. In the end, Emma had given her notice. When the gym owner realized Emma wasn't going to back down, he fired her and hung up. Her mother called the whole idea ludicrous but dropped the argument once she realized Emma's mind was made up.

Her uncle Adrian was understandably concerned given their last conversation but agreed to look after the house in Emma's absence on one condition: she had to keep him in the loop.

"I want to know if you find anything up there, kiddo." Curiosity had gotten the better of him, and when Emma laid out her argument for going—leaving out the bit about the ghost, of course—he agreed it was *possible* there were answers up there they were unlikely to find at home. He also agreed to help Emma pay for the trip.

"Just don't tell Mom, okay? She already thinks I'm nuts."

"She's just worried, Em. We all are."

"I'm fine," Emma argued. "Trust me. Just fine."

Tom and Nessa were cautiously supportive of the endeavor. Both knew the mental toll Miss Nellie's death was taking on Emma and half accepted Emma's contention she was being haunted. They differed, however, in how to approach Emma's quest.

"You can't go around telling people you see ghosts," Tom argued. "You'll end up in the psych ward."

It was Nessa who hit upon the idea of using family research as a cover story.

"If you're sure this girl is family," Nessa said, "then it stands to reason the more holes you fill in on the family tree, the more likely it is you'll find out who she is and hopefully . . . what she wants."

The Greater Annapolis Basin Historical Society and Museum was housed in a restored two-story clapboard house from the turn of the nineteenth century. Its pale gray facade faced bustling Water Street and the still waters of Digby Harbor beyond. Emma sat in her rental car, reviewing the documents and scant few notes she had managed to piece together. She checked her watch: 11:30 a.m. The parking lot around Emma was empty except for one other car, which Emma assumed belonged to one of the museum's employees. An approaching storm darkened the horizon across the harbor, and Emma hoped it would hold off a few more hours. She wanted time to explore. She glanced at her watch again: 11:33 a.m. Twenty-seven minutes before the museum opened.

Emma had recopied the family tree into her notebook to avoid having to pack around a large fragile piece of wrapping paper. She'd taken photos of the painting and the inscriptions on the front and back for reference. The photographs and family documents Emma's mother had brought by were tucked inside a manila folder in her bag. She was ready for answers.

Emma nervously thumbed through her notes, familiarizing herself with the names and dates already seared into her memory.

Nelda Rosemary Roberts
Emigrated 1948 from Canada
Father: Tobias Eugene Roberts
Occupation: Royal Canadian Mounted Police, retired
City of Birth: Digby, Nova Scotia
Mother: Marian Cecilia MacDonald Roberts
Occupation: Seamstress
City of Birth: Digby, Nova Scotia

At the time, Nellie had only been three months old. Tobias and Marian were thirty-nine and thirty-three, respectively. That was a bit old in those days to have a baby, and Emma wondered whether her grandmother had siblings that Tobias and Marian had never told her about. Her uncle had been adamant Nellie was an only child, and he was quite confident that even if there had been siblings, that knowledge would have been passed down so that the child—or children, possibly—would not be forgotten. Emma was torn between possibilities: mother or sister?

It was also possible, as Tom had pointed out the week before, the girl could be someone completely unrelated to the family. Emma considered this. If the specter wasn't someone in the family, tracking down her identity would be much more problematic. Yet Emma was confident, based on the girl's reaction to Marian's photograph and Gran's painting, that she was family . . . immediate family. The sibling tableau was the final nail in the coffin for Emma. As far as she was concerned, the girl was one of two people: Nellie's mother, Marian, or some as yet unknown sister.

None of the immigration forms, however, mentioned other family. Emma added it to the growing list of questions. The makeshift family tree was a start, but apart from this, Emma had little else to go on. She had discovered through several online searches that the Office of the Registrar General would be the most likely place to start looking once she arrived. Her online searches of Nova Scotia had revealed no information, however, on Tobias, Marian, or Nellie.

Emma decided to try the local paper. It was possible, given Digby's small population, that the trio might've been mentioned there. A birth announcement, at least. Small-town papers usually included these. Again, however, she found no matching results to her search. When she called the local newspaper office to see how far back their online archives went, she discovered why.

"Nineteen forties!" the young girl had scoffed. "Don't think so!"

"Oh," Emma said dejectedly. "Sorry to hear that."

"What exactly are you looking for? If you don't mind my asking."

"I'm doing some family research," Emma said, repeating the lie Nessa had suggested. "But all I know so far is that they lived in Digby before moving to the United States. I was hoping to find additional information on the family still there."

"Hmm . . . Well, we have copies of all the papers from back then, but—"

"You do?" Emma interrupted, excitement building in her voice.

"But," the girl continued, "they're all on microfilm or something. Floppy whatever you call them."

"Disks?"

"Yeah, whatever. They're somewhere in the basement, I think."

"I see. Are they accessible to the public? If I went there, I mean."

"I guess. Probably." Her tone suddenly turned noncommittal. "I think the machine is still down there somewhere. We don't get much interest in the old pages anymore, and we're a small paper."

"I understand. It's hard to justify the cost of digitizing when it's not used."

"Exactly." The receptionist snapped her fingers. "Say, have you tried the library? They would have copies, and they might have theirs online already. I can give you their number if you'd like."

"They were my next call. But I'll take the number just the same, please. Thank you for your time."

The local librarian proved more informative, but only slightly.

"We have copies dating back to the late 1800s," the woman explained. She sounded cheerful on the phone. "But most of them aren't archived," she said apologetically. "We've been working our way through them, but the process is time-consuming, unfortunately, and I'm afraid our collection isn't exactly complete. But we do have most of the paper's back issues."

"I see."

"Judith has been handling the archiving. She's really the person you should speak with."

"Is she there? Could I speak with her?"

"I'm sorry, but she's just left on maternity leave."

"Oh."

"I'm sorry." The woman had the good graces to sound halfway sympathetic to Emma's plight. "But anyway, they're here if you'd like to come in and take a look."

Emma was frustrated and disappointed, but it felt equally wrong getting mad at a woman with a newborn baby.

The librarian suggested the local historical society but cautioned they had even fewer documents available online than the library. Emma decided not to call at that point. Her flight had already been booked, so she'd deal with it once she arrived in town.

After talking with her uncle once more, Emma flew to Halifax, Nova Scotia. From there she rented a red two-door Nissan hatchback and drove the three hours across the island to the western edge of Nova Scotia.

On Thursday afternoon at precisely twelve o'clock—the museum's opening—Emma bundled up her research and made her way to the front door. The darkening clouds warned of rain. Masked from the sun, the building's gray exterior blended into the surrounding landscape. A small brass bell mounted to the door chimed as she entered. An older woman looked up from her work behind the counter and smiled as Emma closed the door behind her.

"Hello there."

The woman's smile warmed the room around her and put Emma at ease. A petite woman a few inches shorter than Emma, she wore a pale paisley blouse tucked into a pair of jeans. Wire-rimmed glasses hung from a silver chain around her neck.

"Hello," Emma responded cheerily. "How are you this afternoon?"

"Very well, dear. How are you? Welcome to the museum."

"Thank you. I'm okay, I guess." Emma set the thin brown folder on the counter between them. "I was hoping you could help me."

"Family research?"

"What gave me away?"

The old woman gave a soft laugh, adjusted her blouse, and looked down at Emma's folder. She extended her hand. "My name is Alda Dillon. How can I help?"

"Nice to meet you, Ms. Alda." Emma shook the proffered hand. Though it was frail, Alda's grip was surprisingly strong. "My name is Emma Campbell. I'm looking into some family history. My grandmother and her parents emigrated from Digby in the late forties when she was a few months old. I was hoping to find out more about the family before they left Canada and whether any relations still live in the area." The line, well rehearsed now, rolled effortlessly off Emma's tongue.

"Wonderful."

"I have copies of their birth certificates and immigration papers to the United States, but I haven't had much luck finding anything before 1948 when they left Digby."

The woman took the papers from Emma and gave them a quick scan.

"Roberts," she said thoughtfully. "Not many Roberts left in the area, so that should help us narrow down the search."

"That's encouraging. I also have a family tree I've pieced together from old family photos and papers."

"Oh, well done. That gives us a great place to start." Alda smiled as she shuffled out from behind the counter. "So, where would you like to start?"

"Um," said Emma questioningly. Where *should* she start? She'd been so focused on the information she didn't have that she hadn't thought about what to do next once she got to Digby.

Alda must have seen the befuddlement on her face, because after a brief pause, she patted Emma's arm.

"Why don't we start with property records? You could find out where they lived."

"That'd be great!" There was too much excitement in her voice, and Emma forced herself to calm down. "If it's not too much trouble, I mean. I don't want to interrupt what you were doing."

"That's all right. Now, let's see. Property records are in the back. Follow me, and we'll make a start of it."

As Alda walked by, the scent of lavender from the other side of the room tickled Emma's nose. The scent memory was so intense, Emma turned, fully expecting to see Gran standing there smiling. But Gran wasn't there.

"Coming?"

"What?" Emma spun around to find Alda watching her intently. "Oh, yes, ma'am. Right behind you. Sorry, I just . . . I thought I heard something."

Alda laughed, waving her hand dismissively at Emma. "Oh, this old house creaks all the time, dear. Don't pay any mind to it."

As the museum docent led her through the adjoining rooms, Emma's heart started racing, and a tightness formed in her chest, making it harder to breathe. With each footstep, she felt more and more entombed inside the town's history surrounding her. Every inch of the walls was covered with framed photographs and mementos. Along both sides of the hallways were waist-high bookcases, each filled to capacity. There were school yearbooks organized by school and year; shelves full of photo albums, each labeled with the surname of the donating family; and journals, an entire hallway of nothing but people's most personal thoughts and remembrances. Emma felt strangely intrusive as she fingered the spines of several as they passed by.

Alda led her to what Emma assumed had once been the house's formal dining room. Two turn-of-the-century chandeliers anchored the center of the room. Built-in hutches complete with glass doors and intricate woodwork anchored all four corners. Their robin egg blue color was a pleasant accent against the dull browns, grays, and greens of the room's contents. Here, too, the walls were lined with bookcases.

As Emma drew closer to one, she could see the shelves were labeled. A white label with bold black type read *Property Records.*

"All right, then." Alda sighed. "Just set your things down on the table, dear. We use this as a workspace when people come in for research. Now, let's see what we can find on your family, shall we?" She scanned the volumes. "You said your grandmother left in 1948?"

"Yes, ma'am. That was the date on her immigration papers."

"Right." Alda selected a heavy volume and turned to set it on the large oak table. In the center of the volume was a label in the same black-and-white style as the shelves that read *1940s.*

"If your great-grandparents left in 1948, they would've sold the house to someone," Alda explained as she opened the book. There was an alphabetized index in the front pages. She flipped through the first few pages until she found the *R*'s.

"Roberts," she said, pursing her lips. "Roberts . . . Roberts . . . Roberts…" Her finger scanned down the page without stopping. "Ah, here we are! Roberts. Now, what was your great-grandfather's name again?"

The way Alda looked at her over the top of her glasses made Emma smile. She'd had a professor in college who did that, usually when she was making a pithy, mischievous comeback to a stupid question one of her students had asked.

"Tobias Eugene Roberts."

Alda repeated the name like a mantra as her finger continued scanning the page. "That's curious."

"What?"

"There's no record here for a Tobias Eugene Roberts."

"There's not?"

Alda was still searching up and down the index. "No," she said again with a twinge of remorse. "No Tobias."

"But . . . I don't understand. I know they lived here."

"You're sure?"

"Yes, ma'am, I'm sure. Their immigration papers and birth certificates all list Digby as their place of residence. Digby is also listed as the city of birth for both of my great-grandparents." Her response was clipped but polite. Emma reached for her bag and pulled out the manila folder of documents, from which she produced Tobias's birth certificate. She handed it to Alda.

"Well," Alda fussed, "no mistaking that, is there?"

"No, ma'am."

"No matter." She closed the volume and reshelved it. "We'll just have to try a different approach. Plenty of other avenues to explore."

"Maybe they lived outside of Digby proper," Emma offered. "Do you have records for the county here? Or just inside the city limits?"

"Heavens, no," Alda exclaimed. "But we do have most of them. The local Registrar General's office would have everyone's legal papers. The museum's collection is more of the personal history of the area and is sourced by donation. We do have copies of many old official documents that families have donated, but the vast majority of our collection is personal items. Letters, photographs, journals—"

"Yearbooks, I noticed."

"Precisely. Usually when someone passes and the family doesn't want to keep it. Sometimes they hold on to things for sentimentality, but eventually the family donates it to the museum to keep from throwing it away."

Emma reflected on Alda's words for a moment.

"They had to do something with the house though," she thought out loud.

"Are you sure they sold the house?"

"I'm not sure, honestly. My grandmother was only three months old when they emigrated, and I'm not certain how much of their life in Canada was ever discussed. As for records, all she *did* have are dated *after* 1948."

"Did?"

"She recently passed away."

"I'm sorry for your loss."

"Thank you."

"And no records from your great-grandparents?"

"No, ma'am. Tobias and Marian died before I was born, and there was nothing from their lives in Canada in my grandmother's things. Apart from their immigration papers, of course. And my mother, aunts, and uncles couldn't remember them ever talking about their life in Canada before they moved."

"Of course. Hmm." Alda's right hand was tucked under her chin, and she tapped her lips with her index finger as the two of them considered other options. "Maybe they didn't sell the house."

"What do you mean?"

She shrugged. "Well, as I said, there aren't many Roberts in the area these days. But there were several Roberts in the 1940s. If your great-grandfather had family in the area and they were immigrating to the United States, then it's possible the house was gifted to a family relative. That wouldn't show up in the property records because there was never an actual sale of the home. Perhaps an uncle or a son who was old enough."

"That makes sense."

"Did your grandmother have any siblings? Maybe a brother who was old enough to stay behind when they emigrated?"

"I don't think so. But I do know Tobias had four brothers. We found old photographs of the five of them. But as far as we know, Gran was an only child," replied Emma. Dejection dripped off her words.

Alda cocked her head slightly. Her expression was curious.

"As far as you know?" Alda asked. "You think she did? And perhaps didn't know about it?"

Emma paused, wondering how much to tell this woman. How much was too much information? She chose caution.

"My uncle and I believe it's possible there was an older sibling. We don't have any concrete evidence, just circumstantial bits and pieces that make us question what we know."

Alda sat down across from Emma and leaned forward in her seat, a captive audience for Emma's theory.

"Gracious. You do have a mystery on your hands."

Emma leaned forward. "Think you can help me?"

"Absolutely."

Emma took off the hoodie she was wearing and draped it across a nearby chair. She was wearing a black-and-white T-shirt with *Mizzou* written in gold across her chest. She turned back to Alda with a renewed determination in her eyes. "Okay, then. Where do we go next?"

Alda leaned back in her chair and crossed her arms over her chest. She reminded Emma so much of her own grandmother: the little expressions Alda made, the mischievous twinkle in her eye. Being around the woman both warmed and broke Emma's heart.

"You mentioned your great-grandfather—"

"Tobias."

"Yes. He had four brothers?"

"That's right."

"And you've put together a family tree?"

"Of sorts. Yes, ma'am. We're not sure of its accuracy. We were working off of old family photos and a handful of documents my grandmother had in a safe-deposit box."

"I understand. Why don't we start with that? We can see what we find on everyone else, and hopefully we'll discover something on Tobias and Marian while we're at it."

"Sounds like a plan."

For the rest of the afternoon, Alda and Emma scoured the various rooms downstairs looking for records of her family. They searched subsequent property records, hoping to find a record of some unknown Roberts relative who had sold the family home. They searched the decades preceding 1948 and the one following. Nothing. Census records. Marriage records. Birth records. Death certificates. All yielded nothing. Not one trace. They poured through sixty years of documents in total and didn't find one *hint* of Emma's branch of the Roberts family ever even living in Digby. And more than once, Emma began to question whether she was in the right town. But each time Alda broached the subject, Emma was certain. Her family *had* lived in Digby. That was the one thing—*the one thing*—she was certain of.

It wasn't that they found no record of any Roberts. They found plenty of those. Alda had been right. In the early and mid-twentieth century, the Roberts family was everywhere in Digby County. And surprisingly enough, Emma's family tree proved mostly accurate. They found news articles on several of the brothers and their families. Building off of those discoveries, they turned to school yearbooks. But there the mood changed from frustrating to disconcerting. Alda discovered it first.

"That's odd." Alda was flipping yearbook pages back and forth.

"What's odd?"

"There are missing pages in this yearbook."

Emma leaned forward, and Alda slid the yearbook across to her. It was the 1945–46 edition from the local high school. Emma's eyes widened at the dated hairstyles of the young men and women looking back at her.

"Wow! The hair!"

"That was all the rage back then."

Sure enough, the album went from page thirty-seven to page forty. Pages thirty-eight and thirty-nine were gone.

"Misprint from the publisher, maybe?" Alda offered.

Emma was about to agree when something caught her eye—a tiny paper fragment stuck in the binding. The page wasn't missing; it had been removed.

"Someone ripped out these pages." She showed Alda the fragment left behind.

"Who would do that?"

"Rambunctious children?"

"Probably."

They didn't think much of it until a few minutes later, when Emma discovered missing pages in a second album. Then a third and fourth. All with pages torn out.

"This can't be an accident," Emma said. She'd watched Alda's expression change over the past hour from mildly irritated over kids tearing out pages to increasingly alarmed. They found other evidence of vandalism as they worked as well: pages that had been cut up, newspapers that had been ripped in half. It was an annoyance, to be sure, but the women pressed on with their search.

Despite the setbacks, Emma did discover a treasure trove of information about the Roberts family, and her family tree grew exponentially with name after name being grafted into the trunk. None of them, however, tied back to Tobias, Marian, and Nellie. Emma continued making notes of each discovery they made in her notebook. She hoped to slowly piece things together to figure out who the little ghost girl was. With each missing page they discovered, Emma grew more certain that something *had* happened prior to Tobias and Marian's emigration, something to prompt their abrupt departure from the small coastal town where they had lived their entire lives, abandoning home and family for the United States. A defiant determination set in, and Emma had no intention of walking away. Whoever the girl was, she deserved some bit of peace.

By the time the entry clock chimed half past four, Emma's eyes were running together. It felt at times like she saw names that weren't there, and other times she looked over names that were right in front of her. So, it was with welcome relief that Alda dropped her eyeglasses onto her chest and rubbed her eyes. The glasses lay there unmoving on the tiny brass chain that went around the old woman's neck.

"I'm sorry, dear," she said apologetically. "Time to close up."

"Thank you so much for all your help, Ms. Alda. I really appreciate you taking the time to look through everything with me."

"Ah," she said with a wave of her hand through the empty air, "it was nothing. And it's not like I had anything else to do today. I just hate that we haven't found anything yet on Tobias and Marian."

"They're here somewhere. We just haven't found the right haystack yet."

"What a mess we've made," Alda said with a laugh, glancing at the detritus around them.

It was a warm laugh, and for a moment Emma was reminded of her own grandmother. *Alda and Nellie would have gotten along well,* she thought. Emma smiled and looked around them. They were the only two people there and had been all afternoon.

"All the same, thank you. I'm sure you had other stuff to do today besides a wild-goose chase."

"Now, don't get discouraged," Alda chided. "We know they're here. Tobias, Marian, and Nellie—all their immigration paperwork clearly says Nova Scotia, so we know they're here. Like you said—we just haven't found the haystack. And don't forget, you've fleshed out your family tree quite a lot today."

"That's true. I just wish we could've found *something*."

"We'll find them," Alda said encouragingly. "We will. Besides," she continued, flashing Emma a mischievous grin, "you piqued my curiosity. Now I *have* to find out what happened to them. I love a good mystery. Don't you?"

"I prefer nonfiction, honestly." Emma shrugged.

"Well . . ." Alda smiled, trying to cheer her up. She gestured to the table between them and the piles of books, registers, and miscellaneous papers scattered over it. "You've certainly landed in the middle of one of those, to be sure. It doesn't get any more nonfiction than this, I can promise you."

Emma gave a wry laugh and stood. "Mind if I use the bathroom before I go?"

"Of course! You remember where the key is in the front room?"

"Yes, ma'am. Right next to the phone."

"Just hang it back up when you're done. I'm going to finish this volume while you're gone."

"Okay. Back in a minute."

When Emma returned, Alda was coming out of the back office. She had a slip of paper in her hand, which she handed to Emma.

"Found a news article on the youngest brother that might be of interest."

"Thanks. I'll take a look at it tonight. Right now, I think my eyes are too crossed to read anything else." She rubbed her eyes, praying she could avoid a migraine.

Alda touched Emma's elbow lightly. "Do you need an aspirin? We have some Tylenol in the back office if you need something."

"No, ma'am. Thank you. I have some medication back at the hotel."

"Where are you staying?"

"Seaside Motel." Emma gave the article a quick scan. "Just down the street."

"Oh, that's a cute little place."

"Yes, ma'am." *Cute* wasn't exactly the word Emma would have used to describe it, but she held her tongue. "I'll help you clean up and put all this away."

Alda looked almost hurt at the notion. "You're not coming back tomorrow?"

"Yes, ma'am. But I—"

"Then let's leave it all here," Alda interrupted, setting the book in her hand on the table. "That way we know what we've looked through already. Sound good?"

"You won't get into trouble leaving everything out like this?"

Alda laughed. "My dear, I'm seventy-eight years old. There aren't too many people left I can get in trouble *with*!"

Emma smiled. Alda and her grandmother would have definitely gotten along well.

"True," said Emma, wiping the weariness from her eye. "But it is a pretty big mess we made. Are you sure we shouldn't put at least some of it back?"

Alda shooed her away from the table back to the front. "We'll deal with it once we're done. Sound good?"

Emma nodded. "So . . . I guess I'll see you tomorrow afternoon, then. You open at noon, yes?"

"Generally, yes, but . . ."

Alda went back to her counter and flipped open a small calendar. She scanned it for a few moments. Emma slipped the article into her bag, then tossed it over her shoulder and walked to the front of the museum and stood on the other side of the counter, waiting to see what Alda was going to say.

"I don't have anything else planned for tomorrow," Alda finally said. "Why don't you pop 'round in the morning so we have more time. Is nine o'clock too early for you?"

"It won't be too much trouble?"

Alda gave her a conspiratorial grin. "Our little secret, okay?"

"Okay."

"Good," Alda stated with a nod, closing the argument. "I'll see you at nine, then?"

"Nine sounds just great, Ms. Alda. Thank you. For everything."

A bell sounded behind Emma as the front door of the museum opened, and the two women turned to face it. A middle-aged man in a red-and-blue flannel shirt and faded blue jeans walked in carrying a box in front of him.

"Afternoon, Ms. Alda!" the man called out.

"Afternoon, Franklin!" Alda replied with a bit of a wave. "Just about to close for the day. What brings you in?"

"Old photographs for your collection," he said as he approached the counter and set the box down.

"I'll see you tomorrow, Ms. Alda," interrupted Emma as she took her leave. She nodded a greeting to the man, who returned it with a smile.

"Nine o'clock, de—" A loud clap of thunder outside startled her. "Gracious. You better hurry off before this storm sets in."

"Yes, ma'am. See you tomorrow."

Franklin held the door open for her. As she passed him in the doorway, she caught the faint scent of his cologne. No, *faint* was the wrong word. He had gone swimming in it.

"Thank you," Emma managed to say without coughing.

"You're welcome, Miss?"

"Emma," she offered, continuing to walk as she spoke in hopes there would be fresher air the farther away she got from him. "Have a nice day."

Another roll of thunder ended the conversation as Emma hurried to her car. As the door closed, she could just hear Alda say, "So, what have you brought me today, Franklin?"

VIII

The Seaside Motel looked exactly the way it sounded: a U-shaped midcentury modern cluster of rooms with parking spaces directly in front of each room's ocean-blue front door. Emma shoved her suitcase into the closet, having already put away her clothes in the whitewashed bureau across from the single king sized bed prior to visiting the museum. The room was tastefully decorated in a nautical theme with handcrafted touches, like her bedside lamps, which were made of repurposed antique lobster buoys.

A round table with two chairs sat in front of the window, her backpack waiting patiently in one of them. A plastic to-go bag from a local sandwich shop and a bottle of water were on the table. Emma wanted to fully map out the Roberts family tree in her notebook before she returned to the historical society the next morning. She had lucked out with the sandwich shop, which was just across the street from the motel, because just as she'd made it back to her room, it had begun to rain.

Every light in the room was on, but it still felt dreary with the fog and now the rain. Emma could have opened the curtains had the sun been shining, but her room was close to the street and in full view of the other guests coming in and out of the motel. She had opened them just briefly before she started feeling like an animal at the zoo and reclosed them.

Foul weather continued through the afternoon and into the evening as Emma went through her notes. Even though they had found nothing on Tobias, Marian, or Nellie, they had found plenty on other branches of the family tree. She had discovered one John Aaron Roberts. John Aaron was married to Evelyn Elizabeth Moore and had one daughter Mae, who died in childbirth, and at least five boys. And Emma was only sure of the five because of the photo they had found amongst Nellie's things and Tom's insistence the men in the photograph were siblings. John Aaron was the fourth child of Charles Donald Roberts and had two older brothers and one younger sister. Most of the men who were of age at the time had fought during World War I. One of the brothers had died. One had returned with injuries that would eventually lead him to be wheelchair-bound by the time he was forty.

There were kids. And grandkids. Nieces and nephews. Tons of them. The Roberts family had been very productive in the early twentieth century, and Emma's notepad was filled with page after page of scrunched-up clusters of scribblings.

"This is ridiculous," she finally said, abandoning the notebook. "I need to lay this out so I can see everything."

Emma reached into her bag and retrieved the sheet of wrapping paper she had started with. The sheet nearly covered the entire tabletop and was frayed in several places. Emma quickly realized her original effort had outlived its usefulness. Names and lines had been drawn, marked through, and redrawn several times.

"Nope. That won't work either." She crumpled the sheet into a ball and tossed it into the trash. Glancing around the room, Emma saw an empty patch of wall space over the chest of drawers. "Bingo."

Emma dug through her bag once more and, not finding what she was looking for, snatched the room key off the hook near the door and stepped outside. An overhang protected her from the rain, and Emma danced along the perimeter of the motel to the front desk, where she startled the teenage boy manning the check-in desk as she barged in.

"Hey, sorry. Do you have any Post-it Notes and Scotch tape I could borrow?"

"Sorry?"

"Post-it Notes and Scotch tape," Emma repeated. Catching his befuddled expression, she added, "It's for a work project I'm in the middle of."

That seemed to do the trick.

"Oh." He seemed to understand and opened a desk drawer to see what he could find. He passed Emma a half-used roll of Scotch tape and a square pad of neon pink Post-it Notes. "Will these work?"

"That's great. Thanks so much." Emma tucked them into her hoodie pocket and ducked back outside.

"You're welcome," the kid called out as Emma disappeared into the storm.

Back inside her room, Emma pushed the chest of drawers away from the wall to in front of the door. She pulled a chair over to the bare baby blue wall and wrote *Charles Donald Roberts* on a Post-it. Affixing a small strip of tape to the top and bottom, she stood on the chair and stuck it to the wall near the ceiling.

Hours passed as she methodically assembled the Roberts family tree. Her half-eaten sandwich, now a soggy mess, lay abandoned on the table. Outside, the rain had gone from intense to a drizzling mist. Long after sunset, Emma finally collapsed onto the bed in exhaustion. The red numbers of the hotel alarm clock glared back at her—9:57 p.m. She rubbed her eyes as she yawned.

"I suppose I should take a shower before going to bed," she muttered, not moving.

"Yes," Emma answered herself, "you probably should."

She rolled over, her exhaustion resisting every movement.

"Get up."

Yawning, Emma pushed herself off the bed, walked to the bureau to get some nightclothes, and trudged across the room to the shower. She switched the knob all the way over to *Hot* and began to undress. By the time she was undressed, steam was wafting around the edges of the shower curtain.

The water cascaded over Emma as she ran her hands through her hair, letting it run down her back. She brought up her arms and rested her hands on the shower wall directly in front of her face. She was so tired. Her muscles ached. Her back ached. Everything ached. The hot water felt like a warm shot of whiskey. She needed a good run but decided tonight wasn't the best night for it. One, she had no idea about the layout of Digby. Emma had not seen a single taxi on the road, and if she got lost, she might not be able to find her way back to the motel. And two, the rain had not stopped all evening.

Tomorrow, she thought.

She was so exhausted. The day had been an absolute waste. Not one shred of evidence to confirm Tobias and Marian had lived in Digby before emigrating. Had *ever* lived in Digby. Were it not for the painting and their immigration papers, she would have moved on hours ago. But Alda had insisted they were "closing in" on it, whatever *it* was.

"Family research isn't a quick run around the park, dear," she'd said at one point. *"It's a marathon."*

As encouraging and cheerful as Alda was, by the end of the day, Emma had been starting to wonder if Digby was the right place to be looking. True, Tobias and Marian had been born in Digby, and Digby had been their departure point. But that didn't necessarily mean they had lived here. Emma made a mental note to ask Alda about Canadian emigration patterns tomorrow.

Nothing wrong with covering all your bases, she thought.

Names came back to her. They ran across her mind and out of her mouth as she recited facts and dates to herself. In her mind's eye, they wove their way around one another, forming a tapestry of family. Patterns and redundancies emerged as more names, dates, and relations came back to her. But somewhere deep within the recesses of her brain, the tapestry was frayed. Something was not quite right. But Emma could not put her finger on it. There wasn't anything concrete she could point to, no missing link she had discovered. Perhaps her grandmother's branch of the family had *not* lived in Digby. Maybe they'd lived somewhere else. Maybe . . .

But the painting kept drawing her back. Marian had written *Digby, Nova Scotia* across the bottom of the piece. There was no mistaking that. Someone had once taken the time and effort to write across the back the one word that kept Emma rooted to this place—*home*.

Maybe Digby was the old family homestead, she thought. *The way Gran's house in Rocheport is our family home.*

Emma's mother, aunt, and uncle had moved away as they grew up, but that didn't change the fact that Rocheport was "the family home."

The tapestry in her mind fluttered.

Emma thought of the three siblings with all their children as they all tried squeezing into Gran's tiny little house.

Another flutter. A corner came undone and flapped just a little, as if being pulled by a gentle wind.

Most of the time they spilled out into the yard during the holidays.

The flaw in the tapestry was expanding, ripping into the center of the fabric.

Emma smiled at how Gran had always insisted they get together there instead of somewhere else. Everyone knew there was not enough room. Three kids and their spouses.

Another rip tore through her mind.

Each of Gran's kids had two or more children of their own, and several of the grandchildren were old enough to have boyfriends or girlfriends, spouses or significant others. Not to mention the great-grandchildren.

Another rip.

Emma's mom lived in St. Louis now. Her aunt lived out west.

Another rip. There was something missing.

Her uncle Adi lived in Columbia.

Another rip.

But they all schlepped back to Rocheport for the holidays at Gran's house.

Something Alda found shortly before we stopped.

"That's it!" Emma yelled at the wall as her eyes popped open.

Emma half stumbled out of the shower, wrapped herself in a towel, and raced out of the bathroom. She stood in front of the family tree taped to the wall and read the names of John Aaron and Evelyn's children out loud from left to right.

"Matthias. Bartholomew. Samuel. Mae. Julian," Emma muttered to the wall, trying to will the words onto the pages plastered in front of her.

Five siblings. None of them Tobias. None of them connected to her branch of the family tree. Five siblings. She counted the names again. Read back through the generations before and after.

"Tom could have been wrong about the photograph." Emma said, considering alternatives. "Maybe they were cousins, not siblings. Maybe Tobias belongs to a different branch all together." She folded her arms across her chest and sighed. "Or maybe a completely different tree all together."

But there was still something sticking out like a sore thumb.

"The obituary."

Emma rummaged through her bag for the article Alda had handed her right before closing. Emma had made photocopies of countless documents, spending nearly one hundred Canadian dollars, and it took her several minutes to find what she was looking for. Something Alda had found. Emma remembered her talking about it, but after nearly five hours of researching, she was so worn out and ready to stop, she had barely paid attention.

Finally, toward the bottom of her stack was the document in question. Emma yanked it free from the pile and tossed the rest of the papers onto her bed as she went to stand in front of her makeshift tree.

It was an obituary for Julian David Roberts, dated 1999. Emma's hands trembled as she began to read.

Julian David "Jules" Roberts, age eighty-six of Digby, passed away on Thursday morning, January 10, in Digby General Hospital. Born 1913 in Digby, Jules was the youngest of five sons born to the late John Aaron Roberts and Evelyn Elizabeth Moore. He earned trades as an electrician and heavy-duty mechanic. He was a handyman and mechanic extraordinaire who could fix anything; he was well organized and always had a list on the go. He loved his dog, Arbor, and he loved his family and friends, whether it was a visit or a connection by phone. He had a hearty appetite and enjoyed reading the paper and watching sports and his favourite TV shows. Jules enjoyed drives to take in the beauty of scenery, but his true passion was hunting and fishing and spending time in nature.

Emma skimmed through the relations that were still living.

Besides his parents, he was predeceased by his first wife, Deborah; sister, Mae, who died in childbirth; brothers Matt, Bartholomew, Sam, and Toby; grandson John; mother-in-law, Mildred; sisters-in-law Susan, Gertrude, and Hope.

There it was. Toby. Tobias. Emma looked up at the wall and read the names John Aaron Roberts, Evelyn Elizabeth Moore, and the five children listed below them: Matthias "Matt," Bartholomew, Samuel "Sam," Mae, and Julian "Jules." Her tree was incomplete. There were six children, not five. Six people. Six names. Her hands trembled again as she looked back at the page and reread the obituary.

. . . the youngest of five sons born to the late John Aaron Roberts and Evelyn Elizabeth Moore.

The missing thread of the broken tapestry Emma had spent the afternoon constructing had finally been found. He existed. He was real. She had found him. Emma scratched the sixth and final name across a Post-it and added it to the wall.

"Hi, Toby."

It came out as more of a prayer than a greeting, as if Emma were pleading with him, "Don't go just yet." But Emma felt something else rising within her, something that threatened to kill the euphoria rushing through her body: dread.

Someone, Emma slowly began to realize, had taken painful measures to carefully extract all evidence of Tobias's existence. That was the only thing to explain it. The missing records Alda had fussed over throughout the afternoon, the pages from newspapers that had been removed, journal pages torn out, random photos removed. On their own, they were unsubstantial. They had paid little to no attention to them as the day had progressed. But collectively they presented a mountain of evidence of deliberate, calculating motive, something more sinister than a series of childish acts of vandalism.

But why? Why go through this much trouble? What could possibly have happened in 1948 to make someone want to cut her family's branch out of the Roberts family? A rift in the family, maybe? Sibling rivalry?

Perhaps, Emma thought, her great-grandfather had been mixed up in some shady business dealings before they left. Perhaps that was *why* they left. The possibilities were endless as Emma stood there and considered the logic behind it. Whatever the reason, whoever had done this had been thorough. They hadn't just excised Toby from the records, but his entire branch of the Roberts family tree. That took time and, more importantly, dedication. Emma looked at the piece of paper still in her hand and asked the darkness, "Who did this to you, Toby? Who erased you from the family's history?"

The rain outside was her only reply.

"More importantly . . . why?"

Emma did not need to turn around to know she was not alone. In her pontifications, a presence behind her had gradually became more pronounced. And while Emma felt no desire whatsoever to turn around and face this girl, she also felt almost triumphant. It was a sign from the beyond that she was finally on the right track. But as her elation soared and the fear of her as yet unknown nemesis out there began to sink in, the girl's presence began to unnerve Emma. Not scare, per se, even though it still alarmed Emma when she appeared out of nowhere. But she had slowly come to understand the girl was there not as a torment, but as a guide. Emma considered for a moment the possibility of the girl being caught up in Tobias's dealings, whatever those were.

What happened to you? Emma thought. *How did you die? Natural causes? Or unnatural ones?*

As more and more questions piled inside her mind, Emma began to shiver. Apart from the very threadbare towel wrapped around her midsection, she was naked and wet and dripping all over the carpet. Gooseflesh ran along her extremities, and Emma folded her arms across her chest to conserve her body heat. Her arms were sandpaper as she ran her hands up and down them.

As more and more alarms sounded inside Emma's mind, she felt the girl grow closer. She could feel the specter's energy as it approached, the heat of her radiating against Emma's bare skin. A comforting hand on the shoulder from a friend could be reassuring to a troubled soul, but as Emma felt the ghostly hand rise and reach for her shoulder, she was anything but reassured or comforted.

"No," Emma cried out to the darkness.

The hand paused, hovering just over her shoulder.

"Please," she pleaded. "Don't."

The hand withdrew. Moments later, she was gone, leaving Emma alone to deal with the questions, the mystery, and her dread. Emma stared up at her makeshift family tree. The storm outside had strengthened again and angrily pelted her window.

She stared.

And watched.

And waited.

Waited for the branches to resettle themselves as they adjusted to the newly grafted branch Emma was forcing back into it. Watched to see which limbs embraced the newcomer . . . and which ones rejected it.

Emma again remembered she was still in just a towel, and the carpet beneath her feet was soaked through. It squished between her toes as she moved. She walked back to the bathroom, finished drying off, and got dressed. She needed coffee. It was going to be a long night.

IX

Emma was just finishing her fifth cup of coffee that morning when Alda's blue Hyundai sedan pulled into the museum parking lot. She had been there for nearly an hour already. The previous night's storm had moved on, leaving a dense fogbank in its wake. Emma could just make out the silhouette of the buildings across the street. Everything beyond that was shrouded in gray. Emma, in her haste to get to the museum, had passed it three times because she had been unable to see it until it was too late to make her turn. Before Alda had the chance to switch off her engine and get out, Emma was already standing by her car.

"Morning, Alda," said Emma as she opened the car door for the stunned woman. "Happy Friday!"

"Good heavens, dear! You startled me!"

"I'm sorry."

She offered her hand, which Alda took as she eased herself out of her car. Dressed in jeans and sneakers again, Alda had changed her paisley blouse for one of rich aubergine with a pale cream sweater.

"Did you get any sleep last night, dear? You look positively dreadful." Alda touched Emma's arm. "No offense. Seriously though, are you all right?"

"I need to show you something I discovered last night."

Alda's eyebrows arched in curiosity. "Oh?" she said, intrigued. "Then by all means, let's get inside, shall we? This fog is absolutely wretched."

Emma adjusted her shoulder bag and followed Alda into the building through the rear entrance. A tiny office was in the back with hooks for coats and scarves. A nondescript wooden desk was situated in the corner, and a small empty wicker basket sat on the edge. Alda removed her sweater and hung it up. She dropped her car keys into the basket and relocked the door behind them, then adjusted her glasses.

"Now then," she said as she walked into the museum, switching on the overhead lighting. "What did you need to show me?"

Alda shuffled around the space turning on various lamps, which helped to chase away the darkness. As she did, Emma moved to the dining room, dropped her bag onto the floor, and laid the roll of papers taped together on the closest table. Using the last of her borrowed Scotch tape, Emma had yanked out a dozen blank pages from her notebook the night before, taped them together, and moved the Post-it Notes from the hotel room wall to the paper canvas. She took tchotchkes from their displays and used them as paperweights to keep it flat.

"You said you loved a good mystery yesterday?"

"Yes." Alda cocked a curious eyebrow.

"Well, I believe I found one. One you're probably not going to like."

Alda scowled as she made her way back to the table. "Oh, I don't like the sound of that, dear. More missing documents?"

"It's more than that, Ms. Alda. I think someone has deliberately removed everything that ties back to my side of the family."

Alda nodded and sat down. She took in the names laid out in front of her. Emma watched the older woman in silence as she digested Emma's words.

"I was actually thinking the same thing last night," Alda finally said. Every syllable dripped with worry. She turned and looked up at Emma, who could see the consternation on her face. "But surely that's not possible. I mean, you can't just erase someone, right?"

Emma pulled out the chair next to her and sat down. "Do you remember that article you found right before closing yesterday?"

Alda nodded.

"It was Jules's obituary." Emma handed her the well-thumbed piece of paper. "Take a look at the couple lines I highlighted."

"Born 1913 in Digby, Jules was the youngest of five sons born to the late John Aaron Roberts and Evelyn Elizabeth Moore. Besides his parents, he was predeceased by his first wife, Deborah; sister, Mae, who died in childbirth; brothers Matt, Bartholomew, Sam, and Toby; grandson—oh my word."

"Exactly," said Emma. "Toby. Tobias. Tobias Eugene Roberts."

Alda looked back at the page and reread the article. "We don't know for certain that this Toby"—she pointed to the page—"is *your* Tobias though."

"I do. At least . . . I do *now*." Emma turned back to the family tree on the table. "It took me most of the night to figure it out, but I know for certain that the Toby mentioned in that obituary"—she pointed to the page in Alda's hand—"is the same Tobias we've been looking for all along."

Alda cleared her throat, covering her mouth as she coughed.

"Would you like some water?"

"Yes, please," Alda managed to whisper before coughing again.

Emma returned to the back office, pulled a cold bottle of water from the employee fridge, and came back to the dining room where Alda sat, studying Emma's family tree. She removed the cap and handed it to her.

"Thank you." Alda took several swigs before setting it down on the table. "Did you do all of this last night?"

"I did."

"Gracious, child! Did you get *any* sleep?"

"Not much. But thank goodness for coffee, right?"

Alda smiled. "Now, tell me how you know."

Emma sat down beside her, panning her hand over the pages. "I went through every single document we found yesterday. Every photograph. Every journal entry. Every news—"

"Everything," Alda interrupted. "I understand."

"Right. We found a paper trail for every single person on this tree *except* for Toby."

"But how do you know *your* Toby"—Alda pointed to the pages in front of her—"is the same as *this* Toby?"

"Because of this." Emma reached into her bag, which was hanging on the back of her chair, and pulled out two photographs. She handed the first one to Alda. "This is a photo of Julian Roberts circa 1940."

Alda scanned the photo intently. "Yes."

Emma handed her the second photograph. "This is a photograph from my grandmother's records circa 1931. Take a look at the next-to-last man on the right."

Alda gasped. "You're right. It's the same man." She flipped the photograph over and read the names.

"The man on the far right is my great-grandfather, Toby."

"Right. None of the documents we found yesterday *ever* mentioned a Tobias or Toby. None of them. Do you remember yesterday? The random missing pages from newspapers we kept coming across? The records pages that skipped a page number here and there?"

"The yearbook pages torn out. Yes, I remember."

"Someone has gone through and surgically cut any mention of Toby and his part of the family tree out of history." Alda exhaled deeply. "That's an awful lot of trouble to go through. And"—she raised her hand, still holding the obituary—"it doesn't explain this. If what you're saying is true, and someone deliberately set out to remove your great-grandfather's part of the family—and I'm not saying that's what happened, not yet at least, but if that *is* what happened—how did they miss this? It doesn't make sense with what you're saying."

"It does if you look at the dates."

Alda looked at the photocopy, and *1999* was just visible in the corner of the newspaper page.

"I don't understand."

Emma propped her left arm on the table, resting her head in her palm. "You and I researched everything starting in 1948 and worked our way backward and forward thirty years from that date."

"Yes," Alda said, listening intently. "Because 1948 was when your great-grandparents and grandmother immigrated to America."

"Right. We were looking at everything from 1918 to 1978. This obituary is dated 1999."

Alda began to understand what Emma had been hinting at. "Which means," she chimed in, "whoever did this was already dead by 1999."

"Possibly," replied Emma. "But it could also mean they had moved away from Digby by then."

The old woman pursed her lips as she pondered something for a moment before turning back to the front room.

"What is it?" Emma asked as she followed Ms. Alda. Alda pressed the speakerphone button and dialed a number from memory.

"Something doesn't make sense to me," she said as the phone began ringing.

"*Digby Gazette*," a young woman answered. "How may I direct your call?"

"Franklin Wood, please."

"One moment."

"It doesn't make sense," Alda said to Emma as she was placed on hold, "to get rid of these records."

"What do you mean?"

"Well, apart from the personal items—journals and photos and such—everything here can be found in other places, for one thing. If you know where to look and who to ask."

"So, you're thinking if they stole records from here, then they also—"

Emma was cut short by a cheery male voice booming over the line.

"Franklin Wood speaking."

"Franklin. Hi, it's Alda here at the historical society. How are you?"

"Oh, good morning, Ms. Alda. I'm doing well. How can I help you?"

"This is an odd question, but please bear with me."

"All right. I'm listening."

Emma could hear the confusion in the man's voice.

"Where do you store the old editions of the paper?"

"Well, that depends on how old we're talking. The paper's digital now, so anything that's in the print copy automatically gets placed on the newspaper's webpage."

"And how long has the *Gazette* been doing that?"

"Oh, I'd say about twenty years now. Anything before that is stored on CDs."

"CDs?"

"Yes, ma'am. We hired a few interns back in the nineties, I think, to scan everything into the computer and save it onto CD. It was right after I started working here. Took 'em nearly a year to get through everything."

"How far back do your CDs go?"

Franklin cleared his throat. "Ms. Alda, just exactly how far back are we looking here?"

"Well, 1948 and earlier."

"Forty-eight!" Franklin let out a deep breath that Emma could hear standing a few feet away from the receiver. "Yeah . . . no, those wouldn't be on CD, Ms. Alda. The interns only went back about twenty years or so. Anything before the seventies, I'd say, would still be on microfilm."

"Microfilm."

"Yes, ma'am."

"Why stop with the seventies?"

"No interest would be my guess. There's talk of going back further what with people's interest in researching family lineage these days, but the issue always comes down to money. And small papers usually have very tight budgets."

"I see."

"What's this about, Ms. Alda?"

"Franklin, could you do me a quick favor?"

"Of course."

"Would you check your microfilm collection for the . . . 1940 issues?"

"Any particular issue you're needing?"

Alda cleared her throat, and Emma noticed a new airy tone to Alda's voice as she continued talking. "We're not sure yet. We hope to have a more exact date soon."

"We?"

"A young woman who's in town doing family research. I wanted to check to ensure you had it before I sent her over to your office."

"All right, Ms. Alda. Give me a few minutes, and I'll call you back. You still at the museum?"

"Yes," Alda replied. "You can reach me here."

"A bit early for you to be open, isn't it?"

"Special project."

"I see. And this special project is what prompted you to call?"

"Just covering all the angles, as you reporters say."

"Ms. Alda, what—"

"Thank you, Franklin. You'll call me straight away?"

"All right, I'll call you back in a few."

She hung up the phone and reached for a small phone book under the counter.

"You think they stole documents from other places too, don't you?"

"They had to," Alda replied as she dialed another number. "If they were smart about it, they did. But there's two more places to check."

Alda called the Digby County Justice Centre and the local office of the Registrar General to inquire about records predating 1950. Both were dead ends. Old records at the Justice Centre were stored in the basement, and in 1952 a burst pipe flooded the entire basement level. The flood occurred over the weekend, and no one had noticed until Monday when people came back to work. Everything was lost, including the local office of the Registrar General, which, inconveniently enough, had been located in the basement at the time. It moved to a new location in 1953, having lost every single document in its possession to the flood.

Alda was just putting down the receiver, finished with her call to the Registrar General's office, when the front door burst open. Alda and Emma both jumped. Emma nearly cursed. Alda held a protective hand over her pounding heart.

"Franklin." The raspy word came out with a squeak as she struggled to catch her breath.

The six-foot frame of a clearly agitated Franklin Wood filled the doorway. In his agitation, the door had knocked against the wall, sending several framed photographs to the floor, where they shattered, spraying shards across the room.

"What the hell is going on here?"

X

"Land's sake, Franklin," Alda scolded. "You'll give an old woman a heart attack! And look what you've done!"

"Sorry," he said, his tone softening with embarrassment. "I didn't mean to scare you ladies. I'm sorry."

"Franklin Douglas Wood, how many times have I told you not to go barging into places?"

"I've lost count," he replied dryly.

"Bull in a china shop is what you are, Franklin Wood. Have been since you were a boy."

"It's not my fault I'm taller than everyone else."

"No, it's not, I suppose." Alda's features softened for a moment before rehardening. "But it *is* your fault the way you go storming around town."

"Yes, ma'am."

If it weren't for the fact he was less than three feet away, was twice her size, and could easily swat her like a mosquito, Emma would have found the situation hilarious. A grown man of her father's age, she guessed by his salt-and-pepper hair, was being dressed down like a schoolchild by a woman whose height would not even reach his chest. Yet the deference he showed her was moving. Emma bit her lip to stifle her laughter and focused on the broken glass around her.

Alda reached for a small trash can tucked behind the counter and made her way to the broken glass.

"I'll do it, Ms. Alda," Emma volunteered. She took the can and knelt.

"Thank you, dear."

"I'll . . . help you."

Franklin knelt, and together they began clearing the room. Fortunately for Emma, Franklin's cologne was much less potent than it had been the day before. Emma could actually stomach being around the man without feeling nauseous.

"Thanks," Emma said, slightly annoyed.

"You owe me an explanation about all this," Franklin replied. The look in his emerald eyes made Emma uncomfortable.

"What did you find?" Emma asked.

"You're Emma, am I right? You were here yesterday when I came in."

"Yes, I—"

"I'm sorry," Alda interrupted. "Franklin, this is Miss Emma Campbell from the United States. She's here doing research on her family genealogy. Emma, Mr. Franklin Wood, one of the local journalists who works for the *Digby Gazette*."

He was an imposing figure who filled the space around him. Franklin's towering height and booming voice only accentuated his intimidating persona. Physically fit, he wore a long-sleeve white oxford tucked neatly into a pair of recently pressed black khakis. Leather loafers and a matching belt completed his very professional look. With him he carried a pen and small notebook in his shirt pocket, the top of which could be seen sticking out.

He's a handsome man, Emma thought. *A rather striking man indeed.*

"Pleased to meet you, Mr. Wood," Emma said, extending her hand. Her cheeks reddened as she tried—albeit unsuccessfully—to not meet his gaze.

"And you, Ms. Campbell. Sorry for the scare."

"It's okay. Tell us though, what did you find?"

"No," Alda interrupted. "Finish cleaning up first. Then mystery."

Chastened, Emma and Franklin continued picking up the larger bits of glass while Alda ran the vacuum over the carpet to catch the rest. When she had finished vacuuming and was satisfied everything was in order once more, Alda turned her attention back to Franklin, who had been chatting quietly with Emma.

"There now. Tell us what you found."

"Nothing," he said as he pulled a small notepad and pen from his shirt pocket. "But you already knew that, didn't you?" He eyed Alda, half accusing, half inquiring. "Didn't you?" he repeated.

"I had my suspicions," Alda finally said.

"All right, ladies," Franklin said, opening his notepad. He set it on the counter, clicked the end of his pen, and set to scribbling. "Your turn. Why is the *Gazette* missing its *entire* microfilm collection?"

Alda and Emma gasped.

"All of it?" asked Alda. Emma's hand went to her mouth, half hiding her shock.

Franklin nodded but remained silent. He swiped absently at his hair. Emma noticed he had a habit of running his long fingers through his graying hair whenever he got excited or needed a minute to think.

"Everything?" Emma questioned.

He looked up.

"Every . . . single . . . roll. At least—" He coughed. "Sorry. At least everything from 1910 forward. The really old stuff is still there. I checked. But the rest of it . . . It's all gone."

"From 1910," Alda commented. "Why—"

"The year Tobias was born."

Alda's face paled. She moved to a nearby chair and plopped down with an exasperated sigh. Emma stood there completely dumbfounded. Her mind raced with questions.

Who all was involved?

Was this a family matter? Or someone outside the family exacting vengeance?

Were other family members involved, or just Toby?

And who would go to this much effort to make someone disappear?

"Not to be insensitive, but who . . . is Tobias?"

Franklin wrote the name in his notebook as he asked the question and looked back up at the ladies with expectancy.

"It's a long story," replied Alda.

"No one noticed the films were missing?" Emma asked sheepishly.

"Frankly, I'm not surprised." He took a sip of coffee from his Yeti. "The microfilm archives are shoved in the back of a closet in the basement. No one ever noticed because no one's ever come in asking to see newspapers from back then. Hell, I'm not even sure the machine still works to look at any of it."

"And the newspaper never digitized them?"

Franklin's eyes narrowed as he studied Emma. "What are you saying?"

"I'm not accusing," Emma said quickly, her hands going up. "I'm just trying to understand."

"One of those 'out of sight, out of mind' things, most likely."

"Understandable," Alda said.

"I'm sure if there had been any interest in the older editions, the paper would've digitized them years ago. But up until now, no one has been interested. Now, back to my original question: What is going on here? And who is this Tobias person you mentioned earlier?"

"We're not sure," replied Emma.

"You'll have to do better than that, I'm afraid," Franklin said. His pen hovered over his notepad, ready to take down anything the women said. "I have to tell my editor about this, and she and the police are going to have questions, starting with *why* the museum and an American tourist suspected our records might be missing in the first place."

"I don't like this, Emma." Alda's words trembled as they came out.

"Mr. Wood," began Emma.

"Please, call me Franklin."

"Franklin," Emma continued, "we'll explain everything we can, but-"

"Everything you *can*?"

"I'm afraid most of it still doesn't make sense to us," said Emma.

"I see."

"But can I ask you, Franklin? Could you keep this quiet? At least for now? Until we're able to figure out what's going on?"

"Why would I do that?" He appeared incredulous over the audacity of her question. "A theft has occurred. That's a very serious matter, Ms. Campbell. Even here in the little town of Digby."

"I meant no disrespect, sir. It's just that . . . we don't know what's going on here."

"Conspiracy," Franklin mused. His eyes lit up with excitement, and Emma could see the wheels of his mind turning over the potential headlines emblazoned across the front pages of every major paper in Canada, his name directly tied to all of it. "I like the sound of that."

Alda and Emma exchanged a disconcerted look.

"I think you better show him," Alda finally said.

"Show me what?"

Emma led the reporter into their research room, where her makeshift family tree was still splayed out across the table. She briefly explained why she was in Digby, the Roberts family tree she had pieced together, and the missing documents from the museum, the Registrar General's office, and the Justice Centre. Everything that mentioned her branch of the family tree had been carefully cut out and discarded.

"Damn," muttered Franklin when she was finished, "you *have* uncovered something, haven't you?"

"It seems that way."

"Why?"

"That's the question that's been eluding us for two days," Emma said. "But whoever did this was patient, careful . . ."

"And good," Franklin said. "They managed to do this right under everyone's nose. And the flood at the Justice Centre? You think they're responsible for that too?"

"The clerk just said it was a broken pipe," Alda said. "He didn't say anything about foul play."

"A burst pipe over the weekend." Franklin ran his fingers through his hair. "Convenient. A little too convenient if you ask me."

"You think it was something else?"

The journalist gave a noncommittal shrug. "It's possible. Too early to make a determination on it though."

"Thomas said the pipe that burst was in their office, so even if someone had noticed sooner, most of their records would still have been destroyed."

"Thomas? I thought he retired last year."

Alda shook her head. "No, he's still there."

"And the leak started in their office?"

"Lost everything, he said. Down to the last ink pen."

"Yeah, microfilm doesn't do well in water," Franklin added. He was frantically taking down notes as Emma and Alda spoke.

"He also said," Alda continued, "that the Registrar General's office was scheduled to move to a new location at some point in the coming spring. If the flooding was intentional, the move would've made things harder for them."

"Right," Emma said. "They would've had *two* places to rob instead of just the one, which might've raised suspicions if people found out about the missing records here and at the newspaper. As it was, they were able to kill two birds with one stone, so to speak."

Franklin sighed. He ran his hand through his hair nervously as he scanned the patchwork family tree.

"You know, with all the hair spray you've got up there," Alda teased, "it's not going anywhere."

Emma laughed.

"Oh, hush up."

Emma enjoyed watching their banter. It reminded her so much of her own relationship with her grandmother. Her heart stung at the memory, and Emma unexpectedly found herself on the verge of tears. She turned away and began to tidy up a shelf so as to not be discovered.

"All right," he finally said. "I'll keep this quiet . . . for now."

"Thank you so much, Mr. Franklin!" Emma said as she returned to the table.

"For *now*," he reiterated as he returned his pen and notepad to his khakis. A fresh straight crease ran down the fronts of his legs. "But just until you're able to figure out who's doing this and why."

"I understand." Emma nodded. "Thank you."

"Be careful though," he cautioned as he made his way back to the front door. "If someone—or some*ones*—went to *this* much trouble, I'm guessing there's a *very* dirty little secret in your family they're trying to protect." He glanced warily at Emma. "A secret you might not want to discover."

His words hung in the air like acrid smoke as he closed the door behind him. Emma could hear the engine of a car turning over and driving off as she turned back to Alda, who had hung back as Franklin left.

Dirty little secret, Emma thought. *Maybe it would be better if I left it alone.*

They fell silent, and Emma contemplated their new, much more precarious situation. The central heating unit kicked on, which sent a low buzzing hum through the room as the internal fan pushed out heated air. Alda looked down at the makeshift family tree and then back to the photos of Julian still in her hand. She dropped them onto the table as if the paper were poisoned. Emma could read the woman's expression like an open book.

"You think I should stop digging into this, don't you?"

"Clearly, something happened back then in your family. You don't just wipe away an entire piece of family history like some . . . spill on the kitchen counter mopped up with a dishrag. But Franklin is right. This is different. Someone went to a lot of trouble and took a lot of time to do this."

"I know."

"Are you sure you really want to know what those reasons were?"

Emma considered the question. Collapsing into a chair, she put her head in her hands.

"I don't know, Ms. Alda." She sat up, brushing her hair out of her face with both hands. "On the one hand, I want nothing to do with this. You and Mr. Wood are right. Clearly, something happened in 1948 to my family. And clearly, it was bad enough that someone—inside the family or out—thought it necessary to erase part of the family. I'm not sure I want to keep digging into this."

Alda eyed her thoughtfully. "And on the other?"

Emma looked across the room at the scattered books, photo albums, and records they had scoured over the past two days. Scattered across the broken detritus of her family history lay pieces of the answers she sought. If only she could put the pieces back together.

A movement in the corner of her eye made Emma turn to the doorway and the hall beyond. The girl was standing there. Expectant. Patient. A reminder to Emma of why she had come to Digby in the first place: to uncover the girl's identity.

"I owe it," Emma finally answered, her gaze fixed on the doorway, "to her."

"Her?" Alda asked, turning in the direction of Emma's stare. The doorway was empty as far as she could see. "Her who?"

Emma didn't answer. She was too focused on the girl. Waiting for guidance. Waiting for direction.

Help me, Emma thought, hoping in that moment telepathy was a real thing. *Tell me what to do.*

"Emma? What is it? You see something?"

Emma blinked. Once. Twice. The girl disappeared. The connection severed, Emma turned back to the older woman, who stared at her with confusion.

"I'm sorry. What?"

"Her who?" Alda repeated. "Whom do you owe it to?"

I wish I could tell you, Ms. Alda, Emma thought. But she didn't. Instead, Emma said, "For my grandmother. I must find out, Ms. Alda. Even if it means opening old wounds."

"You know what they say, dear. If you go digging up the past, you never know what may turn up."

"I have to try."

Alda leaned back in her chair, resting her hands in her lap. She gave the family tree a cautious apprehensive eye. After a moment, she nodded curtly, as if reaching her own decision, and looked back at Emma. "Very well, dear. Where do we go from here?"

Emma thought for a moment. "I don't know. How do you find someone who's been erased?"

Alda shrugged. "Now there's the question. One which, I'm afraid, doesn't have a very clear answer."

The hum of the central heating unit cut off, plunging the room into a deafening silence as the two women considered their quandary.

"I don't think we're going to get anywhere looking through official documents. It seems clear whoever did this threw everything away."

"We still have options. Our little thief may have stolen everything here, but the Registrar General's office in Halifax would still have copies."

Emma shook her head. "Tried that. Nothing came up in my research."

"Nothing?"

"No, ma'am. Not a single thing."

"That's strange." Alda walked out of the room.

"Ms. Alda?"

"Just a minute, dear," she called from the front. "I need to make a phone call."

Curiosity got the better of Emma, and she trailed after Alda back to the front parlor, where she was already dialing. She pressed the *Speaker* button so Emma could listen in.

"An old friend of mine works in the Halifax Office of Vital Statistics. Maybe she can help."

"Really?" Emma's pulse quickened with anticipation.

Alda nodded as a female voice began to speak.

"Vital Statistics. How may I direct your call?"

"Margaret McEachern, please."

"Who is calling?"

"Alda Dillon from the Greater Annapolis Basin Historical Society and Museum."

"One moment."

The phone buzzed on the other end twice as the call was transferred.

"Alda, honey! Land's sake, you know, I was just talking to Mark about you last night. I was going to call you this weekend. Everything okay over there?"

Emma listened as Marge and Alda spent the next few minutes catching up on the recent events in their lives. Marge was boisterous with a booming voice and a laugh so hearty it rattled the photos on the wall. Emma wished she could meet the woman in person. Alda finally brought the conversation back around to why she was calling.

"Actually, Marge, I need your help with something."

"Anything! Whatcha got?"

"I have you on speaker. I'm here with Emma Campbell from America."

"Hi, Ms. McEachern," Emma said.

"Honey, call me Marge. Everyone else does."

"Of course. Nice to meet you, Marge. Ms. Alda and I are really hoping you can help us out here."

"What can I do for you, Emma?"

"I'm doing some family research, and so far, I'm coming up empty-handed."

"How so?"

"Well, it's a long story that we're still trying to figure out, but all the records from 1950 back have either been misplaced, stolen, or destroyed, and Ms. Alda said the main office—your office—in Halifax would have copies of all those records, and I was hoping I could get copies of . . . well, anything you can find, really."

"From 1950 back, eh?"

"Yes, ma'am."

"I'm sorry, Emma, but those records aren't here anymore."

"Where are they?"

"Gone."

"Gone?" Emma and Alda asked simultaneously.

"Yes, indeed."

Emma felt a knot rising in her stomach. She crossed her fingers and prayed they weren't facing yet another dead end.

"What do you mean *gone*?" Alda asked.

"Well, you see, Vital Statistics used to be in the city center. Grand old building built in the late 1800s. Gorgeous architecture."

Emma's heart sank. Marge's next words came as no surprise.

"In the early fifties, there was a massive fire downtown. Most of the entire building was destroyed. Several of the surrounding buildings too."

"What about microfilm?"

"This is where it gets dicey. Turns out they were just starting to transfer records over to microfilm back then. But the economy really struggled here in Nova Scotia following the end of the war. A lot of soldiers stayed in Europe as security. Iron Curtain and all that, you know."

"Right."

"Some stayed for the jobs. You could make good money back then with all the construction going on."

"Well, there was a lot to rebuild, eh?" Alda offered.

"That's putting it mildly, to be sure. Many others left with their families and immigrated to America. The fifties were a boom time in the US, and a lot of people wanted in on that."

"Which affected things back here," Emma said.

Alda nodded.

"Those were tough times," Marge said. "Local and provincial government budgets were exceptionally tight in those days. My father was a government employee back then, and I can remember stories from when I was a little girl. The struggles they all had to go through just to get funding for the smallest thing."

"So, microfilming old documents—"

"Was the absolute last thing on anyone's mind."

"So, everything was destroyed." Emma felt like crying. Alda reached across the counter and patted her hand. The touch was almost too much for her to bear, but she pushed forward.

"What about the sprinkler systems or fire extinguishers? None of those worked? Surely a building of that size and historical significance would've had some sort of fire suppression system."

The pause that followed made Emma worried she had offended the woman, but Marge eventually continued her story.

"You'd think so, right? Turns out the requisition form for the funds to install a new sprinkler system . . . was sitting on some bureaucrat's desk waiting for approval."

"Are you serious? God, I'd hate to have been that guy the day after the fire."

"You and me both." Marge laughed. "I'm pretty sure he was reassigned somewhere. Or politely encouraged to pack his box and find gainful employment somewhere else."

Emma sighed as she laid her head on the counter between her crossed arms.

"So, there's nothing left, is there? Nothing to help me in my search?"

"From a government records standpoint, no. Unfortunately not. There was nothing left from the fire. Afterward, the microfilm system was quickly approved by the House of Assembly."

"Go figure."

"After that," Marge continued, "Vital Statistics began the massive task of transferring all paper documents to microfilm across Nova Scotia. Hard copies were left in the regional offices along with a microfilm copy. A second microfilm was sent to Halifax in order to rebuild a central database, if you will."

"Except for Digby." Emma said, dejected.

"What's that?"

"The Digby office lost all their records in a flood prior to the fire." Alda said.

"Flood? What flood? When was this?"

"1952." Alda said. "Burst pipe during the winter destroyed everything."

"I'm sorry to hear that." Marge said. "But if Digby's were all lost . . ."

"Then they would've had nothing on my family to film and send to Halifax."

"Afraid not."

Tears welled up in Emma's eyes as she retreated to the back of the house, leaving Alda to finish up with Marge. Angry footfalls marked her exit from the room. Emma returned to the dining room, where the patchwork of notebook pages lay spread open like an untreated, infected wound. It taunted her silently. Dared her to stop. Dared her to continue.

Emma reached for it and moved to tear it apart, but she stopped short. With the ends caught in her balled up fists, she closed her eyes and took a deep breath to steady herself. Silently, she counted backward from five and imagined the child from her grandma's dining room.

"I need you," Emma whispered.

No answer. She pressed on, muttering to herself in a desperate attempt to will the specter from beyond the grave into the room.

"Help me. You brought me here. To this place. I'm here. But someone has beaten me to it. I don't know what to do. Help me. Help me."

"Emma?"

Emma opened her eyes to find Alda standing at the doorway. The girl was nowhere to be seen.

"Who are you talking to, dear?"

"No one," Emma replied as she cleared her throat and stood up straight again. She wiped her tears with the back of her hand. "Just talking to myself. It seems I've led you on a wild goose chase, Ms. Alda. I'm sorry for wasting your time."

A curious grin spread across the old woman's face.

"What?" Emma asked.

"You remember Jules's obituary?"

"Yes, ma'am. I remember. Why?"

Alda pulled a small index card out from behind her back, where she had been hiding it. It was brown with age.

"On a whim, I decided to check the records."

Emma was too afraid to hope. "Yes."

"And we have some of Julian's personal papers upstairs."

Emma bounded across the room and seized the card from Alda's hand. With trembling hands, she read the comments aloud.

Julian "Jules" Roberts	
Born 1913	Died 1999
Residence	Digby, Nova Scotia
Contents	Seven personal journals Four photo albums Personal letters
Location	F7D3

"But . . . are they there? The thief took everything else."

"Only one way to find out. Come on. Follow me."

They had just stepped into the hallway, heading back up front, when Emma heard a child's giggle behind her. She turned, and there she was. Standing in the doorway to the dining room, she laughed at Emma. Not a malevolent laugh. More amused, the way children sometimes laughed when an adult did something silly.

"Emma? What's the matter, dear?"

"Uh, nothing." Emma thought quickly. "Just something I . . . smelled is all."

Alda walked back down the hall. Emma and the little ghost kept watchful eyes on the woman as she approached.

"Oh." Alda inhaled. "Smells like . . . lavender."

"Is that it?" Emma's eyes never left the little girl.

"Did you put lotion on, dear? Or perfume, maybe?"

"No, ma'am."

"Strange." Alda inhaled again, looking directly at the doorway now. "Wonder where that came from." She shrugged and turned back down the hallway. "Oh well. Plenty of old smells in this place. Now, let's see about those papers, shall we? I'm dying to find out what's up there."

"Right behind you." Emma gave the girl one last glance. "Thank you," she whispered.

The girl laughed again and disappeared like fog, the echo of her laughter dancing down the darkened hallway.

They made their way to the second floor and into what looked to be a bedroom, though there was no bed. Several five-drawer filing cabinets lined the wall, and Alda made straight for the one on the far left.

"*All* of these are diaries?" Emma cried in horror.

"Yes." Alda's cheeriness had not diminished in the slightest with the daunting undertaking. "Read me that location again, would you, dear? At the bottom of the card."

"F7D3."

"Thank you."

"What does it mean?"

"The *F* is what file cabinet it's in." She stopped in front of a cabinet and pointed out the large *7* that had been written in permanent marker along the top. "File cabinet seven, see?"

"And the *D3* is what drawer it's in?"

"Precisely."

Alda opened the third drawer from the top. An assortment of mocha color expandable file wallets filled the drawer. Emma stepped closer and could see each one had a plain white label affixed to the top left corner of the front flap with a person's name on it. Halfway back, they found it —*Julian "Jules" Roberts*. There were two wallets with his name, which initially caught Emma by surprise until she reread the card still in her hand—seven personal journals, four photo albums, and personal letters.

"Oh my God!" Emma screamed with delight. "I can't believe it's still here!"

"Well, in truth, we're not sure *what* is still here," Alda said cautiously, though her beaming smile betrayed the fact she was just as giddy. "Let's get these downstairs. I'll make us a nice cup of tea, and we'll tuck in for the morning and see what we can find, shall we?"

"Tea sounds lovely. Thank you."

"Cream?"

"Uh . . . do you have any honey?"

Alda nodded. "Coming right up."

Emma's first sip of the chamomile tea was like a warm balm spread over her hypercaffeinated vocal cords—instantly soothing with just the right amount sweetness.

"Thank you."

"Now," Alda said, sitting down next to Emma, "where would you like to start?"

"Why don't we save the personal letters for last?" Emma replied. "We can work our way through the journals. See what we find. Then move on to the photos."

"I think you would be best suited for the photos at this point. You've seen these people's faces every day for days now. You'd be more apt to recognize them than I would."

"Okay." Emma nodded. "Then journals. Letters. Then I can work through the photos on my own."

"A sound strategy." Alda beamed, taking a sip of her tea.

They spent the rest of the morning reading Julian's diaries. It was slow going at first, as the man's handwriting was atrocious. Each line was a laborious effort to coax his words into revealing their secrets, but slowly—all too slowly—they began to yield to the ladies' scrutiny. By lunch, Emma could, for the most part, read a line at a slow but steady pace.

Still, she had only managed to get through the first twenty pages or so. Alda's progress was only slightly better. They took a break at eleven thirty, and at precisely twelve o'clock, Alda unlocked the front door and flipped the *Closed* sign over to *Open*. There were already a few tourists waiting outside, which meant Alda would not be free to rejoin the search until the tourists had had their fill. When their explorations led them into the dining room, Emma smiled and apologized for the mess on the table.

"Family research."

A few people asked her how it was going and whether she had found some rich long-lost relative. Most simply nodded, gave her a vacant "Oh" response, and kept on walking. Emma turned back to Julian's diary and continued reading.

The scribbled words twisted and swerved like a cat stretching itself when it first awakens. They sprang from the page, spinning their yarn around Emma. Julian had been an inconsistent journalist at best. Some weeks he wrote daily, then there would be breaks anywhere from a few days to a few months. Each time he had returned to his journal, something significant had been mentioned, as if some unseen hand intended him to record his lowest points. He had been unhappy with his marriage. So, apparently, had his wife, or at least to Julian she'd seemed so. Emma marveled at their commitment to the greater family despite their own personal misery. Things had certainly changed in that respect. People bailed at the first sign of trouble in their marriages now. Few, if any, stuck it out. Fewer marriages survived past the point where the children moved out on their own. But Julian had been committed to his children; that much was clear to Emma. Regardless of how much he might've loathed the woman legally bound to him, he refused to consider divorce.

Shortly after Alda had opened the museum, Emma found something, a single entry in Jules's diary dated February 1947.

That wretched Morrison boy was sent off today. His father says it's for school in England, but people still talk. Postmaster or no, those boys are rotten to the core. Frankly, I'm just glad he's gone. Boys that age get themselves into trouble with nothing to do. Perhaps it's just what the boy needs to grow up and make something of the mess he's made with his life. And Alice's. That poor child.

"Alice?" Emma whispered aloud. "Who's Alice?"

Emma consulted her family tree for the name but came up empty. No Alice. She returned to her reading, picking up a later volume this time in hopes of finding some mention of Toby, Marian, and Nellie. Jules had been an absolute gossip, she discovered. His journals were filled with the goings and comings of the neighbors. She was surprised to discover an hour later that Jules had later entered local politics, even becoming mayor of Digby for a while. Emma slowly warmed to this stranger she only knew from the pages of his diaries. He cared about people. Cared about the town and its inhabitants. And God, did he ever more love to talk.

After an hour of nothing, she set it to the side.

"Clearly, whatever happened in 1947," she murmured, "it severed the family completely. Interesting."

Emma returned to the journal she had been reading before. Three pages in, she found a second entry dated April 1947.

Terrible business. I always knew that Morrison girl was no good for Alice. And now that wretched family has stained ours with their ilk. I told Toby and Cici it would come to no good, but they didn't listen, of course. They don't see the sort of people that family associates themselves with. And now look where it's gotten them. The family is terribly upset by the whole episode, but what's done is done. Can't unpull the trigger once it's been pulled, can you? May God give us strength for the dark days ahead.

Emma leaned forward, staring down at the diary. "Cici? Who the heck is Cici?" She skimmed through her notes and the family tree. No Cici. Emma pulled out her phone and shot a quick text to her uncle.

EMMA
Does the name Cici mean anything to you?
A few seconds came Adi's reply.

UNCLE ADI
Hey kiddo! Cici was Gran's mother's nickname.
Short for Cecilia. Her middle name. Why?

EMMA
We found a few journals belonging to one
of Toby's brothers and the name came up.
I'd never heard it before.

UNCLE ADI
Yep. Cici was what everyone called her.

EMMA
Ok thanks.

UNCLE ADI
No problem. Everything going ok?

EMMA
Its been a rollercoaster. Tell you more next time we talk.

She set her phone on the table and added the name *Cici* in quotation marks by Marian's name on the family tree. Picking up the journal, she reread the entry. "Wait a minute."

"Did you find something, dear?" Alda asked, entering the room.

"I think so. Come and take a look at this. See what you think."

Emma flipped back to the prior entry and passed the book to Alda, who leaned against the edge of the table. Her brow furrowed as she read, clearly displeased by the words on the page.

"Now flip three pages forward and read the entry dated April 1947."

Alda did as instructed, and again, Emma noted Alda's displeasure.

"Well," Alda said, shutting the book firmly. "Clearly some ugly business happened with your family and the Morrisons."

"Do you know them? The Morrisons?"

"I don't recall the name, no. But if Mr. Morrison was the postmaster, there might be records of the family at the Registrar General's office. But, Emma, isn't this getting off topic a little bit? I thought you were looking for your family, not the Morrisons."

"I am." Emma stood and paced around the table, her hands buried deep in her pants pockets. "Hear me out, will you?"

"All right." Alda sat down and watched as Emma took the diary in hand and continued pacing.

"You asked me earlier if Gran had any siblings."

"And you said she didn't."

"Right." Emma nodded. "But listen to this entry again. 'I always knew that Morrison girl was no good for Alice. And now that wretched family has stained ours with their ilk. I told Toby and Cici it would come to no good, but they didn't listen, of course.' Why would my great-grandparents be worried about this kid?"

"You think this Alice person could—"

"Hello?" a man called out from the front room.

"Oh!" Alda darted up from her seat. "Gotta run." She shuffled toward the hallway, calling out, "Be right there."

Emma reread the passage.

Why would they be worried about Alice? she thought. *She must be family. Has to be. It's the only thing that makes sense.*

Emma returned to the pages on the table. Alice wasn't there. Emma knew that already. During the course of her investigations, she had reinserted Toby's branch of the family tree using a different color Post-it Note. She reread the names. Their dates of birth.

She gasped when it finally hit her.

"Of course!"

"Um . . . hi."

Emma spun around to find a woman standing in the archway. Clearly a tourist. Sneakers. Faded denim jeans. A T-shirt that read *I*❤ *Lobster.* She stared at Emma awkwardly.

"Are you okay, miss?" the woman asked. "You were talking to yourself."

It took Emma a moment to process the woman's words. Her head was still spinning from her discovery. Emma plopped down into a chair, her hand clutching the table. The woman took a cautious step forward.

"Are you all right, miss?"

"I think . . ." Emma finally managed to spit out the words. They came reluctantly, like a child being forced out of their favorite hiding place. "I think I just found my grandmother's sister."

"Oh," the woman said cheerily. She raised her hands, shaking them with glee as if she were waving pom-poms. "Yay!"

"Yay," Emma repeated.

The woman lowered her hands and looked around the room. "Well, I'll leave you alone, then. Congrats on finding your great-aunt."

"Thank you," Emma replied. The woman was already gone. Emma could just make out her tinny voice in another room talking with a man.

"Sister," Emma whispered. "Gran had a sister."

Her spin went rigid as a familiar cold presence entered the room. She didn't need to look up to know who was there. Emma took two deep breaths, reminding herself the girl wasn't there to harm, then lifted her head.

She was standing in the hallway, hiding in shadow. Emma moved to get up, but her leaden legs made it difficult to move. "Alice."

It had been Alice in the painting. Alice . . . and Nellie. Sisters at home playing on a tree swing. Emma's eyes watered with emotion. She couldn't wait to tell her grandmother. She reached for her cell phone in her pocket before remembering. Nellie was gone. Emma couldn't call her now, couldn't share her discovery.

Tears welled in her eyes. Emma fought them as best she could, but her emotions were too raw now, and she was thoroughly exhausted. She folded her arms across the table, burying her face to stifle her cries. She wept for the sisters. For what they had lost. For the time stolen from them. Time that only Nellie's recent death had been able to give back.

"My gran," she sobbed, "had a sister."

Emma didn't see Alice when she left, but she felt her absence in the room.

It wasn't until she felt Alda nudging her shoulder that Emma realized she had cried herself to sleep.

"Good heavens, Emma!" Alda exclaimed, taking in the sight of Emma's ragged features and bloodshot eyes. "Whatever is the matter? Why are you crying?"

Emma brushed her residual tears away with the back of her hand and sat up. Alda passed her a handful of tissues, which Emma used to blow her nose and dab her eyes dry.

"Thank you. I'm sorry. I must look a mess."

"What happened?" Alda reached across the table to take her hand. "Did you find something?"

"Gran had a sister," Emma confessed. "Alice."

"The girl from the entries this morning?"

Emma nodded.

"Gracious! And she was your grandmother's sister?"

"Yeah."

"But that's good news, isn't it?" Alda asked, a forced smile on her face.

"Good news. Yeah," Emma repeated.

Alda patted her arm. "Well, now we're really onto it, aren't we? Did you want me to make copies of anything before I shut off the copier?"

"No, ma'am," Emma said, clearing her throat and dabbing her eyes again. "I'll wait and do it later. What time is it?"

"Nearly four. Closing time."

Emma stood and began packing her things. "Guess I must've dozed off there."

"Not surprising," Alda chided. "You were up half the night, remember?"

Emma laughed. "My grandmother would've liked you."

"And I her." Alda's soft tone reminded Emma so much of Nellie. "If she was anything like her granddaughter."

"Until tomorrow, then?"

"Well, the museum is closed on the weekends . . ."

"Oh, well . . . I mean, we can wait until Monday, then. No rush."

"But," Alda pressed, "you could come by my house tomorrow, and we could continue working there."

"I don't want to impose, Ms. Alda. Honestly. It's Saturday, and you've been gracious enough already on this wild-goose chase. Let's just wait until Monday."

"It's no trouble. And besides"—Alda winked, a playful grin stretching across her weathered face—"I love geese."

Emma laughed and began packing her shoulder bag. "Do you mind if I take Julian's stuff with me to read over the weekend? I'll bring them back to you on Monday, of course. Would that be okay?"

"Of course. Of course. Just don't lose anything."

"I won't. I promise."

Alda headed upstairs as Emma rezipped her bag. Emma was about to head for the door when she recognized the box that Franklin had brought in the day before as she was leaving. In between tourists and helping Emma, Alda had started sorting the contents into multiple neat little piles on top of the front counter. Newspaper clippings were arranged in one stack, photographs were in another, and there was even a collection of old school yearbooks. Emma ran her hand absently over several things, not really looking at any of them. She was about to walk past when her hand accidentally brushed too firmly across the stack of photographs and sent them skittering across the table and onto the floor.

"Dang it!" Emma yelled out as she dropped to her knees and began gathering everything up.

"What's wrong?" Alda called down from the stairwell. Delicate measured footsteps began descending.

"Nothing," she replied, a bit too loudly and with more than a hint of guilt in her voice. "I just knocked over a few photographs. I'm sorry. Were these in any particular order?"

"Oh, those," Alda said dismissively as she approached. "No, they're not in any order. Just put them back on the counter, and I'll get to it later."

"Are these from the box Franklin brought in?"

"Yes, he said he was doing some spring cleaning and came across a box of old stuff they didn't need."

"I would've thought a newspaper would want to hang on to its photo collections. Especially if they were taken by someone on staff . . ."

"They keep the negative, to be sure, but the actual photo? Not normally. No need these days with everything on the computer. The museum usually ends up with them. We have quite a substantial photo collection built entirely off people's family donations and local businesses. It's quite fascinating, if you would ever like to see it sometime, that is."

Emma didn't respond.

"Emma?"

No response.

She reached out and touched Emma's arm, startling her. "Sorry, dear. I didn't mean to frighten you. Are you all right?"

"Yes, ma'am."

But Emma's attention was centered on the black-and-white photograph in her hands.

"What is it? You look as if you've seen a ghost."

"This . . . ph-photograph," she finally managed to stutter.

"Photograph?" Alda put her glasses on and peered at the grainy image. "What about it?"

"I've . . . I've seen it . . . before."

"You have?" Alda said with disbelief. "Where?"

"My grandmother." Emma's words were coming more fluidly to her now. "My grandmother had a painting of this tree in her dining room."

"Really? Let me see!"

Emma reluctantly handed her the photograph, and Alda rose and walked to one of the windows to get a better look. It was a photograph of Digby Harbor from the shoreline. Along the left-hand side was a large tree whose branches spread out and over the water. A rope swing had been tied to the largest branch, and a girl sat in it.

"Charming." Alda suddenly realized Emma was still sitting on the floor with a dazed, befuddled look in her eyes. "Oh, my dear, let me help you up."

"I'm fine."

Emma grabbed hold of the counter, a more stable surface than Alda's frail frame, and hoisted herself up off the floor. She walked over to Alda, who was still looking at the photograph.

"You said your grandmother has a copy of this?"

"No," said Emma as she pulled out a chair and took a seat. "She has a painting in her dining room that's nearly identical to this photograph."

"Well, I'll be. That certainly is . . . odd."

"Odd is putting it mildly."

"Where did she get it?"

"It was a wedding present from her mother, Marian. Marian painted it."

"Your great-grandmother was a painter?"

"I never knew her. She died when my mother was just a little girl. But she painted a seascape"—Emma pointed an apprehensive finger toward the photograph—"exactly like that photo. And then she told my grandmother to never let it go. I know because several times I joked with Gran that she needed to update her décor, and she was emphatic about keeping it."

"Same swing? The girl?" Alda was trying hard to wrap her mind around this.

"Same . . . *everything*. Except for the girl. In my grandmother's painting, there are two girls."

"Two?"

Emma nodded.

"Well, I'll be." Alda sighed as she sat down.

"Where was it taken?"

Alda flipped over the print and read, "McCullough House. Digby, Nova Scotia, 1972."

"Where's the McCullough house?"

"Just down the street." Alda perked up suddenly. "You're not going over there, are you?"

"I have to, Ms. Alda."

"Have to? Why?"

"I have to follow this . . . wherever it leads."

"But," protested Alda, "I know the Douglases. They're a young couple. Well, maybe not young. But not old. Late thirties, I'd say. They wouldn't know anything about this."

"But they could possibly lead me to someone who might," said Emma. "What can you tell me about the house now?"

"The house itself? Beautiful property, it is. Old family home in the Victorian style. It's on the main street, dear. Surely you must have seen it on your way into town."

"Probably. But I can't place it right now. And with the fog—"

"Ah, this wretched fog!"

"I could've passed it and just didn't see it. You said the Douglases own the house now? Not the McCulloughs?"

"Yes, the Douglases bought it some time ago. Too big for them if you ask me. But they turned it into a quaint little bed-and-breakfast called the Fishmonger. Quite popular with the tourists."

"How long ago did they buy it?"

"I'd say seven . . . eight years now. Could be longer than that, but I don't think so. Certainly not more than ten."

"Do you remember the previous owners?"

Alda considered the question. "No," she said with a touch of confusion. "Now that you mention it, I don't. Not sure who owned the property before the Douglases."

"Would it be in the property records here?"

"Oh, no." She laughed. "Anything that recent would still be in the courthouse."

"I see."

"The Douglases are good people, Emma." There was a cautionary edge to Alda's words, and Emma took note of it. "Whatever's going on here with your family, I'm sure the Douglases aren't involved."

"I know. But all the same, I'd like to visit the house."

"Very well. Listen, why don't I take a couple of the journals, and we can divide and conquer."

"Oh, I wouldn't want to impose. I mean, it's the weekend. You don't want to be stuck in my family drama all weekend, do you?"

"I don't mind. Truly I don't. And besides that, I'm just as curious as you are. I *have* to know the end of the story now."

"Okay." Emma gave a half smile. "But only if you're sure."

"Very sure, dear. Very sure."

Her grandmother and this woman would have gotten along so well. The thought of it pained Emma.

"Thanks, Ms. Alda. I appreciate all your help."

"Don't mention it."

"Why don't you take the letters? I can work on the journals over the weekend and move on to the photographs once I'm finished."

"A sound solution," Alda replied, taking the stack of correspondence from Emma.

"You said the Douglas house is just down the street, right?"

"Yes, it's just down the street. Turn left and go straight. The house will be on the right-hand side facing the harbor. You can't miss it, but don't"—Alda's expression soured as she raised her finger in a stern warning—"go fretting the Douglases. I'm confident they know nothing about what's going on with your family. Like I said, they only moved in several years ago."

"I understand. I just want to look around and take a few pictures. Maybe see if they can point me to the prior owners. They might know something depending on how long they've lived there."

"True."

Emma held up the photograph. "Do you mind if I get a copy of this one?"

XI

Emma found the Fishmonger easily enough. It was just down Water Street on the right, as Alda had said it would be. The two-story house, now converted into a bed-and-breakfast, had been painted a deep blueberry color with white and red accents. White rocking chairs peppered the wide wraparound porch. A Canadian flag hung from a small metal flagpole mounted to one of the porch columns flanking the stairs that led up to the front door. It swayed lazily in the gentle afternoon breeze.

She switched off the engine and stepped out of her car. The pea gravel crunched under Emma's feet as she listened to seagulls calling out to one another in the distance. The house stood barely a hundred yards from the water's edge with the town harbor directly across. Emma absorbed every sound and smell as she made her way to the front steps. Had her grandmother played in this front lawn, which had long since been converted into guest parking? Had she run up and down the front steps as she played with cousins? Or rocked in one of the near dozen wooden rocking—

"Hiya!"

The greeting startled Emma, and she reacted much like a child caught sneaking into the kitchen for a snack.

"Sorry if I scared you," the woman said, her face reddening slightly with embarrassment. She was standing just off the side of the porch. From ground level, the woman was just tall enough for her head and part of her upper chest to be seen through the porch railing.

"You need a room for the night?"

"I—"

"You're in luck," the woman continued, not hearing Emma's hesitancy. "We've got one room left on the second floor. Queen sized bed. Although if you were wanting a king size, it's currently occupied. But the Hansens are probably checking out tomorrow, so we could put you somewhere else for tonight and then move you into the king suite tomorrow if that's agreeable to you."

Emma had started walking toward the woman as she spoke. The distant sound of children playing in the backyard grew louder as she approached. When she reached the right end of the porch, Emma discovered the railing had a carefully concealed gate blended into it. She opened it and stepped down the stairs, closing the gate behind her.

"Personally, I prefer the queen suites." The woman smiled warmly. "They have a beautiful view of the harbor. Both have dormer windows with bench seating underneath where you can sit and watch the boats come and go. It's quite lovely."

The woman was tall, slightly taller than Emma's five-foot nine frame. She was dressed in faded denim overalls with a green and brown plaid shirt underneath. She wore pink rubber boots with yellow daisies on them, and her hair had been pulled up in a loose haphazard ponytail. She had been planting hosta around the house.

"Oh, look at me," the woman said, throwing up her hands in mock dismay, "prattling on without so much as introducing myself. Hi." She pulled off her dirty work gloves and thrust out her right hand. "I'm Connie. Constance, really. But everyone calls me Connie."

"Emma," she replied as she shook the proffered hand.

"Nice to meet you, Emma." Connie regloved and squatted down. "Let me finish this last hosta, and we'll get you settled. Where are you coming from?"

"America. Missouri."

"Missouri." Connie cocked her head a bit to ponder this. She planted her last hosta and tamped down the earth around it. She stood up, a small trowel and a wooden plant tray in hand. "Hmm, that's . . ." She snapped her fingers in jubilation. "It's in the middle, isn't it? Sorry. I've been trying to teach my daughters the states, but sometimes it can be a bit confusing. Fifty is a lot to keep up with."

"I guess so." Emma smiled, trying not to laugh.

"Well," Connie said as she examined her work. She gave a satisfactory nod at the plants and turned toward the backyard. "Follow me to the back and let me put these away. Then we'll get you settled, shall we?"

She turned without even giving Emma time enough to object, leaving Emma no choice but to follow alongside like a little golden retriever.

"So, what brings you to Digby, Emma? We don't usually get a lot of international visitors in our small town. Unless it's for the golf tournament, of course."

"I came up to do some family—"

Emma's throat clenched midsentence as they rounded the corner of the house and she looked out across the harbor. The knot in her stomach seized, and Emma bent nearly in half and vomited onto the ground.

"Oh, God!" Connie cried out in alarm, startling her daughters, who were playing in the backyard. Both girls looked back at their mother to see what was wrong. "Amelia! Quick! Bring me a chair! Carol, go bring me a glass of cool water from the kitchen! Quickly now!"

"Yes, Mother," the girls replied together as they raced into action. Seconds later, Connie helped Emma into the white plastic chair Amelia had brought. Shortly afterward, Carol appeared in front of her. She held out a small glass of water that had been filled to the brim. The girl wore a slightly disgusted face, which Emma would have found amusing had the circumstances been different.

"I'm sorry." Emma's face flushed with humiliation.

"Are you all right, Emma?" Connie was kneeling on the ground beside her with a worried matronly expression.

"I'm fine," Emma whispered. "Must've been something I ate."

"Did you have tuna?" the younger daughter asked with an air of petulance.

"Carol!"

"Well, Amelia had tuna last week, and it made her twow up," the girl explained, anxious to be of some help to the distressed stranger in their backyard. "Maybe they both ate the same fish!"

"That's enough," Connie rebuked. "Now, you girls run along and play."

Carol was quick in response as she turned and raced away. "It's my turn!"

"Not if I get there first," Amelia said, taking off after her sister.

Emma, who had kept her eyes pinned on the grass in embarrassment up to that point, clutched the plastic arms as she willed herself to look back up. There, across the back lawn, was the harbor.

A dozen boats lay at anchor along the pier jutting out into the tranquil waters . . . just like her grandmother's painting. A large tree anchored the corner of Connie's backyard, which ran right up to the gravelly edge of the seashore. Its branches stretched out over the water, framing the scene beyond. Just like the painting. Two girls—one older, the other younger—played blissfully on a rope swing tied to one of the heavy branches above. Just like the painting. It was identical down to the most minute details. Emma realized her grandmother's prized possession had been painted from this very spot.

Compounding Emma's shock was Alice. Standing with her back against the great tree, she observed the tableau, her attention shifting between the two girls playing and Emma.

The only difference between the two were the girls themselves. Gone were the midcentury jumpers and long-sleeve cotton shirts underneath, replaced by modern-day T-shirts, denim shorts, and sneakers. And instead of pigtails, the younger girl's blond hair was loose and came just above her shoulders. The older girl had much shorter hair, barely covering her neck, and it had been tucked meticulously behind her ears.

"Emma?"

Emma realized she'd been staring and diverted her attention back to the glass of water in her hand. She glanced sheepishly at Connie.

"I'm sorry. I'm not sure what happened just now."

"Are you okay?" Connie asked. "Can you stand?"

"I think so."

Connie tenderly took Emma's arm and helped her to her feet. She held on a few moments to make sure Emma was steady enough on her feet to stay upright before she let go.

"Why don't you come inside?" Connie offered. "I'll make us a nice cup of tea. That should help settle your stomach."

"That sounds lovely. Thank you, Connie."

Connie walked beside her to the back steps of the house and let Emma go up first.

"Girls?" Connie called out. "I'm going inside for a bit with Miss Emma. Don't wander off, okay?"

"Okay," they yelled cheerily before turning back to their play.

After Connie had settled Emma onto one of the long benches flanking the farmhouse table, she made quick work of the tea, chatting the whole time, of course. But Emma was still too dazed to pay any attention. She turned back to the wall of windows looking out onto the backyard and the shoreline. The warmth in her body seemed to drain out onto the oak floors under her feet.

How do I tell her I'm not here for a room?

A woman stepped into the kitchen and was momentarily caught off guard by Emma's presence. "Oh!" she cried with a start. "Didn't expect anyone else in the house this time of day. Sorry about that."

"Sorry if I scared you."

"Emma, this is Sandra," said Connie. The pot had begun to whistle on the stove. Connie wrapped a small towel around the handle and poured the steaming liquid into two dainty little cups.

"Sandra, Emma's a guest from Missouri. She's going to be staying with us."

No. Not a guest.

"Pleasure meeting you, Emma," she said as she stepped across the room and shook Emma's hand. She was roughly Emma's age, Emma surmised. Maybe younger.

"And you, Sandra. Are you a guest here too?"

"I work here in the evenings," she explained as she stepped out of Connie's way.

That explains the business casual, Emma thought, taking in Sandra's pressed black slacks and crisp white oxford. The black sneakers were an unexpected addition. Connie set the teacup in front of Emma.

"Let it cool a bit. It's still very hot."

"Thank you."

"So, we'll likely be seeing a lot of each other," Sandra continued. "Depending on how big a night owl you are."

Emma smiled.

Christ, Emma Campbell. Speak up! Emma chided herself. Instead, she said, "Depending on how sleepy I am, I guess." She sipped the tea. "Hmm . . . good tea. Thank you."

"You're very welcome, Emma," replied Connie. She looked uneasily at Emma. "Are you sure you're all right?"

"Did something happen?" Sandra chimed in. She sat down on the bench next to Connie across from Emma and leaned over the table. She eyed Emma with rapt curiosity.

"She, uh, had an accident in the backyard a few minutes ago."

"It was nothing, honestly," Emma tried to explain. But she knew Connie wasn't buying it. "Just something I ate."

"Where'd you eat today?"

"Sandra!" Connie scolded. "Don't be impertinent. You're as bad as Carol."

"Sorry." Sandra cowered a bit under the older woman's reprimand.

Emma finished her tea, and her stomach felt much better for it. She glanced around the room with its polished features: the classic subway tile backsplash, hardwood floors buffed until they shone like hewn marble.

If the kitchen looks this incredible, there's no way I can afford to stay here.

But Emma felt the tree's pull behind her, like someone standing over her shoulder. Watching everything she did. Quietly judging. Saying nothing.

Afford it or not, this is where I need to be.

"Well, it's almost time I get the girls home and ready for dinner," said Connie as she looked at her watch.

"You don't stay here on the premises?"

"No, there's no room," Connie replied. "Our house is just across the street though, so if you start feeling worse at any point this evening or during the night, please let Sandra know."

"I'll be down here," offered Sandra. "Usually in the dining room studying when I'm done with my chores."

"Studying?"

"I'm taking online classes with the university in Halifax."

"That's great!"

"Sandra is studying business."

"Business administration," she clarified.

"Good for you," Emma cheered. "That's great. How far along are you with your studies?"

"I still have another eighteen months to go, so I'm about halfway. So, what's that? Sophomore? Early junior?"

"Any plans after you're done?"

"I'd like to open my own bed-and-breakfast," replied Sandra as she took the two ladies' empty teacups and saucers and walked toward the kitchen sink. "Tourism is big business here."

"Would you stay here in Digby?"

"Gosh, no!" Sandra set the delicate dishes in the sink, walked back to the table, and sat down. "The Fishmonger's the best B and B in town. Connie would end up putting me out of business."

"I think you'd do well," Connie assured her. "And Digby could always use the extra business."

"Maybe," said Sandra. She shrugged, and Emma could see this was not a new discussion with the women. "I'd still like to strike out on my own. Find some quaint little corner of Nova Scotia and make it mine."

"You're very driven for someone so young."

"Thanks. I had good mentors, and I know what I want."

"And I'm sure you'll do it," said Emma.

"Connie and Dex have been great to work for. Being able to learn the business from the inside out while I'm studying has been a godsend for me. Marketing. Pricing. Day-to-day operations. All of it, you know? The good, the bad, and the ugly."

"I'm sorry," Emma interrupted. "Dex?"

"My husband, Dexter," replied Connie.

"So, Emma, do you need help with your luggage?" Sandra asked.

Crap! Now I'm really stuck.

"Oh, gracious me!" cried Connie as she threw up her hands in disbelief. "I completely forgot about that." She stood and walked out of the room. "You just wait here," she called back to Emma. "Let me grab the book, and we'll see what's available."

There was a brief moment of awkward silence between the two remaining women as they listened to the creaking floors in the front of the house betraying Connie's movements.

"So," began Sandra, "what brings you to Digby?"

"Family research."

"Oh, that's nice. Your family's from here?"

"My maternal grandmother is, yes."

"Okay, let's see," Connie said, interrupting the budding conversation as she returned and laid a spiral book on the table. It was roughly the size of a standard piece of paper, and Emma saw a plethora of Post-it tabs that had been placed along the side to indicate sections. Connie caught hold of a light blue tab and opened the binder. Backed into a corner, Emma finally spoke.

"Connie, I don't—"

"Yes, just as I mentioned outside. One of our queen rooms is available."

"Oh, those are lovely," Sandra added.

"I see," Emma remarked. "It's just that . . . I don't—"

"I'm afraid that's all we have at the moment." Connie's attention was still on the spiral reservations book, so she didn't see Emma's growing unease. "The other four rooms are occupied."

"The queens are the best, Emma," Sandra interrupted again. "Trust me."

While listening, Emma was mentally adding up the remaining balance in her account. She might be able to get a partial refund from the Seaside Motel, but it would never be enough to cover the cost of staying here.

Maybe Uncle Adi would loan me a bit more to cover it, especially if I tell him I'm staying in the old homestead. He might cover it.

"The others are occupied now, but the Hansens are supposed to be leaving tomorrow. I think I mentioned that already. So, the king would be available after we clean the room and change out the linens and toiletries. If you prefer a king sized bed, that is."

"Actually, Connie, Mrs. Hansen said this morning on their way out they were going to stay over a few more days. Something about a tournament or something at the Pines."

"Oh. I see. Well, Emma, I guess the queens are all we have now."

Emma considered her options. She was sitting in her grandmother's house. Her great-grandparents' house. Alice's house. Familial energy emanated off every surface. Every paneled door. Every knob. Every plank on the floor. They had all been touched by her family. *Her* family. This was the last place Alice had lived. The first place her grandmother had lived. She was home. Sure, someone else owned the place, but this was *her* home. It was a part of her. It seemed only fitting that Emma be here. In this house. In these rooms.

With fingers and toes crossed, hoping her uncle wouldn't be too mad at the additional expense, Emma went for it.

"I think the queen room would suit me just fine."

"Excellent." Connie smiled as she made a note of it. "Do you know how many nights you'll be staying?"

"Honestly, I don't. I was telling Sandra I'm here doing some family research, and—"

"Oh, how fun!"

"Well . . . not much fun, to be honest. But it does put me up in the air a bit as to when I'll be leaving."

"I see." Connie flipped through a couple pages. "Well, it looks like the room is available for the next few weeks if you need it."

"Oh, I don't think I'll be here *that* long," Emma protested. "Maybe just another week or two."

"Okay," Connie said, scratching her head with the eraser end of the pencil in her hand. "Why don't I put you down for the next week, and we'll play it by ear."

"Sounds good."

"If things get busier for us, I can let you know so you can book additional nights or make other arrangements. And if you decide to leave earlier, just let Sandra or me know."

"And . . ." Emma hesitated. "Payment?"

"Well," replied Connie, "since you're not sure how long you'll be staying, why don't we go with two nights as a deposit. The rest you can pay as you go or settle the whole thing when you go home. Now that that's settled, why don't we help you with your bags?"

"I can get them. I didn't pack much."

It was a lie. She had brought two large suitcases full as well as a carry-on, but she didn't want the embarrassment of saying she was already checked in to a different hotel.

"But I do need to run an errand first, if that's all right. *Errand, indeed. God, I hope they don't see through that lame excuse.*

"I'll be here," Sandra said. "And if you're feeling better, you could stop by the Shack for some dinner."

"The Shack?"

"The Seafood Shack. It's *the best* in town, trust me. And their biscuits are to *die* for!"

"Sandra's right," agreed Connie. "They are the best seafood place in town. I can highly recommend the lobster bisque."

"Or the clam chowder," offered Sandra.

"That too. And definitely get an extra biscuit. They really are amazing."

Emma nodded. "Sounds delicious. Where is it?"

"The edge of town," replied Sandra. "Get back on Water Street and just keep driving until it dead-ends on Carleton Street. It'll be on your right. You can't miss it. And they do takeout if you'd rather not eat there. Their dining room isn't very big, and Friday nights can be pretty crazy trying to find a table."

"Good to know." Emma stood up from the table and reached into her jeans pocket for her keys. "I think I will do takeout. I still have a lot of reading to do."

"More research?" asked Connie.

"Yes. Ms. Alda and I have been striking out with public records, so now we're combing through old journals and diaries of family relations to see if we can find anything to guide us in the right direction."

"Old family letters! How exciting!"

"Yeah," Sandra chimed in, "I love old history like that. Learning how people lived. What their day-to-day stuff was like. Finding out their dirty secrets."

"I just adore Ms. Alda, don't you?" Connie said. "She truly is just the sweetest little old lady in town."

Emma smiled. "She is indeed."

"I've known Ms. Alda since I was a little girl."

"You grew up here?"

Connie nodded. "Right across the street. We moved back after my mother passed away a few years ago and started the bed-and-breakfast."

"I'm so sorry for your loss."

"Thank you. She had been in failing health for a while—heart condition—and we helped take care of her during those last months. It was her idea to turn this place into a bed-and-breakfast." Connie looked at her watch. "We can chat more tomorrow. I need to get the girls home. And you need to find somewhere to eat dinner."

Connie extended her hand and shook Emma's in farewell. Her grasp was heartfelt and firm, but not hard.

"It was lovely meeting you, Emma. I'm glad you're going to be staying with us at the Fishmonger."

"Me too."

"I'll see you tomorrow for breakfast." And with that, she released Emma's hand and stepped through the back door outside. "Girls!" Emma heard her call through the door. "Time to go!"

"I'll walk you out," said Sandra.

The two women walked through the house to the front porch. As the screen door snapped shut behind them, Sandra pulled out a Canadian ten-dollar note and offered it to Emma.

"Could you do me a favor when you're at the Shack?"

"Okay."

"Could you grab me half a dozen biscuits?"

"Wow! Uh, okay. Are they *really* that good?"

"God, yes!" Sandra's face reddened. "Sorry, you must think I'm quite the pig."

"I would *never* have said that." She balked as she took the bill.

"They make great breakfast sandwiches," Sandra explained. "Sometimes I'll buy a dozen and make up sandwiches. Sausage, bacon. I've even used shrimp sometimes. Wrap them up in aluminum foil and freeze them. They'll last me at least a week."

"Smart thinking."

"Sometimes Connie will buy a batch for breakfast and do the same thing for the restaurant, except she doesn't freeze hers."

"You guys have a restaurant too?"

"Not technically, I guess. We serve breakfast to hotel guests daily, of course, but on the weekends—Saturday and Sunday—we open the dining room and sell to anyone in the community. So, fair warning: don't be too freaked out tomorrow when you come down for breakfast. Dex's pancakes are famous around town."

"No breakfast sandwiches, then?"

"Not tomorrow. Sunday, maybe, but I'd have to check the board."

"I like pancakes."

"Good. And you *have* to try the blueberry marmalade. Connie makes it herself."

"Can't wait."

"I'll see you when you get back. We can take care of the credit card stuff, keys, and everything when you return. Sound good?"

"Sounds great. Thanks, Sandra."

"You're welcome."

Sandra waved goodbye as Emma pulled out of the parking area onto Water Street.

XII

Emma decided to check out of the motel first and then backtrack to the Seafood Shack before returning to the Fishmonger. It took her nearly half an hour to pack all the photos, notecards, and pages she had scattered around the room and taped onto the walls. The motel proprietor wasn't too keen to see her leaving early, but she gave him her best smile and waved as she left the office.

The Seafood Shack was a converted Cape Cod–style bungalow. It was still relatively early for the dinner crowd, but several vehicles already filled the small parking lot. Emma had no more than stepped out of her rental car when she caught the faint scent of butter and garlic wafting through the air. Her stomach practically sang. She loved seafood.

The smells were even more concentrated inside. The aromas were so thick Emma could have thrown a dry piece of toast from one end of the expanded dining room to the other, and it would have landed on the opposite end completely soaked with butter. A piece of driftwood—the words *To Go* painted in yellow across it—hung over a window on the opposite wall. Emma stepped to the window and placed her order with a ruddy cheeked woman roughly her mother's age.

Forty-five minutes later, Emma settled into the upholstered desk chair in her room. She had showered, changed into a comfy pair of sweats and a T-shirt, and put her clothes away in the armoire. Her research, including her night reading, was in her shoulder bag on the bed, except for one of Julian's diaries, which lay on the desk in front of her. Emma planned to flip through it while she ate. But her focus right now was on the takeout boxes from the Shack.

She had taken just a nibble of a biscuit on her way into the Jack-and-Jill-style bathroom she shared with the single room next door. It was so tasty she had stood there in nothing but her underwear and devoured the whole thing. Roughly the size of her fist, the flaky creation was enormous. But it had been that morning since she had last eaten anything substantial, and most of that she had left on the lawn outside. It was tempting to eat the second one, and her stomach growled with disappointment as she walked away. But she'd forced herself into the bathroom. She would save it for her lobster bisque.

"Good thing I bought an extra," she muttered to herself as she opened the covered plastic bowl and set her second biscuit on the lid. Steam rose up to greet her nostrils as she inhaled the buttery aroma. Finishing off her meal was a separate small container filled with a medley of steamed broccoli, asparagus, carrots, and cauliflower. They were lightly dusted with freshly ground black pepper. Emma sampled one of the chopped asparagus pieces. It was perfectly cooked.

And so Emma proceeded to eat as she opened the diary to where she had left off. It didn't take her long. Dated September 1947, Emma read the words aloud.

A sad state of affairs today. Tonight over dinner Toby announced he and Cici are leaving for America in the coming weeks. Seems their position has become untenable with the community since the incident with Alice and the neighbors. And small-town gossip being what it is, things have only gotten worse. Cici was nearly in tears recounting her last visit to the grocery. Practically run out of the shop by women she once called friends for now being *dirty* and *unsuitable*. To be honest,

I'm surprised they're still in Digby. Small towns being what they are, of course.

Matt, of course, being the eldest of us, urged restraint. Said they should just ride it out. That people would eventually move on to something else now with the Morrison boy in school abroad. If he only knew . . .

Emma's mind raced with what-if scenarios. Her heart swelled with sympathy as she read Jules's recounting of her great-grandmother's mistreatment. And to mistreat a woman so heavy with child seemed cruel to Emma. She noted the date—Nellie was born only weeks later. It angered Emma, remembering the bullying she herself had received growing up. First her brothers. Then the cliques at school. Too smart to be counted in the cool girls' club. Too drab to be one of the pretty girls. Emma had gone the four years of high school with her head down, praying she didn't draw the ire of one of the pretty airheads trying to impress her equally cruel friends, or the jugheads always lurking out of sight, waiting to pounce on an easy score. Emma had been anxious to put high school behind her, and to this day she refused to go back.

"What happened to you, Alice?"

Emma considered the question. Clearly, something had happened between "the Morrison boy," as Jules had put it, and Alice. Something distasteful enough to force her parents to leave town.

Sex?

She dismissed the thought. Sex might be a scandalous taboo for small towns, and no doubt the local gossips would have been thrown into a tizzy, but it wouldn't force an entire family to move.

Emma also dismissed the possibility of rape based on the dates in Jules's diary entry. By September 1947, Alice was gone. Whatever happened to her, it had happened prior to September 1947. Otherwise, Jules's entry would have said the *three* of them were leaving Digby, not just Toby and

Cici. It also lined up with what she knew of her grandmother's immigration papers. Digby had been her place of birth and her point of emigration.

"I wonder . . ."

Emma scanned pages as she methodically looked for any other mention of her great-grandparents or of Alice and Nellie. As she ran her right index finger back and forth and down the pages, she sipped the silky smooth broth, munching on the generous chunks of cooked lobster that floated lazily in the creamy dish. Like a true Southern girl, Emma dunked her biscuit into the bisque, using the bread to sop up the excess liquid. What was left was poured over the vegetables. All the while, she perused the diary for answers. She was finishing the last bite of carrot when something crossed her mind.

Did the Morrison boy kill Alice? Is that why he was sent away to England so quickly?

Emma flipped back through several pages, but Jules's entries were surprisingly vague on the matter of Alice and this Morrison boy.

"Dang it, Jules. As big a gossip as you are, there should be *something* in here about what happened."

She sighed, leaning back in the chair. She rested her still-damp hair on the chair's velvet upholstery, closed her eyes, and wrapped her arms around her midsection. Her tummy was full, and she could have easily taken a nap were the sun not already setting outside. In the hallway, she overheard fragments of muffled conversations as the other guests came and went from their rooms. Emma could not be bothered with introductions now though. Those would have to keep until breakfast tomorrow.

For now, at least, she had a long night ahead of her. She disposed of the takeout containers in the trash can located by the door and walked back to the bed to continue reading.

If he did murder Alice, there might be—no, Emma. There won't be records of it. The guy was put on a boat and shipped off to England. Probably right after it happened. No. This got swept under the rug.

"But someone knew," Emma said out loud, sitting down on the bed. "Otherwise his parents wouldn't have sent him overseas."

Emma took in the room around her. The suite had a genteel feel to it. A thick woolen rug partially covered the hardwood floor. Vintage floral wallpaper covered the walls. Emma felt like she was lost in some secret English garden deep in the woods. A cream-colored cotton spread covered the bed. Emma ran her hand over the hand-stitched embroidery. A family heirloom, no doubt. Roses had been woven into the fabric and, over time, had lost their once vibrant colors. Reds had faded into ashen pinks, and the greens of the leaves had weathered to a dull, lifeless hue.

Cherry side tables flanked the bed, and squat round lamps with Tiffany stained glass shades sat atop both. A built-in bench, painted white to match the molding, sat nestled into the dormer just under the window. A thick red velvet cushion topped with fluffy pillows felt comfy as Emma switched on the lamp closest to the window and sat down. She leaned against the wall and brought her knees close to her chest. The velvet fabric was soft against her feet as she tucked an overstuffed satin pillow behind her and settled in for more reading.

The view outside was spectacular, just as Sandra and Connie had both said. The moon's reflection danced across the gentle waters of Digby Harbor. From her vantage point, Emma could see the docks. A fleet of fishing boats bobbed lazily against their moorings. *No doubt*, Emma thought, *some of that catch will end up on tomorrow's menu at the Shack.* Emma suddenly wished she had bought more of those biscuits. Part of her wanted to go downstairs to see if Sandra would have pity on her and give her another one. But she abstained, knowing Sandra had her own plans.

Settling in for what she hoped would be a fruitful read, Emma fluffed up the pillow behind her back and began to read. As she became lost in the long-forgotten stories of strangers, another stranger waited for her outside under the old tree. She sat expectantly on the swing, gazing up at the woman in the window. Her hair, pulled back in pigtails, fluttered in the gathering night winds.

It was deep into the night when Emma finally stopped reading. It was nearly three in the morning. She stood and stretched as far as she could and then bent in half to touch her toes. Emma winced as her lower back and thighs protested her mistreatment.

"Ow."

Emma rubbed her temples. A headache was beginning to take root, and she had no time to be down with a headache. She walked into the bathroom and dug through her toiletries bag for her migraine medication. It wasn't there. Emma next checked her suitcase, thinking the bottle had slipped out during her move from Seaside. It wasn't there either. She went back to the bathroom and searched her toiletries a second time, hoping she had overlooked it. No such luck.

"Don't tell me I left it at the other hotel." Emma muttered. "Great, Emma. Just great."

She needed to take something. Her headache wasn't much at the moment, but Emma knew if she didn't stave off the approaching storm in her head, it would only worsen.

"Maybe Sandra has some Tylenol or something until I can call Seaside. Hopefully housekeeping found it after I checked out."

She stepped outside her room and listened for anyone moving about the house. The second floor was utterly still, and the quiet took her by surprise for a moment before she heard the faint clink of dishes coming from the kitchen. The wood floors were cool against her socked feet as she made her way downstairs, careful not to disturb any of the other guests.

The kitchen door was slightly ajar, the sound of running water luring Emma in. She pushed open the door, and as suspected, Sandra stood there washing dishes. She was still wearing the same clothes from earlier in the day, sans sneakers, which were placed neatly by the back door.

"Good morning," Emma whispered, trying not to take her by surprise.

Sandra gasped and clamped a hand over her mouth.

"Sorry," Emma said apologetically. "I was trying not to scare you."

"Jesus, Emma. You're lucky I caught that naughty word before it left my mouth," she chastised, glancing at the kitchen door. "Otherwise, we'd both be in trouble."

"The door's closed."

"Oh, thank goodness." Sandra sighed, returning to the dinner plate she had dropped when Emma came in. "Don't want to wake anyone up at this time of night." She glanced at the clock on the microwave and gave Emma a puzzled look. "Which begs the question . . . What are *you* doing up this late? Couldn't sleep?"

"I was reading and lost track of time."

"Reading? At this hour?"

"Yeah."

"Did you finish?"

"Not yet. Julian was a prolific journaler. And Ms. Alda took his correspondence to read over the weekend."

"How's it going?"

"I have a headache, so I guess that's promising."

Sandra huffed, amused. "There's some medicine in the cupboard just there," she said, pointing to a floor to ceiling pantry next to the refrigerator. Emma opened the cabinet door and easily found half a dozen bottles of various brands of headache medicine. She popped two Extra Strength Tylenol into her mouth and swallowed. Sandra nudged her arm, and Emma turned to accept the small glass of water being held out.

"Thanks."

"Hope you feel better."

"Me too. I've got too much to do to be sidelined with a headache." Emma handed the glass back, and Sandra set it in the sink with the other dishes that still needed washing. Emma sat down at the breakfast table and rubbed her eyes. "Other than that, I've been reading through my great-uncle's diary all night and—no, wait, my great-great-uncle."

"I don't think he'd mind," Sandra said. She poured herself a glass of water and sat down across from Emma.

"Probably not. I gotta hand it to him though. The man was an absolute gossip."

"Really?"

"Oh, yeah. Anything that went on in Digby, that man was in the middle of it."

"Sounds like a real busybody. No offense."

"None taken. He knew everything that was going on. Whose business was doing well. Whose wasn't. Who needed help. Who was moving out."

"Sounds like a politician."

Emma smiled. "It's funny you say that. He ended up running for mayor when he was older."

"No kidding! That's so cool! Hey, before I forget, how was your dinner?"

"Oh my gosh, it was incredible. And those biscuits!"

"Told ya," Sandra said as she nudged Emma's arm from across the table.

"No wonder you ordered half a dozen. Thanks for suggesting it."

"I'm glad you liked it. Digby doesn't have a lot of places to eat, but the ones we *do* have are pretty good, if I do say so myself."

"I can't wait to try the rest of their menu while I'm here. Are there any other local dishes you recommend? Apart from the biscuits."

"Scallops and lobster are what Digby is famous for, so definitely try both of those. The Shack is the best seafood in the Annapolis Basin, so any way they do it, it's going to be delicious."

"I'll be sure to keep that in mind. Well," Emma said, changing the subject as she glanced up at the wall clock mounted next to the refrigerator, "it's late. And I need to try to get some sleep for a few hours."

"And I need to get everything set up for breakfast."

"You cook too?"

"Nah, Dex does the cooking. But I usually do all the prep work, depending on what the menu is. I handle the time-consuming stuff, really. Chopping the fruits and vegetables. Prepping the scrambled eggs. That sort of thing."

"I'll let you get back to it, then," Emma said as she rose. "Thanks for the Tylenol."

"No problem. Hope you feel better in the morning. See you—" Sandra smiled. "I was going to say 'tomorrow,' but it's already tomorrow, eh? So I guess I'll . . . see you at breakfast, then?"

"Breakfast."

"Bye, Emma."

As Sandra returned to her duties, Emma slipped out of the kitchen and headed back to her room. An antique pie hutch stood next to the staircase, and Emma noticed the shelves were filled with family photos. Her heart leapt as she scanned the smiling faces for a connection between the family who lived here now and her own family from decades earlier. Exhaustion got the better of her, however, and Emma headed into her bedroom.

There was still so much to do, but Emma could barely hold her eyes open. She needed to crash. She set her bag in the chair, switched off the overhead light, pulled back the covers, and crawled into bed. As she lay there semi-comatose, her eyes kept alighting on the remaining diaries. They lay there on the bench seat under the watchful gaze of the moon. Emma turned over away from the window, but she couldn't escape the subtle tug on her from across the room.

"Tomorrow," she whispered to herself. "When you're fresh and rested and can see straight again. I'll finish them tomorrow."

But it was no use. The journals called to her. Emma tossed and turned for nearly twenty minutes before she rolled over onto her back and sighed exasperatedly.

"Fine," she said flatly as she got out of bed. "Have it your way."

She grabbed the two journals and went back to the bed. Switching on one of the bedside lamps, Emma stretched across the bed on her stomach and began to skim read. She had only gotten a few pages in when she found an entry that made her sit up in bed.

May 1941

Today Alice got a tree swing. Toby spent the better part of the day getting it all set up before she got home from school. She and that girl of the postmaster's next door played on the swing all afternoon, watching the boats coming in and out of the harbor. Oh, to be that young again. Helen's a strange one in my opinion, but Cici says she's harmless enough.

There it was. Confirmation. Alice had been Toby and Cici's daughter. And in 1941, she was still young enough to be in school. The entry also gave her Helen's full name and tied her to "the Morrison boy" who had been sent away to England.

Emma rolled over and off the side of the bed, her feet landing with a reverberating thud against the carpet. She grimaced, suddenly remembering the early hour and the fact that everyone else in the house—apart from Sandra in the kitchen—was still sleeping, or at least trying to anyway.

Emma spread the makeshift family tree across the rumpled bed and stared at the faded yellow stickies containing most of the Roberts family. Her pulse quickened as she switched on the overhead light and reached for the pen tucked inside the spirals of her notepad. Flipping to the back where she kept a running list of questions, she added:

Find Helen Morrison.

Find Helen's brother.

Earlier in the day, she had added Toby's missing branch along with his descendants. Three lime-green stickies, a stark contrast to the yellow she'd used for the rest of the family, Toby, Cici, and Nellie stood out amongst the sea of names. Emma's hands were slick with perspiration as she rooted through her bag, found the pad of green Post-its, and wrote:

Alice Roberts

Birth—unknown

Death—early 1947

She affixed it to the chart next to her grandmother Nellie.

"Welcome home, Alice."

As the early-morning winds blew across the harbor outside, rustling the trees, Emma remained very much alone. She stared at the family tree before her, waiting, as she had done earlier, to see who embraced this new truth. And who would reject it.

It had been Alice in the painting. Alice . . . and Nellie. Sisters at home playing on a tree swing. Emma's eyes watered with emotion as she slowly began to understand. Her great-grandmother had painted the sisters as they *would have been*. As they *might* have been had circumstances been different. Two sisters enjoying each other's company in playful abandon. Now Emma understood why the painting had always upset her. It was longing. For what she didn't have. For what she would never have. For what she could have had.

Oh, Gran. I'm so sorry.

As dawn broke across the horizon, Emma's lone upstairs window seemed a beacon to the fishers headed out for the day. With every light and lamp switched on, it guided the boats safely out to harbor.

In the fleeting darkness below, just outside the light's reach, Alice sat on the wooden plank seat of the tree swing. Gazing up at Emma's window, she smiled.

XIII

Emma woke the next morning, still groggy from staying up most of the night. She fumbled her way into the en suite bath, shed her nightclothes, and switched on the shower. It wasn't until she stepped back into her room that Emma remembered—she was in her great-grandparents' house. Her grandmother's house.

The room pulsed with energy as Emma's mind raced. Could this have been the nursery? Could her Gran have slept under the same window Emma had the first few months of her life? The Hansens had the king room across the hall. Had that been Toby and Cici's room? Had Alice played here with her baby sister?

No. Emma caught herself. *Alice died earlier that year. She never met Nellie.*

The weight of that knowledge was a stone inside Emma, anchoring any sliver of joy to the cold, harsh ground. What hurt Emma most was the realization that Cici had painted the siblings in joyous childish abandon not as they *were*, but as they might have been. She had painted it in grief and perhaps guilt. An apology hiding in plain sight, intended to make amends for everything Nellie had missed out on.

Maybe that's why Gran and I were always so close. Both of us desperately wanted a sister, but neither of us ever had one.

Emma checked her phone. It was almost nine thirty, still too early to call her uncle. Her first night in Digby, she had googled the time difference between Nova Scotia and Missouri—two hours.

"Best to wait until lunchtime," Emma said, slipping on her sneakers before heading down for breakfast.

She paused in the hallway, locking her door behind her. The hardwood floors and oak-paneled walls shone in the morning light creeping in through the sheer drapes flanking the windows at both ends of the hall. Gauzy white fabric cascaded down the walls and pooled on the floor beneath the windows. Emma could almost see little Alice playing hide-and-seek with her cousins up here, ducking behind curtains, hiding inside wardrobes or under the beds. There were plenty of places to get into mischief. Emma recalled the shenanigans she and her own cousins had gotten into during family visits to Gran's house. Emma's favorite place to hide was in the back of Gran's closet.

Tucked away behind full-length coats Gran almost never wore and out-of-style dresses she refused to get rid of, Emma would bring her knees up tight against her chest, tucking her feet under her, out of sight from her cousins. There she would sit, soaking in the lavender perfume Gran wore. It hung in the air like a suspended cloud, permeating everything—the fabric, the carpets, even Emma. Now, all these years later, Emma could catch the faintest whiff of lavender and be instantly transported back to that little girl hiding in her grandmother's clothes closet.

Animated chatter from downstairs pulled Emma to the dining room. The smooth varnished banister was cool to the touch as she took each step gingerly, envisaging Alice bounding down the staircase for breakfast each morning.

"There you are!" Connie called out as Emma stepped into the dining room. "I was beginning to worry about you."

"Good morning," she replied sheepishly.

"Sandra said you had a headache last night. Are you feeling any better?"

"Much better. Thank you."

"Have a seat." Connie invited her in. "Sit anywhere you like."

The wall separating the house's original living room and dining room had been removed, and the space had been converted into one large dining area. White cloth–covered tables with seating arrangements of two or four chairs had been positioned through the space. The hardwood floors creaked underfoot, and a beautiful stained glass chandelier hung from the ceiling. Not that the room needed the light. Two bay windows flanked the ornate fireplace, allowing the morning light to pour in.

There were still quite a few people having breakfast, at least twenty by Emma's count. She glanced around the room for an empty table. She recognized Connie's daughters sitting at the table closest to the kitchen, along with an older gentleman with snow-white hair. She assumed he was the girls' grandfather but didn't say anything in case she was wrong. He nodded to her as she caught his eye.

"Morning," she said as she looked around the room.

A middle-aged couple had already seated themselves at one of the window tables, so she decided to sit at the other one closer to the front of the house. As she sat down, Connie's younger daughter, Carol, approached and handed her a well-worn clipboard with a single sheet attached to it: the menu.

"Can I get you something to dwink?"

Emma smiled at the girl, whose face lit up with the attention. Her snaggletoothed smile nearly made Emma burst out laughing.

"Um . . ." She thought for a moment. "I'd like a coffee, please. And maybe a glass of orange juice."

"Do you like cweam and sugar?"

"No, thank you."

"Okay. So . . . coffee and a owange juice."

"Yes, please."

"Okay, thank you."

With that, the little girl bounded out of the room and into the kitchen, where Emma could hear her, even through the closed door, relaying the order to her mother. Emma turned to peruse the menu.

"Adorable child," remarked an older woman at a table close by. She smiled at Emma.

"She is."

"Where are you from, miss? If you don't mind my asking, that is."

"The United States," Emma replied. "From Missouri."

"Missouri." She put a hand to her cheek. "Now, which one is that?"

"It's the one in the middle, Harriet," her husband supplied. "Right smack in the middle. Am I right?" He turned around to Emma for confirmation.

"Yes, sir, that's it. We're right in the middle of the country."

"Thought so. We're your neighbors."

"The Hansens?"

"That's us. My wife, Harriett"—the man indicated his wife—"and I'm Jeremy. Nice to meet you."

Emma shook both their proffered hands. "Emma Campbell."

"Nice to meet you, Emma," Mrs. Hansen said.

Emma was about to respond when the swinging door between the dining area and the kitchen opened and in walked both girls. Carol held a glass of orange juice with both hands so she would not spill it. Her older sister, Amelia, followed slowly behind, holding a steaming cup of coffee on a small saucer. They set their respective glasses on the table and smiled warmly at Emma.

"Here you go," Carol said cheerily.

"Good job, girls," a man added as he approached from across the room.

"Thanks, Dad," they said in unison as they bounded energetically back to the older gentleman seated against the wall.

The younger man stopped at Emma's table. "Hi, Emma," he said with the same cheery voice as his daughters. "I'm Dex."

"Connie's husband, right?"

"That's me."

"Nice to meet you," Emma said, shaking his outstretched hand. "Is Sandra still here, or is she already gone?"

"She leaves at six when Connie or I show up for the breakfast crowd. But she'll be back this evening."

"Well, tell her I said thank you, would you? In case I miss her tonight . . ."

"I will. Now, have you had a chance to look at the menu?"

"No, but Sandra recommended the pancakes."

"With the blueberry marmalade?"

"I think that was it."

The older gentleman across the room interjected over the buzzing crowd around them. "If Sandra suggested it, then it's the marmalade." He laughed.

Dex smiled, amused by what was clearly an inside joke. "That's true."

"Marmalade it is," Emma said.

"Great. Now, what side would you like with that? We offer a fruit medley, oatmeal, sausage, bacon, or ham."

"What kind of fruit?"

"Cantaloupe, blueberries, strawberries, and grapes."

"I'll go with that, please."

"We'll get that started for you," Dex said, accepting the menu from her. "Anything else I can get for you besides the coffee and orange juice?"

"No, thank you. This is fine."

"Okay."

Dex turned and walked back to the kitchen. The couple seated next to Emma were deep in conversation. Emma scanned the room. The guests varied in age. There were plenty of couples, though Emma saw several tables with families. A few toddlers were walking around the room. She took a sip of her coffee just as a young boy, no more than two or three, waddled up to her table.

"Hi," the boy said cheerily. A chubby little hand, sticky with marmalade, waved at her.

"Hi there," replied Emma.

But *hi* seemed to be the only word the child knew. He stood there expectantly, smacking his lips as he peered over the top of Emma's empty table.

Emma had never been good with small children. She liked them; she just didn't have the patience to deal with them. And so, not knowing what else to say, she just smiled at the boy as she took another sip of coffee.

The boy, recognizing he wasn't going to get a treat from this table, furrowed his brow.

"You are just too cute. Do you know that?" Emma laughed as the boy pursed his lips and sauntered off to the next table for something to eat. He next stopped in front of a teenage girl, who cut off a small piece of pancake and handed it to him.

"There ya go, kid."

"Hi," the toddler replied with a satisfied grin. Pancake in hand, he continued making his way around the room. It was only then that Emma noticed everyone was eating pancakes. *Strange*, she thought, *to all be eating the same thing.*

Some were still eating, but most were just enjoying their conversations, no doubt helped along by the endless pot of coffee Dex had in his hand. He made his rounds every few minutes, asking whether someone needed topping off and then disappearing back into the kitchen. The girls flitted back and forth between rooms, alternating between the old man and their mother.

Emma sat quietly as she sipped her coffee. Outside, the weather looked gorgeous, and she could hear birds chirping somewhere. In the distance, someone cranked a lawn mower.

Her suspicions were confirmed about the old man when the younger daughter came bursting through the kitchen door yelling, "Gwandpa! Gwandpa!"

"What is it, Carol?"

"I want to show you something." The child tugged on his hand, trying to get him to stand up and follow her.

"What is it you want to show me?"

"It's outside, Gwandpa!" she explained, still tugging on his hand. "Come on!"

"Okay. Okay." He chuckled as he stood up.

Never letting go of his hand, Carol escorted him out of the room. Dex entered moments later with a plate of three large pancakes and a pot of coffee.

"Here we go." He set the plate in front of her and refilled her coffee cup.

"Thank you."

"Bon appétit!"

"It smells lovely."

"Hot off the griddle. Anything else you need?"

"No, I'm good. Thank you."

"Great." Dex turned apprehensively and said, "I do hope the girls aren't bothering you too much."

A noise outside caught her attention, and Emma saw Carol leading her grandfather around the yard in search of something.

"So, the older gentleman," Emma said. "Is he . . . ?"

"Great-grandfather. Brett Barrett. He's Connie's maternal grandfather. He always comes up on Saturdays to have pancakes with the kids. Family tradition he started when our oldest was just a baby."

"That's so sweet."

"Yeah, it's great having him around still. I don't remember my great-grandfather that well. He passed away when I was just a baby."

"So did mine."

"And the kids certainly love having him around."

"Does he live here in Digby?"

"Close by. He lives in Conway, just around the harbor. You drove through it on your way in."

"Oh, right. I remember a sign for Conway now that you mention it."

"Yeah."

"And he comes in every weekend?"

"Cycles from his house all the way to the Fishmonger."

Emma choked on the coffee she had just taken a sip of. It took her a couple seconds to catch her breath.

"You okay?"

"Fine, thank you. He *cycles* all the way here?"

"Yep. The man has more energy than all of us put together. Eighty-three years old, and he still cycles ten kilometers every day."

"That's incredible. What's his secret?"

"I wish I knew. But he loves it. Says it keeps him young."

"That's . . . impressive. But I don't think a bicycle would be the best vehicle when I visit *my* nieces."

"Do they live close to you?"

"Denver, Colorado, which is about twelve hours driving or a two-hour flight if you're willing to spend the money."

"Twelve hours, yikes. And Connie gets grumpy just driving to Halifax."

"What was that, Dex?"

Emma saw Connie stepping into the room just as Dex was speaking.

"I was just saying how you complain about being in the car for a long time."

"Ugh." She sighed. "I hate being stuck in the car."

"Emma was saying her nieces live twelve hours away."

"Nope." Connie shook her head emphatically. "Not happening. Anyway," she said, turning to Dex, "*you*, mister, are supposed to be helping me in the kitchen."

"Yes, boss," replied Dex, winking at her.

"Enjoy your breakfast," Connie said as they walked away. "Let us know if you need anything else."

"I will. Thank you. And, Connie?"

"Yes?"

Dex stepped around her, letting the door swing closed as Connie stopped to turn back.

"I was wondering if I could talk to you later. When you're finished with breakfast and all?"

"Of course! What about?"

"The house."

"Oh." She arched her eyebrows. "*Now* you've piqued my curiosity."

"I just have a couple questions is all."

"Give me a few minutes to finish with everything in here. Then we can talk."

"Okay, thanks."

Connie disappeared into the kitchen, leaving Emma to her breakfast.

Emma had just taken a bite of fruit when a uniformed police officer stepped into the room. He was smartly dressed in a short sleeve pale blue Oxford and dark navy slacks. A band of yellow ran the length of both pant legs as well as around his officer's cap. Emma noted the crisp straight crease on his trousers. He was clearly a man who took pride in his appearance. Her lack of ironing skills had long been a topic of amusement between her and her grandmother.

An apprehensive hush fell across the room as conversations were cut short and patrons slowly became aware of the man's presence in the room, like a herd of gazelle clocking the presence of a lion on the hunt.

"Morning, Marcus!" Connie called out as she bolted through the revolving door between the kitchen and dining room. She deposited a plate of French toast and a steaming cup of coffee on a nearby table to the delight of a hungry patron. "Grab a seat anywhere. You want the usual?"

"Actually, Connie," the young cop said hesitantly, "I'm here on official business."

Connie, halfway to the kitchen, halted and spun around. "Oh?"

He motioned for her to step closer, and as Connie neared, he whispered something to her that Emma couldn't make out. Emma glanced around the room. Every tense eye was glued to the duo. And then to her. Emma could feel the color draining from her face as she looked to Connie and found herself looking straight into Connie's stricken face.

"Emma Campbell?" Officer Marcus asked, his tone authoritative. He owned the room and knew it. "Of Rocheport, Missouri?"

"Yes, Officer," Emma managed to sputter.

"Would you mind stepping outside for a moment, Ms. Campbell?"

Emma stood and, willing herself to not look around the room, stepped toward the front porch, the officer close beside her. As the door shut behind them, Emma could hear the dining room erupt with chatter.

Emma's legs wobbled, and Officer Marcus caught her by the elbow.

"Why don't you sit down? This shouldn't take long."

But as Emma sat, she realized it made her position untenable. Not only was the officer now standing over her, but his face was in shadow. The morning sun was a spotlight on her face, masking his stolid features.

"My name is Officer Marcus Cameron," the man said, extending his hand.

Emma shook it. He had a firm grip—not overpowering like some men she'd known, but solid nonetheless. He hung his officer's cap off the back of the rocking chair next to her and withdrew a small digital notepad that had been tucked into his armpit.

"Emma Campbell." She laughed nervously, fidgeting with her watch. "But you knew that already."

"What brings you to town, Emma?" He tapped the screen a couple times with the tip of a stylus and began taking notes.

"Family research."

"You're from Digby?"

"My maternal grandmother was born here, yes, sir. She immigrated to the United States in early 1948 with her parents when she was a few months old."

He nodded. "You were staying at the Seaside Motel earlier this week."

"Uh . . . yes, sir."

"What made you move to the Fishmonger?"

"Move?"

"Why did you leave Seaside?"

Crap! How do I answer that?

Officer Cameron watched her closely, cocking his head to one side slightly as she weighed her options.

"I . . . Uh . . ." She was fumbling this. "I liked this place better." Looking up into his steel-blue eyes, Emma could tell he wasn't buying it. "I like old houses."

He didn't answer for a moment, just stood there, waiting for her to explain—or tell the truth. Finally, he knelt in front of her.

"You sure it wasn't something else?"

He had a kind face. His jet-black hair was cut close, and he had the makings of a five o'clock shadow. He was roughly the same age she was, Emma guessed, but his features were weathered, hardened by life's pressures. Up close, she noticed a slight scar that ran for about three inches just above his right eye.

A soldier? He carries himself like one.

"Ms. Campbell?" he asked again, cocking an eyebrow.

The question brought Emma back to herself, and she searched for a response.

"I'm sorry," Emma finally said. "Yes, there was another reason. I have reason to believe the Fishmonger used to belong to my family. I wanted to be here because . . . I don't know. The idea of walking down hallways and in and out of rooms my great-grandparents used to walk was just . . ."

"I understand," he said, noting her response. "And nothing happened at the Seaside specifically?"

The question and slight shift in his voice caught Emma off guard. A tremor ran through her despite the stillness of the weather outside.

"Happened?" she asked, confused by the change in his tone. "I don't - no, sir. Nothing happened. Why do you ask?" Emma searched his eyes for an explanation but found none. She watched him turn back to his tablet and resume writing.

"When did you check out of Seaside?"

"Early yesterday evening. Maybe four or five, I think."

A handful of guests came through the front door onto the porch. Their conversations fell off midsentence when they found Officer Cameron and Emma.

"Morning, Officer," a few of them mumbled as they made their way out to their respective vehicles. The policeman watched them as they began to pull away and drive off. When the last vehicle was gone, he turned back to Emma.

"And that was the last time you were in the room?"

"Yes, sir." Emma leaned forward. "Why are you asking me this? Did something happen after I left?"

Officer Cameron tapped his screen twice more and passed the tablet to her. Emma's grip tightened until her knuckles went white as she stared down at the crime scene photo. Someone had painted *LEAVE* in large capital letters across the wall behind the bed.

"Did you—"

"No," Emma answered, her response emphatic as she shook her head. "No, sir. I didn't do that." Her eyes widened as she zoomed in on the image, noticing the deep reddish color for the first time. "Is that—"

"Paint."

Emma exhaled, leaning back into the rocker. She took note of Marcus's more relaxed posture. He clearly knew what she had been thinking.

"You're sure?"

He nodded but remained quiet, observing her, taking in her every movement. Emma found it unsettling and sat up in the chair, handing the tablet back to him.

"Officer Cameron, I didn't do that. The room was in perfect condition when I checked out of it."

A moment passed between them, and Emma could see the conflict playing havoc with the man's features. Part of him wanted to believe her; part of him didn't.

"Why are you here, Emma?"

"Excuse me?"

"Why did you come back?"

"I—"

"And don't give me the family research excuse," he scolded, wagging the tablet between them. "Whatever this is, whoever did it, you've stepped into something that's a lot more than just family research. And I need to know what."

"I think . . ." *This is crazy. He's going to think you've lost your ever-lovin' mind.* "I think my grandmother's older sister was murdered here."

XIV

"All right. Start from the beginning."

Most of the breakfast crowd had dispersed, and Emma and Officer Cameron had returned the warmth indoors to continue their conversation. Connie had cleared her plate after they'd stepped outside, and Emma's stomach growled in protest as she sat across from the policeman armed with nothing but a cup of coffee.

"Do you mind if I eat while we do this? I'm absolutely starving, Officer Cameron."

"Of course." He stepped into the kitchen for a moment before returning, Connie in tow with a stack of freshly made pancakes and a small bowl of sliced fruit.

"I'm sorry," Connie said. "I didn't know how long you'd be gone and threw everything away." She was nervous. The jittering plates and cups practically danced in her hands as she set them down.

"It's no problem. Thank you for keeping the kitchen open for me."

"Officer, can I get you anything? Coffee or tea, maybe? We still have enough batter for one last order of pancakes if you like."

"No, thank you, Connie. I appreciate the offer though."

Connie nodded and promptly left them to their conversation.

Emma devoured the pancakes. Each of the fluffy rounds had been infused with the warm marmalade, and it ran across the top cake and dripped off the edges. Coupled with homemade maple syrup—also served warm—every morsel melted in Emma's mouth. Normally, she savored her meals, taking time to enjoy each bite one at a time. But she was nervous as hell right now. And starving. And had a policeman sitting right across from her.

To heck with manners, she thought. *If he's locking me up, I'm going with a full stomach.*

"You were saying your grandmother's sister was murdered here."

Emma glanced at the tablet sitting in front of him, now open to the blank cream sheet of notebook paper.

"Yes, sir," Emma said between mouthfuls. "Actually, it's just a working theory at the moment. I don't know enough yet to say one way or the other."

"Let's start with what you *do* know."

Emma started with her grandmother's passing and the surprise stash of documents and photographs they'd discovered. The realization there might be extended family still in Digby. Her conversations with her uncle about the possibility of an older sibling who'd stayed behind or passed away before Toby and Cici left for America.

"I've been working with one of the volunteers at the local historical museum—"

"Ms. Alda?"

"Yes, that's right, but I don't remember her last name."

"It's Dillon," Marcus offered. "Alda Dillon."

Emma acknowledged this and continued with her tale. When she finally revealed her discovery that someone had deliberately disposed of any record of her branch of the family tree, Marcus's eyes widened, and he leaned forward. He had abandoned his notetaking and now sat engrossed in her story.

"So, what made you decide it was murder?"

"Several things," Emma replied, holding up her fingers as she laid out her reasons. "First, there was the diary entry in early 1948 hinting of something distasteful that had happened to Alice. Second, the Morrison boy—clearly guilty in Jules's opinion—being sent away to boarding school in England right after the incident occurred. Finally, the entry from September saying Toby and Cici were moving to America. No mention of Alice."

"And you're certain Alice wasn't sent away or something? Kicked out by the family?"

Emma pondered the idea but ultimately rejected it. "No. None of the diary entries indicate she was thrown out. Something happened, and the families covered it up."

"I see. And you moved from Seaside to the Fishmonger because this used to be the family home?"

Emma nodded, her mouth full of pancakes. From her seat, she could see the girls running around outside playing. They would occasionally run past her on their way to the front of the house, but they never stayed there long. Moments later, they would come thundering past her again as they returned to the backyard. She could hear Brett laughing along with them as they chased him around the yard. She hoped she'd have that much energy at eighty-three. The thought made her think of her grandmother. At seventy-nine, she had already passed away.

Emma wondered what Gran would think of all this were she still alive. So much had happened in the past few days that made Emma question whether she *wanted* to know what was waiting just around the corner. Something terrible must have happened for the family to cut off contact with Tobias's family. And to do so in such an *exact* manner. *That* was the truly scary part of the whole thing. And now this business at Seaside? It worried her.

She forked the last chunk of pancake and brought it up to her mouth as she contemplated the situation.

It would be so easy, she thought to herself, *to leave and forget all about this place. Tell Uncle Adi I was wrong about everything. Just say it was a wild goose chase and leave it at that.*

Alice, however, gave her pause. She deserved peace. Answers. She deserved justice.

"Emma?"

"What?" Emma snapped out of her musings, her head jerking from the window where the girls and Brett were still playing outside back to Officer Cameron. "Sorry. I . . . Uh . . . What was your question?"

"I said you moved from Seaside to here because this was once your family's home?"

"Yes, that's right."

"Anything out of the ordinary happen while you were there?"

Emma considered the question. "My migraine medication."

"You believe it was stolen?"

"No, sir. I think I just forgot to pack it when I moved. I was going to call the front desk this morning to see if housekeeping found it after I left, but now with this—"

"Best let me check on that for you." Marcus pulled his phone from his pants pocket and dialed. Though not on speaker, Emma could just make out the female voice that answered.

"Seaside."

"Yes, this is Officer Cameron."

"Oh hey, Marcus."

"Did housekeeping come across any of Ms. Campbell's belongings when they cleaned the room?"

"No, sir. They never cleaned the room."

"They didn't?"

"No, sir. They took one look at the wall and called me. And I called you."

"And no one's been in the room since then?"

"No, sir."

"Thank you for your time. Have a nice day." He set the phone on the table and turned back to his tablet. "Let me check something else first."

"Sure." Emma watched him scan through a document, slowly dragging his finger across the screen as he made his way down. He then switched to photos taken of the room during their investigation.

"No, not here either."

"Not where?"

"Crime scene inventoried and photographed the room when they were there. No medication was found. Are you sure you packed it?"

"It was in my toiletries bag. I know because I had a headache when I left the museum yesterday and took two pills after I got back to the motel."

"Is it possible you misplaced it after you checked in here?"

"It's possible, yes. But I've searched my room already and can't find it."

"There is another alternative worth considering."

"What's that?"

"That it was taken after you checked in."

Emma blanched at the suggestion. It unsettled her to think someone had been digging through her belongings. Her stomach gurgled, and Emma suddenly regretted those last few bites of pancake.

"Have you discussed this with Connie or Dex?"

"My medication?"

"No, the house and your family's connection to it."

"No, Officer. I was going to this morning once the breakfast shift was over. Ms. Alda said they only bought the Fishmonger about seven or eight years ago. I was hoping they might point me to the seller."

"I see." Marcus rose and strode to the door to the kitchen. "Connie? Dex? Would you mind stepping in for a moment, please?"

They followed Marcus into the dining room and sat down at the table next to Emma. They seemed edgy and nervous.

"What can we do for you, Officer Cameron?" Dex asked, his hand sheltering his wife's across the small table.

"Just some questions that have come up, Dex. Nothing too serious."

"We run a reputable establishment, Officer," Connie noted firmly.

"I know, Connie." Marcus smiled. "And Ms. Campbell is not in any trouble."

Emma noticed the relief in their expressions.

I just want to die. Crawl under the table and just die.

"There was some vandalism down at the Seaside Motel, and we're checking with all the current and former guests."

"Vandalism?" Dex asked.

"Some kids most likely." Marcus glanced at Emma, and she remained quiet. "No need for you to worry. But as Ms. Campbell and I were talking, she mentioned the family research she's been doing up at the museum with Ms. Alda, and she said something rather interesting."

"Oh?" Connie and Dex asked in unison, turning their attention to Emma.

"The research that I have been able to do," she began, "is what led me here."

"To the Fishmonger?"

"Yes. I think this house used to belong to my great-grandparents."

"Oh, how exciting!" Connie said. "So, this is sort of a homecoming for you, I suppose."

"In a sense, yes. My grandmother spent the first few months of her life here, but they immigrated to Missouri after that."

"When was this?"

"She was born in October 1947." Emma noticed in her peripheral that Officer Cameron had resumed taking notes on his tablet.

"Okay."

"I wanted to ask about when you bought the house, about the seller in particular. I was hoping to get in touch with them to see if they could fill in some missing pieces."

"I don't think I'll be of much help to you, I'm afraid."

"No?"

"No. See, we took possession of the house when my mother passed away a few years ago."

Emma's shoulders slumped. "I understand."

"You're sure about the Fishmonger though?" Dex asked, returning to the subject. He was also struggling to control his amusement.

"I am," said Emma apprehensively. "It's why I was sick yesterday outside."

"Sorry?" replied Dex.

"I'm confused," said Connie.

Emma sighed. "How do I explain this without you thinking I'm crazy?"

"Oh, I love any story that starts like that." Dex smirked as he leaned forward in his chair.

"Dexter!"

"Just kidding. Go ahead, Emma."

"My grandmother has a painting in her dining room of your backyard. The tree. The swing. The shoreline. The harbor and boats. All of it. The proportions and sight lines match perfectly down to the last detail."

Emma paused, and Connie and Dex glanced at each other uneasily. Even Officer Cameron had stopped writing and was now staring, mouth agape, at Emma.

"Go on," Dex finally said.

"In the painting, there are two girls playing on the swing. A girl who looks to be in her preteen years is holding a toddler in her arms. So, you can imagine my reaction yesterday when—"

"Oh my God," said Connie as she realized where Emma was going. "The girls."

"Exactly. Your daughters were playing on the swing yesterday when I arrived. And I guess the similarities to my grandmother's painting were just too much."

"Yeah, that would've freaked me out too," said Dex as he ran his hand through his ginger hair.

Connie thought for a moment longer and asked, "But how did you know *this* tree was the same as your grandmother's tree?"

"I've come across a couple things the past few days during my research with Ms. Alda's help at the historical society."

"Sweet woman," Dex commented.

"Yes. We found a photograph of the same tableau. On the back of it, someone had written *McCullough House*."

"Which brought you to us," offered Connie.

"Yes. Ms. Alda told me it was a B and B now. We also found one of my great-great-uncle's personal papers identifying the house and the tree swing in the backyard. I'm not 100 percent certain of everything, but I am fairly certain at this point that *this* house is where she grew up, at least for a few months when she was little."

"So, the two girls in the painting were your grandmother and her sister?" asked Dex.

"Yes, I believe they are."

The trio fell silent as Connie and Dex pondered what Emma had just said. Marcus, for his part, sat quietly making notes.

"So . . . how can we help with your research?"

Emma let out a sigh of relief. "Thank you."

"Don't mention it." He smiled. "You've got me curious now, and Connie and I have always wanted to know more about this old—"

His words were cut off as the kitchen door swung open and knocked against the wall. The girls and Brett stepped into the room, each with grimacing faces.

"Sorry, Mama," the girls said sheepishly.

"What have we told you about swinging that door wide open?"

"Sorry, folks," Brett announced to the room. "Didn't mean to startle you."

But Connie seemed to be the only one frustrated with the incident. Everyone just waved away the apology and returned to their conversations. Dex gave the girls a quick hug.

"You girls go back outside and play."

"But don't leave the backyard," their mother added. "And don't swing that door open again."

"Yes, Mother," replied the girls.

"Why don't you ask Brett?" Dex suggested, watching the door close behind the girls. "He might remember who your mom bought the house from." Dex caught sight of a guest in the hallway trying to get his attention. "Well, back to work. Good luck with your search, Emma."

Connie shooed Dex away and motioned her grandfather over to the table. The old man shook Emma's hand as he took the seat Dex had just vacated.

"Nice to meet you, Emma."

"And you, sir."

"Brett is fine. Officer Cameron, strange seeing you here."

Marcus shook the old man's hand. "Just following up on some things, Mr. Barrett. How are you this morning?"

"Fine." His eyes narrowed as he considered Marcus's words carefully. "Leads, eh?"

"Pops, there was some vandalism down at Seaside last night."

"I see." The old man leaned back in his chair. "Kids these days."

"Pops, do you remember who Mom bought this house from?"

"Why do you ask?"

"It used to belong to Emma's family."

"Really?"

"To my maternal great-grandparents, yes, sir. They lived here with my grandmother Nellie until she was a few months old. And an older daughter, Alice. I was trying to find the seller to see if maybe they remember anything."

"My," said Brett, exhaling deeply. He scratched his head as he thought. "I have to think about that one. It's been a long time since then. If my memory serves me right, the place was empty when my daughter bought the place."

"Empty?"

"Yes. Foreclosure or repossession or something. I can't recall which. But I'm almost certain it was a bank sale."

"What happened to the family who lived here before?" Connie asked.

"Oh, what was their name . . ." Brett scratched his head as he searched his memory for an answer.

"Was it McCullough?" Emma offered.

"Yes," Brett replied, snapping his bony fingers. "Old Judge McCullough. Died in the seventies, I think."

"The photograph I saw was dated 1972."

"No, he passed after that. During all that Nixon nonsense."

"Nixon resigned in '74."

"Yeah." Brett stroked his chin. "That sounds about right. He and my father used to get into a terrible row over it. Papa thought he was a crook, but Judge McCullough thought Nixon was getting the short end of the stick."

"What about his family? Did any of them live in the house after the judge passed away?"

"Not that I recall, no. It was just the old man by the end. His wife had died a few years earlier, and they never had any kids."

"How sad," Connie mused, "dying all alone like that."

Brett humphed. "Oh, he was never alone, Connie girl."

"What do you mean?"

"The old man always had a bottle of whiskey with him."

"So, what happened to the house after he died?" Emma interjected.

"Bank took it over. The old man had used it as collateral on a loan or something, I think. They tried to sell it, but no one wanted the place."

"Seriously?" Emma couldn't believe that. "A grand old house like this? People back home would line up around the block to bid on a place like this."

Brett shook his head. "Too big for most folks around here. Too ostentatious for everyone else. These ornate old houses aren't exactly cheap to maintain either."

"No, I don't guess they are," Emma agreed.

"The bank used it for storage for the longest time," Brett continued. "Oh, I guess about twenty years or so. Right up until Connie's mother here convinced them to sell it to her."

Emma decided to change course. "Mr. Barrett?"

"Brett."

"Brett . . . do you remember my grandmother's family? My grandmother's name was Nellie. Nellie Roberts. Her parents were Tobias and Marian Roberts, maiden name MacDonald. You may have known them as Toby and Cici. They had an older daughter named Alice."

"Do you remember them, Pops?" Connie asked.

"From what little I've been able to find out," Emma added, "Alice would be about your age, maybe a year or two younger or older, but definitely close. And there was a neighbor girl she played with—Helen. I'm not sure of the girl's last name, but I think it might have been Morrison. Helen Morrison. Her father was postmaster at the time."

The old man pursed his lips and thought. Emma saw the deep furrow in his brow and silently hoped he could reach across the decades that had passed and find some small connection to the family she was seeking.

"I'm sorry," he finally said with a shrug. "I've never been good with names, Emma. And I didn't grow up here in Digby. We moved away before I was a teenager. Only moved back after Connie's mother married a Digby man."

"I didn't know that, Pops," Connie said.

Brett smiled. "We wanted to be close to our granddaughter."

"It's okay." Emma sighed. "I'm getting used to dead ends." The words hung uncomfortably in the air until Emma turned to Connie and asked, "So, you didn't grow up here either?"

"Digby, yes. But not in this house," Connie explained. "No, Mom bought this place after I moved to college back in the nineties. We grew up in the house across the street, where Dex and I live now with the girls." She turned to Brett. "When was that? My first year?"

"Sounds right. I know it was fairly quickly because I remember having to decorate this place for Christmas that year. Your mother kept grumbling about how long it was taking since you were away at school."

"That's right! My first Christmas at college! We celebrated that here. I remember that now."

"Was it a bed-and-breakfast back then?"

"No," Brett replied, smiling as he shook his head. "They moved into this ratty old place."

"Mom had always loved this house, so she talked my father into buying it. Then they rented out our old house."

"Was it still called the Fishmonger when you were growing up?"

"Oh, it's been called the fishmonger's house since I was a little kid. Maybe longer than that even." Brett chuckled.

"We shortened it to just the Fishmonger when we opened the bed-and-breakfast," Connie interrupted.

"The original owner," Brett continued, "used to have a big fish market down by the wharf. He'd buy the best stuff that came off the boats every day, then turn around and resell it. Married some city woman from Halifax, if I remember, and built her this big house overlooking the water so she wouldn't feel like she'd moved to the country. Of course, she still felt that way. Digby's never been a big city, you know."

"Didn't she leave him a few years after they were married?" Connie asked. "Or so the story goes."

"Sure did. Talk of the town too." Brett smirked. He glanced around the room to ensure he had the attention of the room. "I was just a boy then, but I remember people gossiping about it like it was yesterday."

"What happened?" Emma asked, her curiosity piqued. She had forgotten her original question by this point.

"Her sister came up from Halifax for a visit, see? And she came with several large trunks. Said she was planning to visit Saint John just across the bay in New Brunswick and then go on out west to see the glaciers. Only, turns out all her trunks were empty."

"Empty?" asked Emma.

"Yes, ma'am. Empty. She stayed for one night." Brett held up a lone index finger for emphasis. "Next day when the fishmonger left for work, the sisters packed up all the wife's clothes, jewelry, books. Everything she wanted to keep—they packed it up. The sister sent for a porter to bring her trunks down to the docks, and they loaded them up on the ferry."

"But how did the wife manage to leave town unnoticed?" Emma asked.

"Here's where the story gets murky. Some folks say the sisters paid someone off in the ticket office to look the other way and not put her name on the passenger list. Some say she snuck onboard during all the hustle and bustle. Ferries can be busy places sometimes, especially when there's a lot of cargo being loaded or unloaded. Bottom line, no one really knows. All folks *do* know is that when the ferry left that day, the wife was on it. And no one ever saw her again."

"What happened to the fishmonger?"

"Turned him mean, it did."

"What do you mean?"

"Angry. He was always angry, mind you. Even as a kid, we knew not to go anywhere near him. But after that? Us kids knew to give the old man a wide berth."

"And he never went after her?"

"Couldn't. Had a business to run. He sent police, of course, but she was long gone by the time they figured out what had happened. Her and the sister both. My guess? They ended up going west. Toronto. Maybe even across the border to the States like your folks."

"Poor man must've been humiliated."

"Oh, folks never let him forget it." Brett huffed. "Became the running joke of the town. Every time a man was having problems at home, men would always say, 'Better check the ferry, or you'll end up like the fishmonger.' "

"Did he stay after that?" Emma asked. "In Digby, I mean."

"Yes, he stayed. He was an old man when he died. Got especially drunk one night—supposedly their wedding anniversary—and fell down the stairs. No one lived in the house after that, apart from the judge, that is. People kept saying the old place was haunted. And then you add what happened to old man McCullough to the mix and—"

"That's absurd," Connie scoffed. "I've never once seen a ghost here. And neither have the girls or Dex."

Brett held up his hand in surrender. "I'm just saying, Constance."

"Well, I don't believe in that nonsense."

Emma started to say she didn't either, but then she remembered the events that had brought her to Digby in the first place and kept her mouth shut.

"Hey, honey, could you help me out for just a bit?" Dex asked Connie as he approached Emma's table. "Marcus, did you need us for anything else?"

"No, I think that about answers everything. Thank you for your time."

"Excuse us for a minute while we tidy up," Connie said, rising from the table. She took Emma's plate and empty cup.

"The pancakes were great, by the way," Emma said. "Compliments to the chef, whichever one of you that is."

Connie cast a look over at Dex, who was almost to the kitchen door. "That was Dex. Best cook in town."

"Glad you liked them, Emma," he called without looking back. The door swung open, and he disappeared behind it.

Emma's cell phone rang, interrupting the conversation, but she didn't recognize the number on the display.

"Hello?"

"Hello? Is this Emma?"

"Who's calling?"

"This is Ms. Alda. From the museum."

"Oh, hi, Ms. Alda! I didn't recognize your phone number."

The reception was spotty, but Emma could just hear Alda's apology. "I'm sorry. I'm calling—"

"I'm sorry, Ms. Alda," Emma interrupted. "I can barely hear you. Hold on and let me walk outside. Excuse me, Officer. Mr. Barrett."

"That's okay," Brett said, rising from his chair. "I need to go check on the girls. Nice to meet you, Emma."

"And I should be going as well," Officer Cameron said, walking Emma out to the front porch again. When they were out of earshot, he said, "How long are you planning to be in Digby?"

"Next few days at least. Why?"

"Don't leave without letting me know." He handed her his card and turned down the steps toward his patrol car.

"Am I a suspect in this?" she called out after him.

"Not yet," Officer Cameron answered without turning back.

Emma watched in horrified silence as he waved goodbye, a bemused smirk on his face, before getting back into his car. It was only when a voice called out, "Hello?" that Emma realized she was still on the line with Alda.

"Hello? You still there?" Emma put her on speakerphone as she walked along the porch and sat down in front of the white rocking chairs.

"Yes, dear. I'm still here."

"That's better. I can hear you now. Now, what were you saying earlier?"

"I said I was calling from home. That's why the phone number was different."

"Oh."

"I wanted to call and check on your progress. I'm coming up empty-handed with your great-great-uncle's correspondence so far. Did you have better luck?"

"I did, actually."

"Really? Why don't you come to my house for lunch? I'd love to see what you've discovered."

"You sure? I wouldn't want to ruin anything you had planned for the day."

Alda laughed. "At my age, the only thing you'd be interrupting is my garden or maybe a bridge game down at the church with the ladies."

"Well, you're on your own with the cards. But I can help with your garden," Emma offered. "My grandmother had quite the garden herself."

"That's very sweet. We'll see. But right now, I want to hear everything about this discovery. Why don't you come on over?"

"I will. I need to contact my uncle first to give him an update, but I'll come over afterward."

"Excellent. Let me give you my address."

"Okay, hold on a minute, and I'll jot it down." Emma opened the notepad app on her cell phone and created a new note. "Okay, go ahead."

"It's 511 Saint Anne Street."

Emma repeated the address.

"I'm on the corner of Saint Anne and East Road. It's a white Colonial. My Hyundai will be parked out front."

"Got it. Give me . . . thirty minutes to an hour?"

"I'll put some coffee on for you," said Alda. "Or would you prefer tea? I have both."

"Don't go to any trouble on my part, Ms. Alda, really. Whatever you're drinking is fine with me."

"No trouble a'tall, dear. I'll see you later today."

Alda was practically giddy as she hung up the phone, and Emma could not help smiling. She saved the note with Alda's address, put her phone back in her pocket, and turned to walk back inside.

In her merriment, Emma never noticed the slight movement of the drapes in the open window behind her, nor had she heard the creak of the wood floors as someone stepped away.

XV

Half an hour later, Emma pulled into the circle drive at 511 Saint Anne Street. It was a cute little white cottage with a well-manicured lawn. An extension had been built onto the front of the house, and a gray green door with a glass insert centered the front facade. The bungalow faced Saint Anne Street, which raced downhill back into the center of town and Digby Harbor.

"Come in! Come in!" Alda cried merrily as she opened the front door when Emma got out of her vehicle.

"How are you this morning?"

"Excited!" A devilish grin stretched across Alda's face. "I can't wait to see what you brought."

Emma's heart leapt as she made her way to the front door, a feeling she realized she hadn't felt since Nellie had died. A sudden pang of anguish threatened to unravel Emma as she crossed the lawn toward this woman who had been from the outset a soothing balm to her frayed grieving heart.

"Come in, dear," Alda said, ushering Emma into the house. It was tastefully decorated with overstuffed furniture. The faint scent of a peppermint candle wafted through the air, tickling Emma's nose. She slipped off her sneakers, feeling the threadbare carpet underfoot.

"Now come inside. I've got a nice pot of coffee all ready to go. And I've put the kettle on just in case. Won't take me no time to have a nice cup of tea ready, if you'd prefer that."

"Oh, you didn't have to go to so much trouble, Ms. Alda."

"No trouble at all, dear."

She led Emma into the kitchen and pulled out a chair for her to sit down. It was only after she was seated that Emma saw the effort Alda had, in fact, gone to despite her protestations of the opposite. A tray of neatly arranged finger sandwiches sat on the table, and Emma could smell the freshly baked loaf of bread resting on the kitchen counter. The jam and butter had already been set on the table between them.

"Tea? Or coffee?"

"Well," Emma said, "I guess coffee since you've already got that made."

"Cream and sugar?"

"No, thank you. Black is fine."

"Coming right up," said Alda as she opened one of the upper cabinet doors and pulled out two blue and red coffee cups with matching saucers. "Now, tell me what you found. You mentioned you found a sister. Possibly?"

"Yes, I think I did."

Emma reached into her shoulder bag and began taking out her research. Alda, having added cream and sugar to her own cup, returned to the table and set the cups down. She pulled out a chair and sat down.

"Have a sandwich," she said as she slid the tray toward Emma.

"Thank you."

"Now . . . tell me everything."

Emma read the diary entries about Alice, the tree swing, and Helen. They compared notes from their respective readings the night before.

"The correspondence was completely worthless," Alda declared. "Mostly business letters during his time as mayor, although some were personal. None of them, however, mentioned anything about the family."

"Nothing about Toby or his side of the family?"

Alda shook her head. "Absolutely nothing. Emma?" Alda took a breath before continuing. "Whatever happened in your family . . . they buried it. And I mean buried it *deep*."

"I think the Morrison boy murdered Alice."

Alda's mouth fell open in shock. Her teacup hung suspended in her hand halfway between the table and her mouth, and it took her several seconds to recover her senses.

"I'm sorry," Alda said, shaking her head in disbelief. "You said *murdered*?"

"Yes, ma'am."

Alda's eyes widened as she set her cup back down. "Have—" She cleared her throat, trying to find her voice. "Have you discovered why?"

"Not yet," Emma said, reaching into her bag for Jules's diaries. "But I can say definitively that Alice *was* my gran's older sister. That much I do know. Here, take a look at these entries I found in Jules Roberts's diaries."

She handed the volume to Alda and pointed out the text in question from 1941.

"Building a tree swing before the girl got home from school. Yes, that's certainly parental."

"Then there's this entry here," Emma said, flipping a few pages to the next bookmark. "Dated April 1947."

Alda read as Emma continued speaking.

"Jules talks of warning Toby and Cici about the Morrisons next door. Said they were the wrong sort of people. That their daughter was a bad influence on Alice."

"Conversations a family would have with each other."

"Exactly."

"But that doesn't necessarily mean this Morrison boy killed Alice," Alda countered. "She could've been sent away. Or been turned out."

"I don't think so. The Morrison boy was sent to England for boarding school in February 1947. That was right after the war ended. England would've been nuts at that time. Certainly no place for a boy on his own. And take a look at this one." She flipped to the entry dated September 1947. "Notice Jules doesn't mention Alice at all, only Toby and Cici. They were the only ones moving to America. What kind of mother abandons her daughter and leaves the country?"

"He doesn't mention your grandmother either though."

"No, he wouldn't. Gran wasn't born until October 1947. She was still pregnant when Jules wrote this."

Alda sat back in her chair, resting her hands in her lap. Emma watched her survey the scattered pages across her dining table. Emma recognized the conflict overshadowing the woman. She had struggled with the same thing as she tried to come to terms with the *possibility* of murder, all the while desperately wanting an alternative but unable to conjure one.

"I'm not saying I agree with you," Alda finally said. "Not just yet."

"But . . . ?"

Alda looked up from the table, and Emma could see the fear in the woman's eyes. "But *if* you're right, are you sure you really want to go digging into this?"

"Sorry?"

"You remember what Franklin said at the museum. This may be a secret you might not want to discover."

"Ms. Alda, I have to know. My family deserves answers. My grandmother deserves answers. I can't sweep this back under the rug."

"But now we're dealing with a lot more people, Emma."

"How so?"

"If this Morrison boy murdered your great-aunt and it was covered up, that implicates not just *your* family, but also the Morrison family."

"Right."

"Now you have a body on your hands. You need to dispose of it. Was she buried somewhere? Taken out to harbor and thrown overboard? Our research so far hasn't discovered anything about the Roberts family being in the fishing industry. And Mr. Morrison was the local postmaster. Now we're dealing with a third party: a fisherman. At the very least a boat owner."

"Yes, but—"

"Then there's the cover-up. How do you explain a girl's sudden disappearance? She was still in school. What do you tell the school? The police?"

"She left on the bus, they could've said."

"But you need a bus ticket for that. And the ticket agent would've been questioned. So would the bus driver."

"Ferry? No, that wouldn't work either. Police would've questioned the captain and the ticket agent."

"Exactly."

"I'm beginning to see your point."

"Which begs the question, Emma . . . Do you still think it's worth it?"

"It may be too late to stop."

Alda cocked an eyebrow, her curiosity piqued. "I'm not sure I like the sound of that."

"Someone broke into my hotel room at the Seaside and left me a message on the wall."

"Broke in! Oh, dear God, Emma! Were you—"

"No, ma'am. I wasn't there. I had already checked out and moved to the Fishmonger."

"What was the message?"

"Leave."

"What?"

"They painted the word *LEAVE* in all caps on the wall."

Alda fidgeted in her chair. "What do the police think?"

"Officially they're saying it was vandalism. Kids having a laugh at tourists' expense."

"And unofficially?"

"I'm pretty sure I'm on a short chain with Officer Cameron the next few days until he can figure out what really happened."

"Marcus Cameron?"

"Yes, ma'am. You know him?"

"It's a small town, Emma." Alda chuckled. "Besides, he's my neighbor. And a good man. Did you tell him why you're—"

"Yeah, he knows why I'm here. And I told him my suspicions about Alice being murdered."

"What did Marcus say?"

"He told me not to leave town without notifying his office first."

Alda took a sip of her tea.

"Besides, I'd like to propose an alternative means to finding out about Alice."

"Yes?" Alda set her cup down and leaned forward, her arms perched on the edge of the table.

"We know the Morrison family lived next door. We know the father was the postmaster during the mid-1940s, and his daughter's name was Helen Morrison."

"Aha! Now I see where you're going."

"We find the Morrisons. Find out who lived next door to the Fishmonger in 1941, and once we have the parents, we circle back to Helen. Alice may have died in 1947, but based on Jules Roberts's diary entries, it's clear that Helen was still living. Heck, she may even still be alive."

"Smart," Alda said. "You should consider going into genealogical research. You have a knack for this."

Emma shrugged. "Ach, maybe."

"So, we find the parents," Alda said. "They lead us to Helen. And Helen, hopefully, will lead us to some answers."

"That's my hope. If she kept a diary, chances are she'd write about her best friend, especially if she lived right next door."

"And," Alda added with a bit of hesitation, "if said best friend's family suddenly left town."

"Agreed. Does the museum have any records of the local postmasters?"

"No. But the Registrar General's office would."

"Which is closed until Monday."

Alda nodded. "Afraid so."

"Well, I guess we stick a pin in it until Monday then."

As they made their way through the pot of coffee and the tray of watercress sandwiches, Alda and Emma formulated a plan of attack. Emma would visit the Registrar General's office on Monday morning and find out who the Digby postmaster was in the 1940s. A quick search online of the Morrison family would turn up the daughter, Helen, they hoped. From her end, Alda would check the museum archives to see if they had anything on the family and pull those records for Emma while she spent the day tracking down the family through the Registrar General's office.

Best-case scenario, they hoped, was they would find Helen still alive. Elderly, yes, but perhaps with enough faculties to remember her childhood best friend and—more importantly—what had happened to that best friend.

Furthermore, a last name would help with a search of school records. The girls were close in age, so it stood to reason that they would be in the same grade. Finding Helen would lead them to Alice. And finding more on Alice's childhood might help Emma discover what had happened to her.

When they had finished the last of the coffee, Emma took the cups and saucers and walked them over to the sink. As she set them inside, she looked out the window.

"What a beautiful view, Ms. Alda," Emma cooed as she looked across the gentle slopes of the wooded landscape. In the distance, downhill from Alda's house, lay the town of Digby, and just beyond that was the wide blue expanse of Digby Harbor. A thin veil of gray fog hung suspended over the water, masking what lay beyond the shore.

"It is, isn't it?"

"I'd never leave this spot, I think."

"Sometimes I don't. Of course, it's much better without the fog. Some days you see all the way to the Gut."

"The Gut?"

"It's the channel that connects the Annapolis Basin to the Bay of Fundy. It's how all the boat traffic gets in and out."

"I see. Julian mentioned the Gut a few times in his diary."

"If you like boat watching, the Gut is where you want to go. My husband and I used to pack a picnic lunch and go up there sometimes. Sit out on the shore and watch the boats sail by."

"Sounds idyllic."

"It's quite nice on a clear day. Especially out by Point Prim."

"What's that?"

"A lighthouse where the Gut opens into the Bay of Fundy. Lots of people go up there on picnics and such. It's not that far from town, actually. You should visit it while you're here. The sunsets are beautiful there. Of course, it probably isn't so nice today, I'm afraid. All this fog . . . I doubt you'd be able to see three feet from the shoreline."

"Is this normal for this time of year?"

"The fog?"

"Yes, ma'am."

"Oh, I don't know." Alda shrugged. "Depends on the winds and water temperatures. Benji would always prattle on about it. Afraid I never did listen much."

Emma noticed the sudden change in Alda's tone and the melancholic expression that swept over her features.

"Sometimes I wish I had," Alda said in a low whisper.

"Benji?"

Alda looked down at her clenched hands on the table. One of the fingernails on her right hand was jagged, like it had caught on something and partially torn off. She rubbed it absently, trying to smooth out the broken edge.

"My husband, Benjamin," she finally replied. "He passed away a long time ago."

"I'm so sorry, Ms. Alda."

Emma walked to the table and rested her hand on Alda's shoulder. Tears wet the corners of her eyes as Alda took a deep breath and exhaled.

"I think I need some air. Let's go sit out on the porch, shall we?"

"Lead the way."

Alda led her to a side door out of the kitchen. She grabbed a faded red cardigan hanging on a hook by the door as she reached for the doorknob. She motioned for Emma to go ahead.

They stepped out onto the side porch and sat down in a matching pair of Adirondack chairs. They were painted bright white, and the backs were set at just the right angle for lounging. The temperature outside was cooler than Emma was used to. Summers in Missouri could be miserably hot and humid. Here in Nova Scotia, however, it was still in the mid-sixties. With the lingering fog and a soft breeze blowing in from the bay, it almost felt cold.

Emma saw boat lights out in the harbor, partially masked by the low-hanging fog. A boat horn would sound occasionally, but other than that, the town lay perfectly still. She watched gulls flying over the docks, diving periodically for a fish or something. It was all so peaceful.

When Alda spoke, Emma was not sure if it was really her who'd spoken or if it had been some other voice carried by the wind.

"They died out there in those waters."

Emma turned to face her, but Alda's attention was fixed on the foggy waters beyond. She looked relaxed, sitting back in her Adirondack right next to Emma. But Emma saw Alda's hands. They were clenched tightly together. Though they looked frail, she saw their strength. It was as if Alda was trying to fight against some impending wave of grief, and only by holding absolutely still could the waves pass by without knocking her over.

"Your husband?" Emma asked gently.

"And my granddaughter."

The confession wrong-footed Emma, and it took her a few seconds to respond to the three little words that seemed to hang in the air between them.

"What happened?"

"They were out in a dinghy fishing when a storm came up unexpectedly. A larger boat wasn't paying attention, what with the storm and all, and didn't see them. They never made it back to shore."

"Oh my God, Ms. Alda. I can't imagine how hard that must've been for you."

"I wanted to die," she replied. A tear ran down her cheek. She swiped it away with the back of her hand. "Victoria would've been about your age right now."

Emma reached across the arm of her chair and placed her left hand over Alda's clenched hands. Alda opened her hands and grasped Emma's between them. They were trembling.

"My son and his wife never visit this place anymore because of it."

"Never?"

"Too painful for them."

"I'm sure."

"Can't say I blame them, mind you. It's hard enough for me to look out the window every day and see that harbor. See where it happened. Always being reminded of the worst day of my life."

"Where's your son now?"

"Toronto. They have a son in college. My son buys me a plane ticket out of Saint John any time I want to visit. It's just across the bay, you know."

"Yes, I think someone else told me that."

"I take the ferry into Saint John and then fly to Toronto." Alda sighed. "But the sight of water brings back bad memories for Taylor."

"Taylor's your son?"

"Yes."

"Have you ever thought of moving closer? So you could see them more regularly?"

Alda smiled as she rubbed her jagged fingernail absently, and Emma could tell from the tilt of her head this was an often-asked question.

"This is where I remember them," she finally said.

"I can understand that."

"I still feel them here sometimes. Like shadows, you know? Shadows of fog. Here one moment. Gone the next."

"Sounds eerie."

"More comforting than frightening, really. It's strange, I know. Of course, I know they're gone. But sometimes . . ."

Alda's words trailed off, and she gazed out over the water. Emma waited a few moments, allowing the older woman to finish, but after Alda did not continue, she prompted her.

"Sometimes?"

Alda blinked.

She was somewhere else, Emma thought. *Some other place.*

Another blink.

Some other time.

"Sometimes . . ."

It was a rough start, like an old carburetor that hadn't been cranked for some time. It would spit and sputter, hesitate even, before coming back to life.

"Sometimes," Alda continued, "when there's a fog, like this one, it feels like they never left. Like . . . if I watch the water closely enough, the dinghy will magically emerge from the mist, and they'll be standing here next to me. Do you believe that?"

Emma paused, and in that moment of contemplation, Alda turned and looked her in the eye. Her gray green eyes seemed to look right through her. Emma felt suddenly exposed and was not sure how she should respond. How much *should* she share with this woman? But she was also afraid, though not of the ridicule and the polite "of course you saw a ghost, dear" comments she would likely have to endure. She was afraid . . . of breathing any more life into this . . . this . . . apparition? This ghost? This troubled soul? The thought sent a tremor through Emma, and she tried subconsciously to throw a veil over any possible answers to Alda's question.

But the wise old woman saw her answer nonetheless. She gave an understanding nod.

"I see," Alda said, replying to her own question. "Perhaps one day you will tell me why you *really* came back."

"I . . ." But Emma's protest stopped with the word. What could she say? Alda was right. There was more to her visit that what she had let on. And Alda knew it. How she knew . . . who knew? Woman's intuition, perhaps.

Or perhaps, Emma thought regretfully, *a grandmother's intuition*. Unsure of what else to say, the women sat there in silence. Hand in hand. Waiting for the long-lost dinghy to emerge. Waiting for Benjamin and Victoria and, in truth, Alice to return.

XVI

The deep tones of the grandfather clock in the hallway startled Emma. She and Alda had been lost in Julian Roberts's world all day. Although the gossipy old man had plenty to say about his neighbors, the government—both local and provincial—and the family in general, on the subject of Toby and his family, the man was strangely silent.

Emma tapped the screen of her cell phone. A photo of her and Nellie came up. It was from Christmas the year before, before Nellie's health had rapidly started going downhill. They were dressed in matching ugly Christmas sweaters and were wearing reindeer horns Emma had found on sale. Big cheesy grins smiled back at Emma, and she couldn't help but laugh.

"Did you find something, dear?"

"No, just laughing at this photo." Emma held up her phone. "It was the last good photo I took with Gran. Her first stroke was just a few days after Christmas last year."

"May I?" Alda reached out a tentative hand. Emma tapped the screen again and handed the phone across the table.

Alda laughed. "Quite the pair you two make."

"Yeah."

"A lot of love in this photo." Alda passed the phone back to Emma. "She looks like she led a full life."

"She did, yes. I think you two would've been good friends if she were still around."

"I'm sure we would have," Alda said, glancing back at the screen.

Emma stood and stretched. "Ow," she moaned. "I've been sitting too long."

"Indeed," Alda said, rising from the dining table where they had been sitting most of the day. Their research lay scattered across the table between them.

"Well, it's late. And I don't want to take up any more of your day than I already have."

"You don't have to rush off. It's no problem."

"Thanks, Ms. Alda. But I still need to call home, talk to my uncle and give him an update on what's happened."

"Well, it was nice to have some company today."

"What are you doing for dinner this evening?"

Alda shrugged. "Oh, I'll be fine. Plenty of leftovers in the refrigerator."

"Come to dinner with me."

Alda thought for a moment. "What did you have in mind?"

"Dinner at the Shack. My treat."

"I'm up for that, I think. Would you mind if I took a bath first?"

"Of course." Emma checked her watch again. "It's about four o'clock now. Why don't we say . . . six o'clock? Is that okay for dinner?"

"Six is perfect."

"Great. I'll come back by and pick you up."

"I can meet you there. It's no problem."

"I don't mind. I like driving."

"All right. Then I will see you at six o'clock." She hugged Emma tightly and whispered in her ear, "It was a good day."

"A very good day."

Alda followed Emma out to her car and waved as she pulled out of the driveway onto Saint Anne Street. From her rearview mirror, Emma could see Alda watching the vehicle as it drove away. She stuck her arm through the open sunroof, waving goodbye as she disappeared down the hill and into town.

That night they dined on freshly made seafood stew with mussels, crab, lobster, and shrimp. The broth had been seasoned with garlic, onions, tomatoes, fennel, saffron, thyme, and bay. The dish had been served with brussels sprouts sautéed in butter and most of the herbs used in the stew, as well as roasted red potatoes that melted in their mouths. Taking a tip from their waitress, the ladies had spooned several teaspoons of the broth over the potatoes. The result was perfection. Emma hadn't planned to order biscuits with the meal since they already had potatoes, but Alda insisted on them.

"You don't come to the Shack, dear heart, and *not* get the biscuits," Alda chided her. "That would be a sin against Maureen."

"Who's Maureen?"

"The owner." Alda grinned mischievously. The wine was starting to go to her head now. "And cook most of the time."

"Well then," replied Emma as she lifted her glass of white wine, "here's to Maureen."

"To Maureen," Alda declared, lifting her glass.

They toasted and then fell into a fit of giggles.

It was a wonderful evening. Alda introduced her to several of the other patrons scattered around the restaurant. Most of them were locals, and Emma got the sense from their reactions to her dinner companion that Alda was a well-regarded member of the community. Emma received firm handshakes from several of the men when they learned that she had helped Alda that day with her gardening.

Emma was knee-deep in conversation with the history teacher from Digby Regional High School on the matter of monarch butterflies—he was a member of the local conservation society and had concerns over the insects' migratory patterns through the central US—when Alda interrupted their conversation to introduce her to a young police officer. When Emma turned, she found herself standing face-to-face with Officer Marcus Cameron. She instantly regretted that last glass of wine with dinner.

"Marcus is also new to Digby," Alda said cheerily.

Emma's stomach moaned in discomfort. She knew a setup when she saw one.

"New? I've been back in Digby for nearly two years now, Ms. Alda."

"Well . . . relatively new."

"Where were you before?" Emma asked.

"Overseas." His answer was polite, but it had a tone that hinted of closed doors.

Emma decided not to push the matter further, but it did confirm her suspicion that Officer Cameron had military experience.

"How's your research coming along?"

"It's slow going," Emma said with a shrug. Out of the corner of her eye, she could see Alda watching them intently, practically giddy with the idea of the two of them.

"Well, good luck with that," the young man said with a smile.

Standing this close and out of uniform, Marcus had a very different feel to Emma. Dressed in a loose hoodie and jeans, he looked . . . nice.

Stop staring, Emma! she chided herself. Emma's face flushed as she took another sip from her glass. *He is handsome though.*

Emma faked a cough, her face hot with embarrassment. She turned away and covered her mouth with her sleeve. Marcus, who was also starting to look uncomfortable, turned to Alda.

"I'll be up this weekend to take a look at that chimney, okay?"

"I'll have a nice cup of tea waiting for you."

"Just don't go poking around in it before I get there," he cautioned. He adjusted his grip on the takeout bag in his hand and looked back at

Emma. Emma was about to say something when he sniffed the air between them. "How much," he asked, drawing his words out, "have you had to drink tonight?"

Oh, God. Now he thinks I'm a drunk. Is my insurance card in the car?

He caught sight of the empty wine bottle on their table and frowned.

"I drank most of it, Officer," Alda said, trying to charm their way out of their predicament.

Marcus glanced between the two of them. "I would feel better if I drove you both home tonight."

Alda was up and out of her chair before Emma had time to even process his words.

"Oh, that sounds lovely, Marcus. Doesn't that sound lovely, Emma? How sweet of you, Marcus dear. Such a good boy. Driving the two of us home just to make sure we don't run off the road somewhere."

More like run someone else off the road, Emma thought.

Marcus smiled.

Did I say that out loud?

"Why don't I take this and wait by the car?" Alda reached for his to-go bag. "You two finish up here. No rush on my account. I'll be drying out in the back seat, Officer."

Emma and Marcus watched as the old woman tottered outside in the darkness. Finding themselves alone, standing in the middle of a crowded restaurant, Emma realized the entire room had been watching.

Kill me now, why don't you.

"I—" Emma stammered. "Let me settle the bill, and I'll meet you outside."

Marcus nodded, clearly uncomfortable with the attention as well, and made a quick exit. Emma paid their tab, paying no heed to the cashier's knowing glances, and left.

The ride back to Alda's house was interminable. As much as Emma had come to enjoy Alda's company, she soon realized that Alda was a chatty drunk. Very, *very* chatty. Emma sat unmoving in the front passenger seat by Marcus. Occasionally, she thought he might be looking at her and stole tiny glances at him. But each time she turned to look, his attention shifted back to the road. Adding to the comedic scene was Alda, safely tucked in the back seat behind reinforced plexiglass like a common criminal.

If only matchmaking were criminal . . .

Minutes later, Marcus's squad car pulled into Alda's driveway. Emma got out and helped her to the front door.

"I'll be by this weekend to work on the chimney, Ms. Alda," Marcus called out to them.

Alda waved behind her, leaning on Emma's arm as they stepped inside the front door.

"He's a good boy," Alda whispered, patting Emma's arm. "Don't you think?"

"Yes, he's a good boy," Emma repeated, desperate to get out of there. "He's very nice."

"And he likes you."

"He *what*?" Emma froze.

Alda grinned. "Ooh!" she squealed. "You like him too, don't you, dear?"

Emma shook her head, exasperated. "You're as bad as my grandmother, Ms. Alda."

She laughed as she made her way into the kitchen.

"Are you going to be okay?" Emma asked.

"I'll be fine, dear. You lovebirds go on. The night is young."

"We are *not* lovebirds. We're not."

But Alda just smiled, pouring herself a glass of water. "Who are you trying to convince here, me or yourself?"

"Good night, Ms. Alda."

"Good night."

"I'll call you Monday with the Morrison names once I find them," Emma said, changing the subject back to business. "Then once I'm done with the Registrar General's office, I'll come back to the museum, and we'll see what we can find. Okay?"

"Sounds like a plan." She sipped her water. "I'll talk to you Monday."

Emma closed the front door behind her, taking a moment to engage the lock in case Alda forgot to do it, and walked back to the car.

"Everything okay?" Marcus asked.

"Yeah. She's fine." Emma fastened her seat belt, and Marcus pulled away. "Thank you, by the way, for taking us home."

"Couldn't have you getting a citation for driving under the influence, now could we?"

"Thanks."

"You're welcome."

Emma turned in her seat to face him. "Did you learn anything this morning? I saw you taking notes the whole time."

"Just listening to the conversation. That's usually the biggest part of any investigation, I've found. Listening to what people have to tell you."

"And what did you hear?" *Is it strange I want to run my fingers through his hair?*

"Too early to tell right now." There was a worried crease along his forehead. "But I don't think it would be wise for you to be out and about by yourself. Not at least until we can figure out what's going on."

"I see."

"Any more messages at the Fishmonger?"

"No. Not yet."

They rode the rest of the way in silence, Marcus's attention on the road, Emma half turned in her seat, her attention on Marcus. When he pulled into the parking lot and killed the engine, Emma said, "You're good with her. Ms. Alda."

"She's a second grandmother to most of us guys. Taught high school history for decades."

"Did she really?"

"Yeah."

Marcus continued speaking, but Emma's thoughts went elsewhere. If Alda had taught at the local high school, then she might have—

"When did she teach?" Emma blurted out.

"When?"

"Yeah. Can you remember when she started?"

Marcus looked out across the water, trying to think. "Well, I'd guess sometime in the sixties or seventies, I think."

Emma's heart sank. Another dead end. "Oh."

"Not the dates you were looking for?"

"No." Emma laid her head back against the headrest. "Sorry. I need earlier than that."

"You still think your aunt was murdered?"

Emma nodded. "Ms. Alda and I are going to try a different approach come Monday."

She briefly explained their new plan to track down Helen Morrison. Marcus seemed impressed with her investigative skills.

"If you ever decide to take up criminal justice, let me know."

Emma laughed. "Miss Emma Marple and Officer Marcus Poirot on the case!"

Their laughter faded into an awkward silence.

Ask him inside for a drink.

But before Emma could talk herself into it, Marcus cut the night short.

"Emma," he said slowly. "Look. Our situation is—"

"You and me, you mean?"

"Yeah. I can't get involved with a suspect in an ongoing investigation."

Suspect?

Every giddy, lovesick emotion inside her fizzled and died with the word. The car felt suddenly stifling, and she opened the passenger window a few inches, letting in the cool summer night air.

"It would cloud my judgement and, more importantly, put my job on the line."

I'm a suspect?

"Emma?"

"When were you going to tell me I'm a suspect?"

Marcus let out a heavy breath. He ran his hand through his hair, scratching the back of his scalp. "A poor choice of words. I'm sorry. You're not a suspect, Emma."

"Then what am I?"

"In a word?"

"Yeah."

"Involved."

Emma nodded, taking in his words. He was right, of course. He was an officer of the law investigating a case that she was at the very heart of. *Conflict of interest* was an understatement. Still, her heart hurt from the blow.

"Good night, Marcus," Emma finally said, opening her door. "Thank you for taking us home tonight. I appreciate it."

"Good night, Emma."

Emma felt his gaze as she trudged up the front steps, fumbled with the key to the front door, and let herself in. As she pushed the front door closed and leaned against it, she heard his car pull away. She slipped her shoes off to soften her footsteps and was bending down to collect them when a young couple stepped out of the drawing room.

"Good evening," the blonde haired woman said, all smiles as she hung on her husband's arm. Her soft curls bounced as she stepped through the entry toward the staircase.

"Good evening," Emma replied, glancing between the husband and wife. The man never spoke, just smiled cordially at her, but Emma noticed the woman's grip on his arm tighten as they walked by.

Awkward.

Emma followed their ascent for a moment before she reached down for her shoes.

"Cute couple, aren't they?"

Emma popped up, startled by the unexpected question. Her head swam from too much wine, and she reached for the doorknob to steady herself.

"Geez!" Emma whispered.

"Sorry," Sandra said. "I didn't mean to scare you."

Emma laughed it off. "Make some noise next time you start sneaking up on me."

"Good day? I haven't seen you since last night."

"It was." Emma fumbled for her room key, which seemed snared on something in her pocket. She pointed her shoes, clutched in her other hand, toward the ceiling. "Who was that?"

"The Rayburns. They come here every May."

"She's certainly possessive, that's for sure."

"Oh, she has reason to be," Sandra said with a smirk.

Emma humphed. "Like I would be interested in her husband."

"Oh, they're married all right," Sandra whispered, leaning in so she couldn't be overheard. "Just not to each other."

Emma was speechless.

"They come here every year. Same week. Same room. Check themselves in as Mr. and Mrs. Rayburn."

"So, how do you know they're not married?"

Sandra's face reddened like a child caught with her hand in the cookie jar. "I . . . Uh . . ."

Emma covered her mouth, suppressing a laugh. "You're busted. Out with it."

"Okay, fine," Sandra replied, crossing her arms over her chest. "International guests have to leave their passports at the front desk for security in case they try to leave without paying the balance on their stay."

"Right." Emma nodded.

"American passports have your full name on the photo page and personal information and emergency contact on the next page. I checked them in last year. She has a different last name *and* a different home address. In a *completely* different city."

"Scandalous," Emma whispered as they both looked up the stairs.

"So, what did you do today?"

"Spent most of the day with Ms. Alda and had dinner at the Seafood Shack."

"And a ride home with Officer Cameron too, I see," Sandra said, grinning from ear to ear.

Emma blushed. "It's not what it seems. We'd had too much to drink with dinner, and he brought us home. Nothing more."

But Sandra wasn't buying it. "Such a knight in shining armor, our little Marcus. I think he likes you, you know."

"Sandra," Emma pleaded, careful not to raise her voice and wake the rest of the house. "It's . . . It's not possible."

Sandra cocked her head to one side and waited for Emma to continue.

"He's a policeman."

"And?"

"And . . . he's investigating something I'm apparently involved in. It would be a conflict of interest."

Sandra's eyes widened. "The break-in at Seaside? How are you involved in that?"

"It was my room they broke into."

"Oh my God. Did they take anything?"

"No." Emma shook her head. "I had already checked out and moved here by the time they broke in."

"Still. Pretty scary. Thank goodness you weren't there."

"Marcus—I mean Officer Cameron—said it was probably some kids having fun with tourists."

Sandra stood there, arms still folded in front of her. Emma could see the hunger for more information in her eyes, but when Emma didn't continue, Sandra unfolded her arms and shuffled her feet.

"Well, I should probably check the drawing room. Clean up a bit. And it's late. I'll let you get some sleep."

"Sandra, quick question for ya. Is there a running trail close by? I'd like to go for a run in the morning if the weather's not too bad."

Sandra's expression lightened. "Oh, yeah. The Sunset Trail is just down the street. You jog?"

Emma nodded. "I'm a physical trainer back home."

"Nice. I love running. Great for clearing the mind, right?"

"You too?"

"Every morning once I get home from my shift."

"Would you mind some company tomorrow?"

"Absolutely not! I'd love to have you along."

"Thanks."

"My shift ends at six when Connie or Dex comes in, so if you'd let me run home and change, I'll come back here and get you."

"Sounds perfect. Thank you, Sandra."

"You're welcome. It'll be fun having someone to run with it. I'm usually out on my own most mornings."

"I'll see you tomorrow, then."

Sandra smiled and turned toward the drawing room. "Have a good night."

"You too."

She had made it halfway to the first landing when a text message came through.

Crap! I was supposed to call Uncle Adi today!

Sure enough, the text was from her uncle.

UNCLE ADI
Just checking on you. Everything okay?

There were also several texts from Nessa and Tom. Emma sat down on the landing, set her sneakers beside her, and started a group text.

EMMA
Hey all! Sorry I haven't called already. Busy digging.

TOM
You had us worried there for a minute. Where you staying?

EMMA
You sitting down? I'm staying at the old Roberts family homestead!

NESSA
What? Seriously?
UNCLE ADI
You talking about Uncle Toby/ Aunt Cici's place?

EMMA
The very one! It's now a B&B. Google 'The Fishmonger.'

A few seconds passed before the texts resumed.

NESSA
OMG! It's gorgeous! Which room are you in?

EMMA
Queen room. 2nd floor. Red décor.

UNCLE ADI
Beautiful old house, Emma. And
you're sure it belonged to the
family?

EMMA
Yes sir. Confirmed with the local
historical museum. The house
belonged to Gran's parents Toby
and Cici Roberts.

TOM
Wow. Sounds awesome. Can't
wait to hear what all you've
discovered.

EMMA
Uncle Adi—guess what? We were
right about Gran. She DID have an
older sister. Can't talk right now.
But she died early 1947. As of now—
I think she might have been
murdered.

TOM
Damn
NESSA
No way! Murdered!
UNCLE ADI
Call me first thing tomorrow morning. Are you okay?

Emma lowered her phone to her lap. Holding it in her hand, she stared at Adi's question. Was she okay? Short answer: no. She wasn't, nor did she feel safe. But she knew how her uncle would react if she told him the truth. He'd have her on the next plane back to Columbia.

EMMA
I'm fine, Uncle Adi. Promise.
I'll call you in the morning
after my run.
A few seconds passed.

UNCLE ADI
I'll be waiting. Have a good night, Em.

EMMA
Love to you all. Night

TOM
Night, Em
NESSA
See you soon! Love ya, girl

Emma pocketed her phone, scooped up her shoes, and made her way up to her room. The bedside lamp cast a warm, magical glow over the room.

Did I leave that light on this morning?

Emma set her shoes by the desk, grabbed a change of nightclothes from the chest of drawers, and stepped into the bathroom to prepare for bed. As she switched off the bathroom light a few minutes later, Emma noticed a small piece of paper folded in half, leaning against the base of the Tiffany lamp.

She crawled into bed, every muscle breathing a weary sigh of relief as she slipped under the cool sheets. Emma reached for the torn page, angling the lampshade so she could get a better look at it. Every ounce of exhaustion vanished as she bolted upright in bed. She dropped the page in her lap, her hands shaking too badly to hold it. Her legs cramped from tightness, and she struggled to catch her breath.

Three words. Three little words scratched into the paper.

You should've left.

Soon after finishing her glass of water, Alda slipped off her shoes just inside the front door and hung her coat in the closet. She meandered through the living room, checking the front window to make sure Marcus and Emma were gone before rambling back into the kitchen.

"They make a cute couple," Alda muttered to herself.

Stepping onto the side porch, she looked out at the bay. The moon was full and illuminated the landscape, but the water—still veiled in fog—remained dark and foreboding. She stood there for several minutes contemplating what to do. Whether it was the buzz from the white wine she'd had with dinner or her mounting anticipation over what new discoveries they would make on Monday, Alda was not the least bit sleepy, which was unusual for her. Normally, she was already in her nightgown and settling down for the night by seven o'clock. But it was after eight, and she felt bursting with energy.

She nearly missed it, could have sworn she had imagined it. But just as Alda was about to go back inside and get ready for bed, she saw—or thought she saw—a little red boat crossing the harbor, a small dinghy with a billowing white canvas sail making its way to shore. And then it was gone.

Alda barely made it to a chair as she fumbled and nearly collapsed onto the deck. She sat there, focused on the spot where the boat had been, and willed it to reappear. It never did. She buried her face in her hands and began to cry.

"I miss you, Benji," she said, sobbing into her palms.

"And I you," came the whisper from across the water. "And I you."

Alda leaned back in her chair and let the grief pass through her. It was almost nine o'clock when she finally rose. Dabbing her tearstained face and eyes with a tissue she always kept in her pocket, she looked back out at the water. Apart from the fog, there was nothing to see.

XVII

The warm summer sun on Emma's face woke her Sunday. She lay basking in it for a moment before remembering the night before. Sitting up, Emma found her barricade still intact. The desk chair was still tucked under the doorknob, the desk blocking the bathroom door.

The note was on her bedside table. She dared not touch it again. Emma sat amongst the plush pillows and soft sheets and considered the fine Victorian prison cell she now found herself locked in. She needed to call Marcus. She *should* have called the night before, but she had chickened out, didn't want to be the damsel in distress.

This was different though. Whoever had broken into her room at Seaside had now done the same here. They had been in her room. Had gone through her things, she guessed.

Thank God, she thought, *I had all my research with me at Ms. Alda's.*

"Crap!" Emma exclaimed, tossing back the covers as she hopped out of bed. "I left my bag in the car when I came back to change before dinner!"

Barefoot and still in the T-shirt and shorts she wore to bed, Emma dashed out of the room and down the stairs. Throwing open the heavy wood door, Emma raced out onto the porch, scanning the vehicles for hers. It wasn't there.

"Where's my car?" Panic rose in the pit of her stomach as Emma searched for her rental. "Where's my car!"

A squad car drove by on Water Street, and Emma remembered. Marcus had driven her and Ms. Alda home. Her vehicle, fingers crossed, was at the Shack. She took a deep breath, her hand on her stomach, as her anxiety began to settle.

"Morning!" Sandra said cheerily as she stepped out onto the porch. "Everything okay?"

"Yeah," Emma said, fumbling for words. "I, uh, forgot my car was still at the Shack. Guess I panicked."

"Want me to run you by there?"

"Would you? Oh, thank you, Sandra. I really appreciate it. All my research and papers are in the back seat, and I'd just feel better, what with everything that's happened, if I had them close by."

Sandra nodded. "Makes sense to me, especially after the break-in at Seaside."

"Let me go grab my keys, and I'll be right back."

"Emma?" Sandra called out, stopping her retreat into the house. "They're, uh, in your hand."

Emma looked down. "Oh, yeah." She laughed, which only made Sandra look at her more curiously. "I guess I'm ready, then."

"Are you sure you're okay?"

"Totally. You ready?"

Sandra wanted to press, Emma could tell, but she didn't. Instead, she guided Emma to her mid-1990s Toyota 4Runner, and the two of them took off. Emma checked the passenger seat for her bag; it was still there, still untouched.

Phew.

"Okay?"

"Yeah," Emma said, waving back. "It's here."

When they had returned to the Fishmonger, Emma remembered to bring her bag in. "Give me ten minutes, and I'll be ready for our run."

"I'll be here on the porch," Sandra replied, taking a seat in one of the rockers.

Emma returned to her room, where she changed into a pair of black leggings and an oversize navy T-shirt. Slipping into her sneakers, she shoved her bag to the back of the wardrobe, grabbed her phone, and locked the door on her way out.

"How far to the beginning of the trail?" Emma asked as they made their way across the Fishmonger's parking lot to Water Street.

"Just a few blocks. It's on the outskirts of town, just past the historical museum."

Traffic was light on Water Street as the duo jogged past the shops toward the Digby Sunset Trail. Most of the shops were still closed; it was still early, and it was Sunday. The weather was perfect to be outside, and Emma soon found herself forgetting about the prior night's terrors. The summer sun beamed down on the women, warming them as they passed the museum. An oversize pickup drove past, the driver tapping his horn in greeting as he waved. Sandra waved back.

Less than a block past the museum, they found the sign for the Digby Sunset Trail. It was a nice path, paved, wide enough for joggers and cyclists to share. As Emma and Sandra ventured farther away from the highway, Emma discovered the trail hugged the shoreline. They passed several hikers the first half mile but soon found themselves alone. The beige gravel crunched underfoot as they walked farther into the countryside. Emma loved being out in nature. She saw people out on the water fishing and remembered Alda's story of her husband and granddaughter. Such a tragic tale.

Houses faded from Emma's line of sight as the trail left town. Soon it was just her and Sandra, with the water on one side and the woods on the other. Benches had been placed strategically along the trail for those who needed to take a rest or wanted to look out over the water. Emma guessed watching the sunset over these waters was quite magical.

"Race you to the lighthouse!" Sandra yelled before making a dash for it, laughing the whole time.

"You're on!"

They ran full on the last few hundred feet before reaching Bear River Lighthouse, the end of the trail. Sandra won. After slapping the side of the lighthouse, she raised her hands in the air, pumping her fists in victory.

"Canada wins! Woo-hoo! Go Team Canada!"

A passerby joined the cheer, catching the women off guard. He laughed as he jogged off in the opposite direction.

"How embarrassing," Sandra said, drinking from the bottle of water in her hand.

They laughed, walking to the water's edge as they caught their breath. Sunlight sparkled off the dancing waters as boats passed. One captain waved at her, blowing his horn as he went past. Emma and Sandra waved back, smiling as they sat down on the bench next to the lighthouse. Emma laid her head back against the wooden structure, closing her eyes as she took a moment to rest and catch her breath. She still ached, and her muscles were stiff and sore. But being out under the warm summer sun kept Emma in good spirits.

Emma sat there, eyes closed, listening to the birds chirping away at one another in the trees. Out across the water, she could just hear the faint cry of a gull. Or perhaps a Canada goose. It reminded her of the long walks she once took with her grandmother along the Missouri River. Nellie had loved to hike, and the river trail had been one of their favorites before time and illness robbed her of it.

Gran, you would've loved this place.

"So, how do you like Digby so far?"

Geez, what a loaded question that is. Emma decided to be more diplomatic. "It's a lovely place. And the bay is beautiful."

"It is that." Sandra took another sip of water.

The distant rumble of an approaching storm ended the conversation. Darkened clouds, heavy with rain, hung ominously over the harbor, blotting out the warm skies beyond. Riding an eastward wind, the clouds moved quickly.

"If we're going to make it back before the storm," Sandra said, "we better head back now, otherwise we'll be caught out in it for sure."

Emma agreed, and the duo took off at a steady pace back toward town. Watching the clouds roll in as they jogged, Emma speculated whether they would make it back without getting wet. It began a race. A race they ultimately lost.

Emma and Sandra had just passed the museum when the clouds burst overhead, releasing large, dense raindrops onto the city. By the time they reached the front porch, they were soaked through. A man and woman Emma hadn't seen before were sitting off to the side of the porch, enjoying the rain. As the women approached, the man ducked back inside.

"You girls will catch your death," the woman called out as Emma and Sandra tried to squeeze off the excess water. "Being out in this."

"Storm caught us by surprise, Mrs. Morrison," Sandra replied.

Morrison? Did she say "Morrison"?

"Forecast last night was for sunshine all day today," Sandra continued. She didn't see Emma's sudden change in posture.

"Oh, you know these early summer storms, Ms. Sandra. They come out of nowhere and disappear as quick as they came."

The front door opened, and the man who had stepped away earlier reappeared holding two towels. He handed one to each of them.

"Here," the man said, a fatherly tone to his words. He looked about her father's age, Emma guessed. "You girls dry yourself off before you catch cold."

"Thank you, Mr. Morrison," Sandra said. "Are these from your room?"

"They are."

"I'll bring some fresh towels up soon to replace them."

"No need to rush," he said. "Judy and I have already had our bath this morning, so we don't need them right away."

"Thank you, Mr. Morrison," Emma said, drying off her hair.

"Don't mention it. You're Ms. Campbell, right? Second floor?"

Emma glanced over at Sandra. Her concerned expression was apparently too obvious, as the old man laughed.

"Sorry if I startled you." He looked back toward the door. "It's a small place. You get to know your neighbors after a few days, if you know what I mean."

"Yes, sir."

"Come and meet my wife," he said, motioning to the woman sitting at the end of the porch.

"I'll take this," Sandra said, collecting the wet towel from Emma. "Can I bring any of you something to drink? A snack, maybe?"

"We're fine, Ms. Sandra. But thank you just the same."

"Emma?"

"No, thank you."

Sandra stepped inside, closing the door behind her, as Emma followed the old man down the porch to where his wife, Judy, was sitting. Her gray skirt swayed with the breeze coming off the water, revealing a stylish pair of black flats on her feet. A red Georgia State zip-up hoodie completed her ensemble.

"Judy, this is Ms. Campbell. Second floor."

"Oh, yes." Her mass of bracelets and charms jangled and danced as a hand shot out from her lap. "Our neighbor across the hallway. Very lovely to meet you, Ms. Campbell. Judy Morrison."

"Al Morrison," her husband added. "Retired. Tampa, Florida."

"Semiretired," Judy corrected him.

Emma shook her hand as Al sat down beside his wife.

"Nice to meet you. Emma Campbell. Physical trainer. Columbia, Missouri."

"Columbia?" Judy repeated. "I know that town. Al, how do we know Columbia?"

"Their football team beat us last season," Al grumbled. Emma noticed his displeasure as he said it.

"Oh, yes, that's right! How could I forget? Our youngest son plays basketball there. Practically tore the family apart when Missouri won that game."

"Yes, ma'am." Emma pulled a third rocker closer to the couple and joined them. They chatted briefly about sports, Al still upset his Georgia Bulldogs had been beaten by the Missouri Tigers. They asked about her research, and Emma told them what she could. After half an hour chatting, Emma asked, "So, why are you guys out here in the rain?"

"Oh, we love the rain. Don't we, Judy?"

"Call it a generational thing, I guess," Judy said. "But I love sitting out on our back porch, cup of coffee in my hand, listening to the rain."

"Makes for good reading weather too."

"More like napping weather, you mean," Judy teased.

Emma's phone rang—her uncle.

"Sorry," she said, standing. "I need to take this."

"Nice to meet you," Judy and Al both called out to her as Emma walked to the opposite end of the porch.

"Hi, Uncle Adi."

"Hey, kiddo." He sounded cheerful, but Emma could also hear the tension in his voice. She sat down and prepared herself for a good lecturing. "Talk to me about this murder."

Forty-five minutes later, she finally hung up the phone. The Morrisons had gone back inside, having listened to enough of the rain, Emma surmised. Her uncle had spent the night searching for last-minute flights to Halifax, and Emma barely managed to talk him out of it. In the end, she had agreed to call him every morning with an update. Fearing he would insist she leave Digby right then, Emma failed to mention the message scrawled across her hotel room wall as well as the message left in her room the night before. She would tell him later. When she got home, maybe. Or perhaps when she figured out what was going on.

Her second call was to Officer Cameron.

Best to get this over with.

The call went to voicemail. Emma was about to hang up when Marcus's outgoing message listed his cell number.

EMMA
Officer Cameron. Emma Campbell.
I received another message last
night.

Her phone rang almost immediately.

"Where are you?"

"I'm at the Fishmonger."

"Anyone with you?"

"No, I'm alone on the porch."

"All right, stay there. I'll be there in a few minutes."

Officer Cameron's squad car pulled into the parking lot soon after. Ducking under an umbrella, he sprinted up the front steps and across the porch to where Emma was still seated. He sat down in the chair next to her, took out his tablet and stylus, and asked her to tell him what had happened.

"After you dropped me off, I went up to my room. The door was locked, but the bedside table lamp was switched on."

"Did you leave it—"

"No, sir. I don't leave lights on."

Marcus shot her a curious look, cocking an eyebrow in disbelief. "Ever?"

"Live with *your* grandmother long enough," Emma explained, "and you learn to switch everything off before you leave a room."

"Makes sense, I guess. From a generational point of view. So, someone had switched on the lamp."

"Yes. And leaning against the base of the lamp was a folded piece of notebook paper."

"Another message?"

Emma nodded.

"What did it say?"

"You should've left."

Marcus's pen paused, hovering over the tablet surface. He looked up at Emma.

"Take me upstairs. I want to see it."

Twenty minutes later, Emma found herself locked in her room again. After calling in the incident, Officer Cameron had taken the page back to police headquarters, where it would be analyzed for potential fingerprints and DNA. A crime scene technician would be by soon to dust the door and the lamp for prints even though Emma repeatedly said she had handled both several times since discovering the note. Still, Marcus wanted to be sure.

When the conversation had turned to moving Emma to a safe house, she put her foot down.

"Absolutely not!" she yelled.

"You need to take this seriously, Emma."

"I'm not going to be held hostage by this coward," Emma insisted.

"And what happens next time? What if this guy does more than leave you a note?"

He's right.

Still, Emma refused.

"Fine," Marcus said, slamming the cover shut on his tablet. "Stay stubborn. If you won't let me move you to a safer location, then I'm moving in here."

"What? No."

"Your bathroom opens to the adjoining room. I've already checked with Dex and Connie, and those guests checked out this morning. They're not expecting new guests until next week. I'll sleep in there until this is settled. You're not to leave the Fishmonger on your own."

"But I'm going to the Registrar General's office tomorrow and meeting with Ms. Alda again. I can't just sit here and do nothing."

Marcus ran a frustrated hand through his hair. "Do you get I'm trying to save your life here?"

"But I'll be—"

"Would you just *let* me do my job, Emma?"

Emma fell silent, realizing the conversation was headed in only one direction.

Marcus watched her, waiting to pounce on any excuse she came up with, but when he realized she had seen his point, he said, "Thank you." He gave her a curt nod. "I'm going to take this to forensics and run home for a change of clothes. Can I trust you to not go anywhere?"

Emma sighed, dropping down onto the bed. "Fine, I'll stay here until you get back, Officer. Could I go downstairs to the kitchen to grab something to eat? I haven't eaten since last night."

"Sure. But do not leave the house."

"I won't. I promise."

The room felt strangely empty as Marcus left. Emma sat on the edge of her bed, listening to his footsteps on the stairs, the forced but cheerful conversation with Dex and Connie in the entry, the soft click of the front door as it closed. She waited for the sound of his engine turning over but couldn't hear it. Emma was about to go downstairs when a soft knock on her door made her spin around.

"Hiya," Connie said. She was smiling, but Emma could see the worry behind it. "I brought you some lunch."

"Thanks, Connie." Emma watched Connie walk across the room and set the tray on the desk.

"It's nothing much. Homemade chicken salad sandwich with a salad. I brought ranch dressing, but I have a few others in the refrigerator if you prefer something else."

"Ranch is fine. Thank you."

"I'm so sorry about last night," Connie said, stepping back to the door. "About your room. Dex and I don't know how someone managed to get in. Did they take anything?"

"No, just left a note."

"Dex is on his way to the hardware store for one of those wireless home security systems. The ones with the cameras, ya know?"

"Yeah."

"We're going to install cameras in the main halls and the stairway for added security."

"Thanks."

"I'll leave you to your lunch. If you need someone to go with you tomorrow . . . I mean, if you have errands to do, I could come with you if you want. You at least wouldn't be alone."

"That's very kind, Connie. Thank you. I'll mention it to Officer Cameron when he comes back."

"Okay." She was halfway out the door when she turned back one last time. "Emma, I really am sorry your room was broken into. I want you to know that Dex and I take our guests' security and privacy very seriously, and we're cooperating fully with the police."

"I know, Connie. I don't blame you guys."

"Okay. Enjoy your lunch."

Connie pulled the door closed, leaving Emma alone in her cell. She glanced out the window at the harbor. The skies were even darker than they had been that morning. Rain pelted the window, and Emma considered the Morrisons' love of rainstorms.

Good napping weather.

She ate half the sandwich before stretching out across the bed, drifting off to sleep within minutes.

The echo of a hard door slam woke Emma up. It was dark out.

How long have I been asleep?

Barefoot, she slipped out of bed and opened her door to hear what was going on. Emma stood there, her bedroom door cracked just enough for half her face to fit through, and listened. Had she imagined the noise in her sleep?

Nothing. Silence. And then . . . muffled voices coming from downstairs. Two voices. One a man's. Angry. Defiant. And aggressive. The other a woman's. Defensive. Frightened. But unyielding.

Emma stepped into the hallway, looking left and right at the other bedrooms. All closed. The Hansens and Morrisons seemed unaffected by the events downstairs. An outburst from the man startled her, and Emma went back for her phone.

I can't be the only one hearing this.

She tapped 911 on the screen. Did Canada have 911? She was about to find out. She pressed the *Call* button. It disconnected. She tried again. The call dropped. She rubbed the sleep out of her eyes and brought the phone close to her face—only one bar of reception.

"Dang it."

She crept back into the hallway and leaned over the banister. The woman's tone was less confident now. Her skin crawled as she heard the fear rising in the woman's voice. She could not, in good conscience, leave her on her own. Mustering her resolve, Emma tiptoed down the stairs to the foyer.

The missing hutch was the first thing she noticed. The open door to the basement was the second. The argument was coming from the basement. Connie and Dex, Emma surmised. Had to be. There were no guest rooms down there, so that eliminated everyone else. But surely they wouldn't be having such a public row with a house full of guests. Then again, how well did she really know them? Marcus, maybe? He'd said yesterday that he was coming back.

Every creak of the floor echoed off the walls as Emma moved toward the open door. The frigid doorframe jolted her body awake as she steadied herself and took a tentative first step into the stairwell. Whitewashed stone walls lined the passageway as she edged farther down the stone stairs.

The voices were closer now but still quite muffled, as if coming through closed doors, and the man was now much more agitated. Emma turned as she reached the bottom of the stairs. A lone bulb partially illuminated the space. Christmas decorations awaiting their season lay patiently on floor to ceiling shelves. Along the wall was a row of neatly stacked plastic tubs holding extra linens for the rooms upstairs; a child's handwritten *LINENS* in all caps scrawled across the front betrayed their contents.

A sliver of light shone along the bottom of a closed door across the room. As Emma watched, two shadows passed back and forth, disturbing the light. Emma was halfway to it when Alice's wispy frame materialized in front of her, blocking Emma's passage.

"Alice," Emma called out, the syllables coming out in a half whisper, half yell. The girl's solemn expression never wavered, nor did she utter a word.

"Alice, I have to help this woman."

Alice didn't budge.

Summoning her courage, Emma took a step forward and reached around the girl for the knob.

Blackness fell upon her as the door opened.

"Ali—"

Emma's cry was cut short by an unseen figure who threw her to the floor and clamped a muscled hand over her mouth. The cold stone floor bit into the exposed portions of her body. She tried to maneuver out from under her assailant, but it was no use. He was much larger than Emma, and his grip was firm. She clenched her teeth shut, biting into his index finger. He howled with enraged pain. With his free hand, he punched Emma's ribs, and she released his finger from her mouth. She gasped for breath, snatching bits of air as best she could, but it was not enough. The hand returned, cutting off her oxygen. She began feeling dizzy and couldn't keep her eyes open. Her eyes were open, yet the darkness cloaked her attacker's identity. His inflamed words were indistinct on Emma's ears and made no sense to her as she fought to remain conscious.

Focus on his voice, Emma instructed herself. *The police will ask about his voice.*

Yet despite his proximity, the attacker's words were strangely muffled. *A mask?*

She reached in vain for the man's face, searching for a mask. She found nothing. Emma attacked his arms next, but he pinned her hands behind her as he sat down on top of her.

"Oh, God, please no!" Emma yelled through the hand still clenched over her mouth.

He twisted her head, shoving her nose into the stone. The scent of fresh paint on the floor combined with raw fish on the man's hands was too much for Emma. She vomited, adding the sickly-sweet odor of her own bodily effluence to an already noxious mix.

"Make him stop!"

Emma felt the pull against her clothes. Could hear the tearing of fabric as she thrashed about, flailing her legs wildly. Desperately trying to move him off her. Thrusting stabs of pain tore through her abdomen. Emma screamed in agony as his hand clamped down on her throat, sealing it shut with his grip. This wasn't happening. This couldn't be happening. Where was everyone? Were they all going to sleep through an assault happening right under their noses?

Help me! Anyone! Please help me!

Through her tears, Emma could see the faint vaporous shadow of Alice. Had she been there this whole time? Was this what she had been trying to protect Emma from? A final thrust from her tormentor seared through Emma's body as she finally understood what was happening. Her eyes widened in horror as she watched Alice's expression change from unresponsive to terrified as a third voice entered the room.

"Alice!" Emma cried. It came out barely a whisper.

The man's grip on her throat tightened. Emma's lungs burned, desperate for air, as she clawed at the hand holding her down. Her eyes glazed over as lack of oxygen began taking its toll on her body. Was she going to die down here? Was that how Alice had died? In her parents' basement? Was this how *she* was going to die?

"Alice, please! Make him stop!"

From the corner of the darkness, closest to the door, Emma could just make out the sound of another man's voice.

"Please!" Emma shouted.

No. Not a man.

"Alice!"

A boy. It was a boy.

"Help me!"

It was then she heard it. The boy wasn't talking. He was laughing.

"Alice!"

"Emma!"

Emma nearly tossed Sandra across the room as she bolted upright in bed. Drenched with sweat, she stared into the frightened faces of Sandra, Officer Marcus Cameron, the Hansens, and the Morrisons. Alice stood across the room in the corner, observing everything. The terrified face she had worn in the basement now appeared contrite, apologetic even.

"Emma?" Sandra approached the bed cautiously this time. "You were having a bad dream."

"Are you all right, Emma?" Officer Cameron questioned.

"Poor dear," Mrs. Hansen added.

"You gave us all a bad fright, young lady," Mr. Hansen added. "We pounded the door for ages 'til Ms. Sandra managed to find the master key."

His wife swatted his back in rebuke.

"Emma?" Sandra asked.

Emma was still too dazed to answer. She looked from the Hansens to Sandra. From Sandra to the Hansens. And finally to Alice, who stood in the corner of the room away from the others.

Sandra took Emma's hand. She gasped.

"You're freezing."

"I'll go downstairs and fix you a hot tea," Mr. Morrison offered. His wife followed suit, casting a cautious glance back at Emma as she stepped out of the room.

"It's okay, Emma. It was just a dream."

"I . . . I'm sorry."

"We were about to phone the police if we couldn't get this door open," Mrs. Hansen offered. "Good thing Officer Cameron showed up when he did."

"You came back?" Emma asked.

"Blasted door," Mr. Hansen continued. "Couldn't get it open."

"I could hear you screaming from downstairs," Marcus said.

Emma felt humiliated. She could feel her face reddening and buried her face in her hands.

"I'm so sorry, Officer. Mr. and Mrs. Hansen. And you, Sandra. God, I'm so embarrassed."

"We're just glad you're all right, Emma," Mr. Hansen said, patting her foot under the covers.

"When we heard you screaming, we thought . . ." began Marcus.

Emma looked up at him, waiting for him to finish. But the cop let the rest of the sentence hang unsaid.

"We thought someone was in here with you," Mr. Hansen said.

"Hurting you," said Mrs. Hansen.

"Well, now that the danger is over," Mr. Hansen said, "we're going downstairs for a game of bridge. You're welcome to join us later. The rain seems to have set in for the day."

"Thank you. I think I'll pass for right now."

The old man nodded as they stepped into the hallway. "You take care, Miss Emma."

"Yes, sir. And again, I'm so sorry for scaring you. I feel like such a child."

"Think nothing of it, my dear," Mrs. Hansen said, trying to be a comfort. "We're just glad you're safe. Would you like one of us to stay with you for a while?"

"Oh, I couldn't."

"I'll stay with her a while," Marcus said.

"Very well. Come along, Jeremy. Let's give this poor girl some space."

The older couple retreated from Emma's room. Moments later, Mr. Morrison appeared, a steaming cup of tea in his hand. Marcus took the cup from him and brought it to Emma's bedside table.

"You okay, Emma?" Mr. Morrison asked.

"Yes, sir. I'll be okay. Just a bad dream. I'm sorry for scaring everyone."

"We'll be downstairs if you need anything."

His departure left just Sandra, who quickly realized she was the third wheel in the room.

"I think I'll go check on everyone downstairs." She put a hand on Emma's shoulder. "Can I get you anything besides the tea?"

"No," Emma whispered, her head hung in embarrassment. "I'm fine."

"Something stronger, maybe?"

Emma smiled and looked up. She reached for Sandra's hand, gripping it tightly. "Thank you."

"Later then, eh?" Sandra winked impishly before turning to Marcus, who was still standing at the foot of the bed. "You'll stay with her for a while?"

"I'll be here."

"Okay." Sandra made her way out and closed the door behind her.

Marcus came and sat on the edge of the bed. His brow was furrowed, his eyes intent on hers. Neither of them spoke as he took her hand. It trembled in the warmth of his touch.

Without speaking, Emma leaned forward, and he wrapped his arms around her, pulling her to him. The heat of his body made her limbs quiver as she snaked her arms around his waist. Burying her head in his chest, she sobbed.

"I was so scared," Marcus whispered in her ear. His words were heavy with emotion as his breath caught in his throat, staving off his own sobs. "I thought I was losing you."

"It was so awful," Emma said between her tears. "I don't think I've ever felt so alone."

"You're not alone anymore," he reassured her, pulling back as he cupped her face in his hands. His eyes were oceans to Emma, swirling with conflicted emotions, and she saw the glimmer of tears forming in the corners.

She reached up and brushed them away with the tips of her fingers. She ran her hand, still wet from his tears, through his soft black hair. Closing his eyes at her touch, Marcus leaned in and kissed her. He was tentative at first, but as Emma reciprocated, the kiss turned hungry. Powerful. Needy.

"I can't," Marcus whispered, finally coming up for air.

"I know," Emma whispered back. Yet neither of them stopped. "I know."

She was the first to pull back. A moment later, Marcus leaned away from her, though he stayed seated on her bed.

"Emma, I need to ask you some questions about tonight."

Emma lay back down, the cool pillow a welcome embrace. "Can it wait until tomorrow?"

Marcus shook his head. "No, it can't. I'm sorry. But there are questions that don't add up that I need you to answer."

She reached for his hand. His skin was warm. Emma could feel the beginnings of a callus in the corner of his palm.

"Promise you won't laugh at me."

He arched an eyebrow but said nothing.

"Promise me that. No matter what."

He pulled her hand to his lips and kissed it softly. "I promise," he whispered. "But you have to tell me everything. No matter how painful. No matter how irrelevant you might think it is."

Emma nodded. "Go get your tablet."

Marcus stepped into the other room and returned soon after with his tablet and stylus. He pulled the desk chair over to the bedside and sat down. Crossing his legs, he opened his notepad.

"Ready?"

"Ready."

"Who's Alice?"

Emma looked across the room.

Marcus followed her line of sight to the empty corner of the room. "Am I missing something here?"

"Alice," Emma answered, her eyes never wavering from the figure in the corner, "was my grandmother's sister. But it would be better, I think, if I started further back. Several weeks back."

"Start where you like," Marcus said. "And I'll save any other questions for the end."

Emma closed her eyes, letting out a long breath.

"I moved in with my grandmother nearly two years ago, when she was first diagnosed."

"With?"

"Cancer. I'd rather not get into the gory details if you don't mind."

"I understand."

"During her final months, Gran began talking about this girl she was seeing."

"A neighborhood kid?"

Emma shook her head. "A ghost."

Marcus's eyes widened, but he said nothing, merely wrote it down.

"At first, I laughed it off. Told her it was the medication making her loopy. Messing with her brain, ya know? But she was adamant. She was seeing this girl plain as I see you right now in that chair."

"Did she know who the girl was?"

"No. Gran said she looked familiar though. As if she was someone she *should* know, but she could never put a name with the face. After Gran died, I started to see her. First it was random places. I'd be cleaning out closets or putting away some of Gran's old things. But soon it was every day. I got the sense she needed help, like something in her life had been left undone and she wanted me to help finish it."

Emma told him about the painting and the photograph of a younger Cici, explaining her initial assertion the girl was Cici—Gran's mother. The writing on the canvas identifying Digby as home. Her thwarted research online turning up nothing and her decision to visit Digby in person.

Marcus listened intently, taking notes as Emma spoke. She told him of her first day with Alda. The repeated dead ends. The random acts of vandalism amongst the records.

"Hold on," Marcus interrupted. "Are you saying these documents were removed?"

"They *were* removed," she assured him.

"How can you be sure?"

"Because I discovered a pattern later that night in my hotel room."

"What did you find?"

"You have to understand I had made notes on every Roberts man, woman, and child we came across that day, and I had a pretty good family tree already mapped out. Ms. Alda found an obituary for Julian Roberts, dated—would you hand me my bag, please? It's in the wardrobe behind my suitcase."

Marcus retrieved the bag and set it in Emma's lap. Rummaging through two compartments, she found her query and passed two pages to Marcus.

"This is Julian's obituary. Dated 1999. Notice the sentence at the end, where it lists the names of the five brothers."

"Toby," Marcus said, looking up from the page. "And you're sure this is *your* Toby? Your great-grandfather?"

"Look at the other page. It's a photograph of the brothers all together. Their names are on the back. We found photographs of Julian from roughly the same time. It's the same man."

Marcus laid his head back and glanced up at the ceiling. "So, let me get this straight. You're saying someone deliberately removed all the records related to Toby and Cici Roberts. Are you sure?"

"And it wasn't just the museum."

He leaned forward, and Emma continued her tale. When Marcus learned the local Registrar General's office and the newspaper office had both been vandalized, his brow furrowed with unease. Each attack seemed random to the naked eye: a flooded basement, a ripped out page here, a missing album there, missing microfilm rolls no one ever asked for. Individually they were inconsequential. Together they formed a pattern, an intent.

He had already grilled her about the messages left at the Seaside Motel and her bedside table, so Emma skipped over those, moving on to Jules's diaries and the revelation that Gran had had an older sister. Alice. And the darker discovery that Alice had died in early 1947 at the hand of "the Morrison boy," presumably Helen's older brother.

"And you're certain this Morrison boy killed her?"

"He raped her." The words were an atomic bomb. Marcus's hand froze as he looked to Emma. "Then he killed her."

"How . . ." Marcus cleared his throat. He fidgeted in his seat, clearly uncomfortable. "How do you know that?"

"My dream."

"Explain."

"Ever since I arrived, I've felt this . . . connection to Alice. Like she's guiding me. Helping me figure this out, ya know? The dream felt like, I don't know . . . a shared memory or something."

"Tell me what happened in the dream."

"Something woke me, and I went downstairs to find the basement door open." A chill went through her as she recalled the dream, and Emma pulled the covers up to her neck. "I heard voices and followed them to a room in the back of the basement. When I opened the door, someone switched off the lights and threw me to the floor. He—" Emma began to cry. "He hurt me." Emma closed her eyes, wiping at her tears. "He hurt me, Marcus."

Marcus leaned forward and caught her hand in his. "You're safe now, Emma. He can't hurt you anymore."

"But that's just it," Emma said, a bit louder than she wanted. She glanced toward the door before continuing, this time in hushed tones. "It wasn't *me* he was hurting. It was Alice. I could feel my clothes being ripped, but there's not a scratch on them. I could feel his . . . his . . ."

"I get it."

"Thank you. It was Alice's memory. She *wanted* me to see it. She wanted me to *know* what had happened to her."

"Okay." He patted her hand and leaned back in his chair. "Okay."

"I'm not crazy."

Marcus chuckled. "You're definitely *not* crazy, Emma Campbell. That much I can tell you for sure." He stared at his tablet. "Anything else you can tell me?"

"No. That's everything that's happened this week."

"All right." He powered down his tablet and closed the cover. "Why don't you try getting some rest. I'll be next door if you need anything." He kissed her forehead and tucked the chair back under the desk.

"Thank you. And I'm sorry for scaring everyone."

He locked her bedroom door as he walked through the Jack-and-Jill bathroom to the adjoining room.

The dreary atmosphere outside permeated Emma's room, casting the space into shadows even though every light in the room had been switched on. Emma sat there in bed staring across the room, and Alice sat primly in the upholstered chair staring back.

"You *were* raped, weren't you?"

Emma didn't need Alice to answer. She knew it already.

"Did he kill you down there?"

No response.

"Will you stay with me until I'm asleep?"

The girl smiled. Emma lay back down and pulled the covers up to her neck. She had so much to tell Alda tomorrow. Sleep slowly took her. The last image she saw as she faded into unconsciousness was of Alice. And for the first time since Nellie's funeral, Emma wasn't so afraid anymore.

XVIII

The rain finally ended later that afternoon, and by dusk the skies had cleared to reveal an ocean of stars overhead. Emma had remained in her room the rest of the day, still badly shaken by her dream. As sunset painted her room in shades of burnt orange, someone knocked on Emma's door. Marcus was there before Emma could even get out of bed. He opened the door to find Mr. and Mrs. Hansen.

"Oh! Officer Cameron. Didn't expect to find you here."

"I'm staying in the adjoining room for now. Did you need something, Mr. Hansen?"

"We were going to ask Emma if she would like to drive out to Point Prim with us to watch the sunset and look at the stars. We would keep an eye on her at all times, Officer," Mr. Hansen pointed out. "She'll be safe with us, I promise you."

"Would you like that, Emma?"

Emma smiled. "Yes, sir. I think I'd like that very much."

"Excellent!" the old man declared, rubbing his hands together. "Why don't you change clothes, and we'll wait for you downstairs."

"Do I have enough time to take a shower?"

"Of course, dear," Mrs. Hansen said. "We'll be downstairs."

They took their leave, and Marcus closed the door.

"That was nice of them."

"It was," Emma said as she pulled a change of clothes from the wardrobe. "How cold does it get at night here?"

"I'd bring a light jacket or sweater. But you should otherwise be okay."

"Thanks," Emma said. "Would you mind going back to your room so I can shower and get dressed?"

She followed him to his room, but just as he was about pull the door shut, Marcus turned.

"We should talk about earlier."

"You promised me tomorrow."

"Not about Alice," he corrected. "I mean . . . the kiss."

Emma kissed him tenderly on the cheek. "You have a job to do. I respect that. When this is over, when you've got this creep and it's over and done with, then we'll talk. Okay?"

He nodded. "Okay."

He locked the door behind him. As Emma stepped away from the door, she suddenly had an overpowering urge to be back in his arms again.

The drive out to Point Prim was thankfully a quiet one. Neither of the Hansens wanted to rehash the awkwardness of the afternoon, and Emma was grateful for it. Just prior to leaving the Fishmonger, Mrs. Hansen had googled the directions to the lighthouse. An automated male voice guided them down the nine kilometers of Lighthouse Road out of town toward their destination. It was a picturesque two-lane road lined with trees. Cottages popped out of the shadows here and there along the way, reminding Emma of the backroads of Missouri. The fog was less dense out here, and Emma wondered for a moment about Digby's topography and if that was what caused the fog to linger the way it did. The alternative reason – Alice – was too unsettling. She had been actively trying to avoid it, yet Alice's connection to this ominous weather was something Emma couldn't deny.

Instead of finding a tranquil spot to watch the sunset, Emma discovered they had stumbled upon Digby's hottest tourist spot. Dozens of people had had the same idea and were camped out along the cliff, watching the last of the boats returning. The Bay of Fundy's waters danced in a kaleidoscope of oranges, reds, and yellows as the waves crashed against the rocky shoreline.

Sandra had packed them a lovely evening picnic basket of goodies, which Mr. Hansen now carried up a gravel trail that led them from the parking lot to the lighthouse. Emma tottered along behind them, carrying a thick blanket for them to spread out on.

A squat white boxy structure with a box-shaped tower attached, Point Prim was practical rather than decorative. Not that it was without its charms, of course.

A bright red stripe ran up the center of each side of the tower, culminating in the red cap. Emma could just make out the wrought iron railing surrounding the glass caged light. It glowed red from the tower's painted interior. Two competing lights—one of man, one of nature—shone on opposite ends of the bay, battling with each other. Or alternatively, Emma considered, talking to each other.

Emma snapped a photo just as Mrs. Hansen said, "This looks like a great little spot. What do you all think?"

"Looks good to me, dear," Mr. Hansen said, setting down the basket as Emma unfolded the blanket and spread it open with Mrs. Hansen's help.

"Didn't realize this spot was so popular," Emma said, taking a seat. "Looks like half the town is out here."

"Nah," Mr. Hansen said. "Most of these folks are tourists like us."

"How do you know?"

"They're up from the Pines," Mrs. Hansen explained. Her husband nodded in agreement. "They always offer a sunset shuttle out to the Point during the summertime for hotel guests."

"That's nice of them."

"Here," she said as she poured wine into a to-go cup and passed it to Emma. "Join us for a drink, will you? It's a lovely cabernet Jeremy picked up in town a few days ago."

"Thank you," Emma said, taking a sip. "Hmm. It's good."

"Isn't it? Oh, I'm glad you like it."

"Now, let's see what Ms. Sandra has cooked up for us," Mr. Hansen said as he started taking things out of the basket.

Sandra had packed half a loaf of bread and an assortment of cheeses and sliced meats with which to make sandwiches. There was a nice-sized Tupperware dish of leftover chicken salad, a packet of RITZ crackers, and several small canisters of different homemade jams and jellies.

"Everything looks so delicious," Mrs. Hansen said, eyeing the chicken salad.

"Ladies first," Mr. Hansen said, handing both of them a plate. "Sunset is breathtaking tonight, isn't it, Harriet?"

"It is indeed, dear."

Emma ate in silence, listening to their banter and the playful teasing, watching the little gestures they made and the way they shared those "perfect bites."

They even still hold hands!

An hour later, the sun had long since set, and the sky lit up with stars. Emma lay back on the blanket, gazing up at the stars while the Hansens were busy discussing the boat traffic coming back into the harbor. She finally got up and stretched her legs.

"Something the matter, Emma?" Mr. Hansen asked.

"No, sir. I'd just like to stretch my legs. Go down to the shoreline for a bit, ya know?"

"Enjoy yourself."

"Do be careful though, dear. The rocks can be dreadfully slippery, and it's quite a drop to the water if you go over," Mrs. Hansen said.

"Harriett's right, Emma. Rough as these waves are tonight, you'd be lucky to make your way out."

"I'll be careful. I promise."

"All right, dear," Mrs. Hansen said.

"If anyone approaches you, be sure to yell as loud as you can."

"I will."

She waved goodbye and continued walking along the trail toward the shoreline. Despite the late hour, people were huddled together on blankets or nestled into folding chairs, captivated by the glorious night sky overhead.

As Emma walked on, she came quite close to the water's edge and pulled up short. Mrs. Hansen had been right. The sheer drop-off was at least ten feet or more. With no one in close proximity, Emma decided to sit down on a craggy rock along the trail.

The crashing waves below sent a gentle spray of refreshing salt water over her as she sat there, watching the moon rise over the bay. The cool water felt good on her face as Emma wiped her face with the back of her hand. She sat there, eyes closed, listening to the thunderous waves as they threw themselves against the stony shore.

When she opened her eyes, it was strangely quiet. Apart from the waves, of course. She checked her phone. It was after ten o'clock. In the distance, Emma could see people collecting their things and preparing to leave. She caught sight of the Hansens and waved. They waved back, motioning toward the car. It was time to leave.

She had only taken a few steps when someone knocked her to the ground, burying her face in the thin topsoil. Emma struggled to get away, but her attacker was too strong. He sat on top of her, pinning her hands behind her back with one hand. The other held Emma's face to the ground. In the darkness, all she could see was rock and a few sprigs of grass.

"Help me!"

The crashing waves threw her words back. His body shifted on top of hers as he leaned down.

"Shut up! Leave the past alone, little girl," came the growled whisper. "Or I'll make sure you join it."

"Get off me! Who are you? What do you want?"

He responded by clutching a handful of Emma's hair, lifting her head up slightly, and slamming it down again. Emma felt the edge of a rock slice her cheek open. She stilled momentarily as the pain jolted through her.

"That's better."

"Please don't hurt me," Emma whimpered.

"Stupid girl," the man snarled. "You're not worth touching."

"Then what do you want?"

"I want you . . . gone."

"What?"

"You heard me. Gone. Forget this place. Forget your trash family. Get back in your car and go home."

She heard the cock of a gun over the waves. Emma's pulse quickened as her body went rigid. The cold steel barrel grazed the side of her head.

"Please."

"Leave! Or else . . ."

He shifted off her and went to get up. Emma wasn't sure what made her do it. Wasn't sure *why* she did it. But in the split second it took for her attacker to stand, Emma's hand, now freed, found a loose rock, spun around, and struck the man's gun arm. Or at least she hoped it was his gun arm. It was too dark for her to see more than a couple inches in front of her. She leapt to her feet, rock in hand, and raised her arm to strike the man a second time.

The man howled in pain from her first blow. He struck Emma across the face as she prepared a second hit, shoving her backward. Emma felt the ground disappear from beneath her.

"Oh, God!" she yelled as she fell backwards into the bay. The icy waters were a thousand knives being driven into her body, and Emma lost her breath as she went under. The waves dashed her against the rock again and again, as if she were a battering ram being driven into the enemy's front gate. The jagged rock tore into her arms as she used them to protect her head and upper body with each successive pummeling.

Each time she was thrown against the rock, Emma managed a fleeting hold on the slippery surface, giving her enough time to take a breath. But she knew she couldn't—wouldn't—last long like this. She had to get out. Her lips began to quiver. Hypothermia wasn't too far off. She had to get out of the water before her limbs started to give out.

Overhead, she could hear the Hansens calling out for her.

"Emma? Emma, dear, where are you?"

"Time to go, Emma." Mr. Hansen's strong voice echoed off the cliff. "Call out, Emma. Where'd you go?"

Emma went to shout, yet each time she opened her mouth, she ended up with a mouthful of seawater. She choked, swallowing half of it.

A rogue wave caught her unprepared and tossed her sideways into the cliff face, slamming the side of her head into the unyielding rock. Her head screamed with pain. The bitter taste of blood and salt water filled her mouth.

She was dying. In that moment, Emma knew she wasn't going to make it. As her body began shutting her extremities down in order to conserve body heat, Emma thought of her grandmother.

"I'm sorry, Gran," Emma cried.

"Come on, Em!" Nellie called out to her. "You've got this."

"I can't."

"Yes, you can."

"I'm so tired, Gran." Emma wrestled with her hold on the rock face. "So tired."

"Emma?" the Hansens called out to her. She could just make out their voices. "Where are you?"

In a break between waves, Emma glanced out across the bay. She remembered then that the ground tapered off into the water at the edge of the Point. If she could only make it to that point, she could more easily maneuver herself out of the water.

"Come on, Em. You can do this."

A wave tossed her limp body against the rock, and Emma reached forward and grabbed hold of an outcropping a foot or so ahead of her. It wasn't much, but it was a foot in the right direction. With each wave that dashed her against the cliffs, Emma moved closer and closer to the Point. Beaten and badly bruised, Emma cried out in agony each time she dug her hands into the rock. Each time she moved a little closer to her target.

The unrelenting waters showed Emma no mercy as they battered her time and again, then pulled her out into the depths. More than once, Emma lost her hold and had to fight her way back to the shoreline.

After nearly half an hour, she reached the Point and pulled herself out of the water. Her feet still dangling over the water's edge, Emma rolled over onto her back. She howled with each movement, every muscle in her body beaten by the night's ordeal. The multiple lacerations on her scalp, arms, and legs stained the gray stone below her a dark crimson. As she lay there on the rocks crying, Emma's only thought was of her grandmother.

"I did it, Gran," she managed between the heaving sobs. "I did it."

"I knew you could, Em," came the whispered reply. "I knew it all along."

When Emma finally began to rouse, she found herself in a hospital room. She had been cleaned and changed into a hospital gown. Her wounds had been bandaged, and judging by the fogginess in her head, she had been given some sort of sedative.

"Don't move."

Sandra.

"I don't think I could even if I wanted to."

Sandra appeared by her bedside. "Here, have some water."

Emma started to laugh but winced as her body reminded her of the ordeal. "Please don't make me laugh," she managed to say.

"Sorry."

"What happened?"

Sandra looked at her with a concerned expression. "You don't remember?"

"She awake?"

A new voice. Emma turned toward the open door and found Officer Cameron standing there with a man in black scrubs.

"Just woke up," Sandra said. "But she doesn't remember anything."

"I remember being attacked," Emma whispered.

Marcus took a step forward as the doctor stepped around him.

"She's exhausted, Officer Cameron. Are you sure this can't wait until morning when she's rested?" The doctor took Emma's wrist between his fingers and measured her pulse against his watch. "Hmm. Stronger than earlier. Good."

"You're . . . You're a doctor?" Emma asked, looking up at his hawkish features.

"Yes, I'm a doctor." He leaned forward, a bit too close for Emma's comfort. "And you, young lady, are lucky to be alive. Do you know where you are?"

Emma's head felt like it was splitting in two. She winced at the brightness of the overhead light.

"Shut off the overhead, will you, Marcus?" the doctor ordered. He turned back to Emma. "Better?"

"Better," she managed to whisper.

"Do you know where you are?"

"Hospital."

"Can you tell me your name?"

"Elizabeth Taylor."

Sandra giggled.

"How did I get here?" Emma answered.

"The Hansens." The words were practically a growl. "They were supposed to keep an eye on you."

"They called emergency services when they found you on the rocks." Sandra explained.

"This wasn't their fault, Marcus," Emma said. "I walked away from them. It was my fault."

"I should've never let you go in the first place."

Emma felt woozy even though she was lying down. She looked up at the physician, who was still standing over her bed. He seemed impossibly tall from this angle.

"How tall are you?"

"Five one," he quipped. Another giggle, this time from a nurse who had slipped into the room. "I've given you a sedative to help with the pain. It'll help you sleep a few hours, but I'm afraid you're in for a world of hurt tomorrow when it wears off."

"Thank you, Doctor."

"We'll monitor her tonight." He was talking to Marcus now. "She doesn't appear to have any broken bones, but a concussion is still probable given the circumstances. We'll run a CT in the morning to be sure."

"Yes, Doctor." Marcus's eyes never left Emma's. "Thank you." Marcus leaned in close. "Emma, can you tell me anything about your attacker?"

"Officer Cameron, can't this wait 'til—"

"No!" He turned back to Emma, who was gazing up at him with cloudy, dreamy eyes. The meds were starting to have an effect. "Emma, what do you remember?"

Her words came out singsongy, drawing out some syllables while cutting others short.

"He came from behind."

"How did you end up in the water?"

"Officer?"

"Just a minute," he pleaded. "How did you end up in the water, Emma?"

"He pushed me."

"Did he say anything before that?"

"Last question, Officer. Then I'm having you removed."

Marcus glared at the doctor, who returned the same arrogant, belligerent stare.

"My patient's health comes before your investigation, Officer Cameron," he stated firmly. "I'm sure the law is on my side on that one."

"Fine. One question." He turned back to Emma. Her expression was dreamy, childlike even. She smiled up at him. "Emma. Did he say anything before he pushed you?"

"You have pretty eyes," Emma teased.

"Time's up. Now out. Or I'll get your superior to do it for you."

Sandra tugged on his sleeve. "It's okay, Marcus. I'll stay with her tonight. You go do what you need to do."

He was halfway to the door when Emma answered.

"He said . . ." She yawned, fading quickly into unconsciousness. "Leave. Or else."

Sandra, the doctor, and Marcus watched in stunned silence as Emma smacked her lips and drifted off to sleep.

XIX

It was just after eight o'clock Monday morning when Alda opened the back door of the museum. Yes, she knew she shouldn't be there. Their official open time wasn't until lunch, but Alda was on a mission, and she could always tell the board she was using the time to sort and catalog the boxes of documents Franklin had brought in last week. With this new line of research Emma had discovered, Helen Morrison was their first real link to Emma's family. Alda was confident Helen would lead them in the right direction.

The back door gave her a bit of trouble as she tried closing it. The interior latch wouldn't engage completely, which meant the door wouldn't stay shut. She tried closing it more forcefully, but no matter how many times she slammed the door, the mechanisms didn't work properly, and the door would swing right back open. After slamming the door closed for the third time—unsuccessfully, of course—Alda held it closed and flipped the deadbolt just above the lock. Finally, the door stayed closed, and Alda breathed a sigh of relief.

She walked to the front desk and began thumbing through the museum index. It took her several minutes, but she finally found what she was looking for.

"Gotcha."

Jubilant, she climbed the stairs to the second floor, the index cards in one hand and a reusable shopping bag in the other. Her head was still foggy from her dinner with Emma, and she leaned on the handrail more heavily today. Alda made a mental note to not have wine again. It always made her unsteady on her feet. But Alda smiled to herself as she climbed the staircase, thinking of the delicious meal and delightful conversation they had shared. She made quick work of it. It wouldn't do to be caught being here. By the time she was finished, the bag was stuffed full.

Her cell phone rang downstairs.

"Silly goose. I must've left it on the counter."

Alda hurried out of the room and rounded the corner to the stairs. In her excitement, she failed to notice the door to the master bedroom was slightly ajar. As her foot hit the third step down, a gruff hand shoved her forward. The phone rang again. Her hands came up out of instinct to break her fall, and in her frightened haste, she let go of the railing. Her spectacles came off as she tipped forward, and Alda screamed in terror as the stairs came closer and closer. Another ring. She had only a moment to glance back at the hooded figure standing at the top of the staircase. But without her glasses, she couldn't tell who it was.

The scream died with the first thud of Alda's head against the pine stairs. Ugly gashes across her forehead and the bridge of her nose opened and stained the eastern white pine treads a deep red as her body tumbled like a ball down the remaining stairs. A jumbled mass of limbs came to rest at the foot of the stairs as the caller was switched over to voicemail.

The hooded figure slowly crept down the stairs, pausing for a moment at Alda's bleeding body to remove one thick work glove. They knelt, and two fingers were laid along the carotid artery in Alda's neck. There was no pulse. The shadow removed their fingers and regloved their pale hand. On the counter beside Alda's cell phone was a box of disinfectant kitchen wipes. The figure plucked one from the container, resealed the lid, and wiped down the area of Alda's neck where their fingers had been. Once done, the murderer wrapped the wipe around Alda's cell phone and pocketed it.

The figure surveyed the room once more to ensure nothing had been missed and quietly slipped out through the back door.

The alarm woke Emma. Dazed and unsure of where she was, she reached for it only to cry out in pain as the needle in her hand moved. A nurse raced into the room and switched off the alarm. Her saline bag needed replacing.

"There, there," she said, trying to calm Emma. "You're in the hospital, Ms. Campbell. You took a nasty fall last night out at the Point."

"Hospital."

"Mm-hmm. Do you remember?"

"I remember."

"Do you remember what happened?"

"No," Emma lied. "It's still all a bit hazy."

"Understandable." The nurse replaced the empty saline bag with a full one and reset the machine. "The doctor will be in shortly. After that, we're going to take some X-rays and a head CT to make sure nothing's broken, okay?"

"Okay."

"Doctor will be in shortly," the nurse said as she walked away.

Sandra lay sleeping on the sofa, unfazed by the noise. Emma didn't have the heart to wake her. She lay there remembering the night before. She thought of Alice. Alone. Victimized. Left for . . . Left for what, exactly? Had she died in the basement assault? Had she survived? She thought of her own attack out at Point Prim, the warning she had been given: leave, or else. What had she gotten herself involved in? Was all this worth it? Maybe Franklin had been right all along. If the family had buried something seventy years ago, did it really need to be dug up?

In the moment, Emma believed Alice's "sharing" had answered the essential question she and Alda had been pursuing: What had happened to precipitate Tobias and Cici leaving town so quickly? And "sharing" was the best description Emma could find to label what had happened to her. Alice had shared her experience with Emma. But why? To warn her? To help her understand? Reflecting on it now, the event generated more questions than answers.

She sat up, her head swimming from a mixture of pain and medication. What the hell had they given her last night? The clock on the nightstand indicated it was just before eight a.m. Emma pulled back her covers and slowly moved to get out of bed. Pain coursed through her body like rivers of acid, yet Emma was determined to get out of bed. Furious at herself for not listening to everyone's warnings, she willed her legs to move as her feet gingerly touched the cool hardwood floor. She was in tears by the time she reached the bathroom.

She stifled her scream with a towel as she took her first look at herself in the mirror. A gash across her left temple down the side of her cheek had been bandaged. Her right eye was black. Dried blood clung to her lower lip, which was split in two places. Her arms had been wrapped in bandages in several places.

"Emma?"

"In here."

"What are you doing up?" Sandra asked, appearing almost instantly by her side. "You could've fallen and hurt herself."

"Worse than this?" She motioned to her face in the mirror.

"Come on. Let's get you back to bed."

"I need a shower."

"After your X-rays and CT, yes." Sandra helped her back to bed, tucking her in.

"Marcus?"

"He had to report in last night. I'm on guard duty until he gets back."

"And the Hansens?"

Sandra shook her head. "I know Marcus read them the riot act. Letting you slip off like that. I've never seen that man so upset."

"It wasn't their fault, Sandra. It was me. I went off on my own. He shouldn't blame them."

"Well . . . he does. And he blames himself for letting you go in the first place."

"Morning, ladies." The doctor from the previous night stepped into the room. "You're looking a lot better than you were last night, Miss Taylor."

"Taylor?"

Sandra laughed. "He asked you your name during the exam, and you said 'Elizabeth Taylor.' "

"Imagine my surprise." The doctor feigned astonishment. "Me, small-town country doctor treating the famous Elizabeth Taylor."

"Where are my diamonds, then?"

He smirked. "In radiology. Come on, let's go look for them."

Sandra helped her into a wheelchair, which the doctor commandeered as soon as she was settled.

"Can you call Ms. Alda for me, please? Let her know what happened and that I won't be able to go to the Registrar General's office today."

"I'll call right now," Sandra said. Standing in the doorway, she watched the doctor wheel Emma down the hall and out of sight. She reached for her cell phone and dialed Ms. Alda's number. It went to voicemail. She hung up, not wanting to scare the lady with the events of the last twenty-four hours.

The hospital released her right before lunch. Her X-rays revealed no broken bones. The CT showed only a mild concussion. She was ordered home to rest and to avoid heavy activity. Sandra drove her back to the Fishmonger.

As Emma shuffled through the front door, she was greeted by a host of her concerned neighbors. The Hansens, Morrisons, and Rayburns welcomed the wounded warrior back to their company as Sandra and Connie fretted over her. Emma passed the pie hutch, now back in its place in front of the basement door. She paused to examine the hardwood floor. There was no indication of the hutch having been moved recently. No scuffs on the floor. No damage to the varnish. Nothing that would suggest anything untoward had happened last night.

And yet . . .

The sight of the door lurking behind it sent shivers through Emma. The girls' laughter coming from the kitchen roused Emma from her wonderings.

"Would you like to go up to your room?" Connie asked, leading her toward the stairs.

"No, please. I'd rather stay down here with everyone if you don't mind. It's too quiet up there all on my own."

"Emma, we're so sorry we left you," Mrs. Hansen said, trying not to cry. "Jeremy and I have been—"

"It was *not* your fault, Mrs. Hansen. Don't beat yourself up over this. I was the one who left you. Not the other way around."

"Still," Mr. Hansen added. "If we'd known this would happen, we would've stayed home last night."

"It wasn't your fault," Emma repeated, patting his arm.

"You should be in bed, Emma," Connie said as Emma moved to sit down in the living room. "I would've brought some breakfast up for you."

"How much did they tell you?"

"Attacked!" Connie exclaimed. "Right here. In Digby. My God, how could something like this happen?"

"Are you hungry?" Mr. Rayburn asked. "Can we get you something to eat?"

"I could eat a little something. Thank you."

"I'll let Dex know," he said.

"I'll come with you," Mrs. Rayburn added as they disappeared into the kitchen.

"You okay?" Al Morrison asked, dropping onto the sofa next to her. "Anything broken?"

"I'm alive," Emma said. "That's about all I can say at this point. Just alive. But no, no broken bones."

"You were lucky," Connie noted.

"Very," Judy Morrison said.

"Can I get you anything?" asked Sandra.

"Any more Tylenol left?"

"Sure thing." Sandra disappeared momentarily. Reappearing next to Emma's table, she handled her two Tylenol and a glass of cool water.

"Here ya go."

"Thanks." She downed the pills and handed Sandra back the empty glass. "Did you call Ms. Alda?"

"I did. But it went to voicemail. I didn't think this was the kind of message you should leave on an elderly woman's voicemail, so I hung up instead."

"Good point," Emma said, her eyes heavy with sleep. "Listen, why don't you all go do whatever it is you had planned today. I'll be fine. I've got plenty of meds and three highly trained guard dogs close by."

"Four, actually, if you count Officer Cameron," Sandra teased.

Emma gave her a thumbs-up. "Four."

It took some encouragement, but the other guests slowly dispersed, leaving for their own activities. Shortly after the Morrisons left to go whale watching, Marcus came in.

"She just dozed off," Dex said, handing him a cup of coffee.

"Probably for the best. She'll hate what I have to tell her anyway."

"What's wrong, Marcus?" Connie asked from the sofa.

Marcus watched Emma for a moment, the smooth rise and fall of her chest with each breath, the relaxed expression on her face.

"Marcus?" Dex asked again. "What's happened?"

"Miss Alda died this morning."

XX

Marcus's words, when he told her, were like stepping through a shattered pane of glass. He had taken her to the drawing room and pulled the heavy pocket doors closed for privacy. Not that it mattered. The rest of the house already knew.

"H-how?" Emma stammered. "How did she die?"

"She fell down the stairs at the museum."

Emma swiped at her tears, which wouldn't stop coming. "This was my fault."

"This was an accident, Emma. Nothing more. It wasn't your fault."

"But if she hadn't been alone—"

"Emergency services said it was almost instantaneous. She wouldn't have felt any pain."

Emma looked away. She did not want that mental image. She fought against it as Marcus continued. But she was beyond hearing him.

Officer Cameron sat down beside Emma. He gave her a moment before reaching into his pocket and pulling out his tablet and stylus. Marcus cleared his throat.

"I need to ask you some questions, Emma. Can you do that for me?"

"It's all my fault." Emma sobbed. She felt numb. Whether from shock or pain from last night's attack, she wasn't sure.

"What do you mean? Why is this your fault?"

"I dragged her into this."

"To what? What did you drag her into, Emma?" Marcus put his hand on Emma's shoulder, giving her a gentle nudge. "Emma, look at me."

Emma wiped her tears with the back of her hand and managed to stop crying long enough to look him in the eye.

Marcus's radio squawked to life. The woman on the other end was asking for his whereabouts. He was wanted back at the station.

"On my way." He looked to Emma. "This wasn't your fault, Emma."

"It was," Emma replied, her voice scratchy from salt water and crying. "I know it was."

"I'll be back as soon as I can." He kissed her tenderly on the cheek. "And then I need to ask you some questions. Do you understand me, Emma?"

She nodded. He kissed her again, this time on her forehead, and left the room. A minute later, Sandra stepped inside.

"I'm so sorry, Emma."

"It's my fault."

"No, don't say that," Sandra implored her, sitting down next to Emma. "You heard what Marcus said. This was an accident."

"I'd . . . I'd like to be alone now, please."

Sandra hugged her before leaving.

An hour later, she was still sitting in the drawing room when Officer Cameron knocked.

"Yes?"

He was in his uniform and looked good. Really good. The dark blue colors and the cut of the fabric accentuated the fact that the man clearly went to the gym more than once a week. Or even twice, for that matter.

"You look nice," Emma managed to say.

"Thanks. You look—"

"Like I just got a woman killed."

He sighed, tossing his cap onto a chair and sitting down next to her. As he drew closer, Emma saw the pained expression on his face.

"I know this is difficult for you right now," he began. His voice had cleared, and there was an official tone to it. "But I do need to ask you some questions."

"Of course. Anything I can do."

"Do you know why Ms. Alda was at the historical society this time of day? It doesn't normally open on Monday until noon. Why was she there so early today?"

"I don't. I'm sorry."

"Was she working on something related to your research?"

"No, I don't think so."

"What makes you say that?"

"I was supposed to go to the Registrar General's office this morning to do some research on a family friend we'd discovered. Helen Morrison. I was going to research their records first and then go to the museum in the afternoon to see what we could find there."

"So, she wasn't expecting you until after lunch?"

"Definitely not."

"And you mentioned a Helen Morrison. Who's Helen?"

"Someone in my research," Emma clarified. "She was childhood friends with my great-aunt Alice."

"The one you believe was murdered."

"Yes, that's right."

"Did she mention anything else she was working on? Any other projects or something?"

Emma considered the question. What had Alda been working on before Emma had walked through the door that first day?

"Only the stuff Franklin brought in last week."

"Franklin? Wood? From the newspaper?"

"That's right. He brought in a box of photos and newspapers and stuff on . . . Thursday, I think. I'm sorry. My days are starting to run together."

"Take your time."

"There was a photograph in one of the boxes of this house," Emma said. "I saw it the next day. It's how I found Connie and Dex. I came straight here."

"Connie's records show you checked in on Friday," Marcus said, consulting his tablet. "Which would mean Franklin came by on Thursday afternoon with the boxes."

"That seems right, I guess. It's possible she was working on stuff from those boxes. She mentioned it in passing when we were at dinner Saturday night. How much time it was going to take her to catalog and file everything."

"When was the last time you spoke to her?"

"Saturday night. When you dropped us off after dinner."

"Nothing Sunday?"

Emma shook her head. "I remember asking Sandra to call her this morning when they were taking me for X-rays. I lost my phone in the ocean and couldn't call her myself."

"What time was this?" he asked, taking notes as they spoke.

"Around eight, I believe. Maybe a little before."

Marcus said nothing, but Emma saw the change in his expression.

"What?"

Marcus shook his head.

"Officer Cameron, what is it?"

"Nothing," he said dismissively. "How long will you be staying in town?"

"A . . . A few more days at least, I think. Why?"

"I'd like you to remain in Digby until we receive the coroner's report."

Emma's face went white. "You think that—I mean, do you . . . Do you suspect foul play?"

"It's just precaution, Emma," Marcus assured her. "Standard procedure. To make sure we didn't miss anything."

"And her family?"

"We're still trying to reach them. Her son and daughter-in-law live in Toronto, but we haven't been able to speak with them yet. Call me if you think of anything else, all right?"

"I will. Thank you, Officer."

"In light of the circumstances," Marcus said, closing the cover on his tablet, "the board of trustees is closing the historical society until after Ms. Alda's funeral, so I'm afraid you won't be able to continue your research for a few days."

Emma felt too dejected to protest. Part of her wanted to push forward. Part of her just wanted to see that mischievous smile one more time.

"I understand," Emma managed to get out. "Thank you for telling me."

Marcus clutched her hand for a moment, then kissed her forehead and excused himself from the room. Emma could hear Dex and Connie in the kitchen but decided against intruding. Dazed with shock and still in quite a lot of pain, she pulled herself up the carved wooden staircase, cognizant of the fact Alda had died on a staircase not two hours earlier. Granted, it was a different one, but a tremor ran through Emma nonetheless as she rounded the landing and forced herself up the second flight of stairs to the second floor.

A strong wind shook the window at the back of the hall as Emma reached the top of the stairs. Her room was directly across the hallway from the stairs. She glanced down the hall to the window facing the backyard and could see the large tree swaying violently. The massive limbs undulated in the gale winds that cut across the bay onto the shore. She approached the window and glanced out at the bleak sky. Streaks of sunlight poked through the clouds, promising a sunny day if only the clouds would move along.

Emma saw the swing and jumped back suddenly, terrified of what she had seen. She shut her eyes tightly, willing her heartbeat to slow down. She kept them shut for several seconds before reopening them and slowly—cautiously—taking a step toward the window. She was still there.

Seated in the tree swing, unmoved by the temper tantrum Mother Nature was throwing around her, Alice sat looking up at the window where Emma now stood. Despite the violent winds blustering outside, neither the girl's dress nor her hair betrayed the unstable weather around her. Quite the opposite. She sat there, swinging ever so gently. Her face looked placid to Emma. Not menacing or foreboding in the slightest.

"Alice," Emma whispered into the glass.

"You see her too, don't you?"

Emma shrieked as she spun around. There, halfway down the hall, stood Amelia. The child seemed almost as terrified as Emma was.

"Sorry," she said sheepishly as Connie came bounding out of the kitchen, the door whacking against the wall.

"Girls?" she yelled.

"Sorry, Connie," Emma called down as she leaned over the railing and looked down at the girls' very worried mother. "That was me."

"You?" The woman laughed. "Emma, you scared me half to death. What happened?"

Emma glanced around her and caught Amelia's pleading expression. Emma knew that look—"please don't tell Mother." She winked at the girl, assuring her she was fine, and saw the full-length mirror on the wall.

"My reflection in the mirror."

Connie sighed. "I've told Dex a hundred times we need to take that thing down. You're not the first person who's been scared by it, Emma. I'll talk to Dex again."

"No, really, it's fine," Emma argued. "I knew it was there. I just . . . I guess with the wind and everything else that's happened today, I wasn't paying attention."

"Not much of a day, is it?" Her tone softened. Connie looked toward the windows and scowled. "And this wind isn't helping matters."

"No."

"Can I bring you some tea or something?"

"No, I think I'm just going to stay inside and read today."

"We have a small library on the third floor if you need something to read. Right at the top of the stairs."

"I'll take a look."

"Dex and I will be here most of the day. The girls too."

"Thanks," Emma said as the woman turned and walked back into the kitchen. As the door opened, she could just hear Dex talking on the phone.

After the kitchen door swung closed, Amelia whispered, "Thank you."

Emma smiled and turned to sit down on the plush green velvet settee pushed against the banister. She patted the spot next to her.

"Come and sit down," she entreated. "I think we need to talk."

"Okay," the girl said sheepishly. "Am I in trouble?"

"No," said Emma. "I just need to ask you a few questions."

The girl approached the settee cautiously. Seeing no hostility in Emma's expression, she plopped down beside her and looked up at the grown-up expectantly.

"What did you mean when you asked me if I saw her too? Who is 'her'?"

"The ghost on the swing," Amelia answered matter-of-factly. "In the backyard. You know, the girl with the pigtails and the funny dress."

"Funny dress?"

"Well, maybe not *laugh* funny," she continued explaining. "I mean *weird* funny. Like something out of an old movie on the telly."

"And you see her?"

"We both do."

"We?"

"Me and Carol. We both see her. Most of the time she's in the swing, but sometimes she comes into the house. We see her in the hallway up here."

"You do?"

"I think you're staying in her bedroom," Amelia continued. "We've seen her go in there loads of times."

"That's an encouraging thought," Emma mumbled. She rubbed her arms, suddenly cold at the thought of a ghost child in her room watching her sleep. "How long have you seen her?"

Amelia thought for a second, cocking her head slightly to ponder the question. "Right after Mom and Dad bought this place. That was where we first saw her." She pointed at the window where Emma had just been standing. "We saw her on the swing outside and ran outside to play with her. But when we got outside, there was no one there."

"She disappeared?"

"We thought so. We told Mom and Dad about her, but they told us it was probably just one of the neighborhood kids who ran off 'cause they were scared of being caught somewhere they shouldn't be. So we went back upstairs to play. And she was standing there"—she pointed again—"in front of the window. Waiting for us."

"Waiting?"

Amelia nodded.

"What did you do?"

"I tried talking to her, but she never talked. She just looked at us for a bit and then walked into your room."

"In there?" Emma pointed toward her door.

"Uh-huh. So, we followed her into the bedroom. Only . . . when we went in, the room was empty. It wasn't like it is now. There was no furniture anywhere. Nowhere for her to hide from us. And we searched *everywhere* for her. She was gone."

"Did you tell your parents about her?"

Another nod. But this one came with a scowl.

"Dad came upstairs and asked us what we were doing looking in all the closets and knocking on the walls and stuff. We told him what happened, but he didn't believe us. Kept saying, 'There's no such thing as ghosts, girls.' "

She stiffened at the last remark and shook her left index finger at Emma, imitating her father.

"Then Mom came up to see what was going on, and when we told her, she made us stop talking about it. And she made us promise not to talk about it again to anyone."

"How many times have you seen her?"

"Loads of times, but always upstairs." Amelia was emphatic on this last point. "She's always upstairs. Either at the window or in the hallway or her bedroom."

"You never see her downstairs?"

She shook her head. "Only once. I don't think she likes it downstairs."

"What makes you say that?"

"This one time, Mom and Dad were bringing up the Christmas decorations from the basement. And me and Carol were playing, see?"

"Yes."

"We were playing hide-and-seek in the basement and wanted her to play with us."

"And she wouldn't?"

"Nope. She just made this weird face and disappeared."

"What kind of weird face?"

"Like she was scared of something down there."

Emma's body went rigid. She now knew exactly what Alice had been frightened of that day.

"Maybe she was scared of the dark," Emma offered.

"Nah, I don't think so."

"And she just disappeared?" She snapped her fingers. "Just like that?"

Amelia put her fingers together and attempted a snap. "Just like that. And she didn't come back for the longest time. Carol said we musta made her mad and that's why she didn't want to play with us anymore."

"But she did come back, didn't she?"

Amelia nodded. "But we never play in the basement anymore when she's here."

"Amelia! Come on, it's your twun."

Emma looked up and saw Carol coming downstairs from the third floor.

"We were playing Candy Land," Amelia explained. "Can I go now?"

"Of course, thank you so much for talking to me."

"You're welcome. But please don't tell Mom or Dad."

"I won't, sweetie. It'll be our little secret."

The girls joined hands and raced back upstairs to continue their board game. Emma heard a door close upstairs. Muffled laughter slid out from under the door and tumbled down to Emma's ears. She sat there listening to their lively chatter before going back to the window.

Alice was still in her swing, looking up at Emma. The two stared at each other for what felt to Emma like an eternity, and then Alice raised a hand and motioned Emma to come outside. Emma froze. Had she imagined that? Or had it been real? She hesitated, and the girl motioned to Emma a second time. Without thinking, Emma turned and hurriedly went downstairs.

She paused at the foot of the stairs, not wanting to alert Connie and Dex to her leaving the house. They would only worry. She turned and went out the front door instead.

The wind whipped and tossed her hair as Emma zigzagged along the side yard toward the back, avoiding the puddles as best she could. She was wearing sneakers and really didn't want to deal with wet sneakers or wet feet.

As she rounded the corner of the house, she saw Alice. She was still there, swinging. She turned to face Emma as she approached. Not smiling. Not frowning. Not reacting at all, Emma realized. It made Emma uneasy, but something compelled her to keep moving forward. She stopped just a few feet from the girl.

"Alice?"

No response.

"Are you Alice?"

Still no response.

"Do you know who I am?" Emma pressed on. "I'm Nellie's granddaughter. Nellie. Your sister."

The girl cocked her head slightly and considered Emma for a moment. Emma wasn't sure what to do, so she just stood there, examining the girl in return. Her dark mahogany color hair glinted as if under a full summer sun despite the clouds and dense fog. Emma's environs were utterly gray, but Alice's . . . Alice looked like she was enjoying a picture-perfect day. The colors of her skin, hair, and clothing were warm. They radiated vibrancy, daring the bleakness around the girl to invade their domain.

A glint of something on the ground behind Alice caught Emma's eye, and her attention was momentarily diverted. A small metal disc protruding out of the soil sparkled in the same distant sunlight that shone on Alice. Emma noticed the soil along the shoreline had been badly beaten up during Sunday's storm. With the soil swept away, something lost—or hidden, Emma considered—had been unearthed.

She turned back to Alice. The swing was empty. The girl was gone. Emma's breathing turned shallow, and she practically threw herself down onto the swing's wooden seat. Her hands trembled as she fumbled to take hold of the rope. Emma closed her eyes, laid her head against the cool rope, and tried to catch her breath.

I hate it when you just vanish like that.

It took a while, but after several minutes had passed, Emma finally opened her eyes. Her hands were no longer shaky, and her breathing had settled. There on the ground lay the disc that had distracted her. She assumed that, at least, was real. The ground around it was more mud than sand, and knowing it was easier to wash dirty feet than dirty shoes, Emma slipped off her sneakers. Careful not to slip in the mud, she walked the few feet to where the object lay half-buried.

It was a locket, she realized as she plucked it from the earth. Its once-silver shell was severely tarnished after being exposed to the elements, and Emma couldn't quite pry it open with her fingernails. The thin chain was brown with dirt, and Emma took another couple steps until she was at the shoreline. She knelt and let the cool waters wash over her newly found treasure. The chain she managed to clean easily, at least the dirt part anyway. No matter how much she rubbed it between her fingers, the metal refused to give her any hint of its original beauty.

Emma saw a fragment of a shell on the sand close by and used it to force the clasp open. A crumbly black piece of paper fell apart in her hand as she opened the locket. If it had been a photograph, it had long since dissolved into useless confetti. She knelt again and rinsed the inside. In tiny block capitals opposite the photograph were engraved words.

To A
Love H

"To A," Emma read out loud. "Love H. A . . . Alice. H . . . Helen."

Emma looked across the foggy gray water. Waves lapped at her feet, rinsing the mud away. She could see silhouettes of fishing boats coming in and out of the harbor. All had their lights on and announced their comings and goings by horn: deep, guttural horns; sharp staccato horns; midtone horns. She thought of Alda's husband, Benjamin, and their granddaughter, who had died in the very waters where she now stood. And of Alice and

Helen standing on this same shore decades earlier. Girls, they were. Lifelong friends, it seemed to Emma.

Where did you go, Alice? Emma pondered. She spun around at the sound of a child's laughter. Alice had returned.

"Where did you go, Alice?" Emma asked again. "Did he kill you in the basement? Is that what happened? What did he do with your body, Alice?"

No response.

"Where are you buried, Alice?"

The girl said nothing but finally raised her arm toward the water, her index finger pointing the way.

"The water. They buried you in the water. Is that it, Alice?"

No response. But she didn't lower her arm. Emma sat back down on the swing, trying to wrap her brain around it.

"You weren't buried in the water. Okay then. Are you here in Digby? Did they hide you somewhere here in town?"

Nothing.

"You're not here. You're not in the harbor. What am I—"

A boat horn echoed off the water. Emma watched as the late ferry chugged away from the docks, headed for Saint John. She sat for several moments, watching the ship disappear into the distant horizon.

"Wait a minute," Emma whispered. Alice turned for the first time and faced her. "You didn't die here, did you, Alice?"

She smiled.

"You left Digby, didn't you?" The ferry horn blew once more. "On the ferry to Saint John."

Emma grabbed her shoes and raced across the back lawn. She reached into her pocket for her phone but remembered she had lost it the day before. She burst into the kitchen, mud and all, to the chagrin of those present. Dex dropped his coffee in his lap. Connie nearly dropped the roast she'd been baking onto the floor.

"Emma!" Sandra said. "What's wrong?"

Emma looked at their startled faces and asked, "Do you have a computer I can borrow?"

XXI

"I don't know why I didn't think of this sooner," Emma chided herself as she opened a web browser.

After she had barged into the kitchen barefoot, Connie had refused her entry until she cleaned up. Like a naughty child, she had followed Dex back into the yard and hosed down her legs and feet, which had been caked with mud. Connie met Emma at the door with a towel Sandra had brought from the laundry room.

"I thought you said you couldn't find anything online," Sandra said as Emma keyed in her search.

"I didn't."

"So . . . what's changed?" Dex asked. "Why do you think you'll find something now?"

"Because," Emma said, turning in her seat to face them. Her expression was that of a child on Christmas morning. "When I searched before, I was only searching Nova Scotia. I never thought to search any of the other provinces because I always assumed Tobias, Cici, and Nellie had gone straight from Digby to America."

"You're thinking they went somewhere else first?" Connie asked.

"No." Emma pointed with her index finger. "I think the three of them did go on to America. But Alice? I think Alice went somewhere else."

"Alice?" Connie and Dex asked simultaneously.

"Her grandmother's older sister," Sandra explained. "But I thought you said she was murdered."

"Murdered?" Connie and Dex yelled.

"It's a long story," Emma explained. "Bottom line: something happened between the Roberts and Morrison families in early 1947 that completely changed both families. Every mention of Alice stops after February 1947. The guy I think was responsible was sent away to England a month later. And after that? Nothing. It's like Alice doesn't even exist."

"You think she was sent away instead?" Sandra asked.

Emma nodded, her face hurting from smiling. "I think she took the ferry to Saint John."

"Saint John?" the trio declared.

"What makes you think that?" Mr. Hansen asked, appearing in the doorway. The women shrieked at the unexpected visitor's arrival.

"Terribly sorry," he said. "I overheard part of your conversation as we were coming in and thought something else had happened. We heard about that poor lady in the museum while we were out on the course."

"Word travels fast in small towns," Dex muttered.

"Indeed," Mr. Hansen said. "Put my wife in a poor state, it did. She's gone upstairs to lie down."

"Can I get her anything?" Sandra asked. "A cup of tea, maybe? Or something to eat?"

"Tea sounds lovely, Ms. Sandra. Thank you."

Sandra excused herself from the room, and Mr. Hansen turned to Connie.

"Your brochure mentioned something of a library, I believe."

"Yes, it's on the third floor. Right at the top of the stairs."

"Wonderful. Then I believe I'll retire to our room for a nice bit of reading."

"Let us know if you need anything, Mr. Hansen," Dex said.

"I will. Thank you." He turned to Emma, his face more serious now. "I assume this is the same Alice from before?"

Emma hesitated. "Yes," she said finally.

He nodded. "Well then, let us hope there are no more . . . incidents tonight."

"One can only hope," Emma retorted.

Mr. Hansen bid them farewell as Sandra stepped out of the kitchen with a tray in her hands. Emma listened to them talking as they made their way upstairs.

Dex finally broke the silence. "Mind telling us what just happened here? What was he talking about, Emma? 'No more incidents.' "

"Did something happen, Emma?" Connie asked.

"Is it weird how he turns up out of nowhere? Right in the middle of people's conversations. Like he walks around eavesdropping on the rest of the world."

Dex chuckled. "Oh, come on, Emma. He's not that strange."

"Isn't he?"

"A bit odd, perhaps," Dex replied. "But I doubt he means any harm by it."

"Still," Emma mused. "It's weird. Anyway . . . Alice. I think Alice took the ferry to Saint John. I don't think she went to America."

"At all?"

"No," Emma said. "I don't think she ever left Canada."

She turned back to the computer screen and pressed *Enter*. They watched as the search results slowly began to come up. Two results down from the search bar, where Emma had keyed *Alice Roberts, Saint John, 1947*, was an obituary.

"Can I print this?"

"Of course," Dex said. Within moments, the inkjet printer spat out a single page. Connie began to read as Emma continued reading the screen.

"Not much here, is there?"

"What's it say?" Dex asked.

"It's just a list of names of people who died that day." Connie explained. "Nothing about Alice at all. Just her name."

"What's this abbreviation after her name?" Emma asked, pointing to the screen.

Connie handed the page to Dex as she leaned in over Emma's shoulder for a better look. "Oh, yeah. You can barely make that out on the photocopy."

"Ever see it before?"

"No." She shook her head. "Dex, have you heard of it?"

"I haven't. Try googling it. See what comes up."

Emma keyed in the acronym—*SEHG, Saint John*—and hit *Enter*. It took them several clicks to find the result they were looking for, but what they discovered came as a total shock. Emma's face turned ashen, and she would've collapsed had she not already been sitting down.

That's not possible.

Connie and Dex leaned forward, reading the screen.

"Oh," said Connie. She put a hand on Emma's shoulder.

"This can't be right," Emma said. "It can't be. Alice died months before this. This has to be the wrong person."

"Emma," Dex said. "There's only one entry for her."

How did I miss it? Toby and Cici's advanced age by the time Gran was born. The shame dumped on to the family, resulting in Toby's family being cut out. The snarky comments from neighbors. "Bad seed," Jules's diary said. How did I not see what was right in front of me?

Five words in bold letters filled the top line of the search results.

Saint Emiliani Home for Girls

"Emma?" Dex asked. His next words came out in a stutter, as if the syllables had to push their way out of his vocal cords. "I hate to be indelicate about this, but . . . are you sure Alice was your grandmother's . . . sister?"

XXII

Once again, the earth had shifted, and Emma found herself falling through the facade of what she'd thought was real into an abyss she had no measure of.

Alice wasn't murdered.

Emma felt light-headed as she stared at the screen, trying to understand how much this was going to change everything. She thought of what her uncle had said of Toby and Cici.

"Poppy and Mimi never talked much about their lives before they moved to St. Louis, so I doubt Mom knew anything, truth be told."

It made total sense now: the sadness they always wore like protective cloaks, the reticence to talk about *any* aspect of their lives in Canada, the age gap between them and Gran, their separation from the rest of the family. They had cut themselves off from everything they knew . . . to protect their granddaughter. To shield her from the nightmare of her origins.

She felt angry at them. Angry they had maintained their silence even after Gran was old enough to understand. Angry they had denied her family access to the greater Roberts family. The aunts they never knew. Cousins. Uncles.

Uncle Adi's words came back.

"We were still kinda young when they passed away, and you never think to ask those kinds of things when you're young, ya know?"

The tumult around her was like mosquitoes buzzing in her ears. Conversations, once full of excitement and revelation, devolved into chaos and uncertainty. Mild irritation morphed into full-blown distraction until Emma could stand it no longer and—

"Quiet! Please!" she shouted.

Silence.

"Thank you. I need to think."

Connie and Dex hung around briefly before excusing themselves to take care of their daily business. Sandra pulled up a chair next to Emma.

"This means Alice wasn't murdered after all, right?" Sandra asked.

"I didn't think places like this still existed anymore," Emma finally said, exchanging a stunned, confused look with Sandra.

Sandra put a hand on her shoulder. "You okay?"

"I'm . . . I'm not sure." Her voice shook, the words too timid to leave her mouth. "It's like . . ."

"Like the earth just opened up and swallowed everything you thought you knew about yourself."

Emma nodded, words still too much an exercise to speak aloud.

She copied and pasted the text into a new search and discovered that Saint Emiliani Home for Girls had been shuttered during the latter half of the twentieth century and was now Saint Thomas Aquinas School—a private school with a hefty price tag to match.

A subsequent search on Saint Thomas Aquinas School yielded a phone number. Emma glanced at the lower right corner of the computer screen: not yet three p.m.

School should still be in session.

"Could I borrow your phone again?"

"Of course," Sandra said, reaching into her pants pocket for her phone.

"Thank you."

Emma dialed the number, putting it on speaker so they could both hear.

"Come on," Emma whispered. "Pick up."

No one answered.

"Maybe you could try again tomorrow morning," Sandra offered. "When school's open."

Just five more rings, Emma thought. *I'll give it five more rings.*

No answer.

Four rings.

"God, I'm shaking I'm so nervous," Sandra said.

Three rings.

"Come on," Emma whispered. "Answer the phone, someone."

Two rings.

"Yes?"

Emma stood, nearly losing her grip on the phone in the sudden movement.

"Yes, hello?"

"Can I help you?"

A woman's voice. No. Not a woman. A teenager.

"Yes, hello. I was trying to reach one of the school administrators, please. I had some questions about a . . . uh . . . about one of the students there."

"I'm sorry, ma'am. They're in meetings most of the day, but I could take a message and have someone call you back as soon as they're available."

"Maybe you could help me, then."

"I'll do my best. How can I help you?"

"My name is Emma Campbell. I'm in Digby, Nova Scotia, doing some family research, and I believe my great-grandmother used to live at the Saint—no, that's not it . . . hang on. The Saint Emiliani Home for Girls."

"Yes, ma'am."

"I was hoping you still had records on hand. Maybe see what her life was like while she was there. Would that be possible?"

"Absolutely, ma'am. All those records are in the basement, but I'm pretty sure Mr. Crosse could show you around and help you find what you're looking for."

"Mr. Crosse? He's the school principal?"

"Oh, no, ma'am. He's the history teacher. Sister Mary Elizabeth is the school principal."

"Great. Could I come by tomorrow morning?"

"Sure thing. Let me check Mr. Crosse's schedule. Bear with me a moment."

"Take your time."

Emma and Sandra sat in rapt attention, listening to the girl mutter to herself as she flipped through pages, searching for Mr. Crosse's schedule.

"Here it is. Sorry that took so long."

"You're fine. Does Mr. Crosse have any availability tomorrow?"

"Yes, ma'am. He has a break between classes from nine to ten o'clock. That's the only time tomorrow he's available, unfortunately."

"That's quite all right. Nine o'clock works perfectly."

"Excellent. I'll put you in his schedule and let him know to be expecting you."

"Should I go straight to his office tomorrow or—"

"No, ma'am. You'll need to come to the front office first. When you arrive tomorrow, use the visitor parking area, and follow the signs to the front office. You wouldn't be able to miss us."

"Thank you," Emma replied, taking quick notes. "Visitor parking. Follow signs to front office."

"Yes, ma'am."

"Thank you so much. I'll see you and Mr. Crosse tomorrow."

"Have a nice day, ma'am. Goodbye."

"Great," Emma said, setting the phone down as she reached for her bag. "Mind if I make one more?"

"Sure."

He answered on the first ring.

"Sandra? Is Emma okay?"

Emma's stomach felt queasy, and her pulse quickened. Sandra covered her mouth, half stifling her laugh. The tips of Emma's ears suddenly felt red-hot.

"It's me. Sandra let me borrow her phone."

"Oh." A slight hint of confusion. "Oh, right. You lost yours."

"Bottom of the ocean, I'm guessing."

"I'll bring you a burner phone when I come by."

"Thanks. Listen. I need a favor."

Emma explained what she had discovered and her appointment with the school's history teacher the following morning.

"Could you take me to Saint John tomorrow?"

Marcus took a moment to answer. "Emma, my shift doesn't end until late tonight, after the last ferry has already left port. And tomorrow morning won't give us enough time to get there by nine o'clock."

"Could we drive?"

He laughed. "It's a six-hour drive. Are you sure you're up for that?"

"For a chance to finally see what happened to Alice, yes, I'm up for it. We can take turns driving so you can get some sleep. And I'll take care of gas and meals. Can you do it?"

"Okay then, Emma. I'll take you."

Sandra gave her a quick high five.

"Thank you, Marcus. I mean Officer Cameron. You've no idea how much this means to me."

"You're welcome. I need to go though. I'll swing by later with that burner phone for you."

"Thanks."

A few minutes after three a.m. Tuesday morning, Emma crept out of her room. Her sneakers in one hand and her backpack full of notes hung on her shoulder, she tiptoed down the staircase. A change of clothes was tucked under her arm. As she reached the first floor, she nearly shrieked as she caught sight of Officer Marcus Cameron standing in the entry waiting. In his hands he held two travel tumblers. Emma prayed it was coffee.

"Morning," she whispered.

"Morning. You sleep well?"

"Not really."

He handed her one of the tumblers, and Emma took a tentative sip. It was coffee. Hot, rich, and slightly sweet.

"I was too excited to sleep," she said. "This is good coffee. You?"

"Off and on. Sandra made it."

"I also whipped up some breakfast sandwiches for you guys to eat on the way," Sandra said, stepping up to stand at Marcus's side. She handed Emma a small brown paper bag that was warm to the touch. "I put orange marmalade on one for you, Emma. That was your favorite, right?"

"Right." Emma set her things down and put on her sneakers.

"And raspberry jam on the other for you, Officer."

"Thanks, Sandra. These should hold us until lunchtime."

"You look comfy." Sandra said.

Emma was dressed in an oversized sweatshirt and jeans. "I brought a change of clothes. Thought maybe we could stop somewhere so I could change before we get to the school."

"You two staying the night? Or coming back on the late ferry?"

"We'll be on the late ferry back tonight," Marcus replied. "The visitation for Ms. Alda is midday Wednesday, so I need to be back for that."

"When is the funeral?" Emma asked.

"Immediately following visitation."

"I'd like to go," Emma said, unsure of herself. "If you think that'd be okay."

"Shouldn't be a problem," Marcus said.

"I didn't know her that long. But she was such a nice woman. And she did a lot for me in what little time we spent together."

"I'm sure you'd be welcome," Sandra said.

Marcus checked his watch. "We better go if you want to be on time for your appointment."

Sandra followed them outside and stood on the porch as they walked to Emma's car.

"Watch out for moose. They're bad this time of night."

"Will do," Marcus said with a wave. "Be back tonight."

Nova Scotia Highway 101—Harvest Highway as the locals call it—reminded Emma a lot of Interstate 70 in Missouri. It was a four-lane highway with a grassy median between and an endless sea of trees on both sides. Emma wondered whether the area was part of a national park. Or alternatively, maybe western Nova Scotia was simply more rural.

The morning sun was still hiding behind approaching storm clouds by the time they were a few miles south of Truro. Emma, having taken the first turn driving, had been on the road for nearly three hours and hadn't seen a single other vehicle on the highway. Marcus, having worked late the night before, had slept most of the way, which was okay. Emma didn't mind the drive alone. It was actually peaceful.

But she couldn't help glancing over at Marcus now and then, her heart melting every time she did. His light snoring. His tousled hair from running his hand through it countless times a day. Emma pondered a life with this man. Settling down in small-town Nova Scotia. She also felt simultaneously guilty. Nessa wanted her to move to New York City. They had planned to move there, talked incessantly about it: conquering the fitness world, becoming celebrity trainers. She still wanted those things. Or did she?

She switched on the radio for something to drown out the silence, but being in the middle of nowhere meant no reception. She reached for her new cell phone—no reception. Emma made a mental note to buy a new phone the moment she got back to Columbia. This burner phone was ridiculous. But it would do for now. Emma turned off the static noise and rolled down the driver's side window an inch or two to let in the cool morning air. It smelled of evergreens.

Emma began to feel a bit peckish. Keeping one hand on the wheel, she reached for one of the bags Sandra had packed. Emma wormed her fingers into the bag labeled *Emma—thank you, Sandra*—looking for a snack. She took her eye off the road for what seemed like just a fraction of a second. But in the blink it took for her to grab hold of her sandwich, a moose stepped into the road.

Emma screamed and twisted the wheel sharply to the left in order to avoid hitting the animal head-on. The scream woke Marcus, who also began screaming as Emma's bag went flying out of her hand and the vehicle left the road and went into the median. The grass was slick with moisture, and Emma braked hard. The car began to spin around and around as it went hurtling down the divide like some demented gymnast.

The whole incident was over in seconds, but when her car finally stopped moving, they found themselves several hundred yards down the highway and facing the opposite direction.

Papers were scattered across the dashboard, and by some weird happenstance, Emma's unopened breakfast sandwich was in her lap.

"Are you okay?" Marcus asked, his voice still panicky.

"I'm okay." Emma's feet were planted firmly on the brake pedal, and it took her several moments before she could mentally force her right hand to release its hold on the steering wheel and put the car into park. "You okay?"

"I'm okay."

Emma was still so terrified she could feel her toes trembling inside her sneakers. She struggled to catch her breath and closed her eyes. She counted backward from ten, and when she reached one, she exhaled one long, deep breath, as if she were trying to expel the fear from her lungs. She opened her eyes and screamed again, making Marcus scream.

"What is it?"

The moose who'd instigated the whole encounter had meandered across the highway and into the median and was now standing right outside Emma's driver's side window. He peered into the car as if he were checking to make sure she was okay. He was so close Emma could see the reflection of the overhead light—which she'd somehow managed to switch on in the melee—in the animal's big black eyes.

She cursed, and the moose jerked its massive head back, perhaps in mild reproach of her foul language. He tossed his head, long ears twitching, and grunted. The moose watched them intently for another second or two, then, deciding there was nothing more to see, turned and wandered back into the woods.

Alone in the dark, Emma sat there stunned, watching the moose disappear into the foliage, half of her cursing the beast and the other half pleading, "Don't leave us alone out here!" As the tip of its tail vanished behind a fir tree, they began to laugh. When she had managed to calm down, Emma opened the car door and stepped out onto the grass. Although the grass was quite slippery, the ground below her was rigid.

Good, she thought, *not muddy. That should make getting out a little easier.*

The silence around them was absolute. In both directions, dark unlit lines of highway stretched out before her. A sea of evergreens swayed hypnotically around the lone woman who dared violate their sanctum. Tree limbs, rubbing bark against bark, signaled and spoke to one another, bound together by some ancient siren's song that only they could hear. Their whispered protestations ran through the air toward the intruder, who heard them as the mere rustling of leaves.

Marcus walked around the vehicle to see what, if any, damage had been done to the car itself. No damage. He took a moment to check each of the tires. No flats.

"Thank God for small miracles," Emma muttered to herself.

Emma leaned against the car and looked up at the starry night above her. It was so quiet out here, these wilds of Nova Scotia. A gentle wind rustled through the trees, grazing her face as it passed by.

Emma.

Emma flinched, her eyes flying open. She knew the voice was in her head, but it still caught her by surprise. "Did you hear that?"

"Hear what?"

Emma, it echoed.

Emma looked around. There was no one there.

Emma, the voice chimed again.

The voice had been as clear as if the speaker were standing right next to her. But it had been in her head, right? Right? It had been one of those id versus ego conversations people have with themselves. Right?

Doubting herself, Emma looked around a second time. She hadn't heard any vehicles approaching. They were still the only car out on the highway. But they were no longer alone.

The wind had fallen still, and the trees had stopped their talking. A dense fog rolled into the area, obscuring Emma's view of the trees on either side of the highway. It surrounded them on all sides, closing in around them until Emma could no longer distinguish where the fog ended and the gray asphalt began.

Emma.

"Emma? Where are you?"

Marcus moved around the vehicle to where Emma was standing.

Emma.

"I heard that," Marcus said.

Emma spun around to see who the speaker was, though she knew already what she was going to find. A hundred yards or so behind her car—west toward Digby—was Alice. Resolute. Determined. Not smiling or frowning. Not menacing or comforting. She was just . . . there. As Emma and Marcus watched, Alice raised a hand and beckoned her to come.

"Tell me you see her," Emma whispered.

She glanced over. Marcus's shocked expression was answer enough. Emma stepped toward Alice, but as she reached the trunk of the car, the fog enveloped Alice, leaving Emma alone once again.

"Alice!" Emma called out.

"Emma, come back! Where'd you go?"

"Alice!"

The fog began to move around her as she took more desperate steps in Alice's direction.

"Alice! Help me, Alice!"

"Emma! I can't see you! Where did you go?"

A twig snapped off to her left, and Emma turned to see what was there. She lost her footing and tripped over a half-exposed rock. Emma went face-first into the dirt and came up spitting out grass. From her knees, she cupped her hands around her mouth and yelled, "Alice!"

She appeared out of the fog mere feet in front of Emma, and Emma sprang back in surprise, ending up on her butt.

"Emma?"

"Alice," Emma whispered. "Help me."

The girl remained silent. She crossed the distance between them and extended a hand to help Emma up. Emma looked at the proffered hand, wondering whether to take it. One side of her brain was telling her to take it.

She's trying to help you up, it told her.

The other half of her brain told her not to.

Unsure of which one to believe, Emma remained frozen to the ground below her. Until the hand reached forward and tenderly brushed a blade of grass out of Emma's hair. She felt that. Felt the hair on her head move as the grass was brushed aside. Felt the slight brush of skin against skin as Alice's fingers withdrew. Emma looked up at the hand, still hovering in front of her. She reached out and took it.

In the seconds it took for Emma to get to her feet, Alice was gone. The fog was gone. The evening wind resumed, and the trees and insects picked up their prior conversations. Emma turned around. She was a few hundred yards from her car now. She didn't think she'd walked that far away from it, but nonetheless, she began walking back.

"Emma!" Marcus called out. He had drifted the opposite direction. "Thank God! Are you all right?"

"I'm fine. You saw her, didn't you?"

Marcus nodded. "I saw her. What do we do?"

Emma reached for the door handle. "We finish this."

"Okay." Marcus stepped around to the driver's side. "But why don't I drive for a while?"

Emma collected her breakfast sandwich and walked around to the passenger side. Marcus cranked the engine, put the car into reverse, and slowly backed out of the median onto the highway and continued to Saint John.

Two hours later, Marcus's cell phone rang. He looked at the screen.

"Headquarters." He pulled over to the side of the highway and turned on the hazard lights.

"Cameron speaking. Hold on, Sam. Calm down. Wait, what?"

"What?" Emma whispered from the passenger seat. The shock on his face made her reach out to touch his arm in support.

"They set fire to the historical society this morning."

"They *what?*"

"Someone set fire to the museum. Yeah, I'm here with Ms. Campbell now. The whole thing?" He looked at Emma, shaking his head. "It's gone."

"Oh my God."

"Can you manage without me a few hours, Sam? I'm halfway to Saint John. Yes, New Brunswick. Yes, the chief knew. I told her last night when I put in the request. Right. Do they know when the fire started? An hour ago. No, she's been with me since three this morning, and I was on surveillance last night. She was at the Fishmonger all night."

They think I did it.

The half conversation was driving Emma insane.

"Have Steve bring the arson team in from Halifax if they need support."

"Arson?" Emma asked.

"Right. We'll be on the late ferry back tonight. Yes. Call me if anything changes. I'll have my phone with me all day. Okay then. Bye." He hung up and tossed the phone onto the dash.

"The museum burned down?"

"Yeah."

"And they think I did it, don't they?"

"No."

Emma began to panic. "Marcus, I heard you. 'She's been with me since three, and I was on surveillance all night.' They actually think I did this?"

"No!" Marcus shouted, turning in his seat. "They're asking because you're an active person of interest in an ongoing case involving vandalism, intimidation, assault, attempted murder, and now arson!"

"Stop shouting!"

Marcus drummed his fingers on the steering wheel. "I'm sorry. I'm as frustrated as you are with this. But all of this started the day you drove into town."

That hurt. Emma balled her fists tight, willing herself not to cry. "So, this is all my fault?"

Marcus blew a long breath out. "I don't think this—any of this—is your fault, Emma. But you've stirred a pot that clearly didn't want to be touched."

"Maybe it would be better if I left it alone. Went home and forgot the whole thing."

Marcus reached for her hand, but Emma pulled away, folding her arms across her chest.

"I think it's too late for that. Whatever this is, Emma. You've got to see it through now."

"I'm not sure I can," Emma stammered, fighting back tears.

"Come on." Marcus nudged her as he put the car back into gear. "Let's go to school."

XXIII

Marcus pulled into the parking lot of Saint Thomas School shortly before nine o'clock. A chilly morning wind off the bay swept through the city and tousled Emma's hair through her partially open window. She checked her makeup in the passenger side mirror.

"Pathetic," she said to herself.

"You look great to me," Marcus said, smiling ear to ear.

"Thanks."

They had stopped at a fast-food joint on the outskirts of Saint John where Emma changed clothes and bought them both a fresh coffee. Her cream summer top, slim-fit jeans, and sandals were quite stylish but were little comfort given the weather. Emma reached for her denim jacket in the back seat, and the two of them hurried across the parking lot to the main entrance.

The three-story edifice of gray Canadian granite loomed over her as they approached. Perfectly aligned windows lined each floor and presented a very orderly appearance. Later two-story additions built of contrasting red brick had been built at both ends, giving it the appearance of an upside-down *U*. Subtle differences in trim work, embellishments (or lack thereof), and color palette gave clues as to the decade in which the wings had been constructed. A very Dickensian structure, Saint Thomas School was, and not in the warm, Christmassy sort of way either. Emma couldn't help but be reminded of Dante's famous line . . .

Abandon all hope, ye who enter here.

It broke her heart knowing her great-grandmother had been relegated to such a dour institution.

"God," Emma muttered aloud.

"I'm not so sure that's the word I'd use," Marcus countered.

"I hear ya."

"So, assuming Alice was already here in April of '47, based on Julian's diary," Marcus said, thinking through their conversations on the ride over, "that would suggest Alice was sent away right after they discovered she was pregnant with the Morrison boy's baby."

"That poor girl." *How lonely she must've been those long months,* Emma thought. "I still can't believe they did it."

"Did what?"

"Abandoned their daughter to this—" Emma pressed her fist to her mouth, fighting back the rage she was feeling. "This hell, Marcus."

Marcus stepped closer and pulled her hand down. "Consider the time, Emma. I know you're angry right now, but think of this from Toby and Cici's perspective."

"Alice was raped, Marcus," Emma said, fuming at his explanation. It angered her even more knowing he was right. "That wasn't her fault. And if a man got a girl pregnant back then, the families would've forced them to marry to avoid this very situation!"

"Not if the shame of marrying down was greater than the shame of an unwed mother-to-be."

"So, they'd rather ship their daughter off to have a baby in secret instead of marrying her off to the poor folks on the wrong side of the tracks?"

"You're still seeing this from the benefit of seventy years," Marcus pressed. "Remember what Julian said in his diaries: Cici was ridiculed out of the grocery store by the very women she once called her friends."

Emma sat down on the hood of the car, still too mad to argue.

"And that was *after* they sent Alice away," he continued. "Can you imagine what their lives would've been like if they *hadn't* sent her away? What *Alice's* life would've been like?"

"Maybe you're right."

Her discovery of Nellie's true mother was a harsh pill for Emma. The lie Toby and Cici had had to commit themselves to. Denying Gran the truth about her mother. The truth of their family still in Canada. All for what? Pride? Shame? Maybe a bit of both, perhaps. A toxic mix if ever there was one.

It had been even harder for her uncle to accept. She'd called him after speaking with Marcus, and he laughed it off when she shared what she had discovered. Laughter turned to anger. Anger turned to denial. Denial turned to hurt. And hurt . . . shattered him.

"I have proof, Uncle Adi," Emma told him, pushing through her own tears. "I'm looking at Alice's obituary right now. She didn't die in early 1947 the way I thought before. She died in October 1947."

But he resisted. "And what makes you think you're right *this* time?"

"I have an appointment with the school history teacher in the morning. He's going to let me go through the records. See what I can find."

Adrian fell silent for a moment. Emma could hear his labored breathing. The ragged exhales to hide the sobs beneath. "Call me when you leave the school."

Emma tucked her arm into Marcus's, steadying herself against the storm of emotions raging in her body and mind as they approached the glass doors, following signage that read *Front Office* with bright red arrows leading the way.

A teenage girl no more than fifteen or sixteen greeted them as they entered the office. Despite her youth, she was dressed quite conservatively, almost spinsterly. She wore an ill-fitting long-sleeve white blouse tucked into a black three-quarter length skirt. Her ginger hair was pulled back into a ponytail, and she wore no jewelry at all, not even a watch.

"Hello. Can I help you?"

Emma's confidence blossomed as the girl gave an approving once-over of her outfit.

"Hi," Emma replied, trying to be cheerful despite her nervousness. "My name is Emma Campbell. I called yesterday and spoke with someone about records from Saint Emiliani. My great-grandmother was a ward here."

The girl looked around the disheveled desk, searching for something.

"Yeah," she said, lifting stacks of paper and books, "Angie left a note here somewhere. Aha!" She snatched a scrap of paper from the edge of her desk. "There it is. Yes. Nine o'clock with Mr. Crosse, is that right?"

"Yes, that's right. He's the history teacher, I believe."

"Yes, ma'am. And a bit of a local historian, so he'll be a great resource if you have any other questions."

"Thank you."

She stood and handed Emma and Marcus clipboards with several pages tucked under the large metal clips.

"If I could have you both sign in, I'll call Mr. Crosse and let him know you're here. Cute jacket, by the way. I love your shoes."

"Thanks."

She picked up the phone and dialed a number while they filled out the sign-in sheet. Name and date were easy enough, but the last two columns left Emma blank. She glanced at Marcus, who had the same puzzled look on his face.

"Host?" she asked the receptionist.

"Put Mr. Crosse down. He—oh, hello, Mr. Crosse. Suzanne here at the front office. Your visitor is here." She paused, holding her index finger up to Emma in that universal gesture of "please wait."

"The one Angie put on your calendar yesterday. They're here to take a look at the Saint Emiliani records. Yes, sir. Okay, thank you." She dropped the receiver back into its cradle and turned to Emma. "He's on his way. Shouldn't be but just a few minutes."

"You were saying about a host," Marcus said.

"Oh, right. Write Mr. Crosse's name there. The school doesn't allow unsupervised visitors, so guests must always have a teacher or one of the security personnel with them."

"Security personnel? At a private school?"

"They're basically just hall monitors." Suzanne shrugged. "If you'd like to sit down until Mr. Crosse gets here?" She motioned to a collection of leather chairs along the wall opposite her. None of them, Emma noticed, looked very comfortable.

"Thank you, but no. I've been in a car all morning, and my legs could use a good stretch."

"All morning?" Suzanne asked, glancing at the clock on her computer screen. "Where are you coming from?"

"That will do, Suzanne," came a singsongy voice from behind them.

Emma turned to find the tall, lanky figure of Sister Mary Elizabeth. Her silver hair was pulled back in a simple bun at the base of her skull. A pair of black half-rimmed reading glasses hung from a thin silver chain around her neck, along with a second silver chain with a pendant of the Crucifixion nestled between two shapeless breasts. She wore a long sleeve white cotton blouse, which was tucked into a long black skirt that stopped exactly two inches from the floor. A pair of black orthopedic shoes peeked out from under her skirt.

She had the face of a prune, wrinkled with two thin lines that barely passed for lips. Emma wondered if the woman had ever smiled in her life.

She had deep-set emerald eyes. Razor-sharp and hardened by time, they bored into Emma. Her gnarled hands were clasped together in front of her as if she were half expecting, half daring you to say something, *anything*, to challenge her authority. And Emma suddenly felt as guilty as a wayward sinner.

"The lady and gentleman have not come all this way to be hounded by your incessant questions, Suzanne," she stated with a prim voice.

"Yes, Sister," the girl said, sufficiently chastened. She turned to her computer and, with head bowed, busied herself with work.

"I am Sister Mary Elizabeth," the woman announced with more than a little piety. "And you are . . . ?"

"Emma Campbell."

"Hello," the nun said, extending her hand.

"Marcus Cameron."

"Hello, sir. You made good time, Ms. Campbell," Sister Mary Elizabeth said, glancing up at the clock on the wall.

"We left Digby early this morning," Emma said, a wink to Suzanne in response to the question she had asked before they were interrupted. "And traffic was light."

"At this hour, I should hope so."

Emma caught the curious look at her bandages on her face and arms. In her haste to leave, she had forgotten to take them off. Feigning embarrassment and hoping sympathy would help their plight, she touched the bandage on her temple.

"Car accident."

"Looks serious."

"She was lucky," Marcus said.

"Indeed."

"I'm very grateful you still have—"

"Yes, I'm afraid you may have come all this way for nothing, Ms. Campbell," Sister Mary Elizabeth interrupted.

"Sorry?"

"You see, the records we have are quite personal and confidential. It would be inappropriate to let the general public walk in and take a look. I'm sure you understand the need to protect these girls' privacy, of course, even if most of them have departed this life, may their souls rest in peace."

She signed the cross across her chest, the beads of her rosary jangling in her right hand as she did.

"But I only want to see one person's records, Sister," Emma pleaded. "My great-grandmother's."

"Perhaps," the wiry woman said dismissively. "Still, you must understand the situation, Ms. Campbell. Unless you have proper documentation authenticating your identity and relation to the person in question, I—"

"I believe I can help with that, Sister," Marcus said, cutting her off. She narrowed her eyes to slits. He reached into his back pocket and set his shield on the counter. "My name is Officer Marcus Cameron. RCMP. Digby Branch."

The nun feigned a glance before looking back to Marcus, sizing him up.

"I wasn't aware police uniforms were so casual these days, Officer Cameron. You expect me to believe this is official business"—she switched back and forth between them—"when you waltz into my office in jeans and a summer dress."

Emma wanted to slap the smirk right off her face. Marcus, however, held firm. He cleared his throat and stared back at her.

"My partner and I," he began, "are here on official business, Sister Mary Elizabeth."

"Is that so?"

"We're investigating a series of events in Digby, which we have reason to believe tie back to a cold murder case."

Sister Mary Elizabeth blinked, the color draining from her prudish face.

Suzanne gasped.

"Our investigation," he continued, "led us to one Alice Roberts, who was admitted to Saint Emiliani Home for Girls in early 1947, where she gave birth to a child later that same year. You pointed out my partner's physical condition earlier. She said it was an accident. That was a lie. The suspect assaulted her, and she was lucky to escape with her life. We are here today, Sister Mary Elizabeth"—Marcus was practically hurling words at the old crow now—"dressed in this manner for *your* sake."

"*My* sake, Officer?"

"Yes, Sister. Considering the price tag of your school and the . . . prominence of the families who send their children to school here, we felt it best to fly under the radar, so to speak. Best to avoid any unpleasant questions from concerned parents. Am I right?"

Emma glanced over at Suzanne, who sat perfectly still in front of her monitor. Her hand was pressed over her mouth, but Emma could just make out the corner of her smile.

"Yes, Officer," Sister Mary Elizabeth finally replied. Her words were hesitant. Unsure. And definitely worried. "I appreciate your tact and sensitivity."

"You're welcome," Marcus said, his words still sharp as knives. "Now, if you would be so kind as to alert Mr. Crosse that his visitors are here, we'll be on our way."

Before the Sister could say anything further, the door to the office opened, and in stepped a balding middle-aged man with a round midsection. Underneath the sickly yellow of his faded cardigan, he wore a crisp white oxford with matching black tie and khakis.

"Ah!" he said, caught off guard by the presence of Sister Mary Elizabeth. "Sister. What a surprise. I thought you'd be in class."

"Mr. Crosse." She said it with such disdain that Emma gave the secretary a nervous look, but Suzanne had started typing furiously at something, trying her best to be invisible. "This is Officers Marcus Cameron and Emma Campbell. They're here to see the Emiliani records downstairs." The woman turned and strode back into her office and promptly closed the door.

"Andrew Crosse," the man said as he approached Emma. "Pleased to meet you."

"Emma Campbell."

"Marcus Cameron."

"Well, now that that's settled." He chuckled. "Suzanne, everything in order?"

"Yes, sir," the girl said, turning her head away from her computer. "They're both signed in."

"Excellent. Well, let's be on our way, shall we?" He stepped aside, holding the office door open for Emma. "This way, if you please, to the right."

Mr. Crosse walked away from the main office down a wide hallway that ran the length of the building. Plush carpeting muffled their footsteps as he took Emma and Marcus past classroom doors with large glass inserts filling the upper half to allow someone—Sister Mary Elizabeth, Emma presumed—to monitor the goings-on of a classroom. They rounded the corner and stopped in front of an elevator. Andrew pressed the down arrow. Behind the closed doors around them, Emma could hear activity in the classrooms as they waited. Teachers giving dictation. Students asking questions. The sudden rap of a ruler against a desk made Emma flinch and brought students' laughter to a sudden halt.

"Not to worry," Mr. Crosse said warmly. "Sister Mary Florence is all bark."

"I don't know," Marcus said, his eyes never leaving the door. "Sounds like she has plenty of bite too."

They stepped into the elevator.

"Sorry you had to witness that. Back at the office, I mean."

"Witness what?"

"School politics, I'm afraid."

"Every office has them, Mr. Crosse," Marcus said.

"Please, call me Andrew."

"For a moment I thought I was going to get detention," Emma joked.

"If I hadn't shown up when I did, you probably would have." He glanced at Emma's shoes. "The Sister's not a fan of open-toed shoes."

Emma's face reddened.

"Oh, it's just a generational thing," Crosse said, trying to reassure her. "She believes bare feet are the pathway to sin and iniquity."

Emma, who was standing just behind him in the cramped elevator box, cocked an eyebrow.

"Seriously?"

"Mm-hmm. Here we are."

The basement level was much quieter and cooler than the floor above. Gooseflesh sprouted up and down Emma's legs as she stepped into the dimly lit hallway. White tile worn from the passage of time replaced the thick carpet, and Emma's sandaled footsteps echoed off the walls as Crosse led them to a small windowless room roughly twenty feet by twenty feet. Industrial fluorescent lighting hummed overhead as Crosse propped the door open. Metal shelving ran floor to ceiling along all four walls. Several four-drawer filing cabinets sat in the center of the room, along with a wood table with four tan folding chairs arranged around it. One of the fluorescent bulbs across the room was going out. It blinked sporadically as Emma looked around the storage room.

"Now then," Andrew said, motioning to the empty chairs. "As I understand it, you're looking for records from the old girls' home, am I right?"

"Yes," Marcus said. "Alice Roberts specifically."

"She was my great-grandmother," Emma added.

"Do you know when this was?"

"It was 1947," Emma said.

"Possibly late 1946," Marcus said. "But no later than April '47."

"Alice Roberts," Andrew repeated, drawing the syllables out as he walked to one of the shelves and pulled down a dusty large volume with *1940s* written on the spine. "Let's see if we can find her, shall we?"

"That's quite a large book for just one decade, Mr. Crosse."

"Andrew," he reminded her. "There was a lot of coming and going back in those days."

"Coming and going?"

Is it possible Alice left this place? Emma thought.

"Yes." Andrew's fingers ran across page after page. "The lucky ones didn't stay very long. They found positions as household staff to some of the wealthier households. Or if they were old enough to marry and could find a suitable man, they married and started homes of their own. Ah, here she is. Alice Roberts."

Emma and Marcus leaned over the table to see the handwritten entries Andrew was pointing out.

"I can make you copies of all this, of course, but basically this is a registrar book of the girls who were living here at the time." He pointed to the labels across the top of the page as he called them out. "You have the girl's name, the date she first entered Saint Emiliani, her record number--"

"Record number?" Marcus asked.

"Those would be personal to one specific girl. Each girl had her own record."

"What would be in these records?" Emma asked.

"Personal information. A bit of backstory on the child. Parentage. Her employment history would be there. Wages. Clothing sizes. Allergies, if she had any. Medical history. Everything pertaining to the girl would've been in her record."

"What are these other columns?" Emma asked, trying to get him back on track.

"Let's see. Name and age of admission . . . And the reason for the girl's departure."

Emma was already one step ahead of him. Using line of sight, she traced the line from Alice's name on the left across the page. Her breath caught as she reached the last column. She knew it was coming, knew what she was going to find, but seeing it in black and white still stung. Her mouth went bitter as nausea overtook her, and Emma sat down. Her knuckles turned white as she gripped the edges of her chair.

"Record number," Andrew continued, unaware of the chasm opening under Emma.

She stared blankly across the table at the file cabinets, and in a moment of elucidation, she understood each one was filled with countless more Alices. Each one someone's daughter. Each one discarded by society. Each one left to wither and die in this place like unwanted fruit on the garden vine.

"The date she left Saint Emiliani."

Emma closed her eyes, preparing herself for the last pronunciation.

"And the reason for the girl's departure."

There it was. The girl's "departure." As if she were merely off on holiday, enjoying a nice day at the beach or hiking through the woods. ETA: unknown. She'd be back soon enough. No need to worry.

"Emma?" Marcus touched her shoulder. "You okay?"

She cleared her throat. Relaxing her grip, Emma fluttered her lashes, whisking away the mist in the corners, and looked up at Crosse.

"Sorry. It was a long drive from Nova Scotia this morning," she lied.

"Would you like me to get either of you a coffee? Water, maybe?"

"No, that's all right," Emma said.

"It's no problem," he assured her. "There's always a fresh pot in the teacher's lounge.

"No, thank you." Emma rose from her chair and glanced down at the open records book. "I'm fine."

"Well, if you change your mind."

"I'll let you know." She sighed, reading the line across the page once again.

Alice Roberts, 15	12 March 1947	R97964	8 Oct 1947	Died in childbirth

"I'm so sorry."

Andrew reached for a box of Kleenex sitting atop a nearby filing cabinet. He gave the box a rough shake, sending a thick layer of dust into the air. He gave it a brush with the back of his hand and passed it to Emma.

"It's all right." She accepted the tissue out of courtesy, but Emma was past tears at this point. "I sort of guessed she was here when she died. Seeing it on paper though . . ."

"Makes it real," Marcus said, finishing her sentence.

"Yeah. Real."

"Would you like to take a break?" Andrew asked. "Maybe step outside and get some air before we continue?"

Emma shook her head. The last thing she wanted was to have an emotional breakdown in front of Sister Mary Sourpuss and a school full of rich kids.

"No, I've come a long way to find Alice." She cleared her throat. "So, let's find her."

"Right," said Andrew, trying to step out of the awkward situation he now found himself in. "Let's find that record, shall we? R97964. Now, let's see . . ." He walked to the other side of the room and scanned the wall of volumes.

"Can we help, Andrew?" asked Marcus.

"Nope. I found it."

He returned to the table and set the volume down. Emma was surprised to see Alice's record was more a box than an actual book. Andrew untied the dark brown string laced around it and carefully opened the cover. Amongst Alice's scant belongings was a bundle of letters neatly tied with a bit of twine.

"May I?"

"Of course."

Emma untied the string and examined the top letter closely. They were addressed to Alex Fischer, not to Alice. The sender was listed as:

Helga Morris
General Post Office
Digby, Nova Scotia

"I don't understand. These letters belong to someone else. Why would they be in Alice's records?"

"Hmm, that is curious." Crosse took a letter from the stack and opened it with delicate fingers. "This one too. Addressed to 'Dear Alex' and signed 'Always your friend, Helga.' "

"Did you find any mention of Helga Morris in your research?" Marcus questioned, opening a third letter.

"No." Emma shrugged. "This is the first I'm hearing of her."

"And who's this Alex Fischer?" Crosse asked. "Have you come across him before?"

"No." Emma sat back down with the stack of letters and began scanning them. "Ms. Alda and I never came across an Alex. Better still, who was Alex . . . to Alice?"

"Most curious," Andrew said, scanning the letter in his hand.

"Could he be the baby's father?" Marcus asked.

"I mean," Crosse tried clarifying, "given the nature of what Saint Emiliani was back then."

"I don't think so," Emma said. "Julian's diaries clearly implicate the Morrison boy."

Crosse opened his mouth to respond, but the crackly voice of Sister Mary Elizabeth over the intercom cut him off.

"Mr. Crosse?"

Andrew rolled his eyes. He looked at his watch. "I have class soon," he whispered to Emma as he turned back to the door and pressed a button next to a speaker mounted on the wall.

"Yes, Sister."

"Your next class begins in ten minutes, Mr. Crosse. Will you and your guests be finishing up soon?"

He glanced back at Emma. "Actually, they left a few minutes ago, Sister. I was just tidying up before going back upstairs."

Emma went to protest, but Crosse held a finger to his lips, urging her to remain silent.

"I see," came the stony reply. "And were they successful with their query?"

"The girl died in childbirth here. October '47, I think. But they got the answers they were looking for, I believe. I don't think they'll be back."

"Very well, Mr. Crosse. Please lock everything up and make sure the lights are all turned off before you return to class."

"Yes, Sister," he said with thinly veiled contempt.

"Good day to you, Mr. Crosse."

"Good day."

And with that, the intercom fell silent.

"But—" Marcus began.

"I know that old crow," Andrew interrupted. "Anything you wanted to photocopy, she'd want to know why. It'd be like the damn Spanish

Inquisition, only in miniature form." He glanced again at his watch. "Why don't you stay for now?"

"But what if she finds us down here?" Emma asked.

Crosse laughed. "Mary Elizabeth has never been in the basement for as long as she's been here."

"But—"

"Don't worry about the Sister. You'll be fine. Trust me. I have to get to class, but as soon as it's done, the kids have lunch period. That gives you at least an hour and a half to look through everything and make copies."

"Is there a machine down here?" Marcus asked.

"Yes." Andrew fumbled in his pocket and pulled out his key ring. After separating one key from the rest, he handed it to Emma. "This key opens the room next door. There're a couple copiers in there. I'll be back in an hour once class is over to help you finish up and help you back upstairs." He took Emma's notebook from the table and scribbled something down before handing it to her. "This is my cell. If you get into any trouble, just text me, and I'll come down."

"What about our car?" Marcus asked. "It's still in the visitors' parking lot. Won't she see it?"

"You can't see the visitor parking lot from the main offices," he explained. "There's a row of hedge and evergreen trees blocking line of sight. I'll be back in one hour."

"One hour," Marcus repeated.

And with that, Emma and Marcus were left on their own, surrounded by too many questions and too few answers.

It took them four letters to figure it out.

Marcus was leaned back in his chair with his feet propped up on the table. "Is it just me, or do these read like Alex is an actual person?"

"I was getting that same impression. Take this letter here. Helga says she included two pounds for Alex as a thank you."

"And she keeps apologizing," Marcus said. "What's up with that?"

"I noticed that too. Every letter she apologizes for what she did."

"And what happened after. Any ideas?"

"Not yet."

"Okay, let's talk this out." He stood, scratched his head, and began pacing around the table. "You're Alice."

"Great," Emma replied sarcastically. "Love where this is going already."

"You've been sent away by your family to a girls' home run by the Church for unwed expecting mothers."

"Right."

"Which means you're not likely to receive mail from them, given the shame of your situation."

"Or," Emma countered, "they cut off all correspondence. From anyone outside."

"Like the person you used to be doesn't exist anym—"

"What?"

"I have an idea." Marcus sent Crosse a text message.

Employee records? From the 40s

Seconds later, his reply came through.

ANDREW CROSSE
Far left corner. Top drawer.

Scrolling through the alphabet, Marcus found her query: Alex Fischer. His file was thin. Clearly, he had not worked at Saint Emiliani very long. Marcus opened it and began reading.

"Bingo. Emma, take a look at this."

"What'd you find?"

Marcus spread the folder open on the table between them. "Alex Fischer. The groundskeeper."

"Nice work, Detective." Emma said. She lightly punched his shoulder.

With the discovery of Alex's identity, the fog of questions began to settle and clear. Childhood friends were seldom abandoned. Alice and Helen's friendship had continued through correspondence after her banishment and Toby and Cici's sudden departure.

As Emma and Marcus examined the dozen or so letters laid out on the table in front of them, the picture became clear enough to make out.

Helen's father had been the postmaster, and it would have been only natural during that time, given the global situation, for children to help out wherever they could, so it could be assumed Helen would have responsibilities at the local post office to help the family.

They had done it right under everyone's noses. The groundskeeper on Alice's end—paid in some way Emma didn't want to think about—would post Alice's letters to Helen. Helen, on the other end, was likely responsible for sorting and putting away mail and would've had no problem pulling out Helga Morris's letters without being caught. Even if someone else had sorted the day's mail, no one knew who Helga Morris was. No one knew where she lived. Correspondence would inevitably end up in the dead letters box, from which Helen could easily collect them without anyone noticing.

"Clever girls," Emma said with pride.

"I have to admit it was genius what they did," Marcus said. "And to use pseudonyms. Genius!"

"Perfect anonymity. And it gave them complete deniability. Even if they were caught, the letters weren't addressed to them."

"Always Alex and Helga. Smart." Marcus nodded. "They must've been really close friends."

"Their whole life. Judging by how many letters are here, I'd say Helen wrote once a week—maybe more than that—the whole time Alice was here."

"Which also means Alice probably smuggled out a letter each week," Marcus said, continuing Emma's train of thought. "Letters that were either stolen or—"

"Or went up in smoke in the fire this morning. Here. Take a look at this one." Emma handed him the letter she had just finished. He read it aloud.

" 'Sixteen today, my dear Alex. Remember when we were little? How we always had our birthday parties together? One big cake for both of us to share. Everyone called us the neighbor twins.' Wait, what?"

"Guess they were born on the same day," Emma said. Taking a heavy breath, she shook her head. "Looks like things got bad after they sent Alice away."

"How so?"

Emma read from the letter. " 'June 1947. My dear Alex, life has become so unbearably insufferable without you. My brothers have poisoned our parents against me. Called me unnatural and ungodly. Father has taken to locking me in my room when I'm not working at the post office. Mother will hardly look at me. Just bursts into tears each time I walk into the room. Please don't hate me for saying this, but I envy you, Alex. You escaped."

"Christ," Marcus said, tossing the trio of letters in his hand back onto the table. "How could anyone live like that? A pariah in your own house."

"Alice gets sent away, and Helen becomes a prisoner in her own home."

"But why?"

"Maybe Helen felt she was responsible for Alice's pregnancy."

"A boy she had introduced Alice to, maybe? It's possible."

"Whatever happened, the families considered both of them equally guilty." She leaned over the table, her eyes wandering from letter to letter.

"All right, girls," Emma entreated. "What am I missing? What are you not saying?"

"If they answer you," Marcus joked, "I'm out of here."

They continued reading.

"Do you notice she never mentions the brothers by name?" Marcus asked after a few minutes.

Emma nodded. "Yeah. She refers to them as *B* and *C*. She does that with everyone in town. Never calls them by their name. Take this one, for example. Helen's talking about one of their schoolteachers, but instead of using her name, she says *'our English teacher.'*"

"Names changed to protect the guilty."

"Or innocent." She sighed. "At this point, I doubt we'll ever know who's who."

Emma passed the letter to Marcus and tenderly opened Helen's final letter to Alice.

" 'Tell my beloved my heart is still his,' " she said out loud.

"She says that in this one." Marcus reached for another letter. "And this one."

Emma did a quick scan of a few letters in front of her. "All of them."

"But . . . who's her beloved?" Marcus asked, his eyes searching the table for an answer.

The line was in each of Helen's letters, which made no sense to Emma or Marcus. Who was Helen talking about? As far as they knew, Alex Fischer had never met Helen, only Alice. And Alice had come over from Nova Scotia alone, so who else would be here besides—

"Oh, God."

"What?"

There was the answer. Right in front of her the whole time. Emma knew now why Helen had repeatedly apologized. She knew why Helen's parents had refused to let her leave the house. She knew why Toby and Cici had taken Nellie and fled to America. She knew whom Helen was talking to with the last line of her letters—*tell my beloved my heart is still* his.

Apart from the baby itself, Emma knew everything. The pieces fell into place, presenting an undeniable scenario Emma couldn't believe and yet couldn't shake off. Letter still in hand, she collapsed into the chair behind her.

"Lovers," Emma whispered to the emptiness around them. "Marcus, what if they were lovers?"

XXIV

By the time Andrew appeared in the doorway, Emma and Marcus had managed to make copies of almost everything: Alice's employment records; her family history; her medical history, including sporadic updates on her pregnancy and how the baby was progressing; Helen's letters; all of it. Near the bottom of the box, she found copies of Alice's death certificate and her grandmother Nellie's birth certificate. She had been born in the very building Emma now found herself in.

What a miserable existence to be born into, thought Emma.

"How's it going?" Andrew asked.

"Almost done." Emma said. "How was class?"

"Ancient Roman history this week."

"Sounds like fun," Marcus said.

"Not to teenagers," he huffed. "You find the copiers?"

"Yes, thank you," Emma said as she walked past him with the last handful of papers to photocopy. "I'm almost done."

"Wow! You work fast." He followed her into the next room as she continued making photocopies. "What did you find out? Did you figure out who Alex and Helga were?"

"I did."

"And?"

Marcus dropped the last few documents into the feed and pressed *Start* as Emma relayed everything they had learned over the past hour: the girls' relationship, Alex the groundskeeper, their secret correspondence and how they'd managed to pull it off.

"Hey, I did have one question though," Emma said.

"What's that?" Andrew asked.

Emma flipped through the photocopies being spit out and handed Andrew a single piece of warm paper. It was Nellie's birth certificate.

"This entry here, for the father?"

Andrew looked where she had pointed. The father was listed as *(Unknown)*.

"Have you ever seen that before?"

"Unknown father?"

"No, the parentheses. I've never seen those used before. What does it mean?"

An awkward silence fell between them, and Emma noticed the glance between Andrew and Marcus.

"Well . . ." This was the last conversation he wanted to have; Emma could see it as plain as the squat nose on Andrew Crosse's face. "You have to remember that back in those days, people swept a lot of things under the rug in order to not offend or embarrass people."

"Alice was raped."

The way Emma said it so calmly that Andrew took a step back, his expression both shocked and sympathetic.

"How did you—"

"You just told me," Emma replied. "It's okay, Mr. Crosse. We assumed as much given everything else we've discovered."

"Yes, well, doctors and the police didn't like using the word on official documents," Andrew explained, "because of the negative societal connotations associated with it, but an unknown father in parentheses was a generally understood code amongst the medical profession that the mother had been raped. I'm sorry."

"Thank you."

"My turn for a question. How did Alice's parents know about the baby? Did you find any correspondence between them during Alice's stay?"

"Only one," Emma clarified. "When they dropped their daughter on Saint Emiliani's doorstep. Dropped her off, paid her room and board, and left. No address. No communication. Nothing."

"That's harsh. So, how did they find out about your grandmother Nellie?"

"We found that out too," Marcus said. "There's an addendum to Alice's death certificate. Saint Emiliani had no contact information for Alice's family. Only these letters from Helga Morris. After Alice died, they notified Helga by mail. A carbon was put in Alice's records."

Marcus handed him a page. Andrew adjusted his wire-frame glasses and read.

October 8, 1947

Dear Mrs. Morris:

We regret to inform you that Ms. Alice Roberts died during childbirth earlier today. Her body was laid to rest this evening in Fernhill Cemetery here in Saint John. Please accept my condolences for your loss.

Before her passing, Alice gave birth to a beautiful baby girl, whom we have named Penelope. She survives and is in good health. While it is understandable that this is a difficult time for your family, immediate attention must be paid to the child in order to secure a proper upbringing for her.

The child will be placed in a temporary home with a loving family through October 16, 1947. If the family wishes to claim the child, please present yourself at the main office of Saint Emiliani between the hours of 9 a.m. and 3 p.m. on or before October 16, 1947. Arrangements will be made to collect and deliver the child to your care forthwith. If you choose not to claim the child, Saint

Emiliani will make arrangements on October 17, 1947, for the child to be
placed for adoption.

    Again, please accept my deepest condolences for your loss.
    With regards,
    Cynthia Skivington
    Saint Emiliani Home for Girls
    Saint John, New Brunswick

"That poor child," Andrew concluded.

"There's a handwritten note on the back dated a week after Alice's death," Emma said, "noting that the family had claimed the baby."

"Alice's parents?" Andrew said. "But how did they—"

"Helen must've told them," Marcus said.

"Makes sense. But how? From what you've just told me, Helen was almost as much a prisoner as Alice."

"We don't know." Marcus shrugged.

"We may never know," Emma said. "Anyone who might know the answer to that, Mr. Crosse, is already gone."

"At least you found the answers you were looking for, I hope."

Emma nodded. "Yes, Mr. Crosse. I have most of them."

"Yes, well . . . I, um, I brought some lunch down for you if you'd like to take a break. I can finish tidying up here."

"Thanks." She shrugged. "But we really shouldn't. We have a funeral back in Digby tomorrow, and there's still one more stop we need to make first."

"But you haven't eaten all morning. You said so yourself. Please, Emma. Stop for a minute and have some lunch."

They couldn't argue there. The sandwiches Sandra had packed had been the only thing they'd eaten since leaving Digby, and they were both now quite peckish. Emma looked to Marcus, letting him decide. His stomach rumbled, settling the matter.

"Thanks," Marcus said.

They were finishing their sandwiches when Andrew stepped into the room.

"What other stop do you need to make?"

"Hmm?"

"You said you had one other stop you needed to make first before leaving town. Where else are you going? If you mind my asking, that is."

"The cemetery," Emma said. "The letter said, 'her body was laid to rest.' Would the church have buried the actual body, do you think? Or would they have cremated her. . .given her situation and there being no family to cover the expense?"

"Definitely not cremation. The Catholic church was staunchly opposed to it back then. Even now, they only marginally condone it. No, according to my research, Saint Emiliani kept a small plot at Fernhill Cemetery on the east side of town. A pauper's grave, honestly."

"I see."

"The cemetery isn't that far away."

"And they could show me where Alice is buried."

"Actually," said Andrew as he perused the photocopied documents again, "it should be on her death certificate."

He found the document and flipped to the back. "There's the plot number."

XXV

"You have my cell," Andrew said, walking them out to the visitor parking lot. "Please call me if I can help in any way."

"Thank you, Mr. Crosse," Emma said, shaking the man's hand. "I really appreciate everything you've done for us."

"Yes, thank you, sir," Marcus added, extending his hand. "You were a great help today."

"It was the least I could do. I'm sorry about your great-grandmother, Ms. Campbell."

"Thank you."

A distant bell rang, and Andrew checked his watch.

"Five-minute bell. I need to get to my next class."

"Of course," Emma said, opening the passenger side door. "Thanks again."

Andrew made it halfway to the entrance before he stopped and ran back to the car. Marcus rolled down his window as Andrew leaned down.

"I don't know if you'd be interested or have time today, but the local historical society is presenting an exhibition in the Saint John Museum of Canadian History on Victorian boarding houses and orphanages. There were several items in our collection that were loaned out for the exhibit."

"They have Alice's things?" asked Emma.

"I don't know specifically, but possibly. It's a pretty extensive exhibit. I don't think there's anything there that would add to what you found here. Anything of relevance was photocopied, and the copies were put on display. The originals would have been kept here. But the exhibit has a lot of personal belongings that have been set up in little vignettes. It's not that far of a drive, and I know the curator. If you have an hour to spare, I could call him to see if he's available for a private tour. Might be worth your time."

Emma glanced at the dashboard. It was almost eleven o'clock. The ferry back to Digby left at four.

"It's on your way. In case you're worried about the time."

"Okay, sounds good," Marcus said. "Text me the address, and we'll stop by."

Andrew's directions were concise, and in less than ten minutes, they pulled up in front of an impressive wood home. Built over one hundred years earlier, its painted plank facade was quite lovely. A sign at the entrance to the driveway advertised "Saint John Museum of Canadian History."

Andrew had called ahead, and Emma and Marcus were met at the door by an elegantly dressed man in his forties named Will, according to his name badge. Will led them to the entrance to the exhibit and was about to begin his rehearsed monologue when Emma stopped him.

"Would you mind if we went through it by ourselves?"

"Certainly, miss," Will replied. "I'll be in and out if either of you need me or have any questions."

"Thank you."

The exhibit was well laid out. It began at the dawn of the Industrial Age and led to the rapid dissolution of families, which resulted in a swift rise in the number of orphans. From there, it moved into boarding houses for children. Oftentimes, the residents were mostly girls who had become pregnant out of wedlock. More often than not, however, the houses held girls—and boys—who were simply abandoned by parents who could no longer afford to clothe and feed the children they had. Emma scanned each vignette for signs of Alice but couldn't find any. Here and there, she spotted tiny markers reading "Donated by Saint Thomas Aquinas School." But as Andrew had pointed out before they'd left the school, there was nothing of importance in the exhibit that she didn't have in her shoulder bag already.

She was feeling a bit disappointed and more than a little tired when they rounded the last corner of the exhibit. Emma could hear other museum guests talking behind her, but she was done. All she wanted right then was to leave. To finish things with the cemetery and make it back to the ferry. To be done with the whole upsetting episode. And then, out of the corner of her eye, Emma caught sight of Alice.

"Emma? What's wrong?" Marcus asked. He wrapped his arm around her as she faltered, fearing she was about to faint.

Emma's pale hand pointed to the last vignette: a girl's dormitory room. A small bed, neatly made, was in the corner. There was a small desk with a lamp and a wooden chair. A bible lay on top of the desk. A chamber pot lay half-hidden under the bed. And there, in the middle of it all, was the girl. She looked to be about five foot six and had a wiry frame. The mannequin had been dressed in a reddish-brown wig parted into pigtails and wore a cream-colored top with a green jumper over it. A green jumper with large white gardenias.

Alice's dress. She knew it.

"That dress," she stated calmly, "belongs to my great-grandmother."

"How do you know that?"

Emma's eyes never left the mannequin. "Because Alice's daughter has a painting in her dining room. And in that painting, Alice is wearing *that* dress."

On the outskirts of Saint John, where Canadian wilderness had long yielded to modern suburbs, lay the secluded rolling hills of Fernhill Cemetery. Aged markers of granite and marble dotted both sides of the one-lane road traversing the property. There were no street markers here, no mileposts to mark the journey. It would've been easy to get lost, which perhaps was the intent of the city planners.

Emma almost missed it. Had Marcus not called her attention to the broken statue, she would have. Deep within the grounds, out of sight of the glitz and glamour of towering Victorian markers of the city's richest, they found a gravel lane. Grass had been allowed to completely overtake it, and markers had been placed right up to the edge on both sides. At the entrance stood a statue—more accurately *half* a statue. Broken at the waist, the top had long since been hauled away. What remained were the lower torso of a grown man and the headless form of a child, its hands clasped together in prayer. "Saint Emiliani" was carved across the base.

"This has to be it," Marcus said.

"I don't think the car will fit," Emma said, judging the width of the lane. "Those markers are too close to the road."

"Can't be too far from here. Pull over, and let's walk."

The ground was soft underfoot as they made their way down the path. Tree limbs stretched out overhead, casting shadows that danced over the road as the wind rustled through the trees. As they crossed a small hill, they saw a fenced plot with a few dozen markers inside it. Centered across the gate was a cross, the initials "SEHG" written in beautiful script at the intersection point.

"This is it," Emma said. "Saint Emiliani Home for Girls."

The gate was so rusty that the handle came away in pieces when Marcus tried to open it. The unoiled hinges screamed at them as Emma pushed it open.

"Would you mind giving me a moment?" Emma asked. "Please."

"Of course. Take as much time as you need. I'll be right here."

Three rows back, she found it: number forty-seven. No name. No date of birth. No date of death. Just a number on a stone marker no bigger than a brick. Emma knelt in front of it and placed a batch of yellow roses she'd purchased on top of it.

"Hello, Alice. My name is Emma. I'm . . . I'm your great-granddaughter. And I've come a very long way to find you." She began to sob. "I'm sorry, Alice. Sorry you were hurt. Sorry your family sent you away. I'm sorry you and Helen never got to live the life you wanted to live. I found your letters." Emma smiled. "She loved you so much, you know that?"

Emma's words failed as her emotions took over, and her tears fell harder down her cheeks. She covered her face with her hands as she bowed over, sobbing.

"S-sorry," she stuttered through her sobs, "you never got to know your daughter."

A warm wind danced across the lawn, kicking up dead leaves as the trees swayed in a wild rhythmic tune only they could hear. It washed across Emma's face, drying her tears as a faint "thank you" touched her ear.

Emma sat up.

"Alice."

The teenage girl was kneeling right in front of her. She looked roughly the same age as she had that day in the dining room. The age she would have been, Emma assumed, when she gave birth to her first and only child. The hand-stitched gardenias on her jumper shimmered in the sunlight like flowers kissed by a gentle spring rain.

"Alice." Emma extended her hand tentatively, not sure how the girl would react.

Alice reached out, taking Emma's hand in hers. She laughed, ultimately tossing her arms around Emma's neck, embracing her as only women can do.

"Thank you for not leaving me," Alice whispered into Emma's ear.

She pulled back, and her eyes shifted to Marcus. She giggled, a childish sound, and gave a sheepish wave.

"He can see you?"

Alice nodded. "He's a good man."

Emma blushed. "Yes. Yes, he is."

They stared at each other a moment longer.

"I'm bringing you home, Alice," Emma finally said. "Home to your daughter. Home to your family."

Alice smiled, leaning her head back to bask in the afternoon sun. Her pigtails flittered about in the breeze.

"I like it here," Alice said, lowering her head to look Emma in the eye again. "But there is something else."

Emma spent the rest of the afternoon filling out paperwork with the funeral home, which oversaw maintenance of Fernhill, to prove the remains in plot forty-seven belonged to Alice Roberts. Once Alice had been properly identified, there was paperwork to identify Emma as immediate family. Once she was recognized as an authorized family member, there was more paperwork authorizing the exhumation and cremation of those remains. And once the family's wishes were carried out, there was yet more paperwork.

Paperwork.

Paperwork.

Paperwork.

It was more than could be accomplished in a single day, the polite funeral director had explained to her. The process would take weeks, and Emma contented herself in the knowledge that she had at least set things in motion. Most of the rest could be filed online or by certified mail, which meant she could return home and tell the family what she had discovered and reunite Alice with the daughter she had never had the chance to get to know. For now, however, they needed to get to the harbor.

As the ferry pulled away from Saint John, scattered raindrops forced everyone inside, and Emma couldn't help but wonder if the gathering storm across the bay was a harbinger of things to come.

It was nearly six thirty when Emma and Marcus finally arrived back at the Fishmonger. As Marcus pulled into the drive, they caught sight of Dex on the front porch. He rose from a rocking chairs as Marcus killed the engine. His cell phone rang.

"The chief."

"I'll meet you inside," Emma said, leaving him in the car to take his call.

Dex must have called into the house for Connie and Sandra, because they had joined him on the porch by the time Emma reached the front steps. Despite the darkness of the storm overhead, which had taken a momentary break, Emma could see the worry lines on Dex's and Connie's faces. Sandra hung back and wouldn't look Emma in the eye.

"Thank goodness you're back," Dex said. "We were starting to get worried about you guys with the storm and all."

"How was the ferry ride back?" Connie asked. Emma could hear the concern in her words, but as she mounted the front steps, she could see the fury in the woman's eyes.

"It was choppy in places but not too bad. I'm just glad to be back on dry land."

"Where's Marcus?" Dex asked.

"He had to take a phone call. His chief, I think."

"At least you made it back safely," Dex said. There was a clear sign of relief in his voice. Connie, on the other hand, still seemed furious. And Sandra seemed suddenly skittish. A flash of lightning illuminated the sky, startling them all.

"Come in, everyone," Connie said. Emma recognized the feigned jollity to the woman's tone. "I've got a pot of tea brewing in the kitchen if anyone would like a cup."

Marcus had ended his call and was halfway to the porch. Emma tried to catch his attention, but he was distracted and noticeably upset.

"Marcus, would you like to come in for a cup of tea? I think I'll fix you a cup. Dex, will you come help me with the cups and saucers?"

She held the door open for Marcus and Dex, hanging back to drape her arm around Emma. As the men stepped away from them, Connie pulled back. She gripped Emma by the shoulders so tight her nails dug into the skin.

"Ow! Connie—"

"What are you mixed up in?"

Emma was too stunned by the question to respond. Connie pushed further.

"The RCMP have been here all day questioning Sandra about a conversation she had with you. And now with the fire and Ms. Alda's death."

"I'm not mixed up in anything," Emma replied. She tried keeping her voice calm to prevent the situation from escalating. "The police are just covering their bases."

"Covering their bases? Why would they need to interview you or Sandra in the first place?"

"Ladies?" Marcus asked. "Coming in?"

"On our way," Connie said cheerily before turning her scowl back on Emma. "We'll talk later."

"Sure."

Connie walked through the living room into the kitchen to join Dex. As she passed, Marcus pointed Emma toward the drawing room.

"Was your chief mad you took the day off?" Emma asked as she sat down on the edge of tufted settee.

"I want you on the next flight out of Nova Scotia."

"What?" That was unexpected.

"You heard me. I want you on the next plane back to America."

"But, Marcus—"

He fell to his knees in front of her and clutched her hands in his so tightly that she winced.

"Please, Emma," he begged. "No more questions. Do this for me. I need you out of Digby. Can you do this for me? Please."

"What happened, Marcus? What did your chief say on that phone call?"

He buried his face in her lap as a half cough, half sob came out.

She leaned forward, pushing him off her lap. His eyes were full of tears. The gleam Emma had first seen in them when they'd met had dulled to a burnished bluish gray. She gripped his shoulders with her hands. "Marcus . . ."

"I need you out of here. It's the only way you'll be safe."

"Tell me what happened. And then I'll go. First thing tomorrow."

Marcus caught his breath. He wiped his nose with the back of his hand, and Emma tried not to grimace.

"Ms. Alda. She . . . She didn't fall, Emma. She was pushed."

"Oh my God." Emma's hands flew to her mouth to stop her from crying out. She shook her head over and over. "No. No, that's not right. You said the coroner ruled it an accidental death."

"He did. But the funeral home sent the body back after finding some distinct bruising."

"Bruising? What kind of bruising?"

"Like those of a fist or open palm hitting the shoulders."

"No," Emma whispered. She pulled him to her as he broke down into heaving sobs. Together they cried, leaning against each other, their tears forming rivulets as they made their way down each other's bodies.

"Here we go," Connie said as she drew back the pocket door separating the sitting room from the living room. "Oh my! I'm sorry. I didn't mean to barge in—"

"It's all right, Connie," Marcus said, getting up from the floor. "You're fine."

"You just heard?"

Marcus turned on her with astonishment. "How did you know? I only just found out when we got back."

Connie's face went red as she glanced at Emma. "RCMP were here earlier. Interviewing everyone. Plus Digby's a small town. You know this place, Marcus. Nobody can keep a secret." She set down a tray with three cups of tea on it. "People have been pretty upset about it since word got out this afternoon." She handed them each a cup and matching saucer.

"Thanks," he said, reaching for a cup. "Who did you hear it from?"

"If you're asking me to throw my neighbors under the proverbial bus, Officer Cameron, I'm sorry. I won't do that." She paused, gauging his reaction. "But if I were an officer, I'd start with the phone records at the coroner's office."

Marcus dragged his hand over his face. "You mean someone in the coroner's office tipped off Franklin and his hounds, is that it?"

Connie smiled nervously. "No comment, Officer." She started backing out of the room. "Well, better go. Loads of work to catch up on with Dex. Anything else you need?"

"No," Emma said. "We'll be fine. Thank you for the tea."

"Night," Connie said timidly. "Bye."

She pulled the pocket door shut, leaving them alone in the room. Emma was about to say something when Marcus put his hand up to keep her from speaking. He pointed to the teacup in his hand. Emma gave him a confused look.

"Not hot," he mouthed as he set the cup down and stood.

Emma brought her cup to her lips. It was tepid. How long, she wondered, had Connie been standing at the door, eavesdropping on their conversation?

Marcus stepped toward the door, intentionally making his footfall louder than it would normally be, and they could hear someone outside scurry away. He reached the door and slid it open enough to poke his head out. There was no one there now. He observed the hallway for a couple minutes to ensure Connie didn't return before he turned back in, closing the door behind him. He stayed close to the door so he could hear if someone tried approaching again.

"Sorry about that," he said, smiling.

"I'm sorry too."

"For what?"

"For Ms. Alda. I know you were close. I wish I could've gotten to know her better."

"She liked you." Marcus grinned. "You brought out the mischief in her, I think."

Emma huffed, but a smile soon spread across her features. "No comment, Officer."

Marcus turned serious as he sat beside her. "Emma, there's something else. Something the chief told me this evening. There were a couple vandalisms while we were gone."

"What? Where?"

"Your room for one."

"Someone broke into my room?"

"Both rooms. Yours and mine. Dex heard someone walking around upstairs while we were gone, and Connie went to check. She didn't see anyone, but your room and mine had been turned out. All your stuff had been gone through, and whoever did it didn't bother cleaning up. The rooms were a right mess: drawers opened, bed covers pulled back."

"Oh, God."

"Connie called the police, and they took a look."

"Did they find anything?"

"They dusted for prints on the doors. Photographed everything. But whoever it was wore gloves."

"Where was the second?"

"Ms. Alda's house."

"Are you kidding me?"

"No. Someone ransacked her study."

"And they just discovered it today?"

"Taylor did when he—"

"Oh, God." Emma's hand flew to her mouth. "Her son. *He* found it?"

Marcus nodded. "Apparently, whoever did it pulled the front door closed when they left, so no one noticed it until Taylor and his family arrived for the funeral service tomorrow."

"That poor man. They must've been terrified."

"They're staying at a hotel until things are settled."

"That's good," Emma said, her teacup trembling in her panicked hand. "Still, knowing someone was digging around in my—"

"They're not here now, Emma." He placed a hand on her shoulder and gave it a slight squeeze. "And you're leaving in the morning."

Emma nodded.

"Good. I'm glad that's settled. You have all the answers you were looking—"

"Not all of them. I still don't know—"

"Who raped Alice. I know. But that is a matter for the police, so let us handle it, okay?"

"And when it's over?"

He leaned in to kiss her. "Always wanted to see the Grand Canyon," Marcus whispered. "Is that close by?"

Emma laughed, returning the kiss. "Oh, sure. Just down the road."

Marcus left the pocket door open when he left the drawing room, walking back to the kitchen. As Emma gathered her bag and made her way upstairs, she could hear Marcus talking with Connie, Dex, and Sandra. As she reached the second floor, Emma passed the Rayburns coming down from their third floor suite.

"Evening, Emma," Mr. Rayburn said. "Haven't seen you around today."

"Yes, sir. I took a day trip over to Saint John, and we left early."

"Lovely town, Saint John," Mrs. Rayburn muttered, her lips pursed. She had stopped two steps up from floor level and now looked down on Emma with condescension.

Emma noticed the suitcase in her hand. "Are you checking out?"

"In the morning," the man replied. "Just tossing a couple of our things in the trunk tonight so we don't have everything to deal with in the morning."

"We no longer feel comfortable staying here," Mrs. Rayburn added, glaring down her nose at Emma. "Since you turned up, it no longer seems suitable for respectable people."

Emma's ears burned with rage, but she was too exhausted to engage this woman. Instead, she turned on her heel and stepped into her room, pausing long enough before she closed it to turn back and say, "Don't let the door hit you on the way out, *Mrs.* Rayburn."

The woman gasped and went to speak, but Mr. Rayburn caught her arm before she could say anything and forced her down the stairs. Emma locked herself in her room and suddenly felt a shiver of fear run through her.

Her room was in shambles. Marcus had been right. All her clothes were strewn across the floor. The trash can had been dumped. The bed had been stripped, and the mattresses were askew. Her toiletry bag had been dumped into the sink. Every drawer was pulled out. Even the rug had been pulled up.

Emma plopped onto the bed, exhaustion taking her will to even move. In the end, she left it the way it was, save the bed. She pushed the mattress back into place and made the bed. As she was pulling back the covers to climb into bed, Emma stopped.

She thought for a moment and then glanced across the room to the window. Acting on some unknown impulse, she went to the window and looked down. There stood Alice, gazing up at her.

"Keep us safe tonight, Alice," she whispered.

Alice never responded.

Emma switched off the lamp and crawled into bed.

XXVI

"Wake up!"

Emma sat bolt upright in bed, ready to pounce on whoever was screaming in her ear. Fists balled, muscles tensed, she went to swing and discovered no one was there. She was alone.

"What?"

Had she been dreaming? Emma considered it but dismissed the notion almost immediately. She had not been dreaming. Someone *had* yelled in her ear. Someone *had* woken her up. Her heart still pounding, Emma glanced at the window.

Alice? Was that you?

Emma threw back the covers and swung out of bed. The cold bit into her bare feet as they landed, throwing Emma off-kilter, and she landed back on the mattress. As she stepped down again, her muscles tensed and began to tremble. It wasn't just the floor that was freezing, she realized. The entire room was frigid.

She tiptoed to her suitcase and threw on sweatpants, a pair of socks, and her hoodie. She went back to the window. The tree swing was empty. Alice wasn't there. Still groggy, Emma stood there staring out at the murky morning fog hovering over the still waters of the bay. A chill went through her, and Emma shuddered as she wrapped her arms around her frame. She ran her hands up and down her arms, trying to warm them.

A noise outside in the hall caught her ear, and Emma spun around in surprise. But the house fell silent again, and Emma started to wonder whether her imagination was just running away with her.

No. Someone yelled.

The red digital display on the alarm clock by the lamp advised it was barely after four in the morning.

The creaky door hinges might as well have been screaming as Emma cracked her door a few inches to peek into the hall. Empty. She opened it a little further and, annoyed at the squeaking hinges, flung it wide open. The hinges howled in protest. Emma stepped into the hallway, looking left and right. She *knew* she had heard someone scream "Wake up."

She stepped toward the staircase, but a quick glance to the right made her stop. The door to the Hansens' room was partially open. The Hansens never left their door open. Ever. Whether they were in or out, the door had always been closed every time Emma had walked by.

She stepped toward it, willing her knees to unlock with each step. The muscles in her legs tightened as Emma hugged the wall. Every step was an exercise of will. Her body willed her to run. Her mind willed her to press on. She took a paperweight from the side table in the hall to use as a weapon. Solid alabaster, the cool stone warmed in her hands as Emma's fingers wrapped around it.

"Hello?"

The Hansens did not answer.

"Mr. Hansen? Mrs. Hansen?"

Nothing.

With a trembling hand, Emma gave the door a gentle push and took a final step forward. She held the stone paperweight in the other, ready to pummel any assailant. She was not, however, ready for what she found.

The paperweight fell to the floor as Emma's hands flew to her mouth to stifle her scream. It landed with a loud *thwack* against the hardwood floor, chipping off the edge of a plank. It rolled across the floor, coming to land next to an upholstered Queen Anne sitting chair.

The Hansens lay dead in their beautiful four-poster king sized bed. The royal blue handles of Connie's chef knives stuck out of their chests. Emma's knees wobbled. Clammy hands clutched at the walls behind her, attempting to keep Emma upright. That was when the scent hit her. Whether from the bitter taste of adrenaline in her mouth or the oxidized scent of blood, Emma's stomach lurched, and she covered her nose and mouth with the sleeve of her hoodie.

She shut her eyes, willing the scene away.

"It's just a dream," she muttered, though her vocal cords were too frozen for any sound to come out. "This isn't real. Wake up, Emma. Wake up. Wake up."

Still glued to the wall, she opened her eyes. They were still there. Still dead. Mr. Hansen looked almost peaceful from this angle, like he had never seen it coming. Emma noticed the half-empty glass of bourbon on the nightstand: Mr. Hansen's favorite nightcap. In the end it had proven to be a blessing. Not so with Mrs. Hansen.

Her eyes bulged as she stared out at Emma. The ghastly display was unnerving to look at.

Pain.

Terror.

Disbelief.

In her final moments, she had reached for her husband, unaware he was already dead, unaware their attacker had dealt with him first. She had been alone in the end. Left without comfort. Without protection.

A trail of blood ran down the sheets and dripped onto the floor. Dark red tendrils stretched outward across the floor, the result of the house's settling and uneven floors, an acrid line of demarcation Emma dared not cross. Between the living . . . and the dead.

Through the haze of fear, a thought rose in her mind. *Marcus.* He was supposed to stay the night. Emma pushed herself away from the wall, and turning her head away from the Hansens, she ran to the window. She wiped her eyes with her sleeves, clearing the tears that clouded her vision. But when she finished, Emma discovered it wasn't her vision that was cloudy. It was the window.

A thick, low fog hovered unaffected outside. Oblivious to what was taking place inside, it shrouded Emma's vision. Desperate to locate Officer Cameron, Emma unfastened the latch and lifted the window.

Leaning out for a better view, she found Marcus's patrol car parked beside hers.

Sprawled out on the ground beside it, out of view from the road, lay the young policeman. She didn't call out for him. It would have done no good. The large splotch of red on his chest told Emma he was dead.

She fled back to her room. She slammed the door behind her and bolted it, locking herself in. Emma dashed across the room and snatched up the burner phone Marcus had brought her the day before, yanking the power cord right out of the wall along with it, and dialed 911. No answer. Only one bar of reception.

Emma cursed.

"Sandra!"

Without stopping to think, Emma disengaged the locks and threw open the bedroom door before racing down the stairs. The heavy door slammed against the wall, but Emma kept going. She slipped on the landing, her socked feet sliding gracelessly across the polished wood floor. Emma landed hard. With her ankle now screaming, she lifted herself up and hobbled the rest of the way down.

An unconscious Sandra lay sprawled across the middle of the living room floor. Emma dropped to her knees by the girl's side. She was lying facedown. A trickle of blood ran down the side of her face, followed the curve of her lips, and pooled in front of her open mouth.

"Sandra!" Emma screamed, checking for a pulse. It was faint. She patted Sandra's face, trying to wake her up. "Sandra, it's Emma."

Sandra didn't answer.

"Come on, Sandra. Wake up now. We have to get outta here."

Emma's ankle protested the kneeling position she was in. She glanced at it, and it was already swelling. Emma moved to take pressure off it and heard the metallic click of a gun being cocked behind her.

"You should've left well enough alone, girl," the man hissed at her in a low voice. Rage dripped off every syllable.

Emma's muscles froze, anchoring her to the hardwood floor.

"You should've heeded my warning out at the Point and left while you had the chance. And left us in peace," he continued. "How did you figure it out? How did you put it all together?"

"The diaries," Emma said, fear tightening her vocal cords.

"What diaries? I got rid of everything that could be traced back to that worthless guttersnipe."

"You missed Julian's diary."

He cursed.

"Should've known. That addle-minded politician never could shut his mouth."

Emma forced the muscles in her legs to move, and she slowly turned to face the culprit.

"You?" She nearly collapsed from shock.

"Yes, me."

"But you don't . . . I mean, she didn't . . . You weren't . . ."

Partial questions formed in Emma's mouth and dissipated into thin air as she tried vocalizing them, for there, some five or six feet away from her, stood Brett Barrett, Connie's grandfather. His bony hand held tight to the cocked revolver, which he had leveled at Emma.

None of it made sense, but then slowly, ever so slowly, the adrenaline coursing through Emma's veins ebbed enough for her brain to take over. One question rose to the forefront.

"Which one are you?" Emma finally asked.

"Which what?"

"Helen said she had two brothers. Brothers she called *B* and *C*. Which brother are you? The older or the younger?"

A wry smile crossed his mouth. "Younger. How much do you know, girl?"

"I know you raped my great-grandmother."

"I did no such thing!" he yelled, raising his arm as he shook the gun at her. Emma's hands came up in the universal sign of surrender. "I'm no rapist, girl! Do you hear me? I'm no rapist!"

"I'm sorry," Emma said calmly, stalling for time. "But if you didn't do it, you know who did. Don't you?"

Brett became suddenly nervous, and Emma made the last connections immediately.

"It was your older brother, wasn't it? The one Helen called *C*."

"Christopher."

"Christopher." Emma repeated.

"How do you know this?"

"Helen's letters."

"Helen never wrote any letters. And what letters she did write went up in smoke with the rest of your family's crap in the fire."

"She wrote letters right under your nose. Letters I found in New Brunswick."

He didn't respond. For Emma, by that point, he didn't need to.

"Now it makes sense," Emma said cautiously.

"Go on," Brett jeered. "Impress me with what you think you know."

"Alice and Helen were lovers."

"Abomination!" He shook the gun at her in a rage. Emma cowered, partially covering Sandra with her own body. "My sister was a normal teenager before that . . . that . . ."

He couldn't even say the word. Emma watched as the old man's face went red with fury.

"You caught them together. Or Christopher did. And then he raped her, didn't he? And you've been covering up his crime your whole life. Haven't you?"

"Wasn't me who covered it up." Brett chuckled maliciously. He pointed an accusing bony finger at her. "*Your* family did that."

"They what?"

His jagged laughter was like cold steel slicing through her, and Emma gripped Sandra's hand to steady her own racing pulse.

"They couldn't have their precious little rich girl tied to the postman's son, now could they? Imagine the scandal. Richest family in town now saddled with the poor folk next door for eternity. The brothers called a meeting. Forced Tobias to send Alice away and paid my father to ship Christopher overseas. They carved and sliced my family up like Christmas turkey and expected us to thank them for the trouble."

"That's why your father locked Helen—"

"Enough!" he yelled, taking a step forward. Emma raised her hands in surrender, placating him, trying to buy time.

Where the hell are the Rayburns? And the Morrisons? Emma thought. *Did he kill them all?*

"You don't get to use my sister as a pawn in your family drama! Do you hear me, girl?"

"Yes, sir." Emma nodded. "Yes, sir. I'm sorry."

Emma sat on the floor, looking up at him. She watched the heave of his chest as he struggled to catch his breath, saw the wild animalistic fever in his eyes. Only once he had calmed did Emma speak.

"You killed Ms. Alda." Her words came out in a whisper. "You pushed her down the stairs and made the whole thing look like an accident."

Brett stood motionless, the revolver trembling in his hand. His eyes glistened with tears, and Emma almost felt sorry for him. She would have felt sorry for him if not for the loaded revolver that was pointed right at her chest and the four—possibly eight—bodies lying dead around her.

He sniffled, dabbing his eyes with his free hand. "I should've burned that place to the ground decades ago and been done with the whole cursed lot of you."

"You destroyed all the family records."

"Clever little girl," he cooed.

"What happened to your sister?" Emma asked, careful to avoid using Helen's name directly.

Brett leaned against the wall, heavy tears running down his cheeks. "My sweet Helen."

"What happened to her, Mr. Barrett? Did your father do something to her?"

Brett's expression switched from grief back to rage instantly.

Wrong question, Emma thought.

"My father never laid a hand on her. A year after Toby and Cici left Digby, Helen took a boat out into the bay. She—" His voice was raw and crackled as the words came out. "She . . . never came back. They said she fell overboard and hit her head."

"But you didn't believe that, did you?"

"Helen was the best swimmer in our family," he cried angrily. "And she certainly would never take a boat out without wearing a life vest. After she died, Mother and Father got rid of everything that was hers, like she never existed."

"And Alice's letters to her?"

He shook his head. "She was smart enough to destroy them. Believe me, if I had known they were still writing each other, I would've put a stop to it."

"What do you think happened that day on the lake?"

"I don't *think*," he snapped. "I *know* what happened. She killed herself. Over that girl. Over that cursed girl."

The vitriol with which he uttered the words caught Emma by surprise. Though he was frail and broken, a dangerous anger flowed through his veins. Emma remembered what Dex had told her over breakfast that first day. Such a lifetime ago, it now seemed.

"The man has more energy than all of us put together. Eighty-three years old, and he still cycles ten kilometers every day."

Any man who had strength enough to bike ten kilometers a day could probably do just about anything he set his mind to. She needed to be cautious.

"How did you do it?"

"What?"

"All of it. The records. The basement flood. The fires."

"Fires?"

"The one in Halifax."

Brett's amused laugh made the hair on her neck stand up. "Oh, that? No. That was just a lucky coincidence."

"You expect me to believe that?"

"Does it matter?"

"How did you get away with it? You were just a kid in 1947. How old were you? Ten? Eleven?"

"Eleven."

"How does an eleven-year-old boy go about destroying . . . Oh. That's it, isn't it? It wasn't just you, was it? Your brother was in on it too, wasn't he?"

"Christopher was dead long before I started."

"I'm sorry."

"Justice," Brett announced flatly.

"Justice!" Emma could barely contain her outrage, her raised voice sending Brett back a step. "You erased an entire family's history!"

"I wanted to wipe you from the face of the earth!" he yelled back. "I wanted the lot of you to just disappear! As if you never existed. And I had four years to plot my revenge."

The animalistic growl in his voice terrified her, and Emma was grateful Sandra was currently unconscious. Otherwise she'd probably be screaming at Emma to loosen her grip on her hand. Still, Emma pressed him. "But *your* brother was the rapist! Where was the justice for Alice? For my grandmother? For Helen?"

"Don't speak that name in my presence, girl! You have no idea how hard it was after it came out! And it always comes out. Gossip is the national pastime of small towns. They crucified my family! The shame we endured because of . . . because . . ."

Unable to get his tongue untied, Brett grew more agitated. He began to pace.

"Because of what those girls did! Having people turn away from us wherever we went, like we were carrying the plague or something. The kids at school . . . the way they'd stare and point and laugh at me when I walked by. None of my friends would even speak to me. My father lost his job. We were humiliated, do you hear? Humiliated! And I was all alone! No friends! No family! No nothing!

"Christopher was never the same after he came home. He was always angry. At me. At our parents. At the townsfolk. At Helen and . . . that girl. He enlisted the day he turned eighteen and shipped off to Vietnam. He left me all alone to . . . to . . ."

"Did he . . . ?"

Brett's voice broke as he forced his next words out. "Bought it his first week there."

"I'm sorry," Emma said, glancing up at the clock. How she wished it were closer to six o'clock.

"Sorry?" He humphed, his anger returning. "Sorry? The paper wouldn't even post his obituary! Even then they shamed us! They wouldn't even acknowledge him then! A war hero, and his own town swept him under the rug like he was nobody! Like he was trash."

Emma could see the mixture of abandonment, grief, and rage on the old man's face—a lethal concoction in anyone, and even more so in a man with a loaded gun . . . and nothing to lose. She decided to try shifting the conversation back to Helen, whom Brett had obviously loved dearly.

"Your sister's last name was Morrison. Why is yours different?"

"Helen's suicide broke my parents' marriage. Papa put a gun in his mouth one night and put an end to his shame. Mother took us boys and moved up north. She remarried after that and started her new family. I was leftovers by that point, a constant reminder of the worst time of her life."

"And the new husband adopted you and Christopher," Emma said, filling in the rest.

"Clever little busybody, aren't you? Too clever. Yes, he adopted me. Just me. He wanted nothing to do with Christopher. But I was never *his* kid. And he never let me forget it either."

"Why did you come back to Digby?"

"I got a job on the ferry when I was fifteen. Scrubbing decks, helping passengers."

"And no one recognized you?"

"I was older, taller, and had a completely different last name. People see what they *want* to see, girl. I rented a room here in town, and on my off days, I put my plan in motion."

"How?"

He laughed. It was the first time Emma could see the tension visibly ease in the old man.

"Right under their noses." He smirked. "I worked several odd jobs around town, including jobs at the local paper and the Justice Centre. The rest was easy."

"And the historical society?"

"That too," he gloated. "Right after retirement, I went through every page in the place until there was nothing left of old Tobias or his wife . . . or his bitch child. I never meant to kill Alda." His tone was unexpectedly contrite. "But I finally had rid our lives of the past, you see? And I couldn't risk you digging up everything I had spent a lifetime trying to bury."

"I'm sorry, Mr. Barrett," Emma said as sympathetically as she could. She glanced at the grandfather clock standing in the corner but was unable to read the dial from this angle. If she could keep stalling him, if she could keep him talking, Connie and Dex would soon arrive for the breakfast service.

"I never meant to reopen old wounds for your family. I just wanted answers for mine."

"I'm sorry too, girl. But you know too much for your own good."

"Brett," she said tenderly, hoping she could coax him into putting the gun down. But the gesture only stiffened his resolve as he raised the gun again and squared his shoulders, preparing to fire. "You don't have to do this. Think of the others. This house is full of guests. If you pull that trigger—"

"Can't be helped now, can it?" he whispered.

"No!"

Alice appeared out of nowhere, standing just to Emma's left, between her and Brett Barrett. Caught by surprise, Brett turned and fired at Alice. The bullet sliced through the shadowy figure and shattered an antique oil lamp sitting on a table in front of the window. The oil exploded in all directions, showering everything in its vicinity. Shards of the etched glass base lay scattered across the floor.

"No, Brett," Alice repeated. "You will not harm anyone else for your crimes."

"You!" In a rage, Brett lunged for Alice. He reached for the girl's neck, and his hand wrapped around . . . nothing. Losing his balance in the attack, he fell face-first into one of the armchairs by the window. Brett scrambled back to his feet, the gun still trained on Alice, who had taken a protective stance between him and Sandra and Emma.

"You ruined my life! Ruined my family! With your godless—"

"And you ruined mine!" Alice shouted. The crystal chandelier overhead shuddered with the outburst. "Have you forgotten that?"

"I didn't do anything!" he reiterated as a dense fog began to fill the room.

Alice, it seemed, was giving Emma cover to escape. Emma glanced behind her. If she could manage to get Sandra to the kitchen, they might be able to slip out the back door.

"I didn't hurt you, Alice! I never touched you!"

"You stood there," Alice yelled, her voice echoing off the rafters of the house, "and watched it happen!"

There it was, Emma realized. The last bit of truth. The laughing boy in her dream of the basement. Brett had watched the whole episode play out, had heard Alice's cries for help. And he'd stood there laughing at her as his brother assaulted fifteen-year-old Alice.

She watched as the old man broke into sobs. A static sizzling noise behind her made Emma look back. The oil had gotten into the outlet just under the window. It sizzled and snapped, sending out sparks as the oil seeped into old electrical wires. Suddenly, the edge of the drapes caught fire. It spread up the cotton fabric quickly. As it traveled upward, the curtain split into pieces, sending bits of burning fabric onto the floor, where they ignited the spilled fuel from the lamp. Soon the backs of the armchairs were ablaze, and the room was quickly filling with smoke.

"You stood there! And you watched it, Brett! You watched him hurt me! You watched him tear my clothes off! You watched him pin me to the floor! And you laughed while he did it."

"No!" Brett brought his hands to his ears, trying to block out the dead girl's words as he sobbed. "I didn't do it! I didn't!"

Emma turned back to Sandra and rolled her over. Using the rising fog as cover, she lifted her upper body and slid her arms around the woman's upper chest just below her armpits. She hoisted her up slowly, careful not to do any more damage, and slowly began stepping backward, away from the confrontation. With Brett's attention focused on Alice, they disappeared into the fog.

"You were there, Brett!" Alice reminded him.

"I didn't do it!"

"Right there!" she continued yelling, pointing at the basement door tucked behind the hutch. "You stood there in the doorway and watched it happen!"

"I didn't do it!"

"In this very house! Right there in that basement! You remember, don't you?"

Something in Brett snapped. Furious, he swung the gun across Alice's face. Had she been real, the blow would've shattered every tooth in her mouth. Shadowy mist swirled through the air before reforming into Alice's face.

"You!" he yelled back at her. "You poisoned my sister with your unnatural ways! It was your fault what happened to her! Your fault! She was a normal little girl before you corrupted her!"

"I loved her!" Alice fumed.

The words sent a tremor through the house, and Emma lost her balance and fell to the floor. She managed to keep her grip on Sandra, protecting her from the fall, but her ankle exploded in pain. She yelled at the sudden sensation, and it took her several moments before she could stand again.

"That wasn't love!" Brett protested. "It was a sin! An abomination!"

Emma watched in horror as the room, once filled with Alice's conjured fog, exploded into flames. The old man yelled in terror as he fell to one knee, cowering in fear. The ceiling close to the window collapsed, weakened from the fire.

"You heard me screaming," Alice continued with a roar. "You heard me calling out for you! You saw me reaching out to you! Reaching out for help!"

"I didn't do it!" He sobbed uncontrollably as the upholstered walls around him were consumed by the raging inferno.

When she reached the kitchen, Emma set Sandra down. Her ankle was now too badly swollen to carry her out of the house. Emma hobbled to the refrigerator and grabbed a bottle of water from the door. She collapsed as she turned back to Sandra. Emma howled as the pain bolted up through her leg. The injury had triggered a migraine, and her head throbbed with each pounding heartbeat. She had to rouse Sandra somehow, or they would both be lost to the fire. Veins of flame ran out in a spiderweb pattern on the floor, following the traces of gasoline-based varnish on the floors into the kitchen.

"A normal girl!" Alice yelled with fury. "That's what your brother kept saying as he did it. 'I'm going to make you a normal girl again.' I can still remember the stench of his breath, you coward! Still smell the rotting fish on his hands as he touched me!"

Desperate and running out of time, Emma crawled across the kitchen and upended the bottle over Sandra's face. Sandra roused, gasping for air after coughing up the cold water. She screamed when she saw the fire spreading around them.

"Sandra!"

"Emma?" She rolled over to find Emma sprawled across the floor. Sandra's hand went to her head and came away bloody from Brett's attack earlier. "What's happening?"

"Hurry!" Emma yelled to her. "We've gotta get out of the house!"

"Where is everyone?" Sandra managed to cough off. Smoke was rapidly filling the room.

"They're gone!"

"Gone?" On hands and knees, Sandra had crawled to Emma's side.

"I twisted my ankle," Emma explained. "Can you help me outside, please?"

Sandra nodded and helped Emma to her feet.

"And what did you do?" Alice screamed. "You stood there laughing! Laughing while your brother hurt me!"

"Who is that?" Sandra asked, turning back to the living room.

"I didn't do it!" Brett sobbed hysterically. "I didn't do it!"

"I'll explain outside!" Emma said over the roaring blaze. Fiery orange fingers had made their way up the kitchen walls and were now spreading across the beadboard ceiling. "Hurry!"

Emma and Sandra crossed the back lawn and stopped at the water's edge. Sandra helped her sit down. Both women were coughing heavily. Emma looked at the house and crawled back another startled step as she gazed up at the inferno. All three floors were now fully engulfed in flames. Windows shattered from the heat, sending sprays of glass across the yard, and angry flames danced out of the now open windows, licking at the house's exterior.

Emma was amazed at how quickly the fire was spreading, but then she remembered the fury in Alice's voice. There was no need of wood to feed this blaze. Alice's blind rage was fuel enough.

"Oh my God!" Emma heard Sandra cry behind her.

Emma looked back and found Sandra gazing up in horror at the blazing inferno. Pained howls from within the house silenced the conversation. They sat clutching each other as they watched black, acrid smoke billow out of the upper floor windows. Emma prayed silently Brett had left no one alive. Anything, she thought, would be better than this.

Neither woman spoke. The noise of the flames and the pained refrain of "I didn't do it" slowly melted into the approaching sirens.

EPILOGUE

On a hot Tuesday in late July, Emma stood close by as two men replaced marker forty-seven with a small marble headstone. By her side, dressed in black, was her uncle Adrian. She nodded graciously to the foreman as the men finished and began packing their equipment to leave. The pudgy man tipped his hard hat and casually walked away.

"I still think we should've taken her out of this lot," Uncle Adi said, dabbing his brow with a handkerchief.

"This is where she wanted to be," Emma said calmly as she stepped forward.

Uncle Adi shrugged but said nothing. He followed her to the shiny new headstone. It wasn't much. Nothing fancy. Certainly nothing on the grand scale of other memorials scattered throughout Fernhill. Emma knelt, careful not to get the hem of her dress dirty, and laid the bouquet of yellow roses on the ground. She ran her hand over the stone.

Alice Roberts
Beloved Daughter and Mother
1932-1947
May She Rest in Peace

"This is a beautiful spot, Em. All nestled under these trees in the shade."

"Yes," Emma replied. "It is beautiful. Are they gone?"

Adrian looked back at the work crew, who were just getting into their truck. "Almost."

A second later, they heard the engine turn over, and the truck pulled away.

"All clear."

Emma opened her bag and took out two items: a trowel and a small nondescript cardboard box.

"You're really doing this?" Adrian asked.

Emma looked back at her uncle. "This was what she wanted, Uncle Adi."

"I know. It's just . . . I hate thinking of her up here all alone."

"She's not alone, Uncle Adi. She's back with her mother."

"Damndest thing," he said with tears in his eyes. "And to think we never would've known if you hadn't come up here looking."

Emma turned back to the stone. "There's a lot we never knew."

The ground was wet from recent rainfall and came away easily. It took only minutes to dig a hole big enough for her purposes. Emma set the trowel aside and surveyed her work. It would do nicely. Satisfied, she turned her attention to the box.

A plastic bag of ashes—her gran's ashes—lay inside. Emma untied the bag and slowly emptied its contents into the hole. The wind, which had been calm, rustled the leaves overhead. Emma looked up at the trees.

"Hope you don't mind," she apologized. "I brought you some company."

Emma covered the ashes and tried to arrange the tufts of grass so no one would know it had been disturbed. Adrian stepped forward and pulled his niece close, and Emma wept against his shoulder.

"Come on," Adrian whispered. "Let's go home now."

"Almost," Emma countered, lifting her head. "We've one more stop to make."

It was midday when they pulled into the parking lot of the Fishmonger. A large "Lot for Sale" sign stood in front of the charred remains of the bed-and-breakfast. A bright red sticker with *REDUCED* written in white block capitals had been posted diagonally across it.

Adrian gasped from the passenger seat. "Dear God. Is this it?"

"This is it." *Poor Connie and Dex*, Emma thought.

She looked across the street to where a smaller sale sign had been posted in their front yard. No one in Digby wanted to live amongst these shadows. Shadows of fog, Ms. Alda had once called them.

Emma longed to see the bay one last time with the sun glinting off its surface, to see sailboats and fishing boats racing across the horizon. Sadly, it was not to be. The fog she so associated with Alice had met her in the bay no sooner than the ferry left Saint John. The closer to Digby they drew, the thicker the fog became. By the time they docked in Nova Scotia, Emma could see only a couple feet in front of them. Locals onboard the ship blamed various storm fronts and pressure systems for the anomaly, but Emma knew better. It was time to put things to rest.

The stone walls of the basement rose out of the ground, encapsulating the pit of blackened wood and ashes that lay piled inside it. Her family's own personal abyss, full of hell and fury—and memories. Memories Emma was more than ready to put behind her.

Only a few of the major support beams were still erect. Thick blackened beams of old-growth wood rose out of the basement, reaching for the light. Only there was no light. Not today anyway. Not for this place. Not for these people. And Emma included herself in that group. They had all been left damaged in some way by what had happened.

They eyed the abyss warily while walking past it to the backyard and the tree swing. As they drew near, the fog thinned and the tree emerged. A ghostly figure in black against a sea of gray.

"Hey!" Adrian said, pointing at the tree. "This is . . . I don't believe it. This is Mom's painting. The one in the dining room back home."

"It is."

"Wow!"

Emma sat down on the swing and looked out across the murky waters. The docks, barely visible, were eerily vacant this time of day. All the scallop and lobster boats had left hours earlier. They would not return until evening, and Emma hoped to be back in Saint John by then, waiting for their return flight to Missouri. Yet despite the emptiness around her, Emma felt strangely comforted by the relative silence.

"Uncle Adi, could you . . . Could you give me a minute?"

"Sure thing, Em. I'll be back by the car."

"Thanks."

As his footsteps receded, Emma began to weep. For Alice. Nellie. Helen. Herself.

So much loss.

So much tragedy.

So much pain.

Warm arms wrapped around Emma and pulled her backward. She leaned into Gran's chest, breathing in the familiar lavender scent. A weathered hand stroked her hair back from where it had fallen into her eyes.

"Why are you crying, Em?" she whispered soothingly. "Tell Gran all about it."

"I'm s-sorry, Gran," Emma stammered, the words coming unevenly through her sobs. "Sorry you never got to say goodbye."

"I'm right here, silly goose," Nellie teased. She laid a hand over Emma's heart. "I've always been here, Emma. I always will be."

Emma's head turned upward to look Nellie in the eye. The gray, once put there by disease and decay, was now gone. Nellie's eyes shone like twin gemstones.

"I love you, Emma girl," Nellie said, kissing her on the forehead.

"I love you too, Gran. I miss you."

"I have to go now."

"I know."

"You'll be all right, Em."

"Bye, Gran."

Nellie stepped toward her mother, who stood waiting by the shore. As she withdrew, the scent of freshly turned earth replaced the lavender. Emma watched as Nellie walked to her mother, still in her teenage visage. They embraced for the first time and slowly vanished into the retreating fog. A minute later, Emma could see the sun off in the distance, peeking through the thinning mist. It reflected off the surface of the water, turning the once-murky waters into shimmering glass.

"I thought I'd find you here."

Emma smiled and, still sitting in the swing, spun around to face Franklin Wood. Dressed in his standard khakis and crisp white oxford, he was too neat for this wreckage of a place. Behind him, still inside the vehicle, sat an older woman watching them curiously.

"How's that?"

He pointed out at the water. The fog was continuing its retreat, leaving a warm clear sky in its wake.

"The fog. Seems to follow you, don't you think?"

Emma nodded but said nothing.

"You here to stir up more trouble?"

"No, I'm not. Just saying goodbye. And how did you know I was here? We only pulled off the ferry a while ago."

"Saw you get out of your car as I was driving by and thought I'd stop and say hello. See what you were up to."

Emma rolled her eyes. "Ever the town snoop, right?"

"Hey!" Franklin frowned, pretending to take offense. "The best journalists don't wait for the story to come to them. We go out looking for it. But I guess that explains the fog this morning. You sure you're here to just say goodbye?"

Emma pointed to her uncle who stood, leaning against their rental car, watching them. "Even brought my uncle this time to keep me out of trouble."

Franklin ran his hand through his hair and looked away. He kicked the ground, slightly embarrassed.

"He really loved you, you know," Franklin said. "Marcus."

The name was a gut punch to Emma, and she reached for the swing to steady herself.

"I'm sorry. I didn't mean to upset you."

"It's fine. Just a lot of loss to deal with."

"Amen to that. Our little town hasn't been in the headlines this much in decades." He glanced at Emma's T-shirt. "You a Yankees fan?"

Emma looked down at her shirt and jeans. She had changed out of the black dress she'd worn to the cemetery while they were on the ferry.

"It was a housewarming present from some friends."

"Housewarming? You moved to New York?"

Emma nodded. "Last month. Someone made an offer on Gran's house while I was up in May."

"So you moved to New York, eh?"

Emma laughed. "My best friend and I always had this dream of being celebrity trainers."

She expected him to laugh, to poke fun at her and Nessa's dreams. But he didn't.

Instead, Franklin simply nodded and said, "I have no doubt you will be one day."

"Thanks."

"But for now, Ms. Campbell, you still owe me a story."

Emma sighed as Adrian walked back from the vehicle to join them.

"Franklin, this is my uncle Adrian." Emma said, rising from the swing. "He came up with me. Uncle Adi, this is Franklin Wood. Journalist for the local paper."

"Pleased to meet you." He shook Adrian's hand before turning back to Emma. "And my story?"

"I do, don't I?"

Franklin nodded.

Emma glanced back at the charred remains of the Fishmonger. So much had happened in that house, and Emma wasn't sure how much of it *should* be shared.

The silence around them grew palpable before Franklin finally spoke.

"Well . . ." He kicked at the ground like a fidgeting child. "Anyway, you hungry?"

"I could eat, I guess. Why?"

"I know this great little place close by. Best seafood you'll ever have. Interested in having lunch with me? My treat, of course. Perhaps you could tell me your side of the story."

"I'm in," Adrian said. "I love seafood."

The trio walked back to their vehicles. Emma looked back at the elderly woman sitting in the front passenger seat of Franklin's car. She waved at Emma when they were a few yards away. "And I see you even brought a chaperone."

"Cute." He smirked. "Actually, we were out running errands when I saw you earlier."

"Oh, right." Emma nodded, smiling. "Errands. Convenient."

"Truth be told, Emma, I think you might be interested in meeting her. And you, of course, Mr. Adrian."

"How so?" Adrian asked.

Franklin stopped and turned to face Emma.

"After you left last time, I was talking to her about the case. I told her how you single-handedly solved a seventy-year-old rape case *and* tracked down a great-grandmother no one in your family ever knew about, and I happened to mention the girl's name during our conversation."

"Okay, Franklin, help me out here." Emma said, shoving her hands in her jeans. "I don't understand."

"Her name is Nancy Lucille Wood . . . née Roberts. My grandmother."

Emma stopped midstep. She looked to her uncle, who was wide-eyed with shock.

"I'm sorry, what?"

Franklin smiled. "Her grandfather was Bartholomew Roberts."

"Toby's brother," Adrian whispered.

"Oh my God," Emma said, her hand going to her gaping mouth as she looked back at the frail, little woman. "So, that means she . . . and you and I are . . . ." Emma was practically giddy with excitement. "Are you sure about this?"

Franklin's Cheshire cat grin was answer enough. "Would you like to come say hello?"

Emma wiped at her tears, nodding. "Yes, please."

Franklin turned and started walking.

They had only made it a few steps when Adrian shouted, "Em, look at that!"

Emma turned. The fog had completely vanished, leaving a picturesque sun hanging high in the sky. Not a cloud could be seen as the sky changed before her eyes from gray to sapphire. A sailboat, its canvas sails unfurled and billowing in the wind coming off the water, skimmed across the surface.

Sitting in their tree swing were Alice and a toddler-aged Nellie. Alice swung gently back and forth with the child sitting in her lap.

"Emma," Adrian whispered.

"I see it."

Alice's green jumper billowed in and out as they swung back and forth. As Emma watched, Alice caught sight of them and turned around in the swing. She clutched Nellie's little hand, and together they waved.

Emma and Adrian both raised a hand and waved back.

"It's Mimi's painting, Em."

"Yes. Mother and daughter together. As it always should have been."

THE END

SIGN UP FOR BOOK CHATS!

Visit www.authorjdnichols.com and sign up for the author's monthly "Book Chats" and gain early-bird access!

- New Book Title Reveals
- New Cover Reveals
- Pre-Order Release Dates
- General On-Sale Dates

Plus

- Exclusive live Q&A sessions with the author after each new book launch! These sessions will not be posted to YouTube and will not be open to the public.

Visit www.authorjdnichols.com and click the *Book Chats* tab to join.

AUTHOR'S NOTE

Thank you for your purchase of *Shadows of Fog*. I hope you enjoyed reading it as much as I enjoyed writing it. I've always loved reading mysteries and stories that make us scared of what goes *"Bump"* in the night. The book you now hold in your hand is the culmination of many a late night, many a "bump in the night," and countless conversations with friends who – by now – are probably tired of listening to me talk about it.

This story began with a painting I picked up at a charity auction. The moment I saw it, some inner voice told me, "This is where your book is set." I had no clue where the painting's locale was, but I followed my muse's instruction and bought it. I subsequently stumbled across a black-and-white photograph of Digby Harbor circa 1926. While the two had their differences, the similarities could not be ignored. So if, dear reader, you were wondering how I chose Digby, Nova Scotia, as the setting of this novel – I didn't. *Digby chose me.*

Sadly, I have not visited Digby (yet). The pandemic hit right as I was beginning my first draft, and life has thrown some pretty hefty curveballs the past few years, which has kept me from visiting. I have tried, using other research methods, to be as faithful to Digby's character and landscape as I can. The Fishmonger and the Shack are my own creations. The historical museum exists; however, the interior and Ms. Alda are patterned after similar museums I have visited and countless sweet grandmother-types who volunteer their time and service to preserving their communities' history.

Please take a moment to post a review of this book on *Amazon* and *Goodreads.com*. Recent studies indicate over ninety percent of readers look at reviews when making the decision to purchase a book.

OVER 90%!

It would be an understatement to say word of mouth and reader reviews/recommendations are the life's blood of any author. In addition to your review, I would also ask one favor: take a selfie with your copy of *Shadows of Fog* and post it to your social media platforms along with a quick review. Thank you in advance for tagging me. My Instagram handle is @authorjdnichols.

ACKNOWLEDGEMENTS

First and foremost, I must give credit for this book to my grandparents, specifically my grandmothers, for instilling in me a love of books and reading. Many an hour I spent stretched out across their living room floors or their front porches with my head buried in a book.

To my mother – for always taking me to the library. For never discouraging me from reading. For never saying "We don't have time" when we walked by a bookstore. And for all the times you scraped and saved so I could buy something when the book fair came to school.

To my father – may he rest in peace – for teaching me the value of an honest day's work. I wish you were here to hold this book in your hand. I miss you every day.

To Mrs. Mary Joe Williams – for nurturing that little kid who loved to read and giving me extra library time. And for the three books you bought on my behalf when I didn't have money to pay for them. I still have those books. If only the world had more teachers like you.

To my best friend David – for putting up with me all these years. For your constant friendship and tireless encouragement. For reading every word I write even if you've already read the three previous drafts. And for the hours we've spent talking about books and the stories we'd write one day.

To my editors Chelsea and Natalia at Enchanted Ink Publishing – your sharp editorial insight helped push me to the best of my current abilities and shape this story into something I am truly proud of. Working with you both has been a pleasure, and I look forward to doing it again.

To my incredibly talented cover designer Sadia Shahid – for being an amazing collaborator. From the outset, you hit it out of the park. Thank you for all your hard work and for always listening to my suggestions (even the ones that didn't make sense). I couldn't be more proud of the end result you put together. I cannot wait to see what the future holds for our future collaborations.

Words cannot describe how grateful I am to you all.

Without you – this book would not exist.

ABOUT THE AUTHOR

Louisiana-born and raised, J.D. Nichols was born into a family of readers and has never known a time that he wasn't reading or making up stories with his cousins. He now lives and works in Columbia, Missouri. When he's not working, J.D. can usually be found enjoying the outdoors or planning his next adventure.

GET UPDATES ON J.D.'S WRITING AND TRAVELS
INSTAGRAM: @authorjdnichols
YOUTUBE: @authorjdnichols
WEBPAGE: www.authorjdnichols.com